Mary Roberts Rinehart

Dangerous Days

OK Publishing 2021

Mary Roberts Rinehart
DANGEROUS DAYS

Historical Novel - WW1

Published by
MUSAICUM
Books

- Advanced Digital Solutions & High-Quality book Formatting -

musaicumbooks@okpublishing.info

2021 OK Publishing

ISBN 978-80-272-7826-8

Contents

Chapter I

Natalie Spencer was giving a dinner. She was not an easy hostess. Like most women of futile lives she lacked a sense of proportion, and the small and unimportant details of the service absorbed her. Such conversation as she threw at random, to right and left, was trivial and distracted.

Yet the dinner was an unimportant one. It had been given with an eye more to the menu than to the guest list, which was characteristic of Natalie's mental processes. It was also characteristic that when the final course had been served without mishap, and she gave a sigh of relief before the gesture of withdrawal which was a signal to the other women, that she had realized no lack in it. The food had been good, the service satisfactory. She stood up, slim and beautifully dressed, and gathered up the women with a smile.

The movement found Doctor Haverford, at her left, unprepared and with his coffee cup in his hand. He put it down hastily and rose, and the small cup overturned in its saucer, sending a smudge of brown into the cloth.

"Dreadfully awkward of me!" he said. The clergyman's smile of apology was boyish, but he was suddenly aware that his hostess was annoyed. He caught his wife's amiable eyes on him, too, and they said quite plainly that one might spill coffee at home-one quite frequently did, to confess a good man's weakness-but one did not do it at Natalie Spencer's table. The rector's smile died into a sheepish grin.

For the first time since dinner began Natalie Spencer had a clear view of her husband's face. Not that that had mattered particularly, but the flowers had been too high. For a small dinner, low flowers, always. She would speak to the florist. But, having glanced at Clayton, standing tall and handsome at the head of the table, she looked again. His eyes were fixed on her with a curious intentness. He seemed to be surveying her, from the top of her burnished hair to the very gown she wore. His gaze made her vaguely uncomfortable. It was unsmiling, appraising, almost-only that was incredible in Clay-almost hostile.

Through the open door the half dozen women trailed out, Natalie in white, softly rustling as she moved, Mrs. Haverford in black velvet, a trifle tight over her ample figure, Marion Hayden, in a very brief garment she would have called a frock, perennial debutante that she was, rather negligible Mrs. Terry Mackenzie, and trailing behind the others, frankly loath to leave the men, Audrey Valentine. Clayton Spencer's eyes rested on Audrey with a smile of amused toleration, on her outrageously low green gown, that was somehow casually elegant, on her long green ear-rings and jade chain, on the cigaret between her slim fingers.

Audrey's audacity always amused him. In the doorway she turned and nonchalantly surveyed the room.

"For heaven's sake, hurry!" she apostrophized the table. "We are going to knit —I feel it. And don't give Chris anything more to drink, Clay. He's had enough."

She went on, a slim green figure, moving slowly and reluctantly toward the drawing-room, her head held high, a little smile still on her lips. But, alone for a moment, away from curious eyes, her expression changed, her smile faded, her lovely, irregular face took on a curious intensity. What a devilish evening! Chris drinking too much, talking wildly, and always with furtive eyes on her. Chris! Oh, well, that was life, she supposed.

She stopped before a long mirror and gave a bit of careless attention to her hair. With more care she tinted her lips again with a cosmetic stick from the tiny, diamond-studded bag she carried. Then she turned and surveyed the hall and the library beyond. A new portrait of Natalie was there, hanging on the wall under a shaded light, and she wandered in, still with her cigaret, and surveyed it. Natalie had everything. The portrait showed it. It was beautiful, smug, complacent.

Mrs. Valentine's eyes narrowed slightly. She stood there, thinking about Natalie. She had not everything, after all. There was something she lacked. Charm, perhaps. She was a cold woman. But, then, Clay was cold, too. He was even a bit hard. Men said that; hard and ambitious, although he was popular. Men liked strong men. It was only the weak they deplored and loved. Poor Chris!

She lounged into the drawing-room, smiling her slow, cool smile. In the big, uncarpeted alcove, where stood Natalie's great painted piano, Marion Hayden was playing softly, carefully posed for the entrance of the men. Natalie was sitting with her hands folded, in the exact center of a peacock-blue divan. The others were knitting.

"Very pretty effect, Toots!" Audrey called. And Miss Hayden gave her the unashamed smile of one woman of the world to another.

Audrey had a malicious impulse. She sat down beside Natalie, and against the blue divan her green gown shrieked a discord. She was vastly amused when Natalie found an excuse and moved away, to dispose herself carefully in a tall, old-gold chair, which framed her like a picture.

"We were talking of men, my dear," said Mrs. Haverford, placidly knitting.

"Of course," said Audrey, flippantly.

"Of what it is that they want more than anything else in the world."

"Children-sons," put in Mrs. Mackenzie. She was a robust, big woman with kindly eyes, and she was childless.

"Women!" called Toots Hayden. She was still posed, but she had stopped playing. Mrs. Haverford's eyes rested on her a moment, disapprovingly.

"What do you say, Natalie?" Audrey asked.

"I hadn't thought about it. Money, probably."

"You are all wrong," said Audrey, and lighted a fresh cigaret. "They want different things at different ages. That's why marriage is such a rotten failure. First they want women; any woman will do, really. So they marry-any woman. Then they want money. After that they want power and place. And when they've got that they begin to want-love."

"Good gracious, Audrey, what a cynical speech!" said Mrs. Mackenzie. "If they've been married all that time —"

"Oh, tut!" said Audrey, rudely.

She had the impulse of the unhappy woman to hurt, but she was rather ashamed of herself, too. These women were her friends. Let them go on believing that life was a thing of lasting loves, that men were true to the end, and that the relationships of life were fixed and permanent things.

"I'm sorry," she said. "I was just being clever! Let's talk about the war. It's the only thing worth talking about, anyhow."

In the dining-room Clayton Spencer, standing tall and erect, had watched the women go out. How typical the party was of Natalie, of her meticulous care in small things and her indifference or real ignorance as to what counted. Was it indifference, really, or was it supreme craftiness, the stupidity of her dinners, the general unattractiveness of the women she gathered around her, the ill-assortment of people who had little in themselves and nothing whatever in common?

Of all the party, only Audrey and the rector had interested him even remotely. Audrey amused him. Audrey was a curious mixture of intelligence and frivolity. She was a good fellow. Sometimes he thought she was a nice woman posing as not quite nice. He didn't know. He was not particularly analytical, but at least she had been one bit of cheer during the endless succession of courses.

The rector was the other, and he was relieved to find Doctor Haverford moving up to the vacant place at his right.

"I've been wanting to see you, Clay," he said in an undertone. "It's rather stupid to ask you how you found things over there. But I'm going to do it."

"You mean the war?"

"There's nothing else in the world, is there?"

"One wouldn't have thought so from the conversation here to-night."

Clayton Spencer glanced about the table. Rodney Page, the architect, was telling a story clearly not for the ears of the clergy, and his own son, Graham, forced in at the last moment to fill a vacancy, was sitting alone, bored and rather sulky, and sipping his third cognac.

"If you want my opinion, things are bad."

"For the Allies? Or for us?"

"Good heavens, man, it's the same thing. It is only the Allies who are standing between us and trouble now. The French are just holding their own. The British are fighting hard, but they're fighting at home too. We can't sit by for long. We're bound to be involved."

The rector lighted an excellent cigar.

"Even if we are," he said, hopefully, "I understand our part of it will be purely naval. And I believe our navy will give an excellent account of itself."

"Probably," Clay retorted. "If it had anything to fight! But with the German fleet bottled up, and the inadvisability of attempting to bombard Berlin from the sea —"

The rector made no immediate reply, and Clayton seemed to expect none. He sat back, tapping the table with long, nervous fingers, and his eyes wandered from the table around the room. He surveyed it all with much the look he had given Natalie, a few moments before, searching, appraising, vaguely hostile. Yet it was a lovely room, simple and stately. Rodney Page, who was by way of being decorator for the few, as he was architect for the many, had done the room, with its plainly paneled walls, the over-mantel with an old painting inset, its lion chairs, its two console tables with each its pair of porcelain jars. Clayton liked the dignity of the room, but there were times when he and Natalie sat at the great table alone, with only the candles for light and the rest of the room in a darkness from which the butler emerged at stated intervals and retreated again, when he felt the oppression of it. For a dinner party, with the brilliant colors of the women's gowns, it was ideal. For Natalie and himself alone, with the long silences between them that seemed to grow longer as the years went on, it was inexpressibly dreary.

He was frequently aware that both Natalie and himself were talking for the butler's benefit.

From the room his eyes traveled to Graham, sitting alone, uninterested, dull and somewhat flushed. And on Graham, too, he fixed that clear appraising gaze that had vaguely disconcerted Natalie. The boy had had too much to drink, and unlike the group across the table, it had made him sullen and quiet. He sat there, staring moodily at the cloth and turning his glass around in fingers that trembled somewhat.

Then he found himself involved in the conversation.

"London as dark as they say?" inquired Christopher Valentine. He was a thin young man, with a small, affectedly curled mustache. Clayton did not care for him, but Natalie found him amusing. "I haven't been over —" he really said 'ovah' —"for ages. Eight months or so."

"Very dark. Hard to get about."

"Most of the fellows I know over there are doing something. I'd like to run over, but what's the use? Nobody around, street's dark, no gayety, nothing."

"No. You'd better stay at home. They-don't particularly want visitors, anyhow."

"Unless they go for war contracts, eh?" said Valentine pleasantly, a way he had of taking the edge off the frequent impertinence of his speech. "No, I'm not going over. We're not popular over there, I understand. Keep on thinking we ought to take a hand in the dirty mess."

Graham spoke, unexpectedly.

"Well, don't you think we ought?"

"If you want my candid opinion, no. We've been waving a red flag called the Monroe Doctrine for some little time, as a signal that we won't stand for Europe coming over here and grabbing anything. If we're going to be consistent, we can't do any grabbing in Europe, can we?"

Clayton eyed him rather contemptuously.

"We might want to 'grab' as you term it, a share in putting the madmen of Europe into chains," he said. "I thought you were pro-British, Chris."

"Only as to clothes, women and filet of sole," Chris returned flippantly. Then, seeing Graham glowering at him across the table, he dropped his affectation of frivolity. "What's the use of our going in now?" he argued. "This Somme push is the biggest thing yet. They're going through the Germans like a hay cutter through a field. German losses half a million already."

"And what about the Allies? Have they lost nothing?" This was Clayton's attorney, an Irishman named Denis Nolan. There had been two n's in the Denis, originally, but although he had disposed of a part of his birthright, he was still belligerently Irish. "What about Rumania? What about the Russians at Lemberg? What about Saloniki?"

"You Irish!" said the rector, genially. "Always fighting the world and each other. Tell me, Nolan, why is it that you always have individual humor and collective ill-humor?"

He felt that that was rather neat. But Nolan was regarding him acrimoniously, and Clayton apparently had not heard at all.

The dispute went on, Chris Valentine alternately flippant and earnest, the rector conciliatory, Graham glowering and silent. Nolan had started on the Irish question, and Rodney baited him with the prospect of conscription there. Nolan's voice, full and mellow and strangely sweet, dominated the room.

But Clayton was not listening. He had heard Nolan air his views before. He was a trifle acid, was Nolan. He needed mellowing, a woman in his life. But Nolan had loved once, and the girl had died. With the curious constancy of the Irish, he had remained determinedly celibate.

"Strange race," Clayton reflected idly, as Nolan's voice sang on. "Don't know what they want, but want it like the devil. One-woman men, too. Curious!"

It occurred to him then that his own reflection was as odd as the fidelity of the Irish. He had been faithful to his wife. He had never thought of being anything else.

He did not pursue that line of thought. He sat back and resumed his nervous tapping of the cloth, not listening, hardly thinking, but conscious of a discontent that was beyond analysis.

Clayton had been aware, since his return from the continent and England days before, of a change in himself. He had not recognized it until he reached home. And he was angry with himself for feeling it. He had gone abroad for certain Italian contracts and had obtained them. A year or two, if the war lasted so long, and he would be on his feet at last, after years of struggle to keep his organization together through the hard times that preceded the war. He would be much more than on his feet. Given three more years of war, and he would be a very rich man.

And now that the goal was within sight, he was finding that it was not money he wanted. There were some things money could not buy. He had always spent money. His anxieties had not influenced his scale of living. Money, for instance, could not buy peace for the world; or peace for a man, either. It had only one value for a man; it gave him independence of other men, made him free.

"Three things," said the rector, apropos of something or other, and rather oratorically, "are required by the normal man. Work, play, and love. Assure the crippled soldier that he has lost none of these, and —"

Work and play and love. Well, God knows he had worked. Play? He would have to take up golf again more regularly. He ought to play three times a week. Perhaps he could take a motor-tour now and then, too. Natalie would like that.

Love? He had not thought about love very much. A married man of forty-five certainly had no business thinking about love. No, he certainly did not want love. He felt rather absurd, even thinking about it. And yet, in the same flash, came a thought of the violent passions of his early twenties. There had been a time when he had suffered horribly because Natalie had not wanted to marry him. He was glad all that was over. No, he certainly did not want love.

He drew a long breath and straightened up.

"How about those plans, Rodney?" he inquired genially. "Natalie says you have them ready to look over."

"I'll bring them round, any time you say."

"To-morrow, then. Better not lose any time. Building is going to be a slow matter, at the best."

"Slow and expensive," Page added. He smiled at his host, but Clayton Spencer remained grave.

"I've been away," he said, "and I don't know what Natalie and you have cooked up between you. But just remember this: I want a comfortable country house. I don't want a public library."

Page looked uncomfortable. The move into the drawing-room covered his uneasiness, but he found a moment later on to revert to the subject.

"I have tried to carry out Natalie's ideas, Clay," he said. "She wanted a sizeable place, you know. A wing for house-parties, and-that sort of thing."

Clayton's eyes roamed about the room, where portly Mrs. Haverford was still knitting placidly, where the Chris Valentines were quarreling under pretense of raillery, where Toots Hayden was smoking a cigaret in a corner and smiling up at Graham, and where Natalie, exquisite and precise, was supervising the laying out of a bridge table.

"She would, of course," he observed, rather curtly, and, moving through a French window, went out onto a small balcony into the night.

He was irritated with himself. What had come over him? He shook himself, and drew a long breath of the sweet night air. His tall, boyishly straight figure dominated the little place. In the half-light he looked, indeed, like an overgrown boy. He always looked like Graham's brother, anyhow; it was one of Natalie's complaints against him. But he put the thought of Natalie away, along with his new discontent. By George, it was something to feel that, if a man could not fight in this war, at least he could make shells to help end it. Oblivious to the laughter in the room behind him, the clink of glass as whiskey-and-soda was brought in, he planned there in the darkness, new organization, new expansions-and found in it a great content.

He was proud of his mills. They were his, of his making. The small iron foundry of his father's building had developed into the colossal furnaces that night after night lighted the down-town district like a great conflagration. He was proud of his mills and of his men. He liked to take men and see them work out his judgment of them. He was not often wrong. Take that room behind him: Rodney Page, dilettante, liked by women, who called him "Roddie," a trifle unscrupulous but not entirely a knave, the sort of man one trusted with everything but one's wife; Chris, too-only he let married women alone, and forgot to pay back the money he borrowed. There was only one man in the room about whom he was beginning to mistrust his judgment, and that was his own son.

Perhaps it was because he had so recently come from lands where millions of boys like Graham were pouring out their young lives like wine, that Clayton Spencer was seeing Graham with a new vision. He turned and glanced back into the drawing-room, where Graham, in the center of that misfit group and not quite himself, was stooping over Marion Hayden. They would have to face that, of course, the woman urge in the boy. Until now his escapades had been boyish ones, a few debts frankly revealed and as frankly regretted, some college mischiefs, a rather serious gambling fever, quickly curbed. But never women, thank God.

But now the boy was through with college, and already he noticed something new in their relationship. Natalie had always spoiled him, and now there were, with increasing frequency, small consultations in her room when he was shut out, and he was beginning to notice a restraint in his relations with the boy, as though mother and son had united against him.

He was confident that Natalie was augmenting Graham's allowance from her own. His salary, rather, for he had taken the boy into the business, not as a partner-that would come later-but as the manager of a department. He never spoke to Natalie of money. Her house bills were paid at the office without question. But only that day Miss Potter, his secretary, had reported that Mrs. Spencer's bank had called up and he had made good a considerable overdraft.

He laid the cause of his discontent to Graham, finally. The boy had good stuff in him. He was not going to allow Natalie to spoil him, or to withdraw him into that little realm of detachment in which she lived. Natalie did not need him, and had not, either as a lover or a husband, for years. But the boy did.

There was a little stir in the room behind. The Haverfords were leaving, and the Hayden girl, who was plainly finding the party dull. Graham was looking down at her, a tall, handsome boy, with Natalie's blonde hair but his father's height and almost insolent good looks.

"Come around to-morrow," she was saying. "About four. There's always a crowd about five, you know."

Clayton knew, and felt a misgiving. The Hayden house was a late afternoon loafing and meeting place for the idle sons and daughters of the rich. Not the conservative old families, who had developed a sense of the responsibility of wealth, but of the second generation of easily acquired money. As she went out, with Graham at her elbow, he heard Chris, at the bridge table.

"Terrible house, the Haydens. Just one step from the Saturday night carouse in Clay's mill district."

When Graham came back, Mrs. Haverford put her hand on his arm.

"I wish you would come to see us, Graham. Delight so often speaks of you."

Graham stiffened almost imperceptibly.

"Thanks, I will." But his tone was distant.

"You know she comes out this winter."

"Really?"

"And-you were great friends. I think she misses you a little."

"I wish I thought so!"

Gentle Mrs. Haverford glanced up at him quickly.

"You know she doesn't approve of me."

"Why, Graham!"

"Well, ask her," he said. And there was a real bitterness under the lightness of his tone. "I'll come, of course, Mrs. Haverford. Thank you for asking me. I haven't a lot of time. I'm a sort of clerk down at the mill, you know."

Natalie overheard, and her eyes met Clayton's, with a glance of malicious triumph. She had been deeply resentful that he had not made Graham a partner at once. He remembered a conversation they had had a few months before.

"Why should he have to start at the bottom?" she had protested. "You have never been quite fair to him, Clay." His boyish diminutive had stuck to him. "You expect him to know as much about the mill now as you do, after all these years."

"Not at all. I want him to learn. That's precisely the reason why I'm not taking him in at once."

"How much salary is he to have?"

"Three thousand a year."

"Three thousand! Why, it will take all of that to buy him a car."

"There are three cars here now; I should think he could manage."

"Every boy wants his own car."

"I pay my other managers three thousand," he had said, still patient. "He will live here. His car can be kept here, without expense. Personally, I think it too much money for the service he will be able to give for the first year or two."

And, although she had let it go at that, he had felt in her a keen resentment. Graham had got a car of his own, was using it hard, if the bills the chauffeur presented were an indication, and Natalie had overdrawn her account two thousand five hundred dollars.

The evening wore on. Two tables of bridge were going, with Denis Nolan sitting in at one. Money in large amounts was being written in on the bridge scores. The air of the room was heavy with smoke, and all the men and some of the women were drinking rather too much. There were splotches of color under the tan in Graham's cheeks, and even Natalie's laughter had taken on a higher note.

Chris's words rankled in Clayton Spencer's mind. A step from the Saturday night carouse. How much better was this sort of thing? A dull party, driven to cards and drink to get through the evening. And what sort of home life were he and Natalie giving the boy? Either this, or the dreary evenings when they were alone, with Natalie sitting with folded hands, or withdrawing to her boudoir upstairs, where invariably she summoned Graham to talk to him behind closed doors.

He went into the library and shut the door. The room rested him, after the babble across. He lighted a cigar, and stood for a moment before Natalie's portrait. It had been painted while he was abroad at, he suspected, Rodney's instigation. It left him quite cold, as did Natalie herself.

He could look at it dispassionately, as he had never quite cared to regard Natalie. Between them, personally, there was always the element she never allowed him to forget, that she had given him a son. This was Natalie herself, Natalie at forty-one, girlish, beautiful, fretful and-selfish. Natalie with whom he was to live the rest of his life, who was to share his wealth and his future, and with whom he shared not a single thought in common.

He had a curious sense of disloyalty as he sat down at his desk and picked up a pad and pencil. But a moment later he had forgotten her, as he had forgotten the party across the hall. He had work to do. Thank God for work.

Chapter II

Natalie was in bed when he went up-stairs. Through the door of his dressing-room he could see her lying, surrounded by papers. Natalie's handsome bed was always covered with things, her handkerchief, a novel, her silk dressing-gown flung over the footboard, sometimes bits of dress materials and lace. Natalie did most of her planning in bed.

He went in and, clearing a space, sat down on the foot of the bed, facing her. Her hair was arranged in a loose knot on top of her head, and there was a tiny space, perhaps a quarter of an inch, slightly darker than the rest. He realized with a little start that she had had her hair touched up during his absence. Still, she looked very pretty, her skin slightly glistening with its night's bath of cold cream, her slim arms lying out on the blue silk eiderdown coverlet.

"I told Doctor Haverford to-night that we would like to give him a car, Natalie," he began directly. It was typical of him, the "we."

"A car? What for?"

"To ride about in, my dear. It's rather a large parish, you know. And I don't feel exactly comfortable seeing him tramping along when most people are awheel. He's not very young."

"He'll kill himself, that's all."

"Well, that's rather up to Providence, of course."

"You are throwing a sop to Providence, aren't you?" she asked shrewdly. "Throwing bread on the waters! I daresay he angled for it. You're easy, Clay. Give you a good dinner-it was a nice dinner, wasn't it?"

"A very nice dinner," he assented. But at the tone she looked up.

"Well, what was wrong?" she demanded. "I saw when I went out that you were angry about something. Your face was awful."

"Oh, come now, Natalie," he protested. "It wasn't anything of the sort. The dinner was all right. The guests were-all right. I may have unconsciously resented your attitude about Doctor Haverford. Certainly he didn't angle for it, and I had no idea of throwing a sop to Providence."

"That isn't what was wrong at dinner."

"Do you really want me to tell you?"

"Not if it's too disagreeable."

"Good heavens, Natalie. One would think I bullied you!"

"Oh, no, you don't bully. It's worse. It's the way you look. Your face sets. Well?"

"I didn't feel unpleasant. It's rather my misfortune that my face —"

"Didn't you like my gown?"

"Very much. It seemed a trifle low, but you know I always like your clothes." He was almost pathetically anxious to make up to her for that moment's disloyalty in the library.

"There!" she said, brushing the papers aside. "Now we're getting at it. Was I anything like as low as Audrey Valentine? Of course not! Her back-You just drive me to despair, Clay. Nothing I do pleases you. The very tone of that secretary of yours to-day, when I told her about that over-draft—it was positively insulting!"

"I don't like overdrafts," he said, without any irritation. "When you want extra amounts you have only to let me know."

"You are always finding fault with me," she complained. "It's either money, or my clothes, or Graham, or something." Her eyes filled. She looked young and absurdly childish. But a talk he had had with the rector was still in his mind. It was while they were still at the table, and Nolan had been attacking the British government.

"We get out of this world largely what we put into it," he had said. "You give largely, Clay, and you receive largely. I rejoice in your prosperity, because you have earned it."

"You think, then," he had asked, "that we only receive as we give? I don't mean material things, of course."

The rector had fixed him with kindly, rather faded old eyes. "That has been my experience," he said. "Happiness for instance only comes when we forget our eternal search for it, and try to make others happy. Even religion is changing. The old selfish idea of saving our own souls has given way largely to the saving of others, by giving them a chance to redeem themselves. Decent living conditions—"

He had gone on, but Clayton had not listened very intently. He had been wondering if happiness was not the thing he had somehow missed. It was then that he had decided to give the car. If, after all, that would make for the rector's happiness—

"I don't want to find fault with you, Natalie," he said gravely. "I would like to see you happy. Sometimes I think you are not. I have my business, but you have nothing to do, and—I suppose you wouldn't be interested in war-work, would you? There are a lot of committees, and since I've been in England I realize what a vast amount is needed. Clothes, you know, and bandages, and-well, everything."

"Nothing to do," she looked up, her eyes wide and indignant. "But of course you would think that. This house runs itself, I suppose."

"Let's be honest, Natalie," he said, with a touch of impatience. "Actually how much time each day do you give this house? You have plenty of trained servants. An hour? Two hours?"

"I'll not discuss it with you." She took up a typewritten sheet and pretended to read it carefully. Clayton had a half-humorous, half-irritated conviction that if he was actually hunting happiness he had begun his search for it rather badly. He took the paper from her, gently.

"What's this?" he inquired. "Anything I should not see?"

"Decorator's estimates for the new house." Her voice was resentful. "You'll have to see them some time."

"Library curtains, gray Chippendale velvet, gold gimp, faced with colonial yellow," he read an item picked at random, "two thousand dollars! That's going some for curtains, isn't it?"

"It's not too much for that sort of thing."

"But, look here, Natalie," he expostulated. "This is to be a country house, isn't it? I thought you wanted chintzed and homey things. This looks like a city house in the country."

He glanced down at the total. The hangings alone, with a tapestry or two, were to be thirty-five thousand dollars. He whistled.

"Hangings alone! And-what sort of a house has Rodney planned, anyhow?"

"Italian, with a sunken garden. The landscape estimates are there, too."

He did not look at them.

"It seems to me you and Rodney have been pretty busy while I've been away," he remarked. "Well, I want you to be happy, my dear. Only—I don't want to tie up a fortune just now. We may get into this war, and if we do —" He rose, and yawned, his arms above his head. "I'm off to bed," he said. "Big day to-morrow. I'll want Graham at the office at 8:30."

She had sat up in bed, and was staring at him. Her face was pale.

"Do you mean that we are going to get into this war?"

"I think it very likely, my dear."

"But if we do, Graham —"

"We might as well face it. Graham will probably want to go."

"He'll do nothing of the sort," she said sharply. "He's all I have. All. Do you think I'm going to send him over there to be cannon-fodder? I won't let him go."

She was trembling violently.

"I won't want him to go, of course. But if the thing comes-he's of age, you know."

She eyed him with thinly veiled hostility.

"You're hard, Clay," she accused him. "You're hard all the way through. You're proud, too. Proud and hard. You'd want to be able to say your son was in the army. It's not because you care anything about the war, except to make money out of it. What is the war to you, anyhow? You don't like the English, and as for French-you don't even let me have a French butler."

He was not the less angry because he realized the essential truth of part of what she said. He felt no great impulse of sympathy with any of the combatants. He knew the gravity of the situation rather than its tragedy. He did not like war, any war. He saw no reason why men should kill. But this war was a fact. He had had no hand in its making, but it was made.

His first impulse was to leave her in dignified silence. But she was crying, and I he disliked leaving her in tears. Dead as was his love for her, and that night, somehow, he knew that it was dead, she was still his wife. They had had some fairly happy years together, long ago. And he felt the need, too, of justification.

"Perhaps you are right, Natalie," he said, after a moment. "I haven't cared about this war as much as I should. Not the human side of it, anyhow. But you ought to understand that by making shells for the Allies, I am not only making money for myself; they need the shells. And I'll give them the best. I don't intend only to profit by their misfortunes."

She had hardly listened.

"Then, if we get into it, as you say, you'll encourage Graham to go?"

"I shall allow him to go, if he feels it his duty."

"Oh, duty, duty! I'm sick of the word." She bent forward and suddenly caught one of his hands. "You won't make him go, Clay?" she begged. "You-you'll let him make his own de-cision?"

"If you will."

"What do you mean?"

"If you'll keep your hands off, too. We're not in it, yet. God knows I hope we won't be. But if I promise not to influence him, you must do the same thing."

"I haven't any more influence over Graham than that," she said, and snapped her finger. But she did not look at him.

"Promise," he said, steadily.

"Oh, all right." Her voice and face were sulky. She looked much as Graham had that evening at the table.

"Is that a promise?"

"Good heavens, do you want me to swear to it?"

"I want you to play fair. That's all."

She leaned back again among her pillows and gathered her papers.

"All right," she said, indifferently. "Have you any preference as to color for your rooms in the new house?"

He was sorry for his anger, and after all, these things which seemed so unimportant to him were the things that made up her life. He smiled.

"You might match my eyes. I'm not sure what color they are. Perhaps you know."

But she had not forgiven him.

"I've never noticed," she replied. And, small bundle of samples in her hand, resumed her reading and her inspection of textiles.

"Good night, Natalie."

"Good night." She did not look up.

Outside his wife's door he hesitated. Then he crossed and without knocking entered Graham's bedroom. The boy was lounging in a long chair by an open fire. He was in his dressing gown and slippers, and an empty whiskey-and-soda glass stood beside him on a small stand. Graham was sound asleep. Clayton touched him on the shoulder, but he slept on, his head to one side, his breathing slow and heavy. It required some little effort to waken him.

"Graham!" said Clayton sharply.

"Yes." He stirred, but did not open his eyes.

"Graham! Wake up, boy."

Graham sat up suddenly and looked at him. The whites of his eyes were red, but he had slept off the dinner wine. He was quite himself.

"Better get to bed," his father suggested. "I'll want you early to-morrow."

"What time, sir?"

He leaned forward and pressed a button beside the mantel-piece.

"What are you doing that for?"

"Ice water. Awfully thirsty."

"The servants have gone to bed. Go down and get it yourself."

Graham looked up at the tone. At his father's eyes, he looked away.

"Sorry, sir," he said. "Must have had too much champagne. Wasn't much else to do, was there? Mother's parties-my God, what a dreary lot!"

Clayton inspected the ice water carafe on the stand and found it empty.

"I'll bring you some water from my room," he said. "And—I don't want to see you this way again, Graham. When a man cannot take a little wine at his own table without taking too much he fails to be entirely a gentleman."

He went out. When he came back, Graham was standing by the fire in his pajamas, looking young and rather ashamed. Clayton had a flash of those earlier days when he had come in to bid the boy good night, and there had always been that last request for water which was to postpone the final switching off of the light.

"I'm sorry, father."

Clayton put his hand on the boy's shoulder and patted him.

"We'll have to do better next time. That's all."

For a moment the veil of constraint of Natalie's weaving lifted between them.

"I'm a pretty bad egg, I guess. You'd better shove me off the dock and let me swim-or drown."

"I'd hardly like to do that, you know. You are all I have."

"I'm no good at the mill."

"You haven't had very much time. I've been a good many years learning the business.'"

"I'll never be any good. Not there. If there was something to build up it would be different, but it's all done. You've done it. I'm only a sort of sublimated clerk. I don't mean," he added hastily, "that I think I ought to have anything more. It's only that-well, the struggle's over, if you know what I mean."

"I'll talk to you about that to-morrow. Get to bed now. It's one o'clock."

He moved to the doorway. Graham, carafe in hand, stood staring ahead of him. He had the courage of the last whiskey-and-soda, and a sort of desperate contrition.

"Father."

"Yes, Graham."

"I wish you'd let me go to France and fly."

Something like a cold hand seemed to close round Clayton's heart.

"Fly! Why?"

"Because I'm not doing any good here. And-because I'd like to see if I have any good stuff in me. All the fellows are going," he added, rather weakly.

"That's not a particularly worthy reason, is it?"

"It's about as worthy as making money out of shells, when we haven't any reason for selling them to the Allies more than the Germans, except that we can't ship to the Germans."

He looked rather frightened then. But Clayton was not angry. He saw Natalie's fine hand there, and the boy's impressionable nature.

"Think that over, Graham," he said gravely. "I don't believe you quite mean it. Good-night."

He went across to his own bedroom, where his silk pajamas, neatly folded, lay on his painted Louis XVI bed. Under his reading lamp there was a book. It was a part of Natalie's decorative scheme for the room; it's binding was mauve, to match the hangings. For the first time since the room had been done over during his absence he picked up the book.

"Rodney's idea, for a cent!" he reflected, looking rather grimly at the cover.

He undressed slowly, his mind full of Graham and the problem he presented. Then he thought of Natalie, and of the little things that made up her life and filled her days. He glanced about the room, beautiful, formal, exquisitely appointed. His father's portrait was gone from over the mantel, and an old French water-color hung there instead. That was too bad of Natalie. Or had it been Rodney? He would bring it back. And he gave a fleeting thought to Graham and his request to go abroad. He had not meant it. It was sheer reaction. But he would talk to Graham.

He lighted a cigaret, and getting into bed turned on his reading lamp. Queer how a man could build, and then find that after all he did not care for the achievement. It was the building alone that was worth while.

He picked up the book from the table, and opened it casually.

> "When first I loved I gave my very soul
> Utterly unreserved to Love's control,
> But Love deceived me, wrenched my youth away,
> And made the gold of life forever gray.
> Long I lived lonely, yet I tried in vain
> With any other joy to stifle pain;
> There is no other joy, I learned to know,
> And so returned to love, as long ago,
> Yet I, this little while ere I go hence,
> Love very lightly now, in self defense."

"Twaddle," said Clayton Spencer, and put the book away. That was the sort of stuff men like Rodney lived on. In a mauve binding, too.

After he had put out the light he lay for a long time, staring into the darkness. It was not love he wanted: he was through with all that. Power was the thing, integrity and power. To yield to no man, to achieve independence for one's soul-not that he put it that way. He formulated it, drowsily: 'Not to give a damn for any one, so long as you're right.' Of course, it was not always possible to know if one was right. He yawned. His conscious mind was drowsing, and from the depths below, released of the sentry of his waking hours, came the call of his starved imagination.

Chapter III

There was no moral to be adduced from Graham's waking the next morning. He roused, reluctantly enough, but blithe and hungry. He sang as he splashed in his shower, chose his tie whistling, and went down the staircase two steps at a time to a ravenous breakfast.

Clayton was already at the table in the breakfast room, sitting back with the newspaper, his coffee at his elbow, the first cigarette of the morning half smoked. He looked rather older in the morning light. Small fine threads had begun to show themselves at the corners of his eyes. The lines of repression from the nostrils to the corners of the mouth seemed deeper. But his invincible look of boyishness persisted, at that.

There was no awkwardness in Graham's "Morning, dad." He had not forgotten the night before, but he had already forgiven himself. He ignored the newspaper at his plate, and dug into his grapefruit.

"Anything new?" he inquired casually.

"You might look and see," Clayton suggested, good-naturedly.

"I'll read going down in the car. Can't stand war news on an empty stomach. Mother all right this morning?"

"I think she is still sleeping."

"Well, I should say she needs it, after last night. How in the world we manage, with all the interesting people in the world, to get together such a dreary lot as that-Lord, it was awful."

Clayton rose and folded his paper.

"The car's waiting," he said. "I'll be ready in five minutes."

He went slowly up the stairs. In her pink bedroom Natalie had just wakened. Madeleine, her elderly French maid, had brought her breakfast, and she was lying back among the pillows, the litter of the early mail about her and a morning paper on her knee. He bent over and kissed her, perfunctorily, and he was quick to see that her resentment of the evening before had survived the night.

"Sleep well?" he inquired, looking down at her. She evaded his eyes.

"Not particularly."

"Any plans for to-day?"

"I'll just play around. I'm lunching out, and I may run out with Rodney to Linndale. The landscape men are there today."

She picked up the newspaper as though to end the discussion. He saw then that she was reading the society news, and he rather more than surmised that she had not even glanced at the black headings which on the first page announced the hideous casualties of the Somme.

"Then you've given the planting contract?"

"Some things have to go in in the fall, Clay. For heaven's sake, don't look like a thunder cloud."

"Have you given the landscape contract?"

"Yes. And please go out. You make my head ache."

"How much is it to be?"

"I don't know. Ask Rodney."

"I'll do nothing of the sort, my dear. This is not Rodney's investment."

"Nor mine, I suppose!"

"All I want you to do, Natalie, is to consult me. I want you to have a free hand, but some one with a sense of responsibility ought to check up these expenditures. But it isn't only that. I'd like to have a hand in the thing myself. I've rather looked forward to the time when we could have the sort of country place we wanted."

"You don't like any of the strings to get out of your fingers, do you?"

"I didn't come up to quarrel, Natalie. I wish you wouldn't force it on me."

"I force it on you," she cried, and laughed in a forced and high-pitched note. "Just because I won't be over-ridden without a protest! I'm through, that's all. I shan't go near the place again."

"You don't understand," he persisted patiently. "I happen to like gardens. I had an idea —I told you about it-of trying to duplicate the old garden at home. You remember it. When we went there on our honeymoon —"

"You don't call that a garden?"

"Of course I didn't want to copy it exactly. It was old and out of condition. But there were a lot of old-fashioned flowers —-However, if you intend to build an Italian villa, naturally —"

"I don't intend to build anything, or to plant anything." Her voice was frozen. "You go ahead. Do it in your own way. And then you can live there, if you like. I won't."

Which was what he carried away with him that morning to the mill. He was not greatly disturbed by her threat to keep her hands off. He knew quite well, indeed, that the afternoon would find her, with Rodney Page, picking her way in her high-heeled shoes over the waste that was some day to bloom, not like the rose of his desire but according to the formal and rigid blueprint which Rodney would be carrying. But in five minutes he had put the incident out of his mind. After all, if it gave her happiness and occupation, certainly she needed both. And his powers of inhibition were strong. For many years he had walled up the small frictions of his married life and its disappointments, and outside that wall had built up an existence of his own, which was the mill.

When he went down-stairs he found that Graham had ordered his own car and was already in it, drawing on his gloves.

"Have to come back up-town early, dad," he called in explanation, and drove off, going at the reckless speed he affected.

Clayton rode down alone in the limousine. He had meant to outline his plans of expansion to Graham, but he had had no intention of consulting him. In his own department the boy did neither better nor worse than any other of the dozens of young men in the organization. If he had shown neither special aptitude for nor interest in the business, he had at least not signally failed to show either. Now, paper and pencil in hand, Clayton jotted down the various details of the new system in their sequence; the building of a forging plant to make the rough casts for the new Italian shells out of the steel from the furnaces, the construction of a new spur to the little railway which bound the old plant together with its shining steel rails. There were questions of supplies and shipping and bank credits to face, the vast and complex problems of the complete new munition works, to be built out of town and involving such matters as the housing of enormous numbers of employees. He scrawled figures and added them. Even with the size of the foreign contract their magnitude startled him. He leaned back, his mouth compressed, the lines from the nostrils to the corners deeper than ever.

He had completely forgotten Natalie and the country house.

Outside the gates to the mill enclosure he heard an early extra being called, and bought it. The Austrian premier had been assassinated. The successful French counter-attack against Verdun was corroborated, also. On the center of the front page was the first photograph to reach America of a tank. He inspected it with interest. So the Allies had at last shown same inventive genius of their own! Perhaps this was but the beginning. Even at that, enough of these fighting mammoths, and the war might end quickly. With the tanks, and the Allied offensive and the evidence of discontent in Austria, the thing might after all be over before America was involved.

He reflected, however, that an early peace would not be an unmixed blessing for him. He wanted the war to end: he hated killing. He felt inarticulately that something horrible was happening to the world. But personally his plans were premised on a war to last at least two years more, until the fall of 1918. That would let him out, cover the cost of the new plant, bring renewals of his foreign contracts, justify those stupendous figures on the paper in his hand.

He wondered, rather uncomfortably, what he would do, under the circumstances, if it were in his power to declare peace to-morrow.

In his office in the mill administration building, he found the general manager waiting. Through the door into the conference room beyond he could see the superintendents of the various departments, with Graham rather aloof and detached, and a sprinkling of the most important foremen. On his desk, neatly machined, was the first tentative shell-case made in the mill machine-shop, an experiment rather than a realization.

Hutchinson, the general manager, was not alone. Opposite him, very neatly dressed in his best clothes, his hat in his hand and a set expression on his face, was one of the boss rollers of the steel mill, Herman Klein. At Clayton's entrance he made a motion to depart, but Hutchinson stopped him.

"Tell Mr. Spencer what you've been telling me, Klein," he said curtly.

Klein fingered his hat, but his face remained set.

"I've just been saying, Mr. Spencer," he said, in good English, but with the guttural accent which thirty years in America had not eliminated, "that I'll be leaving you now."

"Leaving! Why?"

"Because of that!" He pointed, without intentional drama, at the shell-case. "I can't make those shells for you, Mr. Spencer, and me a German."

"You're an American, aren't you?"

"I am, sir. It is not that. It iss that I —" His face worked. He had dropped back to the old idiom, after years of painful struggle to abandon it. "It iss that I am a German, also. I have people there, in the war. To make shells to kill them-no."

"He is determined, Mr. Spencer," said Hutchinson. "I have been arguing with him, but-you can't argue with a German."

Clayton was uneasily aware of something like sympathy for the man.

"I understand how you feel, Klein," he observed. "But of course you know, whether you go or stay, the shells will be made, anyhow."

"I know that."

"You are throwing up a good position."

"I'll try to get another."

The prospective loss of Klein was a rather serious one. Clayton, seated behind his great desk, eyed him keenly, and then stooped to bribery. He mentioned a change in the wage scale, with bonuses to all foremen and rollers. He knew Klein's pride in the mill, and he outlined briefly the growth that was about to be developed. But the boss roller remained obdurate. He understood that such things were to be, but it was not necessary that he assist Germany's enemies against her. Against the determination in his heavy square figure Clayton argued in vain. When, ten minutes later, he went into the conference room, followed by a secretary with a sheaf of papers, the mill was minus a boss roller, and there was rankling in his mind Klein's last words.

"I haf no objection, Mr. Spencer, to your making money out of this war, but I will not."

There had been no insolence in his tone. He had gone out, with his heavy German stolidity of mien unchanged, and had closed the door behind him with quiet finality.

Chapter IV

Graham left the conference that morning in a rather exalted mood. The old mill was coming into its own at last. He had a sense of boyish triumph in the new developments, a feeling of being a part of big activities that would bring rich rewards. And he felt a new pride in his father. He had sat, a little way from the long table, and had watched the faces of the men gathered about it as clearly and forcibly the outlines of the new departure were given out. Hitherto "Spencer's" had made steel only. Now, they were not only to make the steel, but they were to forge the ingots into rough casts; these casts were then to be carried to the new munition works, there to be machined, drilled, polished, provided with fuses, which "Spencer's" were also to make, and shipped abroad.

The question of speeding production had been faced and met. The various problems had been discussed and the bonus system tentatively taken up. Then the men had dispersed, each infected with the drive of his father's contagious force. "Pretty fine old boy," Graham had considered. And he wondered vaguely if, when his time came, he would be able to take hold. For a few minutes Natalie's closetings lost their effect. He saw his father, not as one from whom to hide extravagance and unpaid bills, but as the head of a great concern that was now to be a part of the war itself. He wandered into his father's office, and picked up the shell. Clayton was already at his letters, but looked up.

"Think we rather had them, eh, Graham?"

"Think you did, sir. Carried them off their feet. Pretty, isn't it?" He held up the shell-case. "If a fellow could only forget what the damned things are for!"

"They are to help to end the war," said Clayton, crisply. "Don't forget that, boy." And went back to his steady dictation.

Graham went out of the building into the mill yard. The noise always irritated him. He had none of Clayton's joy and understanding of it. To Clayton each sound had its corresponding activity. To Graham it was merely din, an annoyance to his ears, as the mill yard outraged his fastidiousness. But that morning he found it rather more bearable. He stooped where, in front of the store, the storekeeper had planted a tiny garden. Some small late-blossoming chrysanthemums were still there and he picked one and put it in his buttonhole.

His own office was across the yard. He dodged in front of a yard locomotive, picked his way about masses of lumber and the general litter of all mill yards, and opened the door of his own building. Just inside his office a girl was sitting on a straight chair, her hat a trifle crooked, and her eyes red from crying. He paused in amazement.

"Why, Miss Klein!" he said. "What's the matter?"

She was rather a pretty girl, even now. She stood up at his voice and made an effort to straighten her hat.

"Haven't you heard?" she asked.

"I haven't heard anything that ought to make Miss Anna Klein weep of a nice, frosty morning in October. Unless —" he sobered, for her grief was evident. "Tell me about it."

"Father has given up his job."

"No!"!

"I'm telling you, Mr. Spencer. He won't help to make those shells. He's been acting queer for three or four days and this morning he told your father."

Graham whistled.

"As if it made any difference," she went on irritably. "Some one else will get his job. That's all. What does he care about the Germans? He left them and came to America as soon as he could walk."

Graham sat down.

"Now let's get this," he said. "He won't make shells for the Allies and so he's given up his position. All right. That's bad, but he's a good workman. He'll not have any trouble getting another job. Now, why are you crying?"

"I didn't think you'd want me to stay on."

Putting her fear into words brought back her long hours of terror. She collapsed into the chair again and fell to unquiet sobbing. Graham was disturbed.

"You're a queer girl," he said. "Why should that lose me my most valued assistant?"

When she made no reply he got up and going over to her put a hand on her shoulder. "Tell me that," he said.

He looked down at her. The hair grew very soft and blonde at the nape of her neck, and he ran a finger lightly across it. "Tell me that."

"I was afraid it would."

"And, even if it had, which you are a goose for thinking, you're just as good in your line as your father is in his. I've been expecting any time to hear of your leaving me for a handsomer man!"

He had been what he would have termed jollying her back to normality again. But to his intense surprise she suddenly leaned back and looked up into his face. There was no doubting what he saw there. Just for a moment the situation threatened to get out of hand. Then he patted her shoulders and put the safety of his desk between them.

"Run away and bathe your eyes," he said, "and then come back here looking like the best secretary in the state, and not like a winter thaw. We have the deuce of a lot of work to do."

But after she had gone he sat for some little time idly rapping a pencil on the top of his desk. By Jove! Anna Klein! Of all girls in the world! It was rather a pity, too. She was a nice little thing, and in the last few months she had changed a lot. She had been timid at first, and hideously dressed. Lately she had been almost smart. Those ear-rings now-they changed her a lot. Queer-how things went on in a girl's mind, and a fellow didn't know until something happened. He settled his tie and smoothed back his heavy hair.

During the remainder of the day he began to wonder if he had not been a fatuous idiot. Anna did her work with the thoroughness of her German blood plus her American training. She came back minus her hat, and with her eyes carefully powdered, and not once during the morning was he able to meet her eyes fully. By the middle of the afternoon sex vanity and curiosity began to get the better of his judgment, and he made an excuse, when she stood beside him over some papers, her hand on the desk, to lay his fingers over hers. She drew her hand away quickly, and when he glanced up, boyishly smiling, her face was flushed.

"Please," she said. And he felt hurt and rebuffed. He had no sentiment for her whatever, but the devil of mischief of twenty-two was behind him, urging him on to the eternal experiment. He was very formal with her for the rest of the day, and had the satisfaction of leaving her, at four o'clock, white-faced and miserable over her machine in the little office next to his.

He forgot her immediately, in the attempt to leave the mill without encountering his father. Clayton, he knew, would be staying late, and would be exacting similar tribute to the emergency from the entire force. Also, he had been going about the yard with contractors most of the afternoon. But Graham made his escape safely. It was two hours later when his father, getting into the limousine, noticed the absence of the boy's red car, and asked the gateman how long it had been gone.

"Since about four o'clock, Mr. Spencer."

Suddenly Clayton felt a reaction from the activities of the day. He sank back in the deeply padded seat, and felt tired and-in some odd fashion-lonely. He would have liked to talk to Graham on the way up-town, if only to crystallize his own thoughts. He would have liked to be going home to review with Natalie the day's events, the fine spirit of his men, the small difficulties. But Natalie hated the mention of the mill.

He thought it probable, too, that they were dining out. Yes, he remembered. They were dining at the Chris Valentines. Well, that was better than it might have been. They were not dull, anyhow. His mind wandered to the Valentine house, small, not too well-ordered, frequently noisy, but always gay and extremely smart.

He thought of Audrey, and her curious friendship with Natalie. Audrey the careless, with her dark lazy charm, her deep and rather husky contralto, her astonishing little French songs, which she sang with nonchalant grace, and her crowds of boyish admirers whom she alternately petted and bullied-surely she and Natalie had little enough in common.

Yet, in the last year or so, he had been continually coming across them together-at the club, at luncheon in the women's dining room, at his own house, Natalie always perfectly and expensively dressed, Audrey in the casual garments which somehow her wearing made effective.

He smiled a little. Certain of Audrey's impertinences came to his mind. She was an amusing young woman. He had an idea that she was always in debt, and that the fact concerned her very little. He fancied that few things concerned her very deeply, including Chris. But she knew about food. Her dinners were as casual as her house, as to service, but they were worth eating. She claimed to pay for them out of her bridge winnings, and, indeed, her invitation for to-night had been frankness itself.

"I'm going to have a party, Clay," she had said. "I've made two killings at bridge, and somebody has shipped Chris some ducks. If you'll send me some cigarets like the last, I'll make it Tuesday."

He had sent the cigarets, and this was Tuesday.

The pleasant rolling of the car soothed him. The street flashed by, brilliant with lights that in far perspective seemed to meet. The shop windows gleamed with color. From curb to curb were other cars like the one in which he rode, carrying home other men like himself to whatever the evening held in store. He remembered London at this hour, already dark and quiet, its few motors making their cautious way in the dusk, its throngs of clerks, nearly all women now, hurrying home to whatever dread the night might hold. And it made him slightly more complacent. These things that he had taken for granted before had since his return assumed the quality of luxury.

"Pray God we won't get into it," he said to himself.

He reviewed his unrest of the night before, and smiled at it. Happiness. Happiness came from a sense of achievement. Integrity and power, that was the combination. The respect of one's fellow men, the day's work well done. Romance was done, at his age, but there remained the adventure of success. A few years more, and he would leave the mill to Graham and play awhile. After that-he had always liked politics. They needed business men in politics. If men of training and leisure would only go in for it there would be some chance of cleaning up the situation. Yes, he might do that. He was an easy speaker, and —

The car drew up at the curb and the chauffeur got out. Natalie's car had drawn up just ahead, and the footman was already opening the door. Rodney Page got out, and assisted Natalie to alight. Clayton smiled. So she had changed her mind. He saw Rodney bend over her hand and kiss it after his usual ceremonious manner. Natalie seemed a trifle breathless when she turned and saw him.

"You're early, aren't you?" she said.

"I fancy it is you who are late."

Then he realized that the chauffeur was waiting to speak to him.

"Yes, Jackson?"

"I'm sorry, sir. I guess I'll be leaving at the end of my month, Mr. Spencer."

"Come into the library and I'll talk to you. What's wrong?"

"There's nothing wrong, sir. I have been very well suited. It's only—I used to be in the regular army, sir, and I guess I'm going to be needed again."

"You mean-we are going to be involved?"

"Yes, sir. I think we are."

"There's no answer to that, Jackson," he said. But a sense of irritation stirred him as he went up the steps to the house door. Jackson was a good man. Jackson and Klein, and who knew who would be next?

"Oh, damn the war," he reflected rather wearily.

Chapter V

The winter which preceded the entrance of the United States into the war was socially an extraordinary one. It was marked by an almost feverish gayety, as though, having apparently determined to pursue a policy dictated purely by self interest, the people wished to forget their anomalous position. Like a woman who covers her shame with a smile. The vast number of war orders from abroad had brought prosperity into homes where it had long been absent. Mills and factories took on new life. Labor was scarce and high.

It was a period of extravagance rather than pleasure. People played that they might not think. Washington, convinced that the nation would ultimately be involved, kept its secret well and continued to preach a neutrality it could not enforce. War was to most of the nation a great dramatic spectacle, presented to them at breakfast and in the afternoon editions. It furnished unlimited conversation at dinner-parties, led to endless wrangles, gave zest and point to the peace that made those dinner parties possible, furnished an excuse for retrenchment here and there, and brought into vogue great bazaars and balls for the Red Cross and kindred activities.

But although the war was in the nation's mind, it was not yet in its soul.

Life went on much as before. An abiding faith in the Allies was the foundation stone of its complacency. The great six-months battle of the Somme, with its million casualties, was resulting favorably. On the east the Russians had made some gains. There were wagers that the Germans would be done in the Spring.

But again Washington knew that the British and French losses at the Somme had been frightful; that the amount of lost territory regained was negligible as against the territory still held; that the food problem in the British Islands was acute; that the submarine sinkings were colossal. Our peace was at a fearful cost.

And on the edge of this volcano America played.

When Graham Spencer left the mill that Tuesday afternoon, it was to visit Marion Hayden. He was rather bored now at the prospect. He would have preferred going to the Club to play billiards, which was his custom of a late afternoon. He drove rather more slowly than was his custom, and so missed Marion's invitation to get there before the crowd.

Three cars before the house showed that she already had callers, and indeed when the parlor-maid opened the door a burst of laughter greeted him. The Hayden house was a general rendezvous. There were usually, by seven o'clock, whiskey-and-soda glasses and tea-cups on most of the furniture, and half-smoked cigarets on everything that would hold them, including the piano.

Marion herself met him in the hall, and led him past the drawing-room door.

"There are people in every room who want to be left alone," she volunteered. "I kept the library as long as I could. We can sit on the stairs, if you like."

Which they proceeded to do, quite amiably. From various open doors came subdued voices. The air was pungent with tobacco smoke permeated with a faint scent of late afternoon highballs.

"Tommy!" Marion called, when she had settled herself.

"Yes," from a distance.

"Did you leave your cigaret on the piano?"

"No, Toots dear. But I can, easily."

"Mother," Marion explained, "is getting awfully touchy about the piano. Well, do you remember half the pretty things you told me last night?"

"Not exactly. But I meant them."

He looked up at her admiringly. He was only a year from college, and he had been rather arbitrarily limited to the debutantes. He found, therefore, something rather flattering in the attention he was receiving from a girl who had been out five years, and who was easily the most popular young woman in the gayer set. It gave him a sense of maturity Since the night before he had been rankling under a sense of youth.

"Was I pretty awful last night?" he asked.

"You were very interesting. And —I imagine-rather indiscreet."

"Fine! What did I say?"

"You boasted, my dear young friend."

"Great Scott! I must have been awful."

"About the new war contracts."

"Oh, business!"

"But I found it very interesting. You know, I like business. And I like big figures. Poor people always do. Has it really gone through? I mean, those things do slip up sometimes, don't they.

"It's gone through, all right. Signed, sealed, and delivered."

Encouraged by her interest, he elaborated on the new work. He even developed an enthusiasm for it, to his own surprise. And the girl listened intently, leaning forward so that her arm brushed his shoulder. Her eyes, slightly narrowed, watched him closely. She knew every move of the game she was determining to play.

Marion Hayden, at twenty-five, knew already what her little world had not yet realized, that such beauty as she had had was the beauty of youth only, and that that was going. Late hours, golf, perhaps a little more champagne than was necessary at dinners, and the mornings found her almost plain. And, too, she had the far vision of the calculating mind. She knew that if the country entered the war, every eligible man she knew would immediately volunteer.

At twenty-five she already noticed a change in the personnel of her followers. The unmarried men who had danced with her during her first two winters were now sending flowers to the debutantes, and cutting in on the younger men at balls. Her house was still a rendezvous, but it was for couples like the ones who had preempted the drawing-room, the library and the music room that afternoon. They met there, smoked her cigarets, made love in a corner, occasionally became engaged. But she was of the game, no longer in it.

Men still came to see her, a growing percentage of them married. They brought or sent her tribute, flowers, candy, and cigarets. She was enormously popular at dances. But more and more her dinner invitations were from the older crowd. Like Natalie Spencer's stupid party the night before.

So she watched Graham and listened. He was a nice boy and a handsome one. Also he promised to be sole heir to a great business. If the war only lasted long enough —

"Imagine your knowing all those things," she said admiringly. "You're a partner, aren't you?"

He flushed slightly.

"Not yet. But of course I shall be."

"When you really get going, I wonder if you will take me round and show me how shells are made. I'm the most ignorant person you ever knew."

"I'll be awfully glad to."

"Very well. For that promise you shall have a highball. You're an awful dear, you know."

She placed a slim hand on his shoulder and patted it. Then, leaning rather heavily on him for support, she got to her feet.

"We'll go in and stir up some of the lovers," she suggested. "And if Tommy Hale hasn't burned up the piano we can dance a bit. You dance divinely, you know."

It was after seven when he reached home. He felt every inch a man. He held himself very straight as he entered the house, and the boyish grin with which he customarily greeted the butler had given place to a dignified nod.

Natalie was in her dressing-room. At his knock she told the maid to admit him, and threw a dressing-gown over her bare shoulders. Then she sent the maid away and herself cautiously closed the door into Clayton's room.

"I've got the money for you, darling," she said. From her jewel case she took a roll of bills and held them out to him. "Five hundred."

"I hate to take it, mother."

"Never mind about taking it. Pay those bills before your father learns about them. That's all."

He was divided between gratitude and indignation. His new-found maturity seemed to be slipping from him. Somehow here at home they always managed to make him feel like a small boy.

"Honestly, mother, I'd rather go to father and tell him about it. He'd make a row, probably, but at least you'd be out of it."

She ignored his protest, as she always ignored protests against her own methods of handling matters.

"I'm accustomed to it," was her sole reply. But her resigned voice brought her, as it always had, the ready tribute of the boy's sympathy. "Sit down, Graham, I want to talk to you."

He sat down, still uneasily fingering the roll of bills. Just how far Natalie's methods threatened to undermine his character was revealed when, at a sound in Clayton's room, he stuck the money hastily into his pocket.

"Have you noticed a change in your father since he came back?"

Her tone was so ominous that he started.

"He's not sick, is he?"

"Not that. But-he's different. Graham, your father thinks we may be forced into the war."

"Good for us. It's time, that's sure."

"Graham!"

"Why, good heavens, mother," he began, "we should have been in it last May. We should —"

She was holding out both hands to him, piteously.

"You wouldn't go, would you?"

"I might have to go," he evaded.

"You wouldn't, Graham. You're all I have. All I have left to live for. You wouldn't need to go. It's ridiculous. You're needed here. Your father needs you."

"He needs me the hell of a lot," the boy muttered. But he went over and, stooping down, kissed her trembling face.

"Don't worry about me," he said lightly. "I don't think we've got spine enough to get into the mix-up, anyhow. And if we have —"

"You won't go. Promise me you won't go."

When he hesitated she resorted to her old methods with both Clayton and the boy. She was doing all she could to make them happy. She made no demands, none. But when she asked for something that meant more than life to her, it was refused, of course. She had gone through all sorts of humiliation to get him that money, and this was the gratitude she received.

Graham listened. She was a really pathetic figure, crouched in her low chair, and shaken with terror. She must have rather a bad time; there were so many things she dared not take to his father. She brought them to him instead, her small grievances, her elaborate extravagances, her disappointments. It did not occur to him that she transferred to his young shoulders many of her own burdens. He was only grateful for her confidence, and a trifle bewildered by it. And she had helped him out of a hole just now.

"All right. I promise," he said at last. "But you're worrying yourself for nothing, mother."

She was quite content then, cheered at once, consulted the jewelled watch on her dressing table and rang for the maid.

"Heavens, how late it is!" she exclaimed. "Run out now, dear. And, Graham, tell Buckham to do up a dozen dinner-napkins in paper. Audrey Valentine has telephoned that she has just got in, and finds she hasn't enough. If that isn't like her!"

Chapter VI

Months afterward, Clayton Spencer, looking back, realized that the night of the dinner at the Chris Valentines marked the beginning of a new epoch for him. Yet he never quite understood what it was that had caused the change. All that was clear was that in retrospect he always commenced with that evening, when he was trying to trace his own course through the months that followed, with their various changes, to the momentous ones of the following Summer.

Everything pertaining to the dinner, save the food, stood out with odd distinctness. Natalie's silence during the drive, broken only by his few questions and her brief replies. Had the place looked well? Very. And was the planting going on all right? She supposed so. He had hesitated, rather discouraged. Then:

"I don't want to spoil your pleasure in the place, Natalie —" he had said, rather awkwardly. "After all, you will be there more than I shall. You'd better have it the way you like it."

She had appeared mollified at that and had relaxed somewhat. He fancied that the silence that followed was no longer resentful, that she was busily planning. But when they had almost reached the house she turned to him.

"Please don't talk war all evening, Clay," she said. "I'm so ghastly sick of it."

"All right," he agreed amiably. "Of course I can't prevent the others doing it."

"It's generally you who lead up to it. Ever since you came back you've bored everybody to death with it."

"Sorry," he said, rather stiffly. "I'll be careful."

He had a wretched feeling that she was probably right. He had come back so full of new impressions that he had probably overflowed with them. It was a very formal, extremely tall and reticent Clayton Spencer who greeted Audrey that night.

Afterward he remembered that Audrey was not quite her usual frivolous self that evening. But perhaps that was only in retrospect, in view of what he learned later. She was very daringly dressed, as usual, wearing a very low gown and a long chain and ear-rings of black opals, and as usual all the men in the room were grouped around her.

"Thank heaven for one dignified man," she exclaimed, looking up at him. "Clayton, you do give tone to my parties."

It was not until they went in to dinner that he missed Chris. He heard Audrey giving his excuses.

"He's been called out of town," she said. "Clay, you're to have his place. And the flowers are low, so I can look across and admire you."

There were a dozen guests, and things moved rapidly. Audrey's dinners were always hilarious. And Audrey herself, Clayton perceived from his place of vantage, was flirting almost riotously with the man on her left. She had two high spots of color in her cheeks, and Clayton fancied-or was that in retrospect, too? —that her gayety was rather forced. Once he caught her eyes and it seemed to him that she was trying to convey something to him.

And then, of course, the talk turned to the war, and he caught a flash of irritation on Natalie's face.

"Ask the oracle," said Audrey's clear voice, "Ask Clay. He knows all there is to know."

"I didn't hear it, but I suppose it is when the war will end?"

"Amazing perspicacity," some one said.

"I can only give you my own opinion. Ten years if we don't go in. Possibly four if we do."

There were clamors of dissent.

"None of them can hold out so long."

"If we go in it will end in six months."

"Nonsense! The Allies are victorious now."

"I only gave an opinion," he protested. "One man's guess is just as good as another's. All I contend is that it is going on to a finish. The French and English are not going to stop until they have made the Hun pay in blood for what he has cost them."

"I wish I were a man," Audrey said' suddenly. "I don't see how any man with red blood in his veins can sit still, and not take a gun and try to stop it. Sometimes I think I'll cut off my hair, and go over anyhow. I've only got one accomplishment. I can shoot. I'd like to sit in a tree somewhere and pick them off. The butchers!"

There was a roar of laughter, not so much at the words as at the fierceness with which she delivered them. Clayton, however, felt that she was in earnest and liked her the better for it. He surmised, indeed, that under Audrey's affectations there might be something rather fine if one could get at it. She looked around the table, coolly appraising every man there.

"Look at us," she said. "Here we sit, over-fed, over-dressed. Only not over-wined because I can't afford it. And probably-yes, I think actually-every man at this table is more or less making money out of it all. There's Clay making a fortune. There's Roddie, making money out of Clay. Here am I, serving Clayton's cigarets —I don't know why I pick on you, Clay. The rest are just as bad. You're the most conspicuous, that's all."

Natalie evidently felt that the situation required saving.

"I'm sure we all send money over," she protested. "To the Belgians and all that. And if they want things we have to sell —"

"Oh, yes, I know all that," Audrey broke in, rather wearily. "I know. We're the saviors of the Belgians, and we've given a lot of money and shiploads of clothes. But we're not stopping the war. And it's got to be stopped!"

Clayton watched her. Somehow what she had just said seemed to crystallize much that he had been feeling. The damnable butchery ought to be stopped.

"Right, Audrey," he supported her. "I'd give up every prospect I have if the thing could be ended now."

He meant it then. He might not have meant it, entirely, to-morrow or the day after. But he meant it then. He glanced down the table, to find Natalie looking at him with cynical amusement.

The talk veered then, but still focused on the war. It became abstract as was so much of the war talk in America in 1916. Were we, after this war was over, to continue to use the inventions of science to destroy mankind, or for its welfare? Would we ever again, in wars to come, go back to the comparative humanity of the Hague convention? Were such wickednesses as the use of poison gas, the spreading of disease germs and the killing of non-combatants, all German precedents, to inaugurate a new era of cruelty in warfare.

Was this the last war? Would there ever be a last war? Would there not always be outlaw nations, as there are outlaw individuals? Would there ever be a league of nations to enforce peace?

From that to Christianity. It had failed. On the contrary, there was a great revival of religious faith. Creeds, no. Belief, yes. Too many men were dying to permit the growth of any skepticism as to a future life. We must have it or go mad.

In the midst of that discussion Audrey rose. Her color had faded, and her smile was gone.

"I won't listen any longer," she said. "I'm ready to talk about fighting, but not about dying."

Clayton was conscious that he had had, in spite of Audrey's speech about the wine, rather more to drink than he should have. He was not at all drunk, but a certain excitement had taken the curb off his tongue. After the departure of the women he found himself, rather to his own surprise, delivering a harangue on the Germans.

"Liars and cheats," he said. And was conscious of the undivided attention of the men. "They lied when they signed the Hague Convention; they lie when they claim that they wanted peace, not war; they lie when they claim the mis-use by the Allies of the Red Cross; they lie to the world and they lie to themselves. And their peace offers will be lies. Always lies."

Then, conscious that the table was eying him curiously, he subsided into silence.

"You're a dangerous person, Clay," somebody said. "You're the kind who develops a sort of general hate, and will force the President's hand if he can. You're too old to go yourself, but you're willing to send a million or two boys over there to fight a war that is still none of our business."

"I've got a son," Clayton said sharply. And suddenly remembered Natalie. He would want to boast, she had said, that he had a son in the army. Good God, was he doing it already? He subsided into the watchful silence of a man not entirely sure of himself.

He took no liquor, and with his coffee he was entirely himself again. But he was having a reaction. He felt a sort of contemptuous scorn for the talk at the table. The guard down, they were either mouthing flamboyant patriotism or attacking the Government. It had done too much. It had done too little. Voices raised, faces flushed, they wrangled, protested, accused.

And the nation, he reflected, was like that, divided apparently hopelessly. Was there anything that would unite it, as for instance France was united? Would even war do it? Our problem was much greater, more complicated. We were of every race. And the country was founded and had grown by men who had fled from the quarrels of Europe. They had come to find peace. Was there any humanitarian principle in the world strong enough to force them to relinquish that peace?

Clayton found Audrey in the hall as they moved at last toward the drawing-room. He was the last of the line of men, and as he paused before her she touched him lightly on the arm.

"I want to talk to you, Clay. Unless you're going to play."

"I'd rather not, unless you need me."

"I don't. I'm not playing either. And I must talk to some one."

There was something wrong with Audrey. Her usual insouciance was gone, and her hands nervously fingered the opal beads of her long necklace.

"What I really want to do," she added, "is to scream. But don't look like that. I shan't do it. Suppose we go up to Chris's study."

She was always a casual hostess. Having got her parties together, and having fed them well, she consistently declined further responsibility. She kept open house, her side board and her servants at the call of her friends, but she was quite capable of withdrawing herself, without explanation, once things were moving well, to be found later by some one who was leaving, writing letters, fussing with her endless bills, or sending a check she could not possibly afford to some one in want whom she happened to have heard about. Her popularity was founded on something more substantial than her dinners.

Clayton was liking Audrey better that night than he had ever liked her, though even now he did not entirely approve of her. And to the call of any woman in trouble he always responded. It occurred to him, following her up the stairs, that not only was something wrong with Audrey, but that it was the first time he had ever known her to show weakness.

Chris's study was dark. She groped her way in and turned on the lamp, and then turned and faced him.

"I'm in an awful mess, Clay," she said. "And the worst of it is, I don't know just what sort of a mess it is."

"Are you going to tell me about it?"

"Some of it. And if I don't start to yelling like a tom-cat."

"You're not going to do that. Let me get you something."

He was terrified by her eyes. "Some aromatic ammonia." That was Natalie's cure for everything.

"I'm not going to faint. I never do. Close the door and sit down. And then-give me a hundred dollars, if you have it. Will you?"

"Is that enough?" he asked. And drew out his black silk evening wallet, with its monogram in seed pearls. He laid the money on her knee, for she made no move to take it. She sat back, her face colorless, and surveyed him intently.

"What a comfort you are, Clay," she said. "Not a word in question. Just like that! Yet you know I don't borrow money, usually."

"The only thing that is important is that I have the money with me. Are you sure it's enough?"

"Plenty. I'll send it back in a week or so. I'm selling this house. It's practically sold. I don't know why anybody wants it. It's a poky little place. But-well, it doesn't matter about the house. I called up some people to-day who have been wanting one in this neighborhood and I'm practically sure they'll take it."

"But-you and Chris —"

"We have separated, Clay. At least, Chris has gone. There's a long story behind it. I'm not up to telling it to-night. And this money will end part of it. That's all I'm going to tell about the money. It's a small sum, isn't it, to break up a family!"

"Why, it's absurd! It's —it's horrible, Audrey."

"Oh, it isn't the money. That's a trifle. I just had to have it quickly. And when I learned I needed it of course the banks were closed. Besides, I fancy Chris had to have all there was."

Clayton was puzzled and distressed. He had not liked Chris. He had hated his cynicism, his pose of indifference. His very fastidiousness had never seemed entirely genuine. And this going away and taking all Audrey's small reserve of money —

"Where is he?"

"I don't know. I believe on his way to Canada."

"Do you mean —"

"Oh, no, he didn't steal anything. He's going to enlist in the Canadian army. Or he said so when he left."

"Look here, Audrey, you can't tell me only part of the story. Do you mean to say that Chris has had a magnificent impulse and gone to fight? Or that he's running away from something?"

"Both," said Audrey. "I'll tell you this much, Clay. Chris has got himself into a scrape. I won't tell you about that, because after all that's his story. And I'm not asking for sympathy. If you dare to pity me I'll cry, and I'll never forgive you."

"Why didn't he stay and face it like a man? Not leave you to face it."

"Because the only person it greatly concerned was myself. He didn't want to face me. The thing that is driving me almost mad is that he may be killed over there. Not because I love him so much. I think you know how things have been. But because he went to—well, I think to reinstate himself in my esteem, to show me he's a man, after all."

"Good heavens, Audrey. And you went through dinner with all this to bear!"

"I've got to carry it right along, haven't I? You know how I've been about this war, Clay. I've talked and talked about wondering how our men could stay out of it. So when the smash came, he just said he was going. He would show me there was some good stuff in him still. You see, I've really driven him to it, and if he's killed—"

A surge of resentment against the absent man rose in Clayton Spencer's mind. How like the cynicism of Chris's whole attitude that he should thrust the responsibility for his going onto Audrey. He had made her unhappy while he was with her, and now his death, if it occurred, would be a horror to her.

"I don't know why I burden you with all this," she said, rather impatiently. "I daresay it is because I knew you'd have the money. No, I don't mean that. I'd rather go to you in trouble than to any one else; that's why."

"I hope you always will."

"Oh, I shall! Don't worry." But her attempt at gayety fell flat. She lighted a cigaret from the stand beside her and fell to studying his face.

"What's happened to you?" she asked. "There's a change in you, somehow. I've noticed it ever since you came home. You ought to be smug and contented, if any man should. But you're not, are you?"

"I'm working hard. That's all. I don't want to talk about myself," he added impatiently. "What about you? What are you going to do?"

"Sell my house, pay my debts and live on my own little bit of an income."

"But, good heavens, Audrey! Chris has no right to cut off like this, and leave you. I don't know the story, but at least he must support you. A man can't just run away and evade every obligation. I think I'll have to go after him and give him a talking to."

"No!" she said, bending forward. "Don't do that. He has had a bad scare. But he's had one decent impulse, too. Let him alone, Clay."

She placed the money on the stand, and rose. As she faced him, she impulsively placed her hands on his shoulders.

"I wish I could tell you, Clay," she said, in her low, slightly husky voice, "how very, very much I admire you. You're pretty much of a man, you know. And—there aren't such a lot of them."

For an uneasy moment he thought she was going to kiss him. But she let her hands fall, and smiling faintly, led the way downstairs. Once down, however, she voiced the under lying thought in her mind.

"If he comes out, Clay, he'll never forgive me, probably. And if he is—if he doesn't, I'll never forgive myself. So I'm damned either way."

But ten minutes later, with a man on either side of her, she was sitting at the piano with a cigaret tucked behind her ear, looking distractingly pretty and very gay and singing a slightly indecorous but very witty little French song.

Clayton Spencer, cutting in on the second rubber, wondered which of the many he knew was the real Audrey. He wondered if Chris had not married, for instance, the girl at the piano, only to find she was the woman upstairs. And he wondered, too, if that were true, why he should have had to clear out. So many men married the sort Audrey had been, in Chris's little study, only to find that after all the thing they had thought they were getting was a pose, and it was the girl at the piano after all.

He missed her, somewhat later. She was gone a full half hour, and he fancied her absence had something to do with the money she had borrowed.

Chapter VII

Two things helped greatly to restore Clayton to a more normal state of mind during the next few days. One of them undoubtedly was the Valentine situation. Beside Audrey's predicament and Chris's wretched endeavor to get away and yet prove himself a man, his own position seemed, if not comfortable, at least tenable. He would have described it, had he been a man to put such a thing into words, as that "he and Natalie didn't exactly hit it off."

There were times, too, during those next few days, when he wondered if he had not exaggerated their incompatibility. Natalie was unusually pleasant. She spent some evening hours on the arm of his big chair, talking endlessly about the Linndale house, and he would lean back, smiling, and pretend to a mad interest in black and white tiles and loggias.

He made no further protest as to the expense.

"Tell me," he said once, "what does a fellow wear in this-er-Italian palace? If you have any intention of draping me in a toga and putting vine leaves in my hair, or whatever those wreaths were made of—!"

Natalie had no sense of humor, however. She saw that he meant to be amusing, and she gave the little fleeting smile one gives to a child who is being rather silly.

"Of course," he went on, "we'll have Roman baths, and be anointed with oil afterwards by lady Greek slaves. Perfumed oil."

"Don't be vulgar, Clay." And he saw she was really offended.

While there was actually no change in their relationship, which remained as it had been for a dozen years, their surface life was pleasanter. And even that small improvement cheered him greatly. He was thankful for such a peace, even when he knew that he had bought it at a heavy price.

The other was his work. The directorate for the new munition plant had been selected, and on Thursday of that week he gave a dinner at his club to the directors. It had been gratifying to him to find how easily his past reputation carried the matter of the vast credits needed, how absolutely his new board deferred to his judgment. The dinner became, in a way, an ovation. He was vastly pleased and a little humbled. He wanted terribly to make good, to justify their faith in him. They were the big financial men of his time, and they were agreeing to back his judgment to the fullest extent.

When the dinner was over, a few of the younger men were in no mood to go home. They had dined and wined, and the night was young. Denis Nolan, who had been present as the attorney for the new concern, leaned back in his chair and listened to them with a sort of tolerant cynicism.

"Oh, go home, you fellows," he said at last. "You make me sick. Enough's enough. Why the devil does every dinner like this have to end in a debauch?"

In the end, however, both he and Clayton went along, Clayton at least frankly anxious to keep an eye on one or two of them until they started home. He had the usual standards, of course, except for himself. A man's private life, so long as he was not a bounder, concerned him not at all. But this had been his dinner. He meant to see it through. Once or twice he had seen real tragedy come to men as a result of the recklessness of long dinners, many toasts and the instinct to go on and make a night of it.

Afterward they went to a midnight roof-garden, and at first it was rather dreary. Their youth was only comparative after all, and the eyes of the girls who danced and sang passed over them, to rest on boys in their twenties.

Nolan chuckled.

"Pathetic!" he said. "The saddest sight in the world! Every one of you here would at this moment give up everything he's got to be under thirty."

"Oh, shut up!" some one said, almost savagely.

"Of course, there are compensations," he drawled. "At twenty you want to take the entire bunch home and keep 'em. At thirty you know you can't, but you still want to. At forty and over you don't want them at all, but you think it's damned curious they don't want you."

Clayton had watched the scene with a rather weary interest. He was, indeed, trying to put himself in Graham's place, at Graham's age. He remembered once, at twenty, having slipped off to see "The Black Crook," then the epitome of wickedness, and the disillusionment of seeing women in tights with their accentuated curves and hideous lack of appeal to the imagination. The caterers of such wares had learned since then. Here were soft draperies instead, laces and chiffons. The suggestion was not to the eyes but to the mind. How devilishly clever it all was.

Perhaps there were some things he ought to discuss with Graham. He wondered how a man led up to such a thing.

Nolan bent toward him.

"I've been watching for a girl," he said, "but I don't see her. Last time I was here I came with Chris. She was his girl."

"Chris!"

"Yes. It stumped me, at first. She came and sat with us, not a bad little thing, but-Good Lord, Clay, ignorant and not even pretty! And Chris was fastidious, in a way. I don't understand it."

The ancient perplexity of a man over the sex selections of his friends puckered his forehead.

"Damned if I understand it," he repeated.

A great wave of pity for Audrey Valentine surged in Clayton Spencer's heart. She had known it, of course; that was why Chris had gone away. How long had she known it? She was protecting Chris's name, even now. For all her frivolity, there was something rather big in Audrey. The way she had held up at her dinner, for instance-and he rather fancied that the idea of his going into the army had come from her, directly or indirectly. So Chris, from being a fugitive, was already by way of being a hero to his friends.

Poor Audrey!

He made a mental note to send her some flowers in the morning.

He ordered them on his way down-town, and for some curious reason she was in his mind most of the day. Chris had been a fool to throw away a thing so worth having. Not every man had behind him a woman of Audrey's sort.

Chapter VIII

That afternoon, accompanied by a rather boyishly excited elderly clergyman, he took two hours off from the mill and purchased a new car for Doctor Haverford.

The rector was divided between pleasure at the gift and apprehension at its cost, but Clayton, having determined to do a thing, always did it well.

"Nonsense," he said. "My dear man, the church has owed you this car for at least ten years. If you get half the pleasure out of using it that I'm having in presenting it to you, it will be well worth while. I only wish you'd let me endow the thing. It's likely to cost you a small fortune."

Doctor Haverford insisted that he could manage that. He stood off, surveying with pride not unmixed with fear its bright enamel, its leather linings, the complicated system of dials and bright levers which filled him with apprehension.

"Delight says I must not drive it," he said. "She is sure I would go too fast, and run into things. She is going to drive for me."

"How is Delight?"

"I wish you could see her, Clayton. She-well, all young girls are lovely, but sometimes I think Delight is lovelier than most. She is much older than I am, in many ways. She looks after me like a mother. But she has humor, too. She has been drawing the most outrageous pictures of me arrested for speeding, and she has warned me most gravely against visiting road houses!"

"But Delight will have to be taught, if she is to run the car."

"The salesman says they will send some one."

"They give one lesson, I believe. That's not enough. I think Graham could show her some things. He drives well."

Flying uptown a little later in Clayton's handsome car, the rector dreamed certain dreams. First his mind went to his parish visiting list, so endless, so never cleaned up, and now about to be made a pleasure instead of a penance. And into his mind, so strangely compounded of worldliness and spirituality, came a further dream-of Delight and Graham Spencer-of ease at last for the girl after the struggle to keep up appearances of a clergyman's family in a wealthy parish.

Money had gradually assumed an undue importance in his mind. Every Sunday, every service, he dealt in money. He reminded his people of the church debt. He begged for various charities. He tried hard to believe that the money that came in was given to the Lord, but he knew perfectly well that it went to the janitor and the plumber and the organist. He watched the offertory after the sermon, and only too often as he stood waiting, before raising it before the altar, he wondered if the people felt that they had received their money's worth.

He had started life with a dream of service, but although his own sturdy faith persisted, he had learned the cost of religion in dollars and cents. So, going up town, he wondered if Clayton would increase his church subscription, now that things were well with him.

"After all," he reflected, "war is not an unmixed evil," and outlined a sermon, to be called the Gains of War, and subsequently reprinted in pamphlet form and sold for the benefit of the new altar fund. He instructed Jackson to drive to the parish house instead of to the rectory, so that he might jot down the headings while they were in his mind. They ran like this: Spiritual growth; the nobility of sacrifice; the pursuit of an ideal; the doctrine of thy brother's keeper.

He stopped to speak to Jackson from the pavement.

"I daresay we shall be in frequent difficulties with that new car of ours, Jackson," he said genially. "I may have to ask you to come round and explain some of its mysterious interior to me."

Jackson touched his cap.

"Thank you, sir, I'll be glad to come. But I am leaving Mr. Spencer soon."

"Leaving!"

"Going back to the army, sir."

In the back of his mind the rector had been depending on Jackson, and he felt vaguely irritated.

"I'm sorry to hear it. I'd been counting on you."

"Very sorry, sir. I'm not leaving immediately."

"I sometimes think," observed the rector, still ruffled, "that a man's duty is not always what it appears on the surface. To keep Mr. Spencer-er-comfortable, while he is doing his magnificent work for the Allies, may be less spectacular, but it is most important."

Jackson smiled, a restrained and slightly cynical smile.

"That's a matter for a man's conscience, isn't it, sir?" he asked. And touching his cap again, moved off. Doctor Haverford felt reproved. Worse than that, he felt justly reproved. He did not touch the Gains of War that afternoon.

In the gymnasium he found Delight, captaining a basket-ball team. In her knickers and middy blouse she looked like a little girl, and he stood watching her as, flushed and excited, she ran round the long room. At last she came over and dropped onto the steps at his feet.

"Well?" she inquired, looking up. "Did you get it?"

"I did, indeed. A beauty, Delight."

"A flivver?"

"Not at all. A very handsome car." He told her the make, and she flushed again with pleasure.

"Joy and rapture!" she said. "Did you warn him I am to drive it?"

"I did. He suggests that Graham give you some lessons."

"Graham!"

"Why not?"

"He'll be bored to insanity. That's all. You-you didn't suggest it, did you, daddy?"

With all her adoration of her father, Delight had long recognized under his real spirituality a certain quality of worldly calculation. That, where it concerned her, it was prompted only by love did not make her acceptance of it easier.

"Certainly not," said the rector, stiffly.

"Graham's changed, you know. He used to be a nice little kid. But he's —I don't know what it is. Spoiled, I suppose."

"He'll steady down, Delight."

She looked up at him with clear, slightly humorous eyes.

"Don't get any queer ideas about Graham Spencer and me, Daddy," she said. "In the first place, I intend to choose my own husband. He's to look as much as possible like you, but a trifle less nose. And in the second place, after I've backed the car into a telegraph pole; and turned it over in a ditch, Graham Spencer is just naturally going to know I am no woman to tie to."

She got up and smiled at him.

"Anyhow, I wouldn't trust him with the communion service," she added, and walking out onto the floor, blew shrilly on her whistle. The rector watched her with growing indignation. These snap judgments of youth! The easy damning of the young! They left no room for argument. They condemned and walked away, leaving careful plans in ruin behind them.

And Delight, having gone so far, went further. She announced that evening at dinner that she would under no circumstances be instructed by Graham Spencer. Her mother ventured good-humored remonstrance.

"The way to learn to drive a car," said Delight, "is to get into it and press a few things, and when it starts, keep on going. You've got to work it out for yourself."

And when Clayton, calling up with his usual thoughtfulness that evening, offered Graham as instructor, she refused gratefully but firmly.

"You're a dear to think of it," she said, "and you're a dear to have given Daddy the car. But I'm just naturally going to fight it out in my own way if it takes all winter."

Natalie, gathering her refusal from Clayton's protest, had heaved a sigh of relief. Not that she objected to Delight Haverford. She liked her as much as she liked and understood any young girl, which was very little. But she did not want Graham to marry. To marry would be to lose him. And again, watching Clayton's handsome head above his newspaper, she reflected that Graham was all she had.

Nevertheless, Delight received a lesson in driving from Graham, and that within two days.

On Saturday afternoon, finding the mill getting on his nerves, Clayton suggested to Graham what might be the last golf of the autumn and Graham consented cheerfully enough. For one thing, the offices closed at noon, and Anna Klein had gone. He was playing a little game with Anna —a light-hearted matter of a glance now and then caught and held, a touched hand, very casually done, and an admiring comment now and then on her work. And Anna was blossoming like a flower. She sat up late to make fresh white blouses for the office, and rose early to have abundance of time to dress. She had taken to using a touch of rouge, too, although she put it on after she reached the mill, and took it off before she started for home.

Her father, sullen and irritable these days, would have probably beaten her for using it.

But Anna had gone, and a telephone call to Marion Hayden had told him she was not at home. He thought it possible she had gone to the country club, and accepted his father's suggestion of golf willingly.

From the moment he left the mill Anna had left his mind. He was at that period when always in the back of his mind there was a girl. During the mill hours the girl was Anna, because she was there. In the afternoon it was Marion, just then, but even at that there were entire evenings when, at the theater, a pretty girl in the chorus held and absorbed his entire attention-or at a dance a debutante, cloudy and mysterious in white chiffon, bounded his universe for a few hours.

On this foundation of girl he built the superstructure of his days. Not evil, but wholly ir-responsible. The urge of vital youth had caught him and held him. And Clayton, sitting that day beside him in the car, while Graham drove and the golf clubs rattled in their bags at his feet, remembered again the impulses of his own adolescence, and wondered. There had been a time when he would have gone to the boy frankly, with the anxieties he was beginning to feel. There were so many things he wanted to tell the boy. So many warnings he should have.

But Natalie had stolen him. That was what it amounted to. She had stolen his confidence, as only a selfish woman could. And against that cabal of mother and son he felt helpless. It was even more than that. As against Natalie's indulgence he did not wish to pose as a mentor pointing out always the way of duty.

"How old are you, Graham?" he said suddenly.

"Twenty-two." Graham glanced at him curiously. His father knew his age, of course.

"I was married at your age."

"Tough luck," said Graham. And then: "I'm sorry, father, I didn't mean that. But it's pretty early, isn't it? No time for a good time, or anything."

"I fancy Nature meant men to marry young, don't you? It saves a lot of-complications."

"The girl a fellow marries at that age isn't often the one he'd marry at thirty," said Graham. And feeling that he had said the wrong thing, changed the subject quickly. Clayton did not try to turn it back into its former channel. The boy was uncomfortable, unresponsive. There was a barrier between them, of self-consciousness on his part, of evasion and discomfort on Graham's.

On the way over they had sighted Delight in the new car. She had tried to turn, had backed into a ditch and was at that moment ruefully surveying a machine which had apparently sat down on its rear wheels with its engine pointed pathetically skyward.

Delight's face fell when she recognized them.

"Of course it would have to be you," she said. "Of all the people who might have seen my shame —I'm going on with you. I never want to see the old thing again."

"Anything smashed?" Graham inquired.

"It looks smashed. I can't tell."

It was not until the car was out of the ditch, and Clayton had driven off in Graham's car toward the club that Delight remembered her father's voice the day he had told her Graham would teach her to drive. She stiffened and he was quick to see the change in her manner. The total damage was one flat tire, and while the engine was inflating it, he looked at her. She had grown to be quite pretty. His eyes approved her.

"Better let me come round and give you a few lessons, Delight."

"I'd rather learn by myself, if you don't mind."

"You'll have a real smash unless you learn properly."

But she remained rather obstinately silent.

"What's the matter with me, Delight? You're not exactly crazy about me, are you?"

"That's silly. I don't know anything about you any more."

"That's your fault. You know I've been away for four years, and since I came back I haven't seen much of you. But, if you'll let me come round —"

"You can come if you like. You'll be bored, probably."

"You're being awfully nasty, you know. Here I come to pull you out of a ditch and generally rescue you, and-Come, now, Delight, what is it? There's something. We used to be pals."

"I don't know, Graham," she said truthfully. "I only know-well, I hear things, of course. Nothing very bad. Just little things. I wish you wouldn't insist. It's idiotic. What does it matter what I think?"

Graham flushed. He knew well enough one thing she had heard. Her father and mother had been at dinner the other night, and he had had too much to drink.

"Sorry."

He stopped the pump and put away the tools, all in silence. Good heavens, was all the world divided into two sorts of people: the knockers-and under that heading he placed his father,

Delight, and all those who occasionally disapproved of him-and the decent sort who liked a fellow and understood him?

But his training had been too good to permit him to show his angry scorn. He made an effort and summoned a smile.

"All ready," he said. "And since you won't let me teach you, perhaps I'd better take you home."

"You were going to the club."

"Oh, that's all right. Father's probably found some one."

But she insisted that he drive them both to the club, and turn the car round there. Then, with a grinding of gear levers that made him groan, she was off toward home, leaving Graham staring after her.

"Well, can you beat it?" he inquired of the empty air. "Can you beat it?"

And wounded in all the pride of new manhood, he joined Marion and her rather riotous crowd around the fire inside the clubhouse. Clayton had given him up and was going around alone, followed by a small caddie. The links were empty, and the caddie lonely. He ventured small bits of conversation now and then, looking up with admiration at Clayton's tall figure. And, after a little, Clayton took the bag from him and used him only for retrieving balls. The boy played round, whistling.

"Kinda quiet to-day, ain't it?" he offered, trudging a foot or two behind.

"It is, rather, young man."

"Mostly on Saturdays I caddie for Mr. Valentine. But he's gone to the war."

"Oh, he has, has he?" Clayton built a small tee, and placed his ball on it. "Well, maybe we'll all be going some day."

He drove off and started after the ball. It was not until he was on the green that he was conscious of the boy beside him again.

"How old d'you have to be to get into the army, Mr. Spencer?" inquired the caddie, anxiously. Clayton looked at him quizzically.

"Want to try for it, do you? Well, I'm afraid you'll have to wait a bit."

"I'm older than I look, Mr. Spencer."

"How old are you?"

"Sixteen."

"Afraid you'll have to wait a while," said Clayton and achieved a well-nigh perfect long putt.

"I'd just like to get a whack at them Germans," offered the boy, and getting no response, trudged along again at his heels.

Suddenly it struck Clayton as rather strange that, in all the time since his return from Europe, only four people had shown any but a sort of academic interest in the war, and that, ironically enough, a German had been the first to make a sacrifice for principle. Chris had gone, to get out of trouble. The little caddie wanted to go, to get a "whack" at the madmen of Europe. And Jackson, the chauffeur, was going, giving up his excellent wages to accept the thirty-odd dollars a month of a non-com, from a pure sense of responsibility.

But, among the men he knew best, in business and in the clubs, the war still remained a magnificent spectacle. A daily newspaper drama.

Suddenly Clayton saw Audrey Valentine. She was swinging toward him, her bag with its clubs slung over her shoulder, her hands in the pockets of an orange-colored sweater. In her black velvet tam and short skirt she had looked like a little girl, and at first he did not recognize her. She had seen him, however, and swung toward him.

"Hello, Clay," she called, when they were within hailing distance. "Bully shot, that last."

"Where's your caddie?"

"I didn't want one. I had a feeling that, if I took one, and he lost a ball in these impecunious times of mine, I'd murder him. Saw you at the fifth hole. I'd know your silhouette anywhere."

Under her rakish cap her eyes were rather defiant. She did not want pity; she almost dared him to pity her.

"Come round again with me, Audrey, won't you?"

"I'm off my game to-day. I'll wander along, if you don't mind. I'll probably sneeze or something when you're driving, of course."

"Nothing," he said, gravely approaching his ball, "so adds distance to my drive as a good explosive sneeze just behind it."

They talked very little. Audrey whistled as she walked along with the free swinging step that was characteristic of her, and Clayton was satisfied merely to have her companionship. She was not like some women; a man didn't have to be paying her compliments or making love to her. She even made no comments on his shots, and after a time that rather annoyed him.

"Well?" he demanded, after an excellent putt. "Was that good or wasn't it?"

"Very good," she said gravely. "I am only surprised when you do a thing badly. Not when you do it well."

He thought that over.

"Have you anything in mind that I do badly? I mean, particularly in mind."

"Not very much." But after a moment: "Why don't you make Natalie play golf?"

"She hates it."

He rather wondered if she thought Natalie was one of the things he managed badly.

The sense of companionship warmed him. Although neither of them realized it, their mutual loneliness and dissatisfaction had brought them together, and mentally at least they were clinging, each desperately to the other. But their talk was disjointed:

"I'll return that hundred soon. I've sold the house."

"I wish you wouldn't worry about it. It's ridiculous, Audrey."

And, a hundred yards or so further on, "They wouldn't have Chris in Canada. His heart. He's going into the French Ambulance service."

"Good for Chris."

But she came out very frankly, when they started back to the clubhouse.

"It's done me a lot of good, meeting you, Clay. There's something so big and solid and dependable about you. I wonder —I suppose you don't mind my using you as a sort of anchor to windward?"

"Good heavens, Audrey! If I could only do something."

"You don't have to do a thing." She smiled up at him, and her old audacity was quite gone. "You've just got to be. And-you don't have to send me flowers, you know. I mean, I understand that you're sorry for me, without that. You're the only person in the world I'd allow to be sorry for me."

He was touched. There was no coquetry in her manner. She paid her little tribute quite sincerely and frankly.

"I've been taking stock to-day," she went on, "and I put you among my assets. One reliable gentleman, six feet tall, weight about a hundred and seventy, in good condition. Heavens, what a lot of liabilities you had to off-set!"

He stopped and looked down at her.

"Audrey dear," he said, "what am I to say to all that? What can I do? How can I help?"

"You might tell me-No, that's silly."

"What is silly?"

But she did not answer. She called "Joey!" and gave him her clubs.

"Joey wants to be a soldier," she observed.

"So he says."

"I want to be a soldier, too, Clay. A good soldier."

He suspected that she was rather close to unusual tears.

As they approached the clubhouse they saw Graham and Marion Hayden standing outside. Graham was absently dropping balls and swinging at them. It was too late when Clayton saw the danger and shouted sharply.

A ball caught the caddie on the side of the head and he dropped like a shot.

All through that night Clayton and Audrey Valentine sat by the boy's white bed in the hospital. Clayton knew Graham was waiting outside, but he did not go out to speak to him. He was afraid of himself, afraid in his anger that he would widen the breach between them.

Early in the evening Natalie had come, in a great evening-coat that looked queerly out of place, but she had come, he knew, not through sympathy for the thin little figure on the bed, but as he had known she would come, to plead for Graham. And her cry of joy when the surgeons had said the boy would live was again for Graham.

She had been too engrossed to comment on Audrey's presence there, and Audrey had gone out immediately and left them together. Clayton was forced, that night, to an unwilling comparison of Natalie with another woman. On the surface of their lives, where only they met, Natalie had always borne comparison well. But here was a new standard to measure by, and another woman, a woman with hands to serve and watchful, intelligent eyes, outmeasured her.

Not that Clayton knew all this. He felt, in a vague way, that Natalie was out of place there, and he felt, even more strongly, that she had not the faintest interest in the still figure on its white bed-save as it touched Graham and herself.

He was resentful, too, that she felt it necessary to plead with him for his own boy. Good God, if she felt that way about him, no wonder Graham —

She had placed a hand on Clayton's arm, as he sat in that endless vigil, and bent down to whisper, although no sound would have penetrated that death-like stupor.

"It was an accident, Clay," she pled. "You know Graham's the kindest soul in the world. You know that, Clay."

"He had been drinking." His voice sounded cold and strained to his own ears.

"Not much. Almost nothing, Toots says positively."

"Then I'd rather he had been, Natalie. If he drove that ball out of wanton indifference —"

"He didn't see the boy."

"He should have looked."

In her anger she ceased her sibilant whispering, and stood erect.

"I told him you'd be hard," she said. "He's outside, half-sick with fright, because he is afraid. Afraid of you," she added, and went out, her silks rustling in the quiet corridor.

She had gone away soon after that, the nurse informed him. And toward dawn Clayton left Audrey in the sick room and found Graham. He was asleep in a chair in the waiting-room, and looked boyish and very tired. Clayton's heart contracted.

He went back to his vigil, and let Graham sleep on.

Some time later he roused from a doze in his chair. Graham was across the bed from him, looking down. Audrey was gone. And the injured boy stirred and opened his eyes.

"H-hello, Joey," said Graham, with a catch in his voice.

Joey lay still, his eyes taking in his new surroundings. Then he put out a hand and touched the bandage on his head.

"What I got on?" he demanded, faintly.

Graham caught his father's eyes across the bed, and smiled a shaky, tremulous smile.

"I guess he's all right, Father," he said. And suddenly crumpled up beside the bed, and fell into a paroxysm of silent sobbing. With his arm around the boy's shoulders, Clayton felt in that gray dawn the greatest thankfulness of his life. Joey would live. That cup was taken from his boy's lips. And he and Graham were together again, close together. The boy's grip on his hand was tight. Please God, they would always be together from now on.

Chapter IX

Clayton did not care to tell Natalie of Chris's flight. She would learn it soon enough, he knew, and he felt unwilling to discuss the affair as Natalie would want to discuss it. Not that he cared about Chris, but he had begun to feel a protective interest in Audrey Valentine, an interest that had in it a curious aversion to hearing her name in connection with Chris's sordid story.

He and Natalie met rarely in the next few days. He dined frequently at his club with men connected in various ways with the new enterprise, and transacted an enormous amount of business over the dinner or luncheon table. Natalie's door was always closed on those occasions when he returned, and he felt that with the stubbornness characteristic of her she was still harboring resentment against him for what he had said at the hospital.

He knew she was spending most of her days at Linndale, and he had a vague idea that she and Rodney together had been elaborating still further on the plans for the house. It was the furtiveness of it rather than the fact itself that troubled him. He was open and straightforward himself. Why couldn't Natalie be frank with him?

It was Mrs. Haverford, punctually paying her dinner-call in an age which exacts dinner-calls no longer-even from its bachelors-who brought Natalie the news of Chris's going. Natalie, who went down to see her with a mental protest, found her at a drawing-room window, making violent signals at somebody without, and was unable to conceal her amazement.

"It's Delight," explained Mrs. Haverford. "She's driving me round. She won't come in, and she's forgotten her fur coat. And it's simply bitter outside. Well, my dear, how are you?"

Natalie was well, and said so. She was conscious that Mrs. Haverford was listening with only half an ear, and indeed, a moment later she had risen again and hurried to the window.

"Natalie!" she cried. "Do come and watch. She's turning the car. We do think she drives wonderfully. Only a few days, too."

"Why won't she come in?"

"I'm sure I don't know. Unless she is afraid Graham may be here."

"What in the world has Graham got to do with it?" Natalie's voice was faintly scornful.

"I was going to ask you that, Natalie. Have they quarreled, or anything?"

"I don't think they meet at all, do they?"

"They met once since Clayton gave Doctor Haverford the car. Graham helped her when she had got into a ditch, I believe. And I thought perhaps they had quarreled about something."

"That would imply a degree of intimacy that hardly exists, does it?" Natalie said, sharply.

But Mrs. Haverford had not fought the verbal battles of the parish for twenty years in vain.

"It was the day of that unfortunate incident at the country club, Natalie."

Natalie colored.

"Accident, rather than incident."

"How is the poor child?"

"He is quite well again," Natalie said impatiently "I can not understand the amount of fuss every one makes over the boy. He ran in front of where Graham was driving and got what he probably deserved."

"I understand Clayton has given him a position."

"He has made him an office boy."

"How like dear Clayton!" breathed Mrs. Haverford, and counted the honors as hers. But she had not come to quarrel. She had had, indeed, a frankly benevolent purpose in coming, and she proceeded to carry it out at once.

"I do think, my dear," she said, "that some one ought to tell Audrey Valentine the stories that are going about."

"What has she been doing?" Natalie asked, with her cool smile. "There is always some story about Audrey, isn't there?"

"Do you mean to say you haven't heard?"

"I don't hear much gossip."

Mrs. Haverford let that pass.

"You know how rabid she has been about the war. Well, the story is," she went on, with a certain unction, "that she has driven Chris to enlisting in the Foreign Legion, or something. Anyhow, he sailed from Halifax last week."

Natalie straightened in her chair.

"Are you certain?"

"It's town talk, my dear. Doctor Haverford spoke to Clayton about it some days ago. He rather gathered Clayton already knew."

That, too, was like dear Clayton, Natalie reflected bitterly. He had told her nothing. In her heart she added secretiveness to the long list of Clayton's deficiencies toward her.

"Personally, I imagine they were heavily in debt," Mrs. Haverford went on. "They had been living beyond their means, of course. I like Mrs. Valentine, but I do think, to drive a man to his death, or what may be his death —"

"I don't believe it. I don't believe he went to fight, anyway. He was probably in some sort of a scrape."

"She has sold her house."

Natalie's impulse of sympathy toward Audrey was drowned in her rising indignation. That all this could happen and Audrey not let her know was incredible.

"I haven't seen her recently," she said coldly.

"Nobody has. I do think she might have seen her clergyman. There is a time when only the church can give us the comfort we need, my dear."

And whatever Mrs. Haverford's faults, she meant that quite simply.

"And you say Clay knew?"

"It's rather likely he would. They were golfing together, weren't they, when that caddie was hurt?"

Natalie was not a jealous woman. She had, for years, taken Clay's faithfulness for granted, and her own complacency admitted no chance of such a possibility. But she was quick to realize that she had him at a disadvantage.

"How long have you known it?" she asked him that night, when, after the long dinner was over, she sat with her elbows on the table and faced him across the candles.

He was tired and depressed, and his fine face looked drawn. But he roused and smiled across at her. He had begun to have a feeling that he must make up to Natalie for something-he hardly knew for what.

"Known what, dear?"

"About Chris and Audrey?"

He was fundamentally honest, so he answered her directly.

"Since the day Chris left."

"When was that?"

"The day we dined there."

"And Audrey told you?"

"She had to, in a way. I'm sure she'll tell you herself. She's been rather hiding away, I imagine."

"Why did she have to tell you?"

"If you want the exact truth, she borrowed a small sum from me, as the banks were closed, naturally. There was some emergency —I don't know what."

"She borrowed from you!"

"A very small amount, my dear. Don't look like that, Natalie. She knew I generally carried money with me."

"Oh, I'm not jealous! Audrey probably thinks of you as a sort of grandfather, anyhow. It's not that. It is your keeping the thing from me."

"It was not my secret."

But Natalie was jealous. She had that curious jealousy of her friends which some women are cursed with, of being first in their regard and their confidence. A slow and smoldering anger against Audrey, which had nothing whatever to do with Clayton, darkened her eyes.

"I'm through with Audrey. That's all," she said.

And the man across regarded her with a sort of puzzled wonder.

Her indignation against Clayton took the form of calculation; and she was quick to pursue her advantage. In the library she produced the new and enlarged plans for the house.

"Roddie says he has tried to call you at the mill, but you are always out of your office. So he sent these around to-day."

True to the resolution he had made that night in the hospital, he went over them carefully. And even their magnitude, while it alarmed him, brought no protest from him. After all the mill and the new plant were his toys to play with. He found there something to fill up the emptiness of his life. If a great house was Natalie's ambition, if it gave her pleasure and something to live for, she ought to have it.

She had prepared herself for a protest, but he made none, even when the rather startling estimate was placed before him.

"I just want you to be happy, my dear," he said. "But I hope you'll arrange not to run over the estimate. It is being pretty expensive as it is. But after all, success doesn't mean anything, unless we are going to get something out of it."

They were closer together that evening than they had been for months. And at last he fell to talking about the mill. Natalie, curled up on the chaise longue in her boudoir, listened attentively, but with small comprehension as he poured out his dream, for himself now, for Graham later. A few years more and he would retire. Graham could take hold then. He might even go into politics. He would be fifty then, and a man of fifty should be in his prime. And to retire and do nothing was impossible. A fellow went to seed.

Eyes on the wood fire, he talked on until at last, roused by Natalie's silence, he glanced up. She was sound asleep.

Some time later, in his dressing-gown and slippers, he came and roused her. She smiled up at him like a drowsy child.

"Awfully tired," she said. "Is Graham in?"

"Not yet."

She held up her hands, and he drew her to her feet.

"You've been awfully dear about the house," she said. And standing on tiptoe, she kissed him on the cheek. Still holding both her hands, he looked down at her gravely.

"Do you really think that, Natalie?"

"Of course."

"Then-will you do something in return?"

Her eyes became shrewd, watchful.

"Anything in reason."

"Don't, don't, dear, make Graham afraid of me."

"As if I did! If he is afraid of you, it is your own fault"

"Perhaps it is. But I try-good God, Natalie, I do try. He needs a curb now and then. All boys do. But if we could only agree on it-don't you see how it is now?" he asked, trying to reason gently with her. "All the discipline comes from me, all the indulgence from you. And —I don't want to lose my boy, my dear."

She freed her hands.

"So we couldn't even have one happy evening!" she said. "I won't quarrel with you, Clay. And I won't be tragic over Graham. If you'll just be human to him, he'll come out all right."

She went into her bedroom, the heavy lace of her negligee trailing behind her, and closed the door.

Clayton had a visitor the next morning at the mill, a man named Dunbar, who marked on his visitors' slip, under the heading of his business with the head of the concern, the words, "Private and confidential."

Clayton, looking up, saw a small man, in a suit too large for him, and with ears that projected wide on either side of a shrewd, rather humorous face.

"Mr. Spencer?"

"Yes. Sit down, please."

Even through the closed window the noise of the mill penetrated. The yard-engine whistled shrilly. The clatter of motor-trucks, the far away roar of the furnaces, the immediate vicinity of many typewriters, made a very bedlam of sound. Mr. Dunbar drew his chair closer, and laid a card on the desk.

"My credentials," he explained.

Clayton read the card.

"Very well, Mr. Dunbar. What can I do for you?"

Dunbar fixed him with shrewd, light eyes, and bent forward.

"Have you had any trouble in your mill, Mr. Spencer?"

"None whatever."

"Are you taking any measures to prevent trouble?"

"I had expected to. Not that I fear anything, but of course no one can tell. We have barely commenced to get lined up for our new work."

"May I ask the nature of the precautions?"

Clayton told him, with an uneasy feeling that Mr. Dunbar was finding them childish and inefficient.

"Exactly," said his visitor. "And well enough as far as they go. They don't go far enough. The trouble with you manufacturers is that you only recognize one sort of trouble, and that's a strike. I suppose you know that the Kaiser has said, if we enter the war, that he need not send an army here at all. That his army is here already, armed and equipped."

"Bravado," said Clayton.

"I wonder!"

Mr. Dunbar reached into his breast pocket, and produced a long typed memorandum.

"You might just glance at that."

Clayton read it carefully. It was a list of fires, mostly in granaries and warehouses, and the total loss was appalling.

"All German work," said his visitor. "Arson, for the Fatherland. All supplies for the Allies, you see. I've got other similar lists, here, all German deviltry. And they're only commencing. If we go into the war —"

The immediate result of the visit was that Clayton became a member of a protective league which undertook, with his cooperation, to police and guard the mill. But Mr. Dunbar's last words left him thinking profoundly.

"We're going to be in it, that's sure. And soon. And Germany's army is here. It's not only Germans either. It's the I.W.W., for one thing. We've got a list through the British post-office censor, of a lot of those fellows who are taking German money to-day. They're against everything. Not only work. They're against law and order. And they're likely to raise hell."

He rose to leave.

"How do your Germans like making shells for the Allies?" he asked.

"We haven't a great many. We've had no trouble. One man resigned —a boss roller. That's all."

"Watch him. He's got a grievance."

"He's been here a long time. I haven't an idea he'd do us any harm. It was a matter of principle with him."

"Oh, it's a matter of principle with all of them. They can justify themselves seven ways to the ace. Keep an eye on him, or let us do it for you."

Clayton sat for some time after Dunbar had gone. Was it possible that Klein, or men like Klein, old employees and faithful for years, could be reached by the insidious wickedness of Germany? It was incredible. But then the whole situation was incredible; that a peaceful and home-loving people, to all appearances, should suddenly shed the sheep skin of years of dissimulation, and appear as the wolves of the world.

One of his men had died on the Lusitania, a quiet little chap, with a family in the suburbs and a mania for raising dahlias. He had been in the habit of bringing in his best specimens, and putting them in water on Clayton's desk. His pressed glass vase was still there, empty.

Then his mind went back to Herman Klein. He had a daughter in the mill. She was earning the livelihood for the family now, temporarily. And the Germans were thrifty. If for no other reason he thought Klein would not imperil either his daughter's safety or her salary.

There was a good bit of talk about German hate, but surely there was no hate in Klein.

Something else Dunbar had said stuck in his mind.

"We've got to get wise, and soon. It's too big a job for the regular departments to handle. Every city in the country and every town ought to have a civilian organization to watch and to fight it if it has to. They're hiding among us everywhere, and every citizen has got to be a sleuth, if we're to counter their moves. Every man his own detective!"

He had smiled as he said it, but Clayton had surmised a great earnestness and considerable knowledge behind the smile.

Chapter X

Delight Haverford was to come out in December, but there were times when the Doctor wondered if she was really as keen about it as she pretended to be. He found her once or twice, her usually active hands idle in her lap, and a pensive droop to her humorous young mouth.

"Tired, honey?" he asked, on one of those occasions.

"No. Just talking to myself."

"Say a few nice things for me, while you're about it, then."

"Nice things! I don't deserve them."

"What awful crime have you been committing? Break it to me gently. You know my weak heart."

"Your tobacco heart!" she said, severely. "Well, I've been committing a mental murder, if you want to know the facts. Don't protest. It's done. She's quite dead already."

"Good gracious! And I have reared this young viper! Who is she?"

"I don't intend to make you an accessory, daddy."

But' behind her smile he felt a real hurt. He would have given a great deal to have taken her in his arms and tried to coax out her trouble so he might comfort her. But that essential fineness in him which his worldliness only covered like a veneer told him not to force her confidence. Only, he wandered off rather disconsolately to hunt his pipe and to try to realize that Delight was now a woman grown, and liable to woman's heart-aches.

"What do you think it is?" he asked that night, when after her nightly custom Mrs. Haverford had reached over from the bed beside his and with a single competent gesture had taken away his book and switched off his reading lamp, and he had, with the courage of darkness, voiced a certain uneasiness.

"Who do you think it is, you mean."

"Very well, only the word is 'whom.'"

Mrs. Haverford ignored this.

"It's that Hayden girl," she said. "Toots. And Graham Spencer."

"Do you think that Delight —"

"She always has. For years."

Which was apparently quite clear to them both.

"If it had only been a nice girl," Mrs. Haverford protested, plaintively. "But Toots! She's fast, I'm sure of it."

"My dear!"

"And that boy needs a decent girl, if anybody ever did. A shallow mother, and a money-making father-all Toots Hay den wants is his money. She's ages older than he is. I hear he is there every day and all of Sundays."

The rector had precisely as much guile as a turtle dove, and long, after Mrs. Haverford gave unmistakable evidences of slumber, he lay with his arms above his head, and plotted. He had no conscience whatever about it. He threw his scruples to the wind, and if it is possible to follow the twists of a theological mind turned from the straight and narrow way into the maze of conspiracy, his thoughts ran something like this:

"She is Delight. Therefore to see her is to love her. To see her with any other girl is to see her infinite superiority and charm. Therefore —"

Therefore, on the following Sunday afternoon, the totally unsuspecting daughter of a good man gone wrong took a note from the rector to the Hayden house, about something or other of no importance, and was instructed to wait for an answer. And the rector, vastly uneasy and rather pleased with himself, took refuge in the parish house and waited ten eternities, or one hour by the clock.

Delight herself was totally unsuspicious. The rectory on a Sunday afternoon was very quiet, and she was glad to get away. She drove over, and being in no hurry she went by the Spencer house. She did that now and then, making various excuses to herself, such as liking the police-man at the corner or wanting to see the river from the end of the street. But all she saw that day was Rodney Page going in, in a top hat and very bright gloves.

"Precious!" said Delight to herself. Her bump of reverence was very small.

But she felt a little thrill, as she always did, when she passed the house. Since she could remember she had cared for Graham. She did not actually know that she loved him. She told herself bravely that she was awfully fond of him, and that it was silly, because he never would amount to anything. But she had a little argument of her own, for such occasions, which said that being really fond of any one meant knowing all about them and liking them anyhow.

She stopped the car at the Hayden house, and carried her note to the door. When she went in, however, she was instantly uncomfortable. The place reeked with smoke, and undeniably there was dancing going on somewhere. A phonograph was scraping noisily. Delight's small nose lifted a little. What a deadly place! Coming in from the fresh outdoors, the noise and smoke and bar-room reek stifled her.

Then a door opened, and Marion Hayden was drawing her into a room.

"How providential, Delight!" she said. "You'll take my hand, won't you? It's Graham's dummy, and we want to dance."

The two connecting rooms were full of people, and the air was heavy. Through the haze she saw Graham, and nodded to him, but with a little sinking of the heart. She was aware, however, that he was looking at her with a curious intentness and a certain expectancy. Maybe he only hoped she would let him dance with Toots.

"No, thanks," she said. "Sorry."

"Why not, Delight? Just a hand, anyhow."

"Three good reasons: I don't play cards on Sunday; I don't ever play for money; and I'm stifling for breath already in this air."

She was, indeed, a little breathless.

There was, had she only seen it, relief in Graham's face. She did not belong there, he felt. Delight was-well, she was different. He had not been thinking of her before she came in; he forgot her promptly the moment she went out. But she had given him, for an instant, a breath of the fresh out-doors, and quietness and-perhaps something clean and fine.

There was an insistent clamor that she stay, and Tommy Hale even got down on his knees and made a quite impassioned appeal. But Delight's chin was very high, although she smiled.

"You are all very nice," she said. "But I'm sure I'd bore you in a minute, and I'm certain you'd bore me. Besides, I think you're quite likely to be raided."

Which met with great applause.

But there was nothing of Delight of the high head when she got out of her car and crept up the rectory steps. How could she even have cared? How could she? That was his life, those were the people he chose to play with. She had a sense of loss, rather than injury.

The rector, tapping at her door a little later, received the answer to his note through a very narrow crack, and went away feeling that the way of the wicked is indeed hard.

Clayton had been watching with growing concern Graham's intimacy with the gay crowd that revolved around Marion Hayden. It was more thoughtless than vicious; more pleasure-seeking than wicked; but its influence was bad, and he knew it.

But he was very busy. At night he was too tired to confront the inevitable wrangle with Natalie that any protest about Graham always evoked, and he was anxious not to disturb the new rapprochement with the boy by direct criticism.

The middle of December, which found the construction work at the new plant well advanced, saw the social season definitely on, also, and he found himself night after night going to dinners and then on to balls. There were fewer private dances than in previous Winters, but society had taken up various war activities and made them fashionable. The result was great charity balls.

On these occasions he found himself watching for Audrey, always. She had, with a sort of diabolical cleverness, succeeded in losing herself. Her house was sold, he knew, and he had expected that she would let him know where to find her. She had said she counted on him, and he had derived an odd sort of comfort from the thought. It had warmed him to think that, out of all the people he knew, to one woman he meant something more than success.

But although he searched the gayest crowds with his eyes, those hilarious groups of which she had been so frequently the center, he did not find her. And there had been no letter save a brief one without an address, enclosing her check for the money she had borrowed. She had apparently gone, not only out of her old life, but out of his as well.

At one of the great charity balls he met Nolan, and they stood together watching the crowd.

"Pretty expensive, I take it," Nolan said, indicating the scene. "Orchestra, florist, supper —I wonder how much the Belgians will get."

"Personally, I'd rather send the money and get some sleep."

"Precisely. But would you send the money? We've got to have a quid pro quo, you know-most of us." He surveyed the crowd with cynical, dissatisfied eyes. "At the end of two years of the war," he observed, apropos of nothing, "five million men are dead, and eleven million have been wounded. A lot of them were doing this sort of thing two years ago."

"I would like to know where we will be two years from now."

"Some of us won't be here. Have you seen Lloyd George's speech on the German peace terms? That means going on to the end. A speedy peace might have left us out, but there will be no peace. Not yet, or soon."

"And still we don't prepare!"

"The English tradition persists," said the Irishman, bitterly. "We want to wait, and play to the last moment, and then upset our business and overthrow the whole country, trying to get ready in a hurry.

"I wonder what they will do, when the time comes, with men like you and myself?"

"Take our money," said Nolan viciously. "Tax our heads off. Thank God I haven't a son."

Clayton eyed him with the comprehension of long acquaintance.

"Exactly," he said. "But you'll go yourself, if you can."

"And fight for England? I will not."

He pursued the subject further, going into an excited account of Ireland's grievances. He was flushed and loquacious. He quoted Lloyd George's "quagmire of distrust" in tones raised over the noise of the band. And Clayton was conscious of a growing uneasiness. How much of it was real, how much a pose? Was Nolan representative of the cultured Irishman in America? And if he was, what would be the effect of their anti-English mania? Would we find ourselves, like the British, split into factions? Or would the country be drawn together by trouble until it changed from a federation of states to a great nation, united and unbeatable?

Were we really the melting pot of the world, and was war the fiery furnace which was to fuse us together, or were there elements, like Nolan, like the German-Americans, that would never fuse?

He left Nolan still irritable and explosive, and danced once with Natalie, his only dance of the evening. Then, finding that Rodney Page would see her to her car later, he went home.

He had a vague sense of disappointment, a return of the critical mood of the early days of his return from France. He went to his room and tried to read, but he gave it up, and lay, cigaret in hand, thinking!

There ought to have come to a man, when he reached the middle span, certain compensations for the things that had gone with his youth, the call of adventure, the violent impulses of his early love life. There should come, to take their place, friends, a new zest in the romance of achievement, since other romance had gone, and-peace. But the peace of the middle span of life should be the peace of fulfillment, and of a home and a woman.

Natalie was not happy, but she seemed contented enough. Her life satisfied her. The new house in the day-time, bridge, the theater in the evening or the opera, dinners, dances, clothes-they seemed to be enough for her. But his life was not enough for him. What did he want anyhow? In God's name, what did he want?

One night, impatient with himself, he picked up the book of love lyrics in its mauve cover, from his bedside table. He read one, then another. He read them slowly, engrossingly. It was as though something starved in him was feeding eagerly on this poor food. Their passion stirred him as in his earlier years he had never been stirred. For just a little time, while Natalie danced that night, Clayton Spencer faced the tragedy of the man in his prime, still strong and lusty with life, with the deeper passions of the deepening years, who has outgrown and outloved the woman he married.

A man's house must be built on love. Without love it can not stand.

Natalie, coming in much later and seeing his light still on, found him sleeping, with one arm under his head, and a small black hole burned in the monogrammed linen sheet. The book of poems had slipped to the floor.

The next day she missed it from its place, and Clayton's man, interrogated, said he had asked to have it put away somewhere. He did not care for it. Natalie raised her eyebrows. She had thought the poems rather pretty.

One resolution Clayton made, as a result of that night. He would not see Audrey again if he could help it. He was not in love with her and he did not intend to be. He was determinedly honest with himself. Men in his discontented state were only too apt to build up a dream-woman, compounded of their own starved fancy, and translate her into terms of the first attractive woman who happened to cross the path. He was not going to be a driveling idiot, like Chris and some of the other men he knew. Things were bad, but they could be much worse.

It happened then that when Audrey called him at the mill a day or so later it was a very formal voice that came back to her over the wire. She was quick to catch his tone.

"I suppose you hate being called in business hours, Clay!"

"Not at all."

"That means yes, you know. But I'm going even further. I'm coming down to see you."

"Why, is anything wrong?"

He could hear her laughter, a warm little chuckle.

"Don't be so urgent," she said gayly. "I want to consult you. That's all. May I come?"

There was a second's pause. Then,

"Don't you think I'd better come to see you?"

"I've only a little flat. I don't think you'll like it."

"That's nonsense. Where is it?"

She gave him the address.

"When shall I come?"

"Whenever it suits you. I have nothing to do. Say this afternoon about four."

That "nothing to do" was an odd change, in itself, for Audrey had been in the habit of doling out her time like sweetmeats.

"Where in the world have you been all this time?" he demanded, almost angrily. To his own surprise he was suddenly conscious of a sense of indignation and affront. She had said she depended on him, and then she had gone away and hidden herself. It was ridiculous.

"Just getting acquainted with myself," she replied, with something of her old airy manner. "Good-by."

His irritation passed as quickly as it came. He felt calm and very sure of himself, and rather light-hearted. Joey, who was by now installed as an office adjunct, and who commonly referred to the mill as "ours," heard him whistling blithely and cocked an ear in the direction of the inner room.

"Guess we've made another million dollars," he observed to the pencil-sharpener.

Clayton was not in the habit of paying afternoon calls on women. The number of such calls that he had paid without Natalie during his married life could have been numbered on the fingers of his two hands. Most of the men he knew paid such visits, dropping in somewhere for tea or a highball on the way uptown. He had preferred his club, when he had a little time, the society of other men.

He wondered if he should call Natalie and tell her. But he decided against it. It was possible, for one thing, that Audrey still did not wish her presence in town known. If she did, she would tell Natalie herself. And it was possible, too, that she wanted to discuss Chris, and the reason for his going.

He felt a real sense of relief, when at last he saw her, to find her looking much the same as ever. He hardly knew what he had expected. Audrey, having warned him as to the apartment, did not mention its poverty again. It was a tiny little place, but it had an open fire in the living-room, and plain, pale-yellow walls, and she had given it that curious air of distinction with which she managed, in her casual way, to invest everything about her.

"I hope you observe how neat I am," she said, as she gave him her hand. "My rooms, of course."

"Frightfully so."

He towered in the low room. Audrey sat down and surveyed him as he stood by the fire.

"It is nice to have a man about again."

"Do you mean to say you have been living here, without even visitors, for two months?"

"You'll laugh. Clay, I'm studying!"

"Studying! What?"

"Stenography. Oh, it's not as bad as that. I don't have to earn my living. I've just got to do something for my soul's sake. I went all over the ground, and I saw I was just a cumberer of the earth, and then I thought —"

She hesitated.

"What did you think?"

"If, some time or other, I could release a man to go and fight, it would be the next best thing to giving myself. Not here, necessarily; I don't believe we will ever go in. But in England, anywhere."

"You've released Chris."

"He released himself. And he's not fighting. He's driving an ambulance."

He waited, hoping she would go on. He was not curious, but he thought it might be good for her to talk Chris and the trouble over with some one. But she sat silent, and suddenly asked him if he cared for tea. He refused.

"How's Natalie?"

"Very well."

"And the house?"

"Held up by cold weather now. It should be finished by the end of April."

"Clay," she said, after a moment, "are you going to employ women in the new munition works?"

"In certain departments, yes."

"I have a girl I want work for. She's not trained, of course."

"None of them are. We have to teach them. I can give you a card to the employment department if you want it."

"Thanks."

There was a short silence. She sat looking at the fire, and he had a chance to notice the change in her. She had visualized it herself. Her long ear-rings were gone, and with them some of the insolence they had seemed to accentuate. She was not rouged, and he had thought at first, for that reason, that she looked ill. She was even differently dressed, in something dark and girlish with a boyish white Eton collar.

"I wonder if you think I'm hiding, Clay," she said, finally.

"Well, what are you doing?" He smiled down at her from the hearth-rug.

"Paying my bills! That's not all the truth, either. I'll tell you, Clay. I just got sick of it all. When Chris left I had a chance to burn my bridges and I burned them. The same people, the same talk, the same food, the same days filled with the same silly things that took all my time and gave me nothing."

"How long had you been feeling like that?"

"I don't know. Ever since the war, I suppose. I just got to thinking—"

Her voice trailed off.

"I have some of Chris's Scotch, if you want a high-ball."

"Thanks, no. Audrey, do you hear from Chris?"

"Yes. He's in a dangerous place now, and sometimes at night—I suppose I did force him, in a way. He was doing no good here, and I thought he would find himself over there. But I didn't send him. He——Tell me about making shells."

He was a little bit disappointed. Evidently she did not depend on him enough to tell him Chris's story. But again, she was being loyal to Chris.

He told her about the mill, phrasing his explanation in the simplest language; the presses drilling on white-hot metal; the great anvils; the forge; the machine-shop, with its lathes, where the rough surfaces of the shells were first rough-turned and then machined to the most exact measurements. And finding her interested, he told her of England's women workers, in their khaki-colored overalls and caps, and of the convent-like silence and lack of movement in the filling-sheds, where one entered with rubber-shod feet, and the women, silent and intent, sat all day and all night, with queer veils over their faces, filling shells with the death load.

Audrey listened, her hands clasped behind her head.

"If other women can do that sort of thing, why can't I, Clay?"

"Nonsense."

"But why? I'm intelligent."

"It's not work for a lady."

"Lady! How old-fashioned you are! There are no ladies any more. Just women. And if we aren't measured by our usefulness instead of our general not-worth-a-damn-ness, well, we ought to be. Oh, I've had time to think, lately."

He was hardly listening. Seeing her, after all those weeks, had brought him a wonderful feeling of peace. The little room, with its fire, was cozy and inviting. But he was quite sure, looking down at her, that he was not in danger of falling in love with her. There was no riot in him, no faint stirring of the emotions of that hour with the mauve book.

There was no suspicion in him that the ways of love change with the years, that the passions of the forties, when they come, are to those of the early years as the deep sea to a shallow lake, less easily roused, infinitely more terrible.

"This girl you spoke about, that was the business you mentioned?"

"Yes." She hesitated. "I could have asked you that over the telephone, couldn't I? The plain truth is that I've had two bad months-never mind why, and Christmas was coming, and —I just wanted to see your perfectly sane and normal face again."

"I wish you'd let me know sooner where you were."

She evaded his eyes.

"I was getting settled, and studying, and learning to knit, and-oh, I'm the most wretched knitter, Clay! I just stick at it doggedly. I say to myself that hands that can play golf, and use a pen, and shoot, and drive a car, have got to learn to knit. But look here!"

She held up a forlorn looking sock to his amused gaze. "And I think I'm a clever woman."

"You're a very brave woman, Audrey," he said. "You'll let me come back, won't you?"

"Heavens, yes. Whenever you like. And I'm going to stop being a recluse. I just wanted to think over some things."

On the way home he stopped at his florist's, and ordered a mass of American beauties for her on Christmas morning. She had sent her love to Natalie, so that night he told Natalie he had seen her, and such details of her life as he knew.

"I'm glad she's coming to her senses," Natalie said. "Everything's been deadly dull without her. She always made things go —I don't know just how," she added, as if she had been turning her over in her mind. "What sort of business did she want to see you about?"

"She has a girl she wants to get into the mill."

"Good gracious, she must be changed," said Natalie. And proceeded-she was ready to go out to dinner-to one of her long and critical surveys of herself in the cheval mirror. Recently those surveys had been rather getting on Clayton's nerves. She customarily talked, not to him, but to his reflection over her shoulder, when, indeed, she took her eyes from herself.

"I wonder," she said, fussing with a shoulder-strap, "who Audrey will marry if anything happens to Chris?"

She saw his face and raised her eyebrows.

"You needn't scowl like that. He's quite as likely as not never to come back, isn't he? And Audrey didn't care a pin for him."

"We're talking rather lightly of a very terrible thing, aren't we?"

"Oh, you're not," she retorted. "You think just the same things as I do, but you're not so open about them. That's all."

Chapter XI

Graham was engaged. He hardly knew himself how it had come about. His affair with Marion had been, up to the very moment of his blurted-out "I want you," as light-hearted as that of any of the assorted young couples who flirted and kissed behind the closed doors of that popular house.

The crowd which frequented the Hayden home was gay, tolerant and occasionally nasty. It made ardent love semi-promiscuously, it drank rather more than it should, and its desire for a good time often brought it rather close to the danger line. It did not actually step over, but it hovered gayly on the brink.

And Toots remained high-priestess of her little cult. The men liked her. The girls imitated her. And Graham, young as he was, seeing her popularity, was vastly gratified to find himself standing high in her favor.

Marion was playing for the stake of the Spencer money. In her intimate circle every one knew it but Graham.

"How's every little millionaire?" was Tommy Hale's usual greeting.

She knew only one way to handle men, and with the stake of the Spencer money she tried every lure of her experience on Graham. It was always Marion who on cold nights sat huddled against him in the back seat of the Hayden's rather shabby car, her warm ungloved hand in his. It was Marion who taught him to mix the newest of cocktails, and who later praised his skill. It was Marion who insisted on his having a third, too, when the second had already set his ears drumming.

The effect on the boy of her steady propinquity, of her constant caressing touches, of the general letting-down of the bars of restraint, was to rouse in him impulses of which he was only vaguely conscious, and his proposal of marriage, when it finally came, was by nature of a confession. He had kissed her, not for the first time, but this time she had let him hold her, and he had rained kisses on her face.

"I want you," he had said, huskily.

And even afterward, when the thing was done, and she had said she would marry him, she had to ask him if he loved her.

"I—of course I do," he had said. And had drawn her back into his arms.

He wanted to marry her at once. It was the strongest urge of his life, and put into his pleading an almost pathetic earnestness. But she was firm enough now.

"I don't think your family will be crazy about this, you know."

"What do we care for the family? They're not marrying you, are they?"

"They will have to help to support me, won't they?"

And he had felt a trifle chilled.

It was not a part of Marion's program to enter the Spencer family unwelcomed. She had a furtive fear of Clayton Spencer, the fear of the indirect for the direct, of the designing woman for the essentially simple and open male. It was not on her cards to marry Graham and to try to live on his salary.

So for a few weeks the engagement was concealed even from Mrs. Hayden, and Graham, who had received some stock from his father on his twenty-first birthday, secretly sold a few shares and bought the engagement ring. With that Marion breather easier. It was absolute evidence.

Her methods were the methods of her kind and her time. To allure a man by every wile she knew, and having won him to keep him uncertain and uneasy, was her perfectly simple creed. So she reduced love to its cheapest terms, passion and jealousy, played on them both, and made Graham alternately happy and wretched.

Once he found Rodney Page there, lounging about with the manner of a habitue. It seemed to Graham that he was always stumbling over Rodney those days, either at home, with drawings and color sketches spread out before him, or at the Hayden house.

"What's he hanging around here for?" he demanded when Rodney, having bent over Marion's hand and kissed it, had gone away. "If he could see that bare spot on the top of his head he'd stop all that kow-towing."

"You're being rather vulgar, aren't you?" Marion had said. "He's a very old friend and a very dear one."

"Probably in love with you once, like all the rest?"

He had expected denial from her, but she had held her cigaret up in the air, and reflectively regarded its small gilt tip.

"I'm afraid he's rather unhappy. Poor Rod!"

"About me?"

"About me."

"Look here, Toots," he burst out. "I'm playing square with you. I never go anywhere but here. I—I'm perfectly straight with you. But every time here I find some of your old guard hanging round. It makes me wild."

"They've always come here, and as long as our engagement isn't known, I can't very well stop them."

"Then let me go to father."

"He'll turn you out, you know. I know men, dear old thing, and father is going to raise a merry little hell about us. He's the sort who wants to choose his son's wife for him. He'd like to play Providence." She watched him, smiling, but with slightly narrowed eyes. "I rather think he has somebody in mind for you now."

"I don't believe it."

"Of course you don't. But he has."

"Who?"

"Delight. She's exactly the sort he thinks you'll need. He still thinks you are a little boy, Graham, so he picks out a nice little girl for you. Such a nice little girl."

The amused contempt in her voice made him angry-for Delight rather than himself. He was extremely grown-up and dignified the rest of the afternoon; he stood very tall and straight, and spoke in his deepest voice.

It became rather an obsession in him to prove his manhood, and added to that was the effect of Marion's constant, insidious appeal to the surging blood of his youth. And, day after day, he was shut in his office with Anna Klein.

He thought he was madly in love with Marion. He knew that he was not at all in love with Anna Klein. But she helped to relieve the office tedium.

He was often aware, sitting at his desk, with Anna before him, notebook in hand, that while he read his letters her eyes were on him. More than once he met them, and there was something in them that healed his wounded vanity. He was a man to her. He was indeed almost a god, but that he did not know. In his present frame of mind, he would have accepted even that, however.

Then, one day he kissed her. She was standing very close, and the impulse was quick and irresistible. She made no effort to leave his arms, and he kissed her again.

"Like me a little, do you?" he had asked, smiling into her eyes.

"Oh, I do, I do!" she had replied, hoarsely.

It was almost an exact reversal of his relationship with Marion. There the huskiness was his, the triumphant smile was Marion's. And the feeling of being adored without stint or reservation warmed him.

He released her then, but their relationship had taken on a new phase. He would stand against the outer door, to prevent its sudden opening. And she would walk toward him, frightened and helpless until his arms closed about her. It was entirely a game to him. There were days, when Marion was trying, or the work of his department was nagging him, when he scarcely noticed her at all. But again the mischief in him, the idler, the newly awakened hunting male, took him to her with arms outheld and the look of triumph in his eyes that she mistook for love.

On one such occasion Joey came near to surprising a situation, so near that his sophisticated young mind guessed rather more than the truth. He went out, whistling.

He waited until Graham had joined the office force in the mill lunchroom, and invented an errand back to Graham's office. Anna was there, powdering her nose with the aid of a mirror fastened inside her purse.

Joey had adopted Clayton with a sort of fierce passion, hidden behind a pose of patronage.

"He's all right," he would say to the boys gathered at noon in the mill yard. "He's kinda short-tempered sometimes, but me, I understand him. And there ain't many of these here money kings that would sit up in a hospital the way he did with me."

The mill yard had had quite enough of that night in the hospital. It would fall on him in one of those half-playful, half-vicious attacks that are the humor of the street, and sometimes it was rather a battered Joey who returned to Clayton's handsome office, to assist him in running the mill.

But it was a very cool and slightly scornful Joey who confronted Anna that noon hour. He lost no time in preliminaries.

"What do you think you're doing, anyhow?" he demanded.

"Powdering my nose, if you insist on knowing."

They spoke the same language. Anna knew what was coming, and was on guard instantly.

"You cut it out, that's all."

"You cut out of this office. And that's all."

Joey sat down on Graham's desk and folded his arms.

"What are you going to get out of it, anyhow?" he said with a shift from bullying to argument.

"Out of what?"

"You know, all right."

She whirled on him.

"Now see here, Joey," she said. "You run out and play. I'll not have any little boys meddling in my affairs."

Joey slid off the desk and surveyed her with an impish smile. "Your affairs!" he repeated. "What the hell do I care about your affairs? I'm thinking of the boss. It's up to him if he wants to keep German spies on the place. But it's up to some of us here to keep our eyes open, so that they don't do any harm."

Sheer outrage made Anna's face pale. She had known for some time that the other girls kept away from her, and she had accepted it with the stolidity of her blood. She had no German sympathies; her sympathies in the war lay nowhere.

But-she a spy!

"You get out of here," she said furiously, "or I'll go to Mr. Spencer and complain about you. I'm no more a spy than you are. Not as much! —the way you come sneaking around listening and watching! Now you get out."

And Joey had gone, slowly to show that the going was of his own free will, and whistling. He went out and closed the door. Then he opened it and stuck his head in.

"You be good," he volunteered, "and when the little old U.S. gets to mixing up with the swine over there, I'll bring you a nice fat Hun as a present."

Chapter XII

Two days before Christmas Delight came out. There was an afternoon reception at the rectory, and the plain old house blossomed with the debutante's bouquets and baskets of flowers.

For weeks before the house had been getting ready. The rector, looking about for his accustomed chair, had been told it was at the upholsterer's, or had found his beloved and ragged old books relegated to dark corners of the bookcases. There were always stepladders on the landings, and paper-hangers waiting until a man got out of bed in the morning. And once he put his ecclesiastical heel in a pail of varnish, and slid down an entire staircase, to the great imperilment of his kindly old soul.

But he had consented without demur to the coming-out party, and he had taken, during all the morning of the great day, a most mundane interest in the boxes of flowers that came in every few minutes. He stood inside a window, under pretense of having no place to sit down, and called out regularly,

"Six more coming, mother! And a boy with three ringing across the street. I think he's made a mistake. Yes, he has. He's coming over!"

When all the stands and tables were overflowing, the bouquets were hung to the curtains in the windows. And Delight, taking a last survey, from the doorway, expressed her satisfaction.

"It's heavenly," she said. "Imagine all those flowers for me. It looks"—she squinted up her eyes critically—"it looks precisely like a highly successful funeral."

But a part of her satisfaction was pure pose, for the benefit of that kindly pair who loved her so. Alone in her room, dressed to go down-stairs, Delight drew a long breath and picked up her flowers which Clayton Spencer had sent. It had been his kindly custom for years to send to each little debutante, as she made her bow, a great armful of white lilacs and trailing tiny white rosebuds.

"Fifty dollars, probably," Delight reflected. "And the Belgians needing flannels. It's dreadful."

Her resentment against Graham was dying. After all, he was only a child in Toots Hayden's hands. And she made one of those curious "He-loves-me-he-loves-me-not" arrangements in her own mind. If Graham came that afternoon, she would take it as a sign that there was still some good in him, and she would try to save him from himself. She had been rather nasty to him. If he did not come —

A great many came, mostly women, with a sprinkling of men. The rector, who loved people, was in his element. He was proud of Delight, proud of his home; he had never ceased being proud of his wife. He knew who exactly had sent each basket of flowers, each hanging bunch. "Your exquisite orchids," he would say; or, "that perfectly charming basket. It is there, just beside Mrs. Haverford."

But when Natalie Spencer came in alone, splendid in Russian sables, he happened to be looking at Delight, and he saw the light die out of her eyes.

Natalie had tried to bring Graham with her. She had gone into his room that morning while he was dressing and asked him. To tell the truth, she was uneasy about Marion Hayden and his growing intimacy there.

"You will, won't you, Graham, dear?"

"Sorry, mother. I just can't. I'm taking a girl out."

"I suppose it's Marion."

Her tone caused him to turn and look at her.

"Yes, it's Marion. What's wrong with that?"

"It's so silly, Graham. She's older than you are. And she's not really nice, Graham. I don't mean anything horrid, but she's designing. She knows you are young and-well, she's just playing with you. I know girls, Graham. I —"

She stopped, before his angry gaze.

"She is nice enough for you to ask here," he said hastily.

"She wants your money. That's all."

He had laughed then, an ugly laugh.

"There's a lot of it for her to want."

And Natalie had gone away to shed tears of fury and resentment in her own room.

She was really frightened. Bills for flowers sent to Marion were coming in, to lie unpaid on Graham's writing table. She had over-drawn once again to pay them, and other bills, for theater tickets, checks signed at restaurants, over-due club accounts.

So she went to the Haverfords alone, and managed very effectually to snub Mrs. Hayden before the rector's very eyes.

Mrs. Hayden thereupon followed an impulse.

"If it were not for Natalie Spencer," she said, following that lady's sables with malevolent eyes, "I should be very happy in something I want to tell you. Can we find a corner somewhere?"

And Doctor Haverford had followed her uneasily, behind some palms. She was a thin little woman with a maddening habit of drawing her tight veil down even closer by a contortion of her lower jaw, so that the rector found himself watching her chin rather than her eyes.

"I want you to know right away, as Marion's clergyman, and ours," she had said, and had given her jaw a particularly vicious wag and twist. "Of course it is not announced —I don't believe even the Spencers know it yet. I am only telling you now because I know how dearly" —she did it again —"how dearly interested you are in all your spiritual children. Marion is engaged to Graham Spencer."

The rector had not been a shining light for years without learning how to control his expression. He had a second, too, while she contorted her face again, to recover himself.

"Thank you," he said gravely. "I much appreciate your telling me."

Mrs. Hayden had lowered her voice still more. The revelation took on the appearance of conspiracy.

"In the early spring, probably," she said, "we shall need your services, and your blessing."

So that was the end of one dream. He had dreamed so many-in his youth, of spiritualizing his worldly flock; in middle life, of a bishopric; he had dreamed of sons, to carry on the name he had meant to make famous. But the failures of those dreams had been at once his own failure and his own disappointment. This was different.

He was profoundly depressed. He wandered out of the crowd and, after colliding with a man from the caterer's in a dark rear hall, found his way up the servant's staircase to the small back room where he kept the lares and penates of his quiet life, his pipe, his fishing rods, a shabby old smoking coat, and back files of magazines which he intended some day to read, when he got round to it.

The little room was jammed with old furniture, stripped from the lower floor to make room for the crowd. He had to get down on his knees and crawl under a table to reach his pipe. But he achieved it finally, still with an air of abstraction, and lighted it. Then, as there was no place to sit down, he stood in the center of the little room and thought.

He did not go down again. He heard the noise of the arriving and departing motors subside, its replacement by the sound of clattering china, being washed below in the pantry. He went down finally, to be served with a meal largely supplemented by the left-overs of the afternoon refreshments, ornate salads, fancy ices, and an overwhelming table decoration that shut him off from his wife and Delight, and left him in magnificent solitude behind a pyramid of flowers.

Bits of the afternoon's gossip reached him; the comments on Delight's dress and her flowers; the reasons certain people had not come. But nothing of the subject nearest his heart. At the end of the meal Delight got up.

"I'm going to call up Mr. Spencer," she said. "He has about fifty dollars' worth of thanks coming to him."

"I didn't see Graham," said Mrs. Haverford. "Was he here?"

Delight stood poised for flight.

"He couldn't come because he had enough to do being two places at once. His mother said he was working, and Mrs. Hayden said he had taken Marion to the Country Club. I don't know why they take the trouble to lie to me."

Chapter XIII

Christmas day of the year of our Lord, 1916, dawned on a world which seemed to have forgotten the Man of Peace. In Asia Minor the Allies celebrated it by the capture of a strong Turkish position at Maghdadah. The Germans spent it concentrating at Dead Man's Hill; the British were ejected from enemy positions near Arras. There was no Christmas truce. The death-grip had come.

Germany, conscious of her superiority in men, and her hypocritical peace offers unanimously rejected, was preparing to free herself from the last restraint of civilization and to begin unrestricted submarine warfare.

On Christmas morning Clayton received a letter from Chris. Evidently it had come by hand, for it was mailed in America.

"Dear Clay: I am not at all sure that you will care to hear from me. In fact, I have tried two or three times to write to you, and have given it up. But I am lonelier than Billy-be-damned, and if it were not for Audrey's letters I wouldn't care which shell got me and my little cart.

"I don't know whether you know why I got out, or not. Perhaps you don't. I'd been a fool and a scoundrel, and I've had time, between fusses, to know just how rotten I've been. But I'm not going to whine to you. What I am trying to get over is that I'm through with the old stuff for good.

"God only knows why I am writing to you, anyhow-unless it is because I've always thought you were pretty near right. And I'd like to feel that now and then you are seeing Audrey, and bucking her up a bit. I think she's rather down.

"Do you know, Clay, I think this is a darned critical time. The press, hasn't got it yet, but both the British and the French are hard up against it. They'll fight until there is no one left to fight, but these damned Germans seem to have no breaking-point. They haven't any temperament, I daresay, or maybe it is soul they lack. But they'll fight to the last man also, and the plain truth is that there are too many of them.

"It looks mighty bad, unless we come in. And I don't mind saying that there are a good many eyes over here straining across the old Atlantic. Are we doing anything, I wonder? Getting ready? The officers here say we can't expand an army to get enough men without a draft law. Can you see the administration endangering the next election with a draft law? Not on your life.

"I'm on the wagon, Clay. Honestly, it's funny. I don't mind telling you I'm darned miserable sometimes. But then I get busy, and I'm so blooming glad in a rush to get water that doesn't smell to heaven that I don't want anything else.

"I suppose they'll give us a good hate on Christmas. Well, think of me sometimes when you sit down to dinner, and you might drink to our coming in. If we have a principle to divide among us we shall have to."

Clayton read the letter twice.

He and Natalie lunched alone, Natalie in radiant good humor. His gift to her had been a high collar of small diamonds magnificently set, and Natalie, whose throat commenced to worry her, had welcomed it rapturously. Also, he had that morning notified Graham that his salary had been raised to five thousand dollars.

Graham had shown relief rather than pleasure.

"I daresay I won't earn it, Father," he had said. "But I'll at east try to keep out of debt on it."

"If you can't, better let me be your banker, Graham."

The boy had flushed. Then he had disappeared, as usual, and Clayton and Natalie sat across from each other, in their high-armed lion chairs, and made a pretense of Christmas gayety. True to Natalie's sense of the fitness of things, a small Nuremberg Christmas tree, hung with tiny toys and lighted with small candles, stood in the center of the table.

"We are dining out," she explained. "So I thought we'd use it now."

"It's very pretty," Clayton acknowledged. And he wondered if Natalie felt at all as he did, the vast room and the two men serving, with Graham no one knew where, and that travesty of Christmas joy between them. His mind wandered to long ago Christmases.

"It's not so very long since we had a real tree," he observed. "Do you remember the one that fell and smashed all the things on it? And how Graham heard it and came down?"

"Horribly messy things," said Natalie, and watched the second man critically. He was new, and she decided he was awkward.

She chattered through the meal, however, with that light gayety of hers which was not gayety at all, and always of the country house.

"The dining-room floor is to be oak, with a marble border," she said. "You remember the ones we saw in Italy? And the ceiling is blue and gold. You'll love the ceiling, Clay."

There was claret with the luncheon, and Clayton, raising his glass, thought of Chris and the water that smelled to heaven.

Natalie's mind was on loggias by that time.

"An upstairs loggia, too," she said. "Bordered with red geraniums. I loathe geraniums, but the color is good. Rodney wants Japanese screens and things, but I'm not sure. What do you think?"

"I think you're a better judge than I am," he replied, smiling. He had had to come back a long way, but he made the effort.

"It's hardly worth while struggling to have things attractive for you," she observed petulantly. "You never notice, anyhow. Clay, do you know that you sit hours and hours, and never talk to me?"

"No! Do I? I'm sorry."

"You're a perfectly dreary person to have around."

"I'll talk to you, my dear. But I'm not much good at houses. Give me something I understand."

"The mill, I suppose! Or the war!"

"Do I really talk of the war?"

"When you talk at all. What in the world do you think about, Clay, when you sit with your eyes on nothing? It's a vicious habit."

"Oh, ships and sails and sealing wax and cabbages and kings," he said, lightly.

That afternoon Natalie slept, and the house took on the tomb-like quiet of an establishment where the first word in service is silence. Clay wandered about, feeling an inexpressible loneliness of spirit. On those days which work did not fill he was always discontented. He thought of the club, but the vision of those disconsolate groups of homeless bachelors who gathered there on all festivals that centered about a family focus was unattractive.

All at once, he realized that, since he had wakened that morning, he had been wanting to see Audrey. He wanted to talk to her, real talk, not gossip. Not country houses. Not personalities. Not recrimination. Such talk as Audrey herself had always led at dinner parties: of men and affairs, of big issues, of the war.

He felt suddenly that he must talk about the war to some one.

Natalie was still sleeping when he went down-stairs. It had been raining, but a cold wind was covering the pavement with a glaze of ice. Here and there men in top hats, like himself, were making their way to Christmas calls. Children clinging to the arms of governesses, their feet in high arctics, slid laughing on the ice. A belated florist's wagon was still delivering Christmas plants tied with bright red bows. The street held more of festivity to Clayton than had his house. Even the shop windows, as he walked toward Audrey's unfashionable new neighborhood, cried out their message of peace. Peace-when there was no peace.

Audrey was alone, but her little room was crowded with gifts and flowers.

"I was hoping you would come, Clay," she said. "I've had some visitors, but they're gone. I'll tell them down-stairs that I'm not at home, and we can really talk."

"That's what I came for."

And when she had telephoned; "I've had a letter from Chris, Audrey."

She read it slowly, and he was surprised, when she finally looked up, to find tears in her eyes.

"Poor old Chris!" she said. "I've never told you the story, have I, Clay? Of course I know perfectly well I haven't. There was another woman. I think I could have understood it, perhaps, if she had been a different sort of a woman. But —I suppose it hurt my pride. I didn't love him. She was such a vulgar little thing. Not even pretty. Just-woman."

He nodded.

"He was fastidious, too. I don't understand it. And he swears he never cared for her. I don't believe he did, either. I suppose there's no explanation for these things. They just happen. It's the life we live, I dare say. When I look back-She's the girl I sent into the mill."

He was distinctly shocked.

"But, Audrey," he protested, "you are not seeing her, are you?"

"Now and then. She has fastened herself on me, in a way. Don't scowl like that. She says she is straight now and that she only wants a chance to work. She's off the stage for good. She-danced. That money I got from you was for her. She was waiting, up-stairs. Chris was behind with her rent, and she was going to lose her furniture."

"That you should have to do such a thing!" he protested. "It's —well, it's infamous."

But she only smiled.

"Well, I've never been particularly shielded. It hasn't hurt me. I don't even hate her. But I'm puzzled sometimes. Where there's love it might be understandable. Most of us would hate to have to stand the test of real love, I daresay. There's a time in every one's life, I suppose, when love seems to be the only thing that matters."

That was what the poet in that idiotic book had said: "There is no other joy."

"Even you, Clay," she reflected, smilingly. "You big, grave men go all to pieces, sometimes."

"I never have," he retorted.

She returned Chris's letter to him.

"There," she said. "I've had my little whimper, and I feel better. Now talk to me."

The little clock was striking six when at last he rose to go. The room was dark, with only the glow of the wood fire on Audrey's face. He found her very lovely, rather chastened and subdued, but much more appealing than in her old days of sparkle and high spirits.

"You are looking very sweet, Audrey."

"Am I? How nice of you!"

She got up and stood on the hearth-rug beside him, looking up at him. Then, "Don't be startled, Clay," she announced, smilingly. "I am going to kiss you-for Christmas."

And kiss him she did, putting both hands on his shoulders, and rising on her toes to do it. It was a very small kiss, and Clayton took it calmly, and as she intended him to take it. But it was, at that, rather a flushed Audrey who bade him good-night and God bless you.

Clayton took away with him from that visit a great peace and a great relief. He had talked out to her for more than an hour of the many things that puzzled and bewildered him. He had talked war, and the mill, and even Graham and his problems. And by talking of them some of them had clarified. A little of his unrest had gone. He felt encouraged, he had a new strength to go on. It was wonderful, he reflected, what the friendship of a woman could mean to a man. He was quite convinced that it was only friendship.

He turned toward home reluctantly. Behind him was the glow of Audrey's fire, and the glow that had been in her eyes when he entered. If a man had such a woman behind him...

He went into his great, silent house, and the door closed behind him like a prison gate.

For a long time after he had gone, Audrey, doors closed to visitors, sat alone by her fire, with one of his roses held close to her cheek.

In her small upper room, in a white frame cottage on the hill overlooking the Spencer furnaces, Anna Klein, locked away from prying eyes, sat that same Christmas evening and closely inspected a tiny gold wrist-watch. And now and then, like Audrey, she pressed it to her face.

Not the gift, but the giver.

Chapter XIV

Having turned Dunbar and his protective league over to Hutchinson, the general manager, Clayton had put him out of his mind. But during the week after Christmas he reached the office early one morning to find that keen and rather shabby gentleman already there, waiting.

Not precisely waiting, for he was standing by one of the windows, well back from it, and inspecting the mill yard with sharp, darting glances.

"Hello, Dunbar," said Clayton, and proceeded to shed his fur-lined coat. Dunbar turned and surveyed him with the grudging admiration of the undersized man for the tall one.

"Cold morning," he said, coming forward. "Not that I suppose you know it." He glanced at the coat.

"I thought Hutchinson said that you'd gone away."

"Been to Washington. I brought something back that will interest you."

From inside his coat he produced a small leather case, and took from it a number of photographs.

"I rather gathered, Mr. Spencer," he said dryly, "when I was here last that you thought me an alarmist. I don't know that I blame you. We always think the other fellow may get it, but that we are safe. You might glance at those photographs."

He spread them out on the desk. Beyond the windows the mill roared on; men shouted, the locomotive whistled, a long file of laborers with wheelbarrows went by. And from a new building going up came the hammering of the riveting-machines, so like the rapid explosions of machine guns.

"Interesting, aren't they?" queried Dunbar. "This is a clock-bomb with a strap for carrying it under a coat. That's a lump of coal-only it isn't. It's got enough explosive inside to blow up a battleship. It's meant for that, primarily. That's fire-confetti —damnable stuff-understand it's what burned up most of Belgium. And that's a fountain-pen. What do you think of that? Use one yourself, don't you? Don't leave it lying around. That's all."

"What on earth can they do with a fountain-pen?"

"One of their best little tricks," said Mr. Dunbar, with a note of grudging admiration in his voice. "Here's a cut of the mechanism. You sit down, dip your pen, and commence to write. There's the striking pin, or whatever they call it. It hits here, and-good night!"

"Do you mean to say they're using things like that here?"

"I mean to say they're planning to, if they haven't already. That coal now, you'd see that go into your furnaces, or under your boilers, or wherever you use it, and wouldn't worry, would you?"

"Are these actual photographs?"

"Made from articles taken from a German officer's trunk, in a neutral country. He was on his way somewhere, I imagine."

Clayton sat silent. Then he took out his fountain-pen and surveyed it with a smile.

"Rather off fountain-pens for a time, I take it!" observed Dunbar. "Well, I've something else for you. You've got one of the best little I.W.W. workers in the country right here in your mill. Some of them aren't so bad-hot air and nothing else. But this fellow's a fanatic. Which is the same as saying he's crazy."

"Who is he?"

"Name's Rudolph Klein. He's a sort of relation to the chap that got out. Old man's been sore on him, but I understand he's hanging around the Klein place again."

Clayton considered.

"I don't remember him. Of course, I can't keep track of the men. We'll get rid of him."

Mr. Dunbar eyed him.

"That's the best thing you can think of?"

"I don't want him round, do I?"

"Nine of you men out of ten say that. You'd turn him loose and so warn him. Not only that, but he'll be off on his devil's work somewhere. Perhaps here. Perhaps elsewhere. And we want him where we can find him. See here, Mr. Spencer, d'you ever hear of counter-espionage?"

Clayton never had, but the term explained itself.

"Set a spy to watch a spy," said Dunbar. "Let him think he's going on fine. Find his confederates. Let them get ready to spring something. And then-get them. Remember," he added with sarcasm, "we're still neutral. You can't lock a man up because he goes around yelling 'Down with capital!' The whole country is ready to yell it with him. And, even if you find him with a bomb under his coat, labeled 'made in Germany,' it's hard to link Germans up with the thing. He can say that he always buys his bombs in Germany. That they make the best bombs in the world. That he likes the way they pack 'em, and their polite trade methods."

Clayton listened, thinking hard.

"We have a daughter of Klein's here. She is my son's secretary."

Dunbar glanced at him quickly, but his eyes were on the window.

"I know that."

"Think I should get rid of her?"

Dunbar hesitated. He liked Clayton Spencer, and it was his business just then to know something about the Kleins. It would be a good thing for Clayton Spencer's boy if they got rid of the girl.

On the other hand, to keep her there and watch her was certainly a bigger thing. If she stayed there might be trouble, but it would concern the boy only. If she left, and if she was one link in the chain to snare Rudolph, there might be a disaster costing many lives. He made his decision quickly.

"Keep her, by all means," he said. "And don't tell Mr. Graham anything. He's young, and he'd be likely to show something. I suppose she gets considerable data where she is?"

"Only of the one department. But that's a fair indication of the rest."

Dunbar rose.

"I'm inclined to think there's nothing to that end of it," he said. "The old chap is sulky, but he's not dangerous. It's Rudolph I'm afraid of."

At the luncheon hour that day Clayton, having finished his mail, went to Graham's office. He seldom did that, but he was uneasy. He wanted to see the girl. He wanted to look her over with this new idea in his mind. She had been a quiet little thing, he remembered; thorough, but not brilliant. He had sent her to Graham from his own office. He disliked even the idea of suspecting her; his natural chivalry revolted from suspecting any woman.

Joey, who customarily ate his luncheon on Clayton's desk in his absence, followed by one of Clayton's cigarets, watched him across the yard, and whistled as he saw him enter Graham's small building.

"Well, what do you think of that?" he reflected. "I hope he coughs before he goes in."

But Clayton did not happen to cough. Graham's office was empty, but there was a sound of voices from Anna Klein's small room beyond. He crossed to the door and opened it, to stand astonished, his hand on the door-knob.

Anna Klein was seated at her desk, with her luncheon spread before her on a newspaper, and seated on the desk, a sandwich in one hand, the other resting on Anna's shoulder, was Graham. He was laughing when Clayton opened the door, but the smile froze on his face. He slid off her desk.

"Want me, father?"

"Yes," said Clayton, curtly. And went out, leaving the door open. A sort of stricken silence followed his exit, then Graham put down the sandwich and went out, closing the door behind him. He stood just inside it in the outer room, rather pale, but looking his father in the eyes.

"Sorry, father," he said. "I didn't hear you. I —"

"What has that to do with it?"

The boy was silent. To Clayton he looked furtive, guilty. His very expression condemned him far more than the incident itself. And Clayton, along with his anger, was puzzled as to his best course. Dunbar had said to leave the girl where she was. But-was it feasible under these circumstances? He was rather irritated than angry. He considered a flirtation with one's stenographer rotten bad taste, at any time. The business world, to his mind, was divided into two kinds of men, those who did that sort of thing, and those who did not. It was a code, rather than a creed, that the boy had violated.

Besides, he had had a surprise. The girl who sat laughing into Graham's face was not the Anna Klein he remembered, a shy, drab little thing, badly dressed, rather sallow and unsmiling. Here was a young woman undeniably attractive; slightly rouged, trim in her white blouse, and with an air of piquancy that was added, had he known it, by the large imitation pearl earrings she wore.

"Get your hat and go to lunch, Graham," he said. "And you might try to remember that a slightly different standard of conduct is expected from my son, here, than may be the standard of some of the other men."

"It doesn't mean anything, that sort of fooling."

"You and I may know that. The girl may not."

Then he went out, and Graham returned unhappily to the inner room. Anna was not crying; she was too frightened to cry. She had sat without moving, her hand still clutching her untouched sandwich. Graham looked at her and tried to smile.

"I'm gone, I suppose?"

"Don't you worry about that," he said, with boyish bravado. "Don't you worry about that, little girl."

"Father will kill me," she whispered. "He's queer these days, and if I go home and have to tell him —" She shuddered.

"I'll see you get something else, if the worst comes, you know."

She glanced up at him with that look of dog-like fidelity that always touched him.

"I'll find you something good," he promised.

"Something good," she repeated, with sudden bitterness. "And you'll get another girl here, and flirt with her, and make her crazy about you, and —"

"Honestly, do you like me like that?"

"I'm just mad about you," she said miserably.

Frightened though he was, her wretchedness appealed to him. The thought that she cared for him, too, was a salve to his outraged pride. A moment ago, in the other room, he had felt like a bad small boy. As with Marion, Anna made him feel every inch a man. But she gave him what Marion did not, the feeling of her complete surrender. Marion would take; this girl would give.

He bent down and put his arms around her.

"Poor little girl!" he said. "Poor little girl!"

Chapter XV

The gay and fashionable crowd of which Audrey had been the center played madly that winter. The short six weeks of the season were already close to an end. By mid-January the south and California would have claimed most of the women and some of the men. There were a few, of course, who saw the inevitable catastrophe: the Mackenzies had laid up their house-boat on the west coast of Florida. Denis Nolan had let his little place at Pinehurst. The advance wave of the war tide, the increased cost of living, had sobered and made thoughtful the middle class, but above in the great businesses, and below among the laboring people, money was plentiful and extravagance ran riot.

And Audrey Valentine's world missed her. It refused to accept her poverty as an excuse, and clamored for her. It wanted her to sit again at a piano, somewhere, anywhere, with a lighted cigaret on the music-rack, and sing her husky, naive little songs. It wanted her cool audacity. It wanted her for week-end parties and bridge, and to canter on frosty mornings on its best horses and make slaves of the park policemen, so that she might jump forbidden fences. It wanted to see her oust its grinning chauffeurs, and drive its best cars at their best speed.

Audrey Valentine leading a cloistered life! Impossible! Selfish!

And Audrey was not cut out for solitude. She did not mind poverty. She found it rather a relief to acknowledge what had always been the fact. But she did mind loneliness. And her idea of making herself over into something useful was not working out particularly well. She spent two hours a day, at a down-town school, struggling with shorthand, and her writing-table was always littered with papers covered with queer hooks and curves, or with typed sheets beginning:

"Messrs Smith and Co.,: Dear Sirs."

Clayton Spencer met her late in December, walking feverishly along with a book under her arm, and a half-desperate look in her eyes. He felt a little thrill when he saw her, which should have warned him but did not.

She did not even greet him. She stopped and held out her book to him.

"Take it!" she said. "I've thrown it away twice, and two wretched men have run after me and brought it back."

He took it and glanced at it.

"Spelling! Can't you spell?"

"Certainly I can spell," she said with dignity. "I'm a very good speller. Clay, there isn't an 'i' in business, is there?"

"It is generally considered necessary to have two pretty good eyes in business." But he saw then that she was really rather despairing. "There is, one 'i,' " he said. "It seems foolish, doesn't it? Audrey dear, what are you trying to do? For heaven's sake, if it's money?"

"It isn't that. I have enough. Honestly, Clay, I just had some sort of an idea that I'd been playing long enough. But I'm only good for play. That man this morning said as much, when we fussed about my spelling. He said I'd better write a new dictionary."

Clayton threw back his head and laughed, and after a moment she laughed, too. But as he went on his face was grave. Somebody ought to be looking after her. It was not for some time that he realized he carried the absurd little spelling-book. He took it back to the office with him, and put it in the back of a drawer of his desk. Joey, coming in some time later, found him, with the drawer open, and something in his hands which he hastily put away. Later on, Joey investigated that drawer, and found the little book. He inspected it with a mixture of surprise and scorn.

"Spelling!" he muttered. "And a hundred dollar a month girl to spell for him!"

It was Rodney Page who forced Audrey out of her seclusion.

Rodney had had a prosperous year, and for some time his conscience had been bothering him. For a good many years he had blithely accepted the invitations of his friends-dinners, balls, week-end and yachting parties, paying his way with an occasional box of flowers. He decided, that last winter of peace, to turn host and, true to instinct, to do the unusual.

It was Natalie who gave him the suggestion.

"Why don't you turn your carriage-house into a studio, and give a studio warming, Roddie? It would be fun fixing it up. And you might make it fancy dress."

Before long, of course, he had accepted the idea as of his own originating, and was hard at work.

Rodney's house had been his father's. He still lived there, although the business district had encroached closely. And for some time he had used the large stable and carriage-house at the rear as a place in which to store the odd bits of furniture, old mirrors and odds and ends that he had picked up here and there. Now and then, as to Natalie, he sold some of them, but he was a collector, not a merchant. In his way, he was an artist.

In the upper floor he had built a skylight, and there, in odd hours, he worked out, in watercolor, sketches of interiors, sometimes for houses he was building, sometimes purely for the pleasure of the thing.

The war had brought him enormous increase in his collection. Owners of French chateaus, driven to poverty, were sending to America treasures of all sorts of furniture, tapestries, carpets, old fountains, porcelains, even carved woodwork and ancient mantels, and Rodney, from the mixed motives of business and pride, decided to exhibit them.

The old brick floor of the stable he replaced with handmade tiles. The box-stalls were small display-rooms, hung with tapestries and lighted with candles in old French sconces. The great carriage-room became a refectory, with Jacobean and old monastery chairs, and the vast loft overhead, reached by a narrow staircase that clung to the wall, was railed on its exposed side, waxed as to floor, hung with lanterns, and became a ballroom.

Natalie worked with him, spending much time and a prodigious amount of energy. There was springing up between them one of those curious and dangerous intimacies, of idleness on the woman's part, of admiration on the man's, which sometimes develop into a wholly spurious passion. Probably Rodney realized it; certainly Natalie did not. She liked his admiration; she dressed, each day, for Rodney's unfailing comment on her clothes.

"Clay never notices what I wear," she said, once, plaintively.

So it was Rodney who brought Audrey Valentine out of her seclusion, and he did it by making her angry. He dropped in to see her between Christmas and New-years, and made a plea.

"A stable-warming!" she said. "How interesting! And fancy dress! Are you going to have them come as grooms, or jockeys? If I were going I'd go as a circus-rider. I used to be able to stand up on a running horse. Of course you're having horses. What's a stable without a horse?"

He saw she was laughing at him and was rather resentful.

"I told you I have made it into a studio."

But when he implored her to go, she was obdurate.

"Do go away and let me alone, Rodney," she said at last. "I loathe fancy-dress parties."

"It won't be a party without you."

"Then don't have it. I've told you, over and over, I'm not going out. It isn't decent this year, in my opinion. And, anyhow, I haven't any money, any clothes, any anything. A bad evening at bridge, and I shouldn't be able to pay my rent."

"That's nonsense. Why do you let people say you are moping about Chris? You're not."

"Of course not."

She sat up.

"What else are they saying?"

"Well, there's some talk, naturally. You can't be as popular as you have been, and then just drop out, without some gossip. It's not bad."

"What sort of talk?"

He was very uncomfortable.

"Well, of course, you have been pretty strong on the war stuff?"

"Oh, they think I sent him!"

"If only you wouldn't hide, Audrey. That's what has made the talk. It's not Chris's going."

"I'm not hiding. That's idiotic. I was bored to death, if you want the truth. Look here, Rodney. You're not being honest. What do they say about Chris and myself?"

He was cornered.

"Is it-about another woman?"

"Well, of course now and then-there are always such stories. And of course Chris —"

"Yes, they knew Chris." Her voice was scornful. "So they think I'm moping and hiding because-How interesting!"

She sat back, with her old insolent smile.

"Poor Chris!" she said. "The only man in the lot except Clay Spencer who is doing his bit for the war, and they-when is your party, Roddie?"

"New-year's Eve."

"I'll come," she said. And smiling again, dangerously, "I'll come, with bells on."

Chapter XVI

There had been once, in Herman Klein the making of a good American. He had come to America, not at the call of freedom, but of peace and plenty. Nevertheless, he had possibilities.

Taken in time he might have become a good American. But nothing was done to stimulate in him a sentiment for his adopted land. He would, indeed, have been, for all his citizenship papers, a man without a country but for one thing.

The Fatherland had never let go. When he went to the Turnverein, it was to hear the old tongue, to sing the old songs. Visiting Germans from overseas were constantly lecturing, holding before him the vision of great Germany. He saw moving-pictures of Germany; he went to meetings which commenced with "Die Wacht am Rhine." One Christmas he received a handsome copy of a photograph of the Kaiser through the mail. He never knew who sent it, but he had it framed in a gilt frame, and it hung over the fireplace in the sitting-room.

He had been adopted by America, but he had not adopted America, save his own tiny bit of it. He took what the new country gave him with no faintest sense that he owed anything in return beyond his small yearly taxes. He was neither friendly nor inimical.

His creed through the years had been simple: to owe no man money, even for a day; to spend less than he earned; to own his own home; to rise early, work hard, and to live at peace with his neighbors. He had learned English and had sent Anna to the public school. He spoke

English with her, always. And on Sunday he put on his best clothes, and sat in the German Lutheran church, dozing occasionally, but always rigidly erect.

With his first savings he had bought a home, a tiny two-roomed frame cottage on a bill above the Spencer mill, with a bit of waste land that he turned into a thrifty garden. Anna was born there, and her mother had died there ten years later. But long enough before that he had added four rooms, and bought an adjoining lot. At that time the hill had been green; the way to the little white house had been along and up a winding path, where in the spring the early wild flowers came out on sunny banks, and the first buds of the neighborhood were on Klein's own lilac-bushes.

He had had a magnificent sense of independence those days, and of freedom.

He voted religiously, and now and then in the evenings he had been the moderate member of a mild socialist group. Theoretically, he believed that no man should amass a fortune by the labor of others. Actually he felt himself well paid, a respected member of society, and a property owner.

In the early morning, winter and summer, he emerged into the small side porch of his cottage and there threw over himself a pail of cold water from the well outside. Then he rubbed down, dressed in the open air behind the old awning hung there, took a dozen deep breaths and a cup of coffee, and was off for work. The addition of a bathroom, with running hot water, had made no change in his daily habits.

He was very strict with Anna, and with the women who, one after another, kept house for him.

"I'll have no men lounging around," was his first instruction on engaging them. And to Anna his solicitude took the form almost of espionage. The only young man he tolerated about the place was a distant relative. Rudolph Klein.

On Sunday evenings Rudolph came in to supper. But even Rudolph found it hard to get a word with the girl alone.

"What's eating him, anyhow," he demanded of Anna one Sunday evening, when by the accident of a neighbor calling old Herman to the gate, he had the chance of a word.

"He knows a lot about you fellows," Anna had said. "And the more he knows the less he trusts you. I don't wonder."

"He hasn't anything on me."

But Anna had come to the limit of her patience with her father at last.

"What's the matter with you?" she demanded angrily one night, when Herman had sat with his pipe in his mouth, and had refused her permission to go to the moving-pictures with another girl. "Do you think I'm going on forever like this, without a chance to play? I'm sick of it. That's all."

"You vill not run around with the girls on this hill." He had conquered all but the English "w." He still pronounced it like a "v."

"What's the matter with the girls on this hill?" And when he smoked on in imperturbable silence, she had flamed into a fury.

"This is free America," she reminded him. "It's not Germany. And I've stood about all I can. I work all day, and I need a little fun. I'm going."

And she had gone, rather shaky as to the knees, but with her head held high, leaving him on the little veranda with his dead pipe in his mouth and his German-American newspaper held before his face. She had returned, still terrified, to find the house dark and the doors locked, and rather than confess to any one, she had spent the night in a chair out of doors.

At dawn she had heard him at the side of the house, drawing water for his bath. He had gone through his morning program as usual, by the sounds, and had started off for work without an inquiry about her. Only when she heard the gate click had she hammered at the front door and been admitted by the untidy servant.

"Fine way to treat me!" she had stormed, and for a part of that day she was convinced that she would never go back home again. But fear of her father was the strongest emotion she knew, and she went back that night, as usual. It not being Herman's way to bother with greetings, she had passed him on the porch without a word, and that night, winding a clock before closing the house, he spoke to her for the first time.

"There is a performance at the Turnverein Hall to-morrow night. Rudolph vill take you."

"I don't like Rudolph."

"Rudolph viii take you," he had repeated, stolidly. And she had gone.

He had no conception of any failure in himself as a parent. He had the German idea of women. They had a distinct place in the world, but that place was not a high one. Their function was to bring children into the world. They were breeding animals, and as such to be carefully watched and not particularly trusted. They had no place in the affairs of men, outside the home.

Not that he put it that way. In his way he probably loved the girl. But never once did he think of her as an intelligent and reasoning creature. He took her salary, gave her a small allowance for car-fare, and banked the rest of it in his own name. It would all be hers some day, so what difference did it make?

But the direst want would not have made him touch a penny of it.

He disliked animals. But in a curious shame-faced fashion he liked flowers. Such portions of his garden as were useless for vegetables he had planted out in flowers. But he never cut them and brought them into the house, and he watched jealously that no one else should do so. He kept poisoned meat around for such dogs in the neighborhood as wandered in, and Anna had found him once callously watching the death agonies of one of them.

Such, at the time the Spencer mill began work on its new shell contract, was Herman Klein, sturdily honest, just according to his ideas of justice, callous rather than cruel, but the citizen of a world bounded by his memories of Germany, his life at the mill, and his home.

But, for all that, he was not a man the German organization in America put much faith in. Rudolph, feeling his way, had had one or two conversations with him early in the war that had made him report adversely.

"Let them stop all this fighting," Herman had said. "What matter now who commenced it? Let them all stop. It is the only way."

"Sure, let them stop!" said Rudolph, easily. "Let them stop trying to destroy Germany."

"That is nonsense," Herman affirmed, sturdily. "Do you think I know nothing? I, who was in the Prussian Guard for five years. Think you I know nothing of the plan?"

The report of the German atrocities, however, found him frankly incredulous, and one noon hour, in the mill, having read the Belgian King's statement that the German army in Belgium had protected its advance with women and children, Rudolph found him tearing the papers to shreds furiously.

"Such lies!" he cried. "It is not possible that they should be believed."

The sinking of the Lusitania, however, left him thoughtful and depressed. In vain Rudolph argued with him.

"They were warned," he said. "If they chose to take the chance, is it Germany's fault? If you tell me not to put my hand on a certain piece in a machine and I do it anyhow, is it your fault if I lose a hand?"

Old Herman eyed him shrewdly.

"And if Anna had been on the ship, you think the same, eh?"

Rudolph had colored.

For some time now Rudolph had been in love with Anna. He had not had much encouragement. She went out with him, since he was her only means of escape, but she treated him rather cavalierly, criticized his clothes and speech, laughed openly at his occasional lapses into sentiment, and was, once in a long time, so kind that she set his heart leaping.

Until the return of Graham Spencer, all had gone fairly well. But with his installment in the mill, Rudolph's relations with Anna had changed. She had grown prettier-Rudolph was not observant enough to mark what made the change, but he knew that he was madder about her than ever. And she had assumed toward him an attitude of almost scornful indifference. The effect on his undisciplined young mind was bad. He had no suspicion of Graham. He only knew his own desperate unhappiness. In the meetings held twice weekly in a hall on Third Street he was reckless, advocating violence constantly. The conservative element watched him uneasily; the others kept an eye on him, for future use.

The closing week of the old year found the situation strained in the Klein house. Herman had had plenty of opportunities for situations, but all of them had to do directly or indirectly with the making of munitions for the Allies. Old firms in other lines were not taking on new men. It was the munition works that were increasing their personnel. And by that time the determination not to assist Germany's enemies had become a fixed one.

The day after Christmas, in pursuit of this idea, he commanded Anna to leave the mill. But she had defied him, for the second time in her, life, her face pale to the lips.

"Not on your life," she had said. "You may want to starve. I don't."

"There is plenty of other work."

"Don't you kid yourself. And, anyhow, I'm not looking for it. I don't mind working so you can sit here and nurse a grouch, but I certainly don't intend to start hunting another job."

She had eyed him morosely. "If you ask me," she continued, "you're out of your mind. What's Germany to you? You forgot it as fast as you could, until this war came along. You and Rudolph! You're long distance patriots, you are."

"I will not help my country's enemies," he had said doggedly.

"Your country s enemies. My word! Isn't this your country? What's the old Kaiser to you?"

He had ordered her out of the house, then, but she had laughed at him. She could always better him in an argument.

"Suppose I do go?" she had inquired. "What are you going to live on? I'm not crazy in the head, if you are."

She rather thought he would strike her. He had done it before, with the idea of enforcing discipline. If he did, she would leave him. Let him shift for himself. He had taken her money for years, and he could live on that. But he had only glared at her.

"We would have done better to remain in Germany," he said. "America has no respect for parents. It has no discipline. It is a country without law."

She felt a weakening in him, and followed up her advantage.

"And another thing, while we're at it," she flung at him. "Don't you go on trying to shove Rudolph down my throat. I'm off Rudolph for keeps."

She flung out her arm, and old Herman saw the gleam of something gold on her wrist. He caught her hand in his iron grip and shoved up her sleeve. There was a tiny gold wrist-watch there, on a flexible chain. His amazement and rage gave her a moment to think, although she was terrified.

"Where did you get that?"

"The mill gave them to the stenographers for Christmas."

"Why did you not tell me?"

"We're not talking much these days, are we?"

He let her go then, and that night, in the little room behind Gustav Shroeder's saloon, he put the question to Rudolph. Because he was excited and frightened he made slow work of his inquiry, and Rudolph had a moment to think.

"Sure," he replied. "All the girls in the executive offices got them."

But when the meeting was over, Rudolph did not go back to his boarding-house. He walked the streets and thought.

He had saved Anna from her father. But he was of no mind to save her from himself. She would have to account to him for that watch.

Anna herself lay awake until late. She saw already the difficulties before her. Herman was suspicious. He might inquire. There were other girls from the mill offices on the hill. And he might speak to Rudolph.

The next evening she found Rudolph waiting for her outside the mill gate. Together they started up what had been, when Herman bought the cottage, a green hill with a winding path. But the smoke and ore from the mill had long ago turned it to bareness, had killed the trees and shrubbery, and filled the little hollows where once the first arbutus had hidden with cinders and ore dust. The path had become a crooked street, lined with wooden houses, and paved with worn and broken bricks.

Where once Herman Klein had carried his pail and whistled bits of Shubert as he climbed along, a long line of blackened men made their evening way. Untidy children sat on the curb, dogs lay in the center of the road, and women in all stages of dishabille hung over the high railings of their porches and watched for their men.

Under protest of giving her a lift up the hill, Rudolph slipped his hand through Anna's left arm.

Immediately she knew that the movement was a pretext. She could not free herself.

"Be good, now," he cautioned her. "I've got you. I want to see that watch."

"You let me alone."

"I'm going to see that watch."

With his free hand he felt under her sleeve and drew down the bracelet.

"So the mill gave it to you, eh? That's a lie, and you know it."

"I'll tell you, Rudolph," she temporized. "Only don't tell father. All the girls have watches, and I wanted one. So I bought it."

"That's a lie, too."

"On the installment plan," she insisted. "A dollar a week, that's straight. I've paid five on it already."

He was almost convinced, not quite. He unfastened it awkwardly and took it off her wrist. It was a plain little octagonal watch, and on the back was a monogram. The monogram made him suspicious again.

"It's only gold filled, Rudolph."

"Pretty classy monogram for a cheap watch." He held it close; on the dial was the jeweler's name, a famous one. He said nothing more, put it back on Anna's arm and released her. At the next corner he left her, with a civil enough good-bye, but with rage in his heart.

Chapter XVII

The New-year, destined to be so crucial, came in cheerfully enough. There was, to be sure, a trifle less ostentation in the public celebrations, but the usual amount of champagne brought in the most vital year in the history of the nation. The customary number of men, warmed by that champagne, made reckless love to the women who happened to be near them and forgot it by morning. And the women themselves presented pictures of splendor of a peculiar gorgeousness.

The fact that almost coincident with the war there had come into prominence an entirely new school of color formed one of the curious contrasts of the period. Into a drab world there flamed strange and bizarre theatrical effects, in scenery and costume. Some of it was beautiful, most of it merely fantastic. But it was immediately reflected in the clothing of fashionable women. Europe, which had originated it, could use it but little; but great opulent America adopted it and made it her own.

So, while the rest of the world was gray, America flamed, and Natalie Spencer, spending her days between dressmakers and decorators, flamed with the rest.

On New-year's Eve Clayton Spencer always preceded the annual ball of the City Club, of which he was president, by a dinner to the board of governors and their wives. It was his dinner. He, and not Natalie, arranged the seating, ordered the flowers, and planned the menu. He took considerable pride in it; he liked to think that it was both beautiful and dignified. His father had been president before him, and he liked to think that he was carrying on his father's custom with the punctilious dignity that had so characterized him.

He was dressed early. Natalie had been closeted with Madeleine, her maid, and a hair-dresser, for hours. As he went down-stairs he could hear her voice raised in querulous protest about something.

When he went into the library Buckham was there stooping over the fire, his austere old face serious and intent.

"Well, another year almost gone, Buckham!" he said.

"Yes, Mr. Spencer."

"It would be interesting to know what the New-year holds."

"I hope it will bring you peace and happiness, sir."

"Thank you."

And after Buckham had gone he thought that rather a curious New-year's wish. Peace and happiness! Well, God knows he wanted both. A vague comprehension of the understanding the upper servants of a household acquire as to the inner life of the family stirred in him; how much they knew and concealed under their impassive service.

When Natalie came down the staircase a few minutes later she was swathed in her chinchilla evening wrap, and she watched his face, after her custom when she expected to annoy him, with the furtive look that he had grown to associate with some unpleasantness.

"I hate dressing for a ball at this hour," she said, rather breathlessly. "I don't feel half-dressed by midnight."

Madeleine, in street costume, was behind her with a great box.

"She has something for my hair," she explained. Her tone was nervous, but he was entirely unsuspicious.

"You don't mind if I don't go on to Page's, do you? I'm rather tired, and I ought to stay at the club as late as I can."

"Of course not. I shall probably pick up some people, anyhow. Everybody is going on."

In the car she chattered feverishly and he listened, lapsing into one of the silences which her talkative spells always enforced.

"What flowers are you having?" she asked, finally.

"White lilacs and pussy-willow. Did your orchids come?"

"Thanks, yes. But I'm not wearing them. My gown is flame color. They simply shrieked."

"Flame color?"

"A sort of orange," she explained. And, in a slightly defiant tone: "Rodney's is a costume dance, you know."

"Do you mean you are in fancy dress?"

"I am, indeed."

He was rather startled. The annual dinner of the board of governors of the City Club and their wives was a most dignified function always. He was the youngest by far of the men; the women were all frankly dowagers. They represented the conservative element of the city's social life, that element which frowned on smartness and did not even recognize the bizarre. It was old-fashioned, secure in its position, influential, and slightly tedious.

"There will be plenty in fancy dress."

"Not at the dinner."

"Stodgy old frumps!" was Natalie's comment. "I believe you would rather break one of the ten commandments than one of the conventions," she added.

It was when he saw her coming down the staircase in the still empty clubhouse that he realized the reason for her defiant attitude when she acknowledged to fancy dress. For she wore a peacock costume of the most daring sort. Over an orange foundation, eccentric in itself and very short, was a vivid tunic covered with peacock feathers on gold tissue, with a sweeping tail behind, and on her head was the towering chest of a peacock on a gold bandeau. She waved a great peacock fan, also, and half-way down the stairs she paused and looked down at him, with half-frightened eyes.

"Do you like it?"

"It is very wonderful," he said, gravely.

He could not hurt her. Her pleasure in it was too naive. It dawned on him then that Natalie was really a child, a spoiled and wilful child. And always afterward he tried to remember that, and to judge her accordingly.

She came down, the upturned wired points of the tunic trembling as she stepped. When she came closer he saw that she was made up for the costume ball also, her face frankly rouged, fine lines under her eyes, her lashes blackened. She looked very lovely and quite unfamiliar. But he had determined not to spoil her evening, and he continued gravely smiling.

"You'd better like it, Clay," she said, and took a calculating advantage of what she considered a softened mood. "It cost a thousand dollars."

She went on past him, toward the room where the florist was still putting the finishing touches to the flowers on the table. When the first guests arrived, she came back and took her place near him, and he was uncomfortably aware of the little start of surprise with which she burst upon each new arrival, In the old and rather staid surroundings of the club she looked out of place-oriental, extravagant, absurd.

And Clayton Spencer suffered. To draw him as he stood in the club that last year of our peace, 1916, is to draw him not only with his virtues but with his faults; his over emphasis on small things; his jealousy for his dignity; his hatred of the conspicuous and the unusual.

When, after the informal manner of clubs, the party went in to dinner, he was having one of the bad hours of his life to that time. And when, as was inevitable, the talk of the rather serious table turned to the war, it seemed to him that Natalie, gorgeous and painted, represented the very worst of the country he loved, indifference, extravagance, and ostentatious display.

But Natalie was not America. Thank God, Natalie was not America.

Already with the men she was having a triumph. The women, soberly clad, glanced at each other with raised eye-brows and cynical smiles. Above the band, already playing in the ballroom, Clayton could hear old Terry Mackenzie paying Natalie extravagant, flagrant compliments.

"You should be sitting in the sun, or on a balcony," he was saying, his eyes twinkling. "And pretty gentlemen with long curls and their hats tucked under their arms should be feeding you nightingale tongues, or whatever it is you eat."

"Bugs," said Natalie.

"But-tell me," Terry bent toward her, and Mrs. Terry kept fascinated eyes on him. "Tell me, lovely creature-aren't peacocks unlucky?"

"Are they? What bad luck can happen to me because I dress like this?"

"Frightfully bad luck," said Terry, jovially. "Some one will undoubtedly carry you away, in the course of the evening, and go madly through the world hunting a marble balustrade to set you on. I'll do it myself if you'll give me any encouragement."

Perhaps, had Clayton Spencer been entirely honest with himself that night, he would have acknowledged that he had had a vague hope of seeing Audrey at the club. Cars came up, discharged their muffled occupants under the awning and drove away again. Delight and Mrs. Haverford arrived and he danced with Delight, to her great anxiety lest she might not dance well. Graham came very late, in the wake of Marion Hayden.

But Audrey did not appear.

He waited until the New-year came in. The cotillion was on then, and the favors for the midnight figure were gilt cornucopias filled with loose flowers. The lights went out for a moment on the hour, the twelve strokes were rung on a triangle in the orchestra, and there was a moment's quiet. Then the light blazed again, flowers and confetti were thrown, and club servants in livery carried round trays of champagne.

Clayton, standing glass in hand, surveyed the scene with a mixture of satisfaction and impatience. He found Terry Mackenzie at his elbow.

"Great party, Clay," he said. "Well, here's to 1917, and may it bring luck."

"May it bring peace," said Clayton, and raised his glass.

Some time later going home in the car with Mrs. Mackenzie, quiet and slightly grim beside him, Terry spoke out of a thoughtful silence.

"There's something wrong with Clay," he said. "If ever a fellow had a right to be happy-he has a queer look. Have you noticed it?"

"Anybody married to Natalie Spencer would develop what you call a queer look," she replied, tartly.

"Don't you think he is in love with her?"

"If you ask me, I think he has reached the point where he can't bear the sight of her. But he doesn't know it."

"She's pretty."

"So is a lamp-shade," replied Mrs. Terry, acidly. "Or a kitten, or a fancy ice-cream. But you wouldn't care to be married to them, would you?"

It was almost dawn when Natalie came in. Clayton had not been asleep. He had got to thinking rather feverishly of the New-year. Without in any way making a resolution, he had determined to make it a better year than the last; to be more gentle with Natalie, more under-standing with Graham; to use his new prosperity wisely; to forget his own lack of happiness in making others happy. He was very vague about that. The search of the ages the rector had called happiness, and one found it by giving it.

To his surprise, Natalie came into his bedroom, looking like some queer oriental bird, vivid and strangely unlike herself.

"I saw your light. Heavens, what a party!"

"I'm glad you enjoyed it. I hope you didn't mind my not going on."

"I wish you had. Clay, you'll never guess what happened."

"Probably not. What?"

"Well, Audrey just made it, that's all. Funny! I wish you'd seen some of their faces. Of course she was disgraceful, but she took it off right away. But it was like her-no one else would have dared."

His mouth felt dry. Audrey-disgraceful!

"It was in the stable, you know, I told you. And just at midnight the doors opened and a big white horse leaped in with Audrey on his back. No saddle-nothing. She was dressed like a bare-back rider in the circus, short tulle skirts and tights. They nearly mobbed her with joy." She yawned. "Well, I'm off to bed."

He roused himself.

"A happy New-year, my dear."

"Thanks," she said, and wandered out, her absurd feathered tail trailing behind her.

He lay back and closed his eyes. So Audrey had done that, Audrey, who had been in his mind all those sleepless hours; for he knew now that back of all his resolutions to do better had been the thought of her.

He felt disappointed and bitter. The sad disillusion of the middle years, still heroically cling-ing to faiths that one after another destroyed themselves, was his.

Chapter XVIII

Audrey was frightened. She did not care a penny's worth what her little world thought. Indeed, she knew that she had given it a new thrill and so had won its enthusiastic approval. She was afraid of what Clayton would think.

She was absurdly quiet and virtuous all the next day, gathered out her stockings and mended them; began a personal expenditure account for the New-year, heading it carefully with "darning silk, 50 cents"; wrote a long letter to Chris, and-listened for the telephone. If only he would call her, so she could explain. Still, what could she explain? She had done it. It was water over the dam-and it is no fault of Audrey's that she would probably have spelled it "damn."

By noon she was fairly abject. She did not analyze her own anxiety, or why the recollection of her escapade, which would a short time before have filled her with a sort of unholy joy, now turned her sick and trembling.

Then, in the middle of the afternoon, Clay called her up. She gasped a little when she heard his voice.

"I wanted to tell you, Audrey," he said, "that we can probably use the girl you spoke about, rather soon."

"Very well. Thank you. Is-wasn't there something else, too?"

"Something else?"

"You are angry, aren't you?"

He hesitated.

"Surprised. Not angry. I haven't any possible right to be angry."

"Will you come up and let me tell you about it, Clay?"

"I don't see how that will help any."

"It will help me."

He laughed at that; her new humility was so unlike her.

"Why, of course I'll come, Audrey," he said, and as he rang off he was happier than he had been all day.

He was coming. Audrey moved around the little room, adjusting chairs, rearranging the flowers that had poured in on New-year's day, brushing the hearth. And as she worked she whistled. He would be getting into the car now. He would be so far on his way. He would be almost there. She ran into her bedroom and powdered her nose, with her lips puckered, still whistling, and her heart singing.

But he scolded her thoroughly at first.

"Why on earth did you do it," he finished. "I still can't understand. I see you one day, gravity itself, a serious young woman-as you are to-day. And then I hear-it isn't like you, Audrey."

"Oh yes, it is. It's exactly like me. Like one me. There are others, of course."

She told him then, making pitiful confession of her own pride and her anxiety to spare Chris's name.

"I couldn't bear to have them suspect he had gone to the war because of a girl. Whatever he ran away from, Clay, he's doing all right now."

He listened gravely, with, toward the end, a jealousy he would not have acknowledged even to himself. Was it possible that she still loved Chris? Might she not, after the fashion of women, be building a new and idealized Chris, now that he had gone to war, out of his very common clay?

"He has done splendidly," he agreed.

Again the warmth and coziness of the little room enveloped him. Audrey's low huskily sweet voice, her quick smile, her new and unaccustomed humility, and the odd sense of her understanding, comforted him. She made her indefinite appeal to the best that was in him.

Nothing so ennobles a man as to have some woman believe in his nobility.

"Clay," she said suddenly, "you are worrying about something."

"Nothing that won't straighten out, in time."

"Would it help to talk about it?"

He realized that he had really come to her to talk about it. It had been in the back of his head all the time.

"I'm rather anxious about Graham."

"Toots Hayden?"

"Partly."

"I'm afraid she's got him, Clay. There isn't a trick in the game she doesn't know. He had about as much chance as I have of being twenty again. She wants to make a wealthy marriage, and she's picked on Graham. That's all."

"It isn't only Marion. I'm afraid there's another girl, a girl at the mill-his stenographer. I have no proof of anything. In fact, I don't think there is anything yet. She's in love with him, probably, or she thinks she is. I happened on them together, and she looked-Of course, if what you say about Marion is true, he can not care for her, even, well, in any way."

"Oh, nonsense, Clay. A man-especially a boy-can love a half-dozen girls. He can be crazy about any girl he is with. It may not be love, but it plays the same tricks with him that the real thing does."

"I can't believe that."

"No. You wouldn't."

She leaned back and watched him. How much of a boy he was himself, anyhow! And yet how little he understood the complicated problems of a boy like Graham, irresponsible but responsive, rich without labor, with time for the sort of dalliance Clay himself at the same age had had neither leisure nor inclination to indulge.

He was wandering about the room, his hands in his pockets, his head bent. When he stopped:

"What am I to do with the girl, Audrey?"

"Get rid of her. That's easy."

"Not so easy as it sounds."

He told her of Dunbar and the photographs, of Rudolph Klein, and the problem as he saw it.

"So there I am," he finished. "If I let her go, I lose one of the links in Dunbar's chain. If I keep her?"

"Can't Natalie talk to him? Sometimes a woman can get to the bottom of these things when a man can't. He might tell her all about it."

"Possibly. But I think it unlikely Natalie would tell me."

She leaned over and patted his hand impulsively.

"What devils we women are!" she said. "Now and then one of us gets what she deserves. That's me. And now and then one of us get's something she doesn't deserve. And that's Natalie. She's over-indulgent to Graham."

"He is all she has."

"She has you."

Something in her voice made him turn and look at her.

"That ought to be something, you know," she added. And laughed a little.

"Does Natalie pay his debts?"

"I rather think so."

But that was a subject he could not go on with.

"The fault is mine. I know my business better than I know how to handle my life, or my family. I don't know why I trouble you with it all, anyhow. You have enough." He hesitated. "That's not exactly true, either. I do know. I'm relying on your woman's wit to help me. I'm wrong somehow."

"About Graham?"

"I have a curious feeling that I am losing him. I can't ask for his confidence. I can't, apparently, even deserve it. I see him, day after day, with all the good stuff there is in him, working as little as he can, drinking more than he should, out half the night, running into debt-good heavens, Audrey, what can I do?"

She hesitated.

"Of course, you know one thing that would save him, Clay?"

"What?"

"Our getting into the war."

"I ought not to have to lose my boy in order to find him. But-we are going to be in it."

He had risen and was standing, an elbow on the mantel-piece, looking down at her.

"I suppose every man wonders, once in a while, how he'd conduct himself in a crisis. When the Lusitania went down I dare say a good many fellows wondered if they'd have been able to keep their coward bodies out of the boats. I know I did. And I wonder about myself now. What can I do if we go into the war? I couldn't do a forced march of more than five miles. I can't drill, or whatever they call it. I can shoot clay pigeons, but I don't believe I could hit a German coming at me with a bayonet at twenty feet. I'd be pretty much of a total loss. Yet I'll want to do something."

And when she sat, very silent, looking into the fire: "You see, you think it absurd yourself."

"Hardly absurd," she roused herself to look up at him. "If it is, it's the sort of splendid absurdity I am proud of. I was wondering what Natalie would say."

"I don't believe it lies between a man and his wife. It's between him and his God."

He was rather ashamed of that, however, and soon after he went away.

Chapter XIX

Natalie Spencer was finding life full of interest that winter. Now and then she read the headings in the newspapers, not because she was really interested, but that she might say, at the dinner-party which was to her the proper end of a perfect day:

"What do you think of Turkey declaring her independence?"

Or:

"I see we have taken the Etoile Wood."

Clayton had overheard her more than once, and had marveled at the dexterity with which, these leaders thrown out, she was able to avoid committing herself further.

The new house engrossed her. She was seeing a great deal of Rodney, too, and now and then she had fancied that there was a different tone in Rodney's voice when he addressed her. She never analyzed that tone, or what it suggested, but it gave her a new interest in life. She was always marceled, massaged, freshly manicured. And she had found a new facial treatment. Clayton, in his room at night, could hear the sharp slapping of flesh on flesh, as Madeleine gently pounded certain expensive creams into the skin of her face and neck.

She refused all forms of war activity, although now and then she put some appeal before Clayton and asked him if he cared to send a check. He never suggested that she answer any of these demands personally, after an experience early in the winter.

"Why don't you send it yourself?" he had asked. "Wouldn't you like it to go in your name?"

"It doesn't matter. I don't know any of the committee."

He had tried to explain what he meant.

"You might like to feel that you are doing something."

"I thought my allowance was only to dress on. If I'm to attend to charities, too, you'll have to increase it."

"But," he argued patiently, "if you only sent them twenty-five dollars, did without some little thing to do it, you'd feel rather more as though you were giving, wouldn't you?"

"Twenty-five dollars! And be laughed at!"

He had given in then.

"If I put an extra thousand dollars to your account to-morrow, will you check it out to this fund?"

"It's too much."

"Will you?'

"Yes, of course," she had agreed, indifferently. And he had notified her that the money was in the bank. But two months later the list of contributors was published, and neither his name nor Natalie's was among them.

Toward personal service she had no inclination whatever. She would promise anything, but the hour of fulfilling always found her with something else to do. Yet she had kindly impulses, at times, when something occurred to take her mind from herself. She gave liberally to street mendicants. She sent her car to be used by those of her friends who had none. She was lavish with flowers to the sick-although Clayton paid her florist bills.

She was lavish with money-but never with herself.

In the weeks after the opening of the new year Clayton found himself watching her. He wondered sometimes just what went on in her mind during the hours when she sat, her hands folded, gazing into space. He could not tell. He surmised her planning, always planning; the new house, a gown, a hat, a party.

But late in January he began to think that she was planning something else. Old Terry Mackenzie had been there one night, and he had asserted not only that war was coming, but that we would be driven to conscription to raise an army.

"They've all had to come to it," he insisted. "And we will, as sure as God made little fishes. You can't raise a million volunteers for a war that's three thousand miles away."

"You mean, conscription among the laboring class?" Natalie had asked naively, and there had been a roar of laughter.

"Not at all," Terry had said. And chuckled. "This war, if it comes, is every man's burden, rich and poor. Only the rich will give most, because they have most to give."

"I think that's ridiculous," Natalie had said.

It was after that that Clayton began to wonder what she was planning.

He came home late one afternoon to find that they were spending the evening in, and to find a very serious Natalie waiting, when he came down-stairs dressed for dinner. She made an effort to be conversational, but it was a failure. He was uneasily aware that she was watching him, inspecting, calculating, choosing her moment. But it was not until they were having coffee that she spoke.

"I'm uneasy about Graham, Clay."

He looked up quickly.

"Yes?"

"I think he ought to go away somewhere."

"He ought to stay here, and make a man of himself," he came out, almost in spite of himself. He knew well enough that such a note always roused Natalie's antagonism, and he waited for the storm. But none came.

"He's not doing very well, is he?"

"He's not failing entirely. But he gives the best of himself outside the mill. That's all."

She puzzled him. Had she heard of Marion?

"Don't you think, if he was away from this silly crowd he plays with, as he calls it, that he would be better off?"

"Where, for instance?"

"You keep an agent in England. He could go there. Or to Russia, if the Russian contract goes through."

He was still puzzled.

"But why England or Russia?"

"Anywhere out of this country."

"He doesn't have to leave this country to get away from a designing woman."

From her astonished expression, he knew that he had been wrong. She was not trying to get him away from Marion. From what?

She bent forward, her face set hard.

"What woman?"

Well, it was out. She might as well know it. "Don't you think it possible, Natalie, that he may intend to marry Marion Hayden?"

There was a very unpleasant half-hour after that. Marion was a parasite of the rich. She had abused Natalie's hospitality. She was designing. She played bridge for her dress money. She had ensnared the boy.

And then:

"That settles it, I should think. He ought to leave America. If you have a single thought for his welfare you'll send him to England."

"Then you hadn't known about Marion when you proposed that before?"

"No. I knew he was not doing well. And I'm anxious. After all, he's my boy. He is —"

"I know," he supplemented gravely. "He is all you have. But I still don't understand why he must leave America."

It was not until she had gone up-stairs to her room, leaving him uneasily pacing the library floor, that he found the solution. Old Terry Mackenzie and his statement about conscription. Natalie wanted Graham sent out of the country, so he would be safe. She would purchase for hint a shameful immunity, if war came. She would stultify the boy to keep him safe. In that hour of clear vision he saw how she had always stultified the boy, to keep him safe. He saw her life a series of small subterfuges, of petty indulgences, of little plots against himself, all directed toward securing Graham immunity-from trouble at school, from debt, from his own authority.

A wave of unreasoning anger surged over him, but with it there was pity, too; pity for the narrowness of her life and her mind, pity for her very selfishness. And for the first time in his life he felt a shamefaced pity for himself. He shook himself violently. When a man got sorry for himself—

Chapter XX

Rudolph Klein had not for a moment believed Anna's story about the watch, and on the day after he discovered it on her wrist he verified his suspicions. During his noon hour he went up-town and, with the confident swagger of a certain type of man who feels himself out of place, entered the jeweler's shop in question.

He had to wait for some little time, and he spent it in surveying contemptuously the contents of the show-cases. That even his wildest estimate fell far short of their value he did not suspect, but his lips curled. This was where the money earned by honest workmen was spent, that women might gleam with such gewgaws. Wall Street bought them, Wall Street which was forcing this country into the war to protect its loans to the Allies. America was to pull England's chestnuts out of the fire that women, and yet more women, might wear those strings of pearls, those glittering diamond baubles.

Into his crooked mind there flashed a line from a speech at the Third Street hall the night before: "War is hell. Let those who want to, go to hell."

So-Wall Street bought pearls for its women, and the dissolute sons of the rich bought gold wrist-watches for girls they wanted to seduce. The expression on his face was so terrible that the clerk behind the counter, waiting to find what he wanted, was startled.

"I want to look at gold wrist-watches," he said. And eyed the clerk for a trace of patronage.

"Ladies?"

"Yes."

He finally found one that was a duplicate of Anna's, and examined it carefully. Yes, it was the same, the maker's name on the dial, the space for the monogram on the back, everything.

"How much is this one?"

"One hundred dollars."

He almost dropped it. A hundred dollars! Then he remembered Anna's story.

"Have you any gold-filled ones that look like this?"

"We do not handle gold-filled cases."

He put it down, and turned to go. Then he stopped.

"Don't sell on the installment plan, either, I suppose?" The sneer in his voice was clearer than his anxiety. In his mind, he already knew the answer.

"Sorry. No."

He went out. So he had been right. That young skunk had paid a hundred dollars for a watch for Anna. To Rudolph it meant but one thing.

That had been early in January. For some days he kept his own counsel, thinking, planning, watching. He was jealous of Graham, but with a calculating jealousy that set him wondering how to turn his knowledge to his own advantage. And Anna's lack of liberty comforted him somewhat. He couldn't meet her outside the mill, at least not without his knowing it.

He established a system of espionage over her that drove her almost to madness.

"What're you hanging round for?" she would demand when he stepped forward at the mill gate. "D'you suppose I never want to be by myself?"

Or:

"You just go away, Rudolph Klein. I'm going up with some of the girls."

But she never lost him. He was beside her or at her heels, his small crafty eyes on her. When he walked behind her there was a sensuous gleam in them.

After a few weeks she became terrified. There was a coldness of deviltry in him, she knew. And he had the whip-hand. She was certain he knew about the watch, and her impertinence masked an agony of fear. Suppose he went to her father? Why, if he knew, didn't he go to her father?

She suspected him, but she did not know of what. She knew he was an enemy of all government, save that of the mob, that he was an incendiary, a firebrand who set on fire the brutish passions of a certain type of malcontents. She knew, for all he pretended to be the voice of labor, he no more represented the honest labor of the country than he represented law and order.

She watched him sometimes, at the table, when on Sundays he ate the mid-day meal with them; his thin hatchet face, his prominent epiglottis. He wore a fresh cotton shirt then, with a flaming necktie, but he did not clean his fingernails. And his talk was always of tearing down, never of building up.

"Just give us time, and we'll show them," he often said. And "them" was always the men higher up.

He hated policemen. He and Herman had had many arguments about policemen. Herman was not like Rudolph. He believed in law and order. He even believed in those higher up. But he believed very strongly in the fraternity of labor. Until the first weeks of that New-year, Herman Klein, outside the tyranny of his home life, represented very fairly a certain type of workman, believing in the dignity and integrity of his order. But, with his failure to relocate himself, something went wrong in Herman. He developed, in his obstinate, stubborn, German head a suspicion of the land of his adoption. He had never troubled to understand it. He had taken it for granted, as he took for granted that Anna should work and turn over her money to him.

Now it began to ask things of him. Not much. A delegation of women came around one night and asked him for money for Belgian Relief. The delegation came, because no one woman would venture alone.

"I have no money for Belgians," he said. He would not let them come in. "Why should I help the Belgians? Liars and hypocrites!"

The story went about the neighborhood, and he knew it. He cared nothing for popularity, but he resented losing his standing in the community. And all along he was convinced that he was right; that the Belgians had lied. There had been, in the Germany he had left, no such will to wanton killing. These people were ignorant. Out of the depths of their ignorance they talked.

He read only German newspapers. In the little room back of Gustav Shroeder's he met only Germans. And always, at his elbow, there was Rudolph.

Until the middle of January Rudolph had not been able to get him to one of his incendiary meetings. Then one cold night while Anna sewed by the lamp inside the little house,

Rudolph and Herman walked in the frozen garden, Herman with his pipe, Rudolph with the cheap cigarets he used incessantly. Anna opened the door a crack and listened at first. She was watchful of Rudolph, always, those days. But the subject was not Anna.

"You think we get in, then?" Herman asked.

"Sure."

"But for what?"

"So 'Spencers' can make more money out of it," said Rudolph bitterly. "And others like them. But they and their kind don't do the dying. It's the workers that go and die. Look at Germany!"

"Yes. It is so in Germany."

"All this talk about democracy-that's bunk. Just plain bunk. Why should the workers in this country kill the workers in another? Why? To make money for capital-more money."

"Ja," Herman assented. "That is what war is. Always the same. I came here to get away from war."

"Well, you didn't get far enough. You left a king behind, but we've got a Czar here."

Herman was slowly, methodically, following an earlier train of thought.

"I am a workman," he said. "I would not fight against other workmen. Just as I, a German, will not fight against other Germans."

"But you would sit here, on the hill, and do nothing."

"What can I do? One man, and with no job."

"Come to the meeting to-night."

"You and your meetings!" the old German said impatiently. "You talk. That's all."

Rudolph lowered his voice.

"You think we only talk, eh? Well, you come and hear some things. Talk! You come," he coaxed, changing his tone. "And we'll have some beer and schnitzel at Gus's after. My treat. How about it?"

Old Herman assented. He was tired of the house, tired of the frozen garden, tired of scolding the slovenly girl who pottered around all day in a boudoir cap and slovenly wrapper. Tired of Anna's rebellious face and pert answers.

He went inside the house and put a sweater under his coat, and got his cap.

"I go out," he said, to the impassive figure under the lamp. "You will stay in."

"Oh, I don't know. I may take a walk."

"You will stay in," he repeated, and followed Rudolph outside. There he reached in, secured the key, and locked the door on the outside. Anna, listening and white with anger, heard his ponderous steps going around to the back door, and the click as he locked that one also.

"Beast!" she muttered. "German schwein."

It was after midnight when she heard him coming back. She prepared to leap out of her bed when he came up-stairs, to confront him angrily and tell him she was through. She was leaving home. But long after she had miserably cried herself to sleep, Herman sat below, his long-stemmed pipe in his teeth, his stockinged feet spread to the dying fire.

In that small guarded hail that night he had learned many surprising things, there and at Gus's afterward. The Fatherland's war was already being fought in America, and not only by Germans. The workers of the world had banded themselves together, according to the night's speakers. And because they were workers they would not fight the German workers. It was all perfectly simple. With the cooperation of the workers of the world, which recognized no country but a vast brotherhood of labor, it was possible to end war, all war.

In the meantime, while all the workers all over the world were being organized, one prevented as much as possible any assistance going to capitalistic England. One did some simple thing-started a strike, or sawed lumber too short, or burned a wheat-field, or put nails in harvesting machinery, or missent perishable goods, or changed signal-lights on railroads, or drove copper nails into fruit-trees, so they died. This was a pity, the fruit-trees. But at least they did not furnish fruit for Germany's enemies.

So each one did but one thing, and that small, so small that it was difficult to discover. But there were two hundred thousand men to do them, according to Rudolph, and that meant a great deal.

Only one thing about the meeting Herman had not liked. There were packages of wicked photographs going about. Filthy things. When they came to him he had dropped them on the floor. What had they to do with Germany's enemies, or preventing America from going into the war?

Rudolph laughed when he dropped them.

"They won't bite you!" he had said, and had stooped to pick them up. But Herman had kept his foot on them.

So-America would go into the war against the Fatherland, unless many hundreds of thousands did each their little bit. And if they did not, America would go in, and fight for England to control the seas, and the Spencer plant would make millions of shells that honest German workers, sweat-brothers of the world, might die.

He remembered word for word the peroration of the evening's speech.

"We would extend the hand of brotherhood to the so-called enemy, and strangle the cry for war in the fat white throats of the blood-bloated money-lenders of Wall Street, before it became articulate."

He was very tired. He stooped and picked up his shoes, and with them in his hand, drawn to his old-time military erectness, he stood for some time before the gilt-framed picture on the wall. Then he went slowly and ponderously up-stairs to bed.

Chapter XXI

From the moment, the day before Christmas, when Graham had taken the little watch from his pocket and fastened it on Anna's wrist, he was rather uneasily aware that she had become his creature. He had had no intention of buying Anna. He was certainly not in love with her. But he found her amusing and at times comforting.

He had, of course, expected to lose her after the unlucky day when Clayton had found them together, but Dunbar had advised that she be kept on for a time at least. Mentally Graham figured that the first of January would see her gone, and the thought of a Christmas present for her was partly compounded of remorse.

He had been buying a cigaret case for Marion when the thought came to him. He had not bought a Christmas present for a girl, except flowers, since the first year he was at college. He had sent Delight one that year, a half-dozen little leather-bound books of poetry. What a precious young prig he must have been! He knew now that girls only pretended to care for books. They wanted jewelry, and they got past the family with it by pretending it was not real, or that they had bought it out of their allowances. One of Toots' friends was taking a set of silver fox from a man, and she was as straight as a die. Oh, he knew girls, now.

The next day he asked Anna Klein: "What would you like for Christmas?"

Anna, however, had insisted that she did not want a Christmas present.

Later on, however, she had seen a watch one of the girls on the hill had bought for twelve dollars, and on his further insistence a day or so later she had said:

"Do you really want to know?"

"Of course I do."

"You oughtn't to spend money on me, you know."

"You let me attend to that. Now, out with it!"

So she told him rather nervously, for she felt that twelve dollars was a considerable sum. He had laughed, and agreed instantly, but when he went to buy it he found himself paying a price that rather startled him.

"Don't you lose it, young lady!" he admonished her when, the day before Christmas, he fastened it on her wrist. Then he had stooped down to kiss her, and the intensity of feeling in her face had startled him. "It's a good watch," he had said, rather uneasily; "no excuse for your being late now!"

All the rest of the day she was radiant.

He meant well enough even then. He had never pretended to love her. He accepted her adoration, petted and teased her in return, worked off his occasional ill humors on her, was indeed conscious sometimes that he was behaving extremely well in keeping things as they were.

But by the middle of January he began to grow uneasy. The atmosphere at Marion's was bad; there was a knowledge of life plus an easy toleration of certain human frailties that was as insidious as a slow fever. The motto of live and let live prevailed. And Marion refused to run away with him and marry him, or to let him go to his father.

In his office all day long there was Anna, so yielding, so surely his to take if he wished. Already he knew that things there must either end or go forward. Human emotions do not stand still; they either advance or go back, and every impulse of his virile young body was urging him on.

He made at last an almost frenzied appeal to Marion to marry him at once, but she refused flatly.

"I'm not going to ruin you," she said. "If you can't bring your people round, we'll just have to wait."

"They'd be all right, once it is done."

"Not if I know your father! Oh, he'd be all right-in ten years or so. But what about the next two or three? We'd have to live, wouldn't we?"

He lay awake most of the night thinking things over. Did she really care for him, as Anna cared, for instance? She was always talking about their having to live. If they couldn't manage on his salary for a while, then it was because Marion did not care enough to try.

For the first time he began to question Marion's feeling for him. She had been rather patronizing him lately. He had overheard her, once, speaking of him as a nice kid, and it rankled. In sheer assertion of his manhood he met Anna Klein outside the mill at the noon hour, the next day, and took her for a little ride in his car. After that he repeatedly did the same thing, choosing infrequented streets and roads, dining with her sometimes at a quiet hotel out on the Freeland road.

"How do you get away with this to your father?" he asked her once.

"Tell him you're getting ready to move out to the new plant, and we're working. He's not round much in the evenings now. He's at meetings, or swilling beer at Gus's saloon. They're a bad lot, Graham, that crowd at Gus's."

"How do you mean, bad?"

"Well, they're Germans, for one thing, the sort that shouts about the Fatherland. They make me sick."

"Let's forget them, honey," said Graham, and reaching under the table-cloth, caught and held one of her hands.

He was beginning to look at things with the twisted vision of Marion's friends. He intended only to flirt a little with Anna Klein, but he considered that he was extremely virtuous and, perhaps, a bit of a fool for letting things go at that. Once, indeed, Tommy Hale happened on them in a road-house, sitting very quietly with a glass of beer before Graham and a lemonade in front of Anna, and had winked at him as though he had received him into the brotherhood of those who were seeing life.

Then, near the end of January, events took another step forward. Rudolph Klein was discharged from the mill.

Clayton, coming down one morning, found the manager, Hutchinson, and Dunbar in his office. The two men had had a difference of opinion, and the matter was laid before him.

"He is a constant disturbing element," Hutchinson finished; "I understand Mr. Dunbar's position, but we can't afford to have the men thrown into a ferment, constantly."

"If you discharge him you rouse his suspicions and those of his gang," said Dunbar, sturdily.

"There is a gang, then?"

"A gang! My God!"

In the end, however, Clayton decided to let Rudolph go. Hutchinson was insistent. Production was falling down. One or two accidents to the machinery lately looked like sabotage. He had found a black cat crudely drawn on the cement pavement outside his office-door that very morning, the black cat being the symbol of those I.W.W.'s who advocated destruction.

"What about the girl?" Dunbar asked, when the manager had gone.

"I have kept her, against my better judgment, Mr. Dunbar."

For just a moment Dunbar hesitated. He knew certain things that Clayton Spencer did not, things that it was his business to know. The girl might be valuable one of these days. She was in love with young Spencer. The time might come when he, Dunbar, would need to capitalize that love and use it against Rudolph and the rest of the crowd that met in the little room behind Shroeder's saloon. It was too bad, in a way. He was sorry for this man with the strong, repressed face and kindly mouth, who sat across from him. But these were strange times. A man could not be too scrupulous.

"Better keep her on for a month or two, anyhow," he said. "They're up to something, and I miss my guess if it isn't directed against you."

"How about Herman Klein?"

"Nothing doing," stated Mr. Dunbar, flatly. "Our informer is tending bar at Gus's. Herman listens and drinks their beer, but he's got the German fear of authority in him. He's a beer socialist. That's all."

But in that Mr. Dunbar left out of account the innate savagery that lurked under Herman's phlegmatic surface.

"You don't think it would do if she was moved to another office?"

"The point is this." Dunbar moved his chair forward. "The time may come when we will need the girl as an informer. Rudolph Klein is infatuated with her. Now I understand that she has a certain feeling of-loyalty to Mr. Graham. In that case" —he glanced at Clayton —"the welfare of the many, Mr. Spencer, against the few."

For a long time after he was gone Clayton sat at his desk, thinking. Every instinct in him revolted against the situation thus forced on him. There was something wrong with Dunbar's reasoning. Then it flashed on him that Dunbar probably was right, and that their points of view were bitterly opposed. Dunbar would have no scruples, because he was not quite a gentleman. But war was a man's game. It was not the time for fine distinctions of ethics. And Dunbar was certainly a man.

If only he could talk it over with Natalie! But he knew Natalie too well to expect any rational judgment from her. She would demand at once that the girl should go. Yet he needed a woman's mind on it. In any question of relationship between the sexes men were creatures of impulse, but women had plotted and planned through the ages. They might lose their standards, but never their heads. Not that he put such a thought into words. He merely knew that women were better at such things than men.

That afternoon, as a result of much uncertainty, he took his problem to Audrey. And Audrey gave him an answer.

"You've got to think of the mill, Clay," she said. "The Dunbar man is right. And all you or any other father of a boy can do is to pray in season, and to trust to Graham's early training."

And all the repressed bitterness in Clayton Spencer's heart was in his answer.

"He never had any early training, Audrey. Oh, he had certain things. His manners, for instance. But other things? I ought not to say that. It was my fault, too. I'm not blaming only Natalie. Only now, when it is all we have to count on —"

He was full of remorse when he started for home. He felt guilty of every disloyalty. And in masculine fashion he tried to make up to Natalie for the truth that had been wrung from him. He carried home a great bunch of roses for her. But he carried home, too, a feeling of comfort and vague happiness, as though the little room behind him still reached out and held him in its warm embrace.

Chapter XXII

In the evening of the thirty-first of January Clayton and Graham were waiting for Natalie to come down to dinner when the bell rang, and Dunbar was announced. Graham welcomed the interruption. He had been vaguely uneasy with his father since that day in his office when Clayton had found him on Anna Klein's desk. Clayton had tried to restore the old friendliness of their relation, but the boy had only half-heartedly met his advances. Now and then he himself made an overture, but it was the almost timid advance of a puppy that has been beaten. It left Clayton discouraged and alarmed, set him to going back over the past for any severity on his part to justify it. Now and then he wondered if, in Graham's frequent closetings with Natalie, she did not covertly undermine his influence with the boy, to increase her own.

But if she did, why? What was going on behind the impassive, lovely mask that was her face.

Dunbar was abrupt, as usual.

"I've brought you some news, Mr. Spencer," he said. He looked oddly vital and alive in the subdued and quiet room. "They've shown their hand at last. But maybe you've heard it."

"I've heard nothing new."

"Then listen," said Dunbar, bending forward over a table, much as it was his habit to bend over Clayton's desk. "We're in it at last. Or as good as in it. Unrestricted submarine warfare! All merchant-ships bound to and from Allied ports to be sunk without warning! We're to be allowed-mark this, it's funny! —we're to be allowed to send one ship a week to England, nicely marked and carrying passengers only."

There was a little pause. Clayton drew a long breath.

"That means war," he said finally.

"Hell turned over and stirred up with a pitch-fork, if we have any backbone at all," agreed Dunbar. He turned to Graham. "You young fellows'll be crazy about this."

"You bet we will," said Graham.

Clayton slipped an arm about the boy's shoulders. He could not speak for a moment. All at once he saw what the news meant. He saw Graham going into the horror across the sea. He saw vast lines of marching men, boys like Graham, boys who had frolicked through their careless days, whistled and played and slept sound of nights, now laden like pack-animals and carrying the implements of death in their hands, going forward to something too terrible to contemplate.

And a certain sure percentage of them would never come back.

His arm tightened about the boy. When he withdrew it Graham straightened.

"If it's war, it's my war, father."

And Clayton replied, quietly:

"It is your war, old man."

Dunbar turned his back and inspected Natalie's portrait. When he faced about again Graham was lighting a cigaret, and Natalie herself was entering the room. In her rose-colored satin she looked exotic, beautiful, and Dunbar gave her a fleeting glance of admiration as he bowed. She looked too young to have a boy going to war. Behind her he suddenly saw other women, thousands of other women, living luxurious lives, sheltered and pampered, and suddenly called on to face sacrifice without any training for it.

"Didn't know you were going out," he said. "Sorry. I'll run along now."

"We are dining at home," said Natalie, coldly. She remained standing near the door, as a hint to the shabby gentleman with the alert eyes who stood by the table. But Dunbar had forgotten her already.

"I came here right away," he explained, "because you may be having trouble now. In fact, I'm pretty sure you will. If we declare war to-morrow, as we may?"

"War!" said Natalie, and took a step forward.

Dunbar remembered her.

"We will probably declare war in a day or two. The Germans..."

But Natalie was looking at Clayton with a hostility in her eyes she took no trouble to conceal.

"I hope you'll be happy, now. You've been talking war, wanting war-and now you've got it."

She turned and went out of the room. The three men in the library below heard her go up the stairs and the slam of her door behind her. Later on she sent word that she did not care for any dinner, and Clayton asked Dunbar to remain. Practical questions as to the mill were discussed, Graham entering into them with a new interest. He was flushed and excited. But Clayton was rather white and very quiet.

Once Graham took advantage of Dunbar's preoccupation with his asparagus to say:

"You don't object to the aviation service, father?"

"Wherever you think you can be useful."

After coffee Graham rose.

"I'll go and speak to mother," he said. And Clayton felt in him a new manliness. It was as though his glance said, "She is a woman, you know. War is men's work, work for you and me. But it's hard on them."

Afterward Clayton was to remember with surprise how his friends gathered that night at the house. Nolan came in early, his twisted grin rather accentuated, his tall frame more than usually stooped. He stood in the doorway of the library, one hand in his pocket, a familiar attitude which made him look oddly boyish.

"Well!" he drawled, without greeting. "They've done it. The English have got us. We hadn't a chance. The little Welshman —"

"Come in," Clayton said, "and talk like an American and not an Irishman. I don't want to know what you think about Lloyd George. What are you going to do?"

"I was thinking," Nolan observed, advancing, "of blowing up Washington. We'd have a fresh start, you see. With Washington gone root and branch we would have some sort of chance, a clear sweep, with the capital here or in Boston. Or London."

Clayton laughed. Behind Nolan's cynicism he felt a real disturbance. But Dunbar eyed him uncertainly. He didn't know about some of these Irish. They'd fight like hell, of course, if only they'd forget England.

"Don't worry about Washington," Clayton said. "Let it work out its own problems. We will have our own. What do you suppose men like you and myself are going to do? We can't fight."

Nolan settled himself in a long chair.

"Why can't we fight?" he asked. "I heard something the other day. Roosevelt is going to take a division abroad-older men. I rather like the idea. Wherever he goes there'll be fighting. I'm no Rough Rider, God knows; but I haven't spent a half hour every noon in a gymnasium for the last ten years for nothing. And I can shoot."

"And you are free," Clayton observed, quietly.

Nolan looked up.

"It's going to be hard on the women," he said. "You're all right. They won't let you go. You're too useful where you are. But of course there's the boy."

When Clayton made no reply Nolan glanced at him again.

"I suppose he'll want to go," he suggested.

Clayton's face was set. For more than an hour now Graham had been closeted with his mother, and as the time went on, and no slam of a door up-stairs told of his customary method of leaving a room, he had been conscious of a growing uneasiness. The boy was soft; the fiber in him had not been hardened yet, not enough to be proof against tears. He wanted desperately to leave Nolan, to go up and learn what arguments, what coaxing and selfish whimperings Natalie was using with the boy. But he wanted, also desperately, to have the boy fight his own fight and win.

"He will want to go, I think. Of course, his mother will be shaken just now. It'll all new to her. She wouldn't believe it was coming."

"He'll go," Nolan said reflectively. "They'll all go, the best of them first. After all, we've been making a lot of noise about wanting to get into the thing. Now we're in, and that's the first price we pay-the boys."

A door slammed up-stairs, and Clayton heard Graham coming down. He passed the library door, however, and Clayton suddenly realized that he was going out.

"Graham!" he called.

Graham stopped, and came back slowly.

"Yes, father," he said, from the doorway.

"Aren't you coming in?"

"I thought I'd go out for a hit of a spin, if you don't mind. Evening, Mr. Nolan."

The boy was shaken. Clayton knew it from his tone. All the fine vigor of the early evening was gone. And an overwhelming rage filled him, against Natalie, against himself, even against the boy. Trouble, which should have united his house, had divided it. The first threat of trouble, indeed.

"You can go out later," he said rather sharply. "We ought to talk things over, Graham. This is a mighty serious time."

"What's the use of talking things over, father? We don't know anything but that we may declare war."

"That's enough, isn't it?"

But he was startled when he saw Graham's face. He was very pale and his eyes already looked furtive. They were terribly like Natalie's eyes sometimes. The frankness was gone out of them. He came into the room, and stood there, rigid.

"I promised mother to get her some sleeping-powders."

"Sleeping-powders!"

"She's nervous."

"Bad things, sleeping-powders," said Nolan. "Get her to take some setting-up exercises by an open window and she'll sleep like a top."

"Do you mind, if I go, father?"

Clayton saw that it was of no use to urge the boy. Graham wanted to avoid him, wanted to avoid an interview. The early glow of the evening faded. Once again the sense of having lost his son almost overwhelmed him.

"Very well," he said stiffly. And Graham went out.

However, he did not leave the house. At the door he met Doctor Haverford. And Delight, and Clayton heard the clergyman's big bass booming through the hall.

"—like a lamb to the slaughter!" he was saying. "And I a man of peace!"

When he came into the library he was still holding forth with an affectation of rage.

"I ask you, Clayton," he said, "what refuge is there for a man of peace? My own child, leading me out into the night, and inquiring on the way over if I did not feel that the commandment not to kill was a serious error."

"Of course he's going," she said. "He has been making the most outrageous excuses, just to hear mother and me reply to them. And all the time nothing would hold him back."

"My dear," said the rector solemnly. "T shall have to tell you something. I shall have to lay bare the secrets of my heart. How are you, Nolan? Delight, they will not take me. I have three back teeth on a plate. I have never told you this before. I did not wish to ruin your belief that I am perfect. But —"

In the laugh that greeted this Graham returned. He was, Clayton saw, vaguely puzzled by the rector and rather incredulous as to Delight's attitude.

"Do you really want him to go?" he asked her.

"Of course. Aren't you going? Isn't everybody who is worth anything going? I'd go myself if I could. You don't know how lucky you are."

"But is your Mother willing?"

"Why, what sort of a mother do you think I have?"

Clayton overheard that, and he saw Graham wince. His own hands clenched. What a power in the world a brave woman was! And what evil could be wrought by a woman without moral courage, a selfish woman. He brought himself up short at that.

Others came in. Hutchinson, from the mill. Terry Mackenzie, Rodney Page, in evening clothes and on his way from the opera to something or other. In a corner Graham and Delight talked. The rector, in a high state of exaltation, was inclined to be oratorical and a trifle noisy. He dilated on the vast army that would rise overnight, at the call. He considered the raising of a company from his own church, and nominated Clayton as its captain. Nolan grinned sardonically.

"Precisely," he said dryly. "Clayton, because he looks like a Greek god, is ideally fitted to lead a lot of men who never saw a bayonet outside of a museum. Against trained fighting men. There's a difference you know, dominie, between a clay pigeon and a German with a bomb in one hand and a saw-toothed bayonet in the other."

"We did that in the Civil War."

"We did. And it took four years to fight a six-months war."

"We must have an army. I daresay you'll grant that."

"Well, you can bet on one thing; we're not going to have every ward boss who wants to make a record raising a regiment out of his henchmen and leading them to death."

"What would you suggest?" inquired the rector, rather crestfallen.

"I'd suggest training men as officers. And then—a draft."

"Never come to it in the world." Hutchinson spoke up. "I've heard men in the mill talking. They'll go, some of them, but they won't be driven. It would be civil war."

Clayton glanced at Graham as he replied. The boy was leaning forward, listening.

"There's this to be said for the draft," he said. "Under the volunteer system the best of our boys will go first. That's what happened in England. And they were wiped out. It's every man's war now. There is no reason why the few should be sacrificed for the many."

"And there's this, too," Graham broke in. He was flushed and nervous. "A fellow would have to go. He wouldn't be having to think whether his going would hurt anybody or not. He wouldn't have to decide. He'd—just go."

There was a little hush in the room. Then Nolan spoke.

"Right-o!" he said. "The only trouble about it is that it's likely to leave out some of us old chaps, who'd like to have a fist in it."

Hutchinson remained after the others had gone. He wanted to discuss the change in status of the plant.

"We'll be taken over by the government, probably," Clayton told him. "They have all the figures, capacity and so on. The Ordnance Department has that in hand."

Hutchinson nodded. He had himself made the report.

"We'll have to look out more than ever, I suppose," he said, as he rose to go. "The government is guarding all bridges and railways already. Met a lot of National Guard boys on the way."

Graham left when he did, offering to take him to his home, and Clayton sat for some time alone, smoking and thinking. So the thing had come at last. A year from now, and where would they all be? The men who had been there to-night, himself, Graham? Would they all be even living? Would Graham —?

He looked back over the years. Graham a baby, splashing water in his bath and shrieking aloud with joy; Graham in his first little-boy clothes, riding a velocipede in the park and bringing in bruises of an amazing size and blackness; Graham going away to school, and manfully fixing his mind on his first long trousers, so he would not cry; Graham at college, coming in with the winning crew, and stumbling, half collapsed, into the arms of a waiting, cheering crowd. And the Graham who had followed his mother up the stairs that night, to come down baffled, thwarted, miserable.

He rose and threw away his cigar. He must have the thing out with Natalie. The boy's soul was more important than his body. He wanted him safe. God, how he wanted him safe! But he wanted him to be a man.

Natalie's room was dark when he went in. He hesitated. Then he heard her in bed, sobbing quietly. He was angry at himself for his impatience at the sound. He stood beside the bed, and forced a gentleness he did not feel.

"Can I get you anything?" he asked.

"No, thank you." And he moved toward the lamp. "Don't turn the light on. I look dreadful."

"Shall I ring for Madeleine?"

"No. Graham is bringing me a sleeping-powder."

"If you are not sleepy, may I talk to you about some things?"

"I'm sick, Clay. My head is bursting."

"Sometimes it helps to talk out our worries, dear." He was still determinedly gentle.

He heard her turning her pillow, and settling herself more comfortably.

"Not to you. You've made up your mind. What's the use?"

"Made up my mind to what?"

"To sending Graham to be killed."

"That's hardly worthy of you, Natalie," he said gravely. "He is my son, too. I love him at least as much as you do. I don't think this is really up to us, anyhow. It is up to him. If he wants to go?"

She sat up, suddenly, her voice thin and high.

"How does he know what he wants?" she demanded. "He's too young. He doesn't know what war is; you say so yourself. You say he is too young to have a position worth while at the plant, but of course he's old enough to go to war and have a leg shot off, or to be blinded, or something." Her voice broke.

He sat down on the bed and felt around until he found her hand. But she jerked it from him.

"You promised me once to let him make his own decision if the time came."

"When did I promise that?"

"In the fall, when I came home from England."

"I never made such a promise."

"Will you make it now?"

"No!"

He rose, more nearly despairing than he had ever been. He could not argue with a hysterical woman. He hated cowardice, but far deeper than that was his conviction that she had already exacted some sort of promise. And the boy was not like her in that respect. He regarded a promise as almost in the nature of an oath. He himself had taught him that in the creed of a gentleman a promise was a thing of his honor, to be kept at any cost.

"You are compelling me to do a strange and hateful thing," he said. "If you intend to use your influence to keep him out, I shall have to offset it by urging him to go. That is putting a very terrible responsibility on me."

He heard her draw her breath sharply.

"If you do that I shall leave you," she said, in a frozen voice.

Suddenly he felt sorry for her. She was so weak, so childish, so cowardly. And this was the nearest they had come to a complete break.

"You're tired and nervous," he said. "We have come a long way from what I started out to say. And a long way from-the way things used to be between us. If this thing, to-night, does not bring two people together —"

"Together!" she cried shrilly. "When have we been together? Not in years. You have been married to your business. I am only your housekeeper, and Graham's mother. And even Graham you are trying to take away from me. Oh, go away and let me alone."

Down-stairs, thoughts that were almost great had formulated themselves in his mind; that to die that others might live might be better than to live oneself; that he loved his country, although he had been shamefaced about it; that America was really the melting-pot of the world, and that, perhaps, only the white flame of war would fuse it into a great nation.

But Natalie made all these thoughts tawdry. She cheapened them. She found in him nothing fine; therefore there was probably nothing fine in him. He went away, to lie awake most of the night.

Chapter XXIII

But, with the breaking off of diplomatic relations, matters remained for a time at a standstill. Natalie dried her eyes and ordered some new clothes, and saw rather more of Rodney Page than was good for her.

With the beginning of February the country house was far enough under way for it to be promised for June, and Natalie, the fundamentals of its decoration arranged for, began to haunt old-furniture shops, accompanied always by Rodney.

"Not that your taste is not right, Natalie," he explained. "It is exquisite. But these fellows are liars and cheats, some of them. Besides, I like trailing along, if you don't mind."

Trailing along was a fairly accurate phrase. There was scarcely a day now when Natalie's shining car, with its two men in livery, did not draw up before Rodney's office building, or stand, as unostentatiously as a fire engine, not too near the entrance of his club. Clayton, going in, had seen it there once or twice, and had smiled rather grimly. He considered its presence there in questionable taste, but he felt no uneasiness. Determined as he was to give Natalie such happiness as was still in him to give, he never mentioned these instances.

But a day came, early in February, which was to mark a change in the relationship between Natalie and Rodney.

It started simply enough. They had lunched together at a down-town hotel, and then went to look at rugs. Rodney had found her rather obdurate as to old rugs. They were still arguing the matter in the limousine.

"I just don't like to think of all sorts of dirty Turks and Arabs having used them," she protested. "Slept on them, walked on them, spilled things on the —? ugh!"

"But the colors, Natalie dear! The old faded 'copper-tones, the dull-blues, the dead-rose! There is a beauty about age, you know. Lovely as you are, you'll be even lovelier as an old woman."

"I'm getting there rather rapidly."

He turned and looked at her critically. No slightest aid that she had given her beauty missed his eyes, the delicate artificial lights in her hair, her eyebrows drawn to a hair's breadth and carefully arched, the touch of rouge under her eyes and on the lobes of her ears. But she was beautiful, no matter what art had augmented her real prettiness. She was a charming, finished product, from her veil and hat to her narrowly shod feet. He liked finished things, well done. He liked the glaze on a porcelain; he liked the perfect lacquering on the Chinese screen he had persuaded Natalie to buy; he preferred wood carved into the fine lines of Sheraton to the trees that grow in the Park, for instance, through which they were driving.

A Sheraton sideboard was art. Even certain forms of Colonial mahogany were art, although he was not fond of them. And Natalie was-art. Even if she represented the creative instincts of her dressmaker and her milliner, and not her own-he did not like a Louis XV sofa the less that it had not carved itself.

Possibly Natalie appealed then to his collective instinct, he had not analyzed it. He only knew that he liked being with her, and he was not annoyed, certainly, by the fact that he knew their constant proximity was arousing a certain amount of comment.

So:

"You are very beautiful," he said with his appraising glance full on her. "You are quite the loveliest woman I know."

"Still? With a grown son?"

"I am not a boy myself, you know."

"What has that to do with it?"

He hesitated, then laughed a little.

"I don't know," he said. "I didn't mean to say that, exactly. Of course, that fact is that I'm rather glad you are not a debutante. You would be giving me odds and ends of dances if you were, you know, and shifting me as fast as possible. As it is —"

The coquetry which is a shallow woman's substitute for passion stirred in her.

"Well? I'm awfully interested."

He turned and faced her.

"I wonder if you are!"

"Go on, Roddie. As it is??"

"As it is," he said, rather rapidly, "you give me a great deal of happiness. I can't say all I would like to, but just being with you-Natalie, I wonder if you know how much it means to me to see you every day."

"I like it, or I wouldn't do it."

"But —I wonder if it means anything to you?"

Curiously enough, with the mere putting it into words, his feeling for her seemed to grow. He was even somewhat excited. He bent toward her, his eyes on her face, and caught one of her gloved hands. He was no longer flirting with a pretty woman. He was in real earnest. But Natalie was still flirting.

"Do you want to know why I like to be with you? Because of course I do, or I shouldn't be."

"Does a famishing man want water?"

"Because you are sane and sensible. You believe, as I do, in going on as normally as possible. All these people who go around glooming because there is a war across the Atlantic! They are so tiresome. Good heavens, the hysterical attitude of some women! And Clay!"

He released her hand.

"So you like me because I'm sensible! Thanks."

"That's a good reason, isn't it?"

"Good God, Natalie, I'm only sensible because I have to be. Not about the war. I'm not talking about that. About you."

"What have I got to do with your being sensible and sane?"

"Just think about things, and you'll know."

She was greatly thrilled and quite untouched. It was a pleasant little game, and she held all the winning cards. So she said, very softly:

"We mustn't go on like this, you know. We mustn't spoil things."

And by her very "we" let him understand that the plight was not his but theirs. They were to suffer on, she implied, in a mutual, unacknowledged passion. He flushed deeply.

But although he was profoundly affected, his infatuation was as spurious as her pretense of one. He was a dilettante in love, as he was in art. His aesthetic sense, which would have died of an honest passion, fattened on the very hopelessness of his beginning an affair with Natalie. Confronted just then with the privilege of marrying her, he would have drawn back in dismay.

Since no such privilege was to be his, however, he found a deep satisfaction in considering himself hopelessly in love with her. He was profoundly sorry for himself. He saw himself a tragic figure, hopeless and wretched. He longed for the unattainable; he held up empty hands to the stars, and by so mimicking the gesture of youth, he regained youth.

"You won't cut me out of your life, Natalie?" he asked wistfully.

And Natalie, who would not have sacrificed this new thrill for anything real in the world, replied:

"It would be better, wouldn't it?"

There was real earnestness in his voice when he spoke. He had dramatized himself by that time.

"Don't take away the only thing that makes life worth living, dear!"

Which Natalie, after a proper hesitation, duly promised not to do.

There were other conversations after that. About marriage, for instance, which Rodney broadly characterized as the failure of the world; he liked treading on dangerous ground.

"When a man has married, and had children, he has fulfilled his duty to the State. That's all marriage is-duty to the State. After that he follows his normal instincts, of course."

"If you are defending unfaithfulness?"

"Not at all. I admire faithfulness. It's rare enough for admiration. No. I'm recognizing facts. Don't you suppose even dear old Clay likes a pretty woman? Of course he does. It's a total difference of view-point, Natalie. What is an incident to a man is a crime to a woman."

Or:

"All this economic freedom of women is going to lead to other freedoms, you know."

"What freedoms?"

"The right to live wherever they please. One liberty brings another, you know. Women used to marry for a home, for some one to keep them. Now they needn't, but-they have to live just the same."

"I wish you wouldn't, Rodney. It's so-cheap."

It was cheap. It was the old game of talking around conversational corners, of whispering behind mental doors. It was insidious, dangerous, and tantalizing. It made between them a bond of lowered voices, of being on the edge of things. Their danger was as spurious as their passion, but Natalie, without humor and without imagination, found the sense of insecurity vaguely attractive.

Fundamentally cold, she liked the idea of playing with fire.

Chapter XXIV

When war was not immediately declared the rector, who on the Sunday following that eventful Saturday of the President's speech to Congress had preached a rousing call to arms, began to feel a bit sheepish about it.

"War or no war, my dear," he said to Delight, "it made them think for as much as an hour. And I can change it somewhat, and use it again, if the time really comes."

"Second-hand stuff!" she scoffed. "You with your old sermons, and Mother with my old dresses! But it was a good sermon," she added. "I have hardly been civil to that German laundress since."

"Good gracious, Delight. Can't you remember that we must love our enemies?"

"Do you love them? You know perfectly well that the moment you get on the other side, if you do, you'll be jerking the cross off your collar and bullying some wretched soldier to give you his gun."

He had a guilty feeling that she was right.

It was February then, and they were sitting in the parish house. Delight had been filling out Sunday-school reports to parents, an innovation she detested. For a little while there was only the scratching of her pen to be heard and an occasional squeal from the church proper, where the organ was being repaired. The rector sat back in his chair, his fingertips together, and whistled noiselessly, a habit of his when he was disturbed. Now and then he glanced at Delight's bent head.

"My dear," he commented finally.

"Just a minute. That wretched little Simonton girl has been absent three Sundays out of four. And on the fourth one she said she had a toothache and sat outside on the steps. Well, daddy?"

"Do you see anything of Graham Spencer now?"

"Very little." She looked at him with frank eyes. "He has changed somehow, daddy. When we do meet he is queer. I sometimes think he avoids me."

He fell back on his noiseless whistling. And Delight, who knew his every mood, got up and perched herself on the arm of his chair.

"Don't you get to thinking things," she said. And slipped an arm around his neck.

"I did think, in the winter —"

"I'll tell you about that," she broke in, bravely. "I suppose, if he'd cared for me at all, I'd have been crazy about him. It isn't because he's good looking. I — well, I don't know why. I just know, as long as I can remember, I — however, that's not important. He thinks I'm a nice little thing and lets it go at that. It's a good bit worse, of course, than having him hate me."

"Sometimes I think you are not very happy."

"I'm happier than I would be trying to make him fall in love with me. Oh, you needn't be shocked. It can be done. Lots of girls do it. It isn't any moral sense that keeps me from it, either. It's just pride."

"My dear!"

"And there's another angle to it. I wouldn't marry a man who hasn't got a mind of his own. Even if I had the chance, which I haven't. That silly mother of his-she is silly, daddy, and selfish-Do you know what she is doing now?"

"We ought not to discuss her. She —"

"Fiddlesticks. You love gossip and you know it."

Her tone was light, but the rector felt that arm around his neck tighten. He surmised a depth of feeling that made him anxious.

"She is trying to marry him to Marion Hayden."

The rector sat up, almost guiltily.

"But-are you sure she is doing that?"

"Everybody says so. She thinks that if he is married, and there is a war, he won't want to go if he has a wife." She was silent for a moment. "Marion will drive him straight to the devil, daddy."

The rector reached up and took her hand. She cared more than she would admit, he saw. She had thought the thing out, perhaps in the long night-when he slept placidly. Thought and suffered, he surmised. And again he remembered his worldly plans for her, and felt justly punished.

"I suppose it is hard for a father to understand how any one can know his little girl and not love her. Or be the better for it."

She kissed him and slid off the arm of his chair.

"Don't you worry," she said cheerfully. "I had to make an ideal for myself about somebody. Every girl does. Sometimes it's the plumber. It doesn't really matter who it is, so you can pin your dreams to him. The only thing that hurts is that Graham wasn't worth while."

She went back to her little cards, but some ten minutes later the rector, lost in thought, heard the scratching of her pen cease.

"Did you ever think, daddy," she said, "of the influence women have over men? Look at the Spencers. Mrs. Spencer spoiling Graham, and making her husband desperately unhappy. And —"

"Unhappy? What makes you think that?"

"He looks unhappy."

The rector was startled. He had an instant vision of Clayton Spencer, tall, composed, hand-some, impeccably clothed. He saw him in the setting that suited him best, the quiet elegance of his home. Clayton unhappy! Nonsense. But he was uneasy, too. That very gravity which he had noticed lately, that was certainly not the gravity of an entirely happy man. Clayton had changed, somehow. Was there trouble there? And if there were, why?

The rector, who reduced most wretchedness to terms of dollars and cents, of impending bills and small deprivations found himself at a loss.

"I am sure you are wrong," he objected, rather feebly.

Delight eyed him with the scorn of nineteen for fifty.

"I wonder what you would do," she observed, "if mother just lay around all day, and had her hair done, and got new clothes, and never thought a thought of her own, and just used you as a sort of walking bank-account?"

"My dear, I really can not —"

"I'll tell you what you'd do," she persisted. "You'd fall in love with somebody else, probably. Or else you'd just naturally dry up and be made a bishop."

He was extremely shocked at that, and a little hurt. It took her some time to establish cheerful relations again, and a very humble apology. But her words stuck in the rector's mind. He made a note for a sermon, with the text: "Her children arise up, and call her blessed; her husband also, and he praiseth her."

He went quietly into the great stone building and sat down. The organist was practicing the Introit anthem, and half way up the church a woman was sitting quietly.

The rector leaned back, and listened to the music. He often did that when he had a sermon in his mind. It was peaceful and quiet. Hard to believe, in that peace of great arches and swelling music, that across the sea at that moment men were violating that fundamental law of the church, "Thou shalt not kill."

The woman turned her head, and he saw that it was Audrey Valentine. He watched her with kindly, speculative eyes. Self-reliant, frivolous Audrey, sitting alone in the church she had so casually attended-surely that was one of the gains of war. People all came to it ultimately. They held on with both hands as long as they could, and then they found their grasp growing feeble and futile, and they turned to the Great Strength.

The organist had ceased. Audrey was kneeling now. The rector, eyes on the gleaming cross above the altar, repeated softly:

"Save and deliver us, we humbly beseech Thee, from the hands of our enemies; that we, being armed with Thy defense, may be preserved evermore from all perils."

Audrey was coming down the aisle. She did not see him. She had, indeed, the fixed eyes of one who still looks inward. She was very pale, but there was a new look of strength in her face, as of one who has won a victory.

"To glorify Thee, who are the only giver of all victory, through the merits of thy Son, Jesus Christ our Lord," finished the rector.

Chapter XXV

On the last day of February Audrey came home from her shorthand class and stood wearily by the window, too discouraged even to remove her hat. The shorthand was a failure; the whole course was a failure. She had not the instinct for plodding, for the meticulous attention to detail that those absurd, irrational lines and hooks and curves demanded.

She could not even spell! And an idiot of an instructor had found fault with the large square band she wrote, as being uncommercial. Uncommercial! Of course it was. So was she uncommercial. She had dreamed a dream of usefulness, but after all, why was she doing it? We would never fight. Here we were, saying to Germany that we had ceased to be friends and letting it go at that.

She might go to England. They needed women there. But not untrained women. Not, she thought contemptuously, women whose only ability lay in playing bridge, or singing French chansons with no particular voice.

After all, the only world that was open to her was her old world. It liked her. It even understood her. It stretched out a tolerant, pleasure-beckoning hand to her.

"I'm a fool," she reflected bitterly. "I'm not happy, and I'm not useful. I might as well play. It's all I can do."

But her real hunger was for news of Clayton. Quite suddenly he had stopped dropping in on his way up-town. He had made himself the most vital element in her life, and then taken himself out of it. At first she had thought he might be ill. It seemed too cruel otherwise. But she saw his name with increasing frequency in the newspapers. It seemed to her that every relief organization in the country was using his name and his services. So he was not ill.

He had tired of her, probably. She had nothing to give, had no right to give anything. And, of course, he could not know how much he had meant to her, of courage to carry on. How the memory of his big, solid, dependable figure had helped her through the bad hours when the thought of Chris's defection had left her crushed and abject.

She told herself that the reason she wanted to see Natalie was because she had neglected her shamefully. Perhaps that was what was wrong with Clay; perhaps he felt that, by avoiding Natalie, she was putting their friendship on a wrong basis. Actually, she had reached that point all loving women reach, when even to hear a beloved name, coming out of a long silence, was both torture and necessity.

She took unusual pains with her dress that afternoon, and it was a very smart, slightly rouged and rather swaggering Audrey who made her first call in weeks on Natalie that afternoon.

Natalie was a little stiff, still slightly affronted.

"I thought you must have left town," she said. "But you look as though you'd been having a rest cure."

"Rouge," said Audrey, coolly. "No, I haven't been entirely resting."

"There are all sorts of stories going about. That you're going into a hospital; that you're learning to fly; that you're in the secret service?"

"Just because I find it stupid going about without a man!" Natalie eyed her shrewdly, but there was no self-consciousness in Audrey's face. If the stories were true, and there had been another woman, she was carrying it off well.

"At least Chris is in France. I have to go, when I go, without Clay. And there is no excuse whatever."

"You mean-he is working?"

"Not at night. He is simply obstinate. He says he is tired. I don't really mind any more. He is so hatefully heavy these days."

"Heavy! Clay!"

"My dear!" Natalie drew her chair closer and lowered her voice. "What can one do with a man who simply lives war? He spends hours over the papers. He's up if the Allies make a gain, and impossible if they don't. I can tell by the very way he slams the door of his room when he comes home what the news is. It's dreadful."

Audrey flushed.

"I wish there were more like him."

But Natalie smiled tolerantly.

"You are not married to him. I suppose the war is important, but I don't want it twenty-four hours a day. I want to forget it if I can. It's hideous."

Audrey's mouth twitched. After all, what was the good of talking to Natalie. She would only be resentful.

"How is the house coming on?" she asked.

She had Natalie on happy ground there. For a half-hour she looked at blueprints and water-color sketches, heard Rodney's taste extolled, listened to plans for a house-party which she gathered was, rather belatedly, to include her. And through it all she was saying to herself,

"This is his wife. This is the woman he loves. He has had a child by her. He is building this house for her. He goes into her room as Chris came into mine. And she is not good enough. She is not good enough."

Now that she had seen Natalie, she knew why she had not seen her before. She was jealous of her. Jealous and contemptuous. Suddenly she hated Natalie. She hated her because she was Clayton Spencer's wife, with all that that implied. She hated her because she was unworthy of him. She hated her because she loved Clay, and hated her more because she loved herself more than she loved him.

Audrey sat back in her chair and saw that she had traveled a long way along a tragic road. For the first time in her brave and reckless life she was frightened. She was even trembling. She lighted a cigaret from the stand at Natalie's elbow to steady herself.

Natalie chattered on, and Audrey gave her the occasional nod that was all she needed. She thought,

"Does he know about her? Is he still fooled? She is almost beautiful. Rodney is falling in love with her, probably. Does he know that? Will he care terribly if he finds it out? She looks cold, but one can't tell, and some men-has she a drop of honest, unselfish passion in her?"

She got up suddenly.

"Heavens, how late it is!" she said. "I must run on."

"Why not stay on to dinner? Graham is seldom home, and we can talk, if Clay doesn't."

The temptation to see Clay again was strong in Audrey. But suddenly she knew that she did not want to see them together, in the intimacy of their home. She did not want to sit between them at dinner, and then go away, leaving them there together. And something fundamentally honest in her told her that she had no right to sit at their table.

"I'll come another time, if you'll ask me. Not to-day," she said. And left rather precipitately. It hurt her, rather, to have Natalie, with an impulsive gesture, gather the flowers out of a great jar and insist on her carrying them home with her. It gave her a miserable sense of playing unfairly.

She walked home. The fresh air, after Natalie's flower-scented, overheated room, made her more rational. She knew where she stood, anyhow. She was in love with Clayton Spencer. She had, she reflected cynically, been in love before. A number of times before. She almost laughed aloud. She had called those things love, those sickly romances, those feeble emotions!

Then her eyes filled with unexpected tears. She had always wanted some one to make her happy. Now she wanted to make some one happy. She cared nothing for the cost. She would put herself out of it altogether. He was not happy. Any one could see that. He had everything, but he was not happy. If he belonged to her, she would live to make him happy. She would —

Suddenly she remembered Chris. Perhaps she did not know how to hold a man's love. She had not held him. He had protested that she was the only woman he had ever loved, but all the time there had been that other girl. How account for her, then?

"He did not think of me," she reflected defiantly, "I shall not think of him."

She was ashamed of that instantly. After all, Chris was doing a man's part now. She was no longer angry with him. She had written him that, over and over, in the long letters she had made a point of sending him. Only, she did not love him any more. She thought now that she never had loved him.

What about the time when he came back? What would she do then? She shivered.

But Chris, after all, was not to come back. He would never come back again. The cable was there when she reached her apartment —a cold statement, irrefutable, final.

She had put the flowers on the table and had raised her hands to unpin her hat when she saw it. She read it with a glance first, then slowly, painfully, her heart contracted as if a hand had squeezed it. She stood very still, not so much stricken as horrified, and her first conscious thought was of remorse, terrible, gasping remorse. All that afternoon, while she had been hating Natalie and nursing her love for Clay, Chris had been lying dead somewhere.

Chris was dead.

She felt very tired, but not faint. It seemed dreadful, indeed, that she could be standing there, full of life, while Chris was dead. Such grief as she felt was for him, not for herself. He had loved life so, even when he cheapened it. He had wanted to live and now he was dead. She, who did not care greatly to live, lived on, and he was gone.

All at once she felt terribly alone. She wanted some one with her. She wanted to talk it all out to some one who understood. She wanted Clay. She said to herself that she did not want him because she loved him. All love was dead in her now. She wanted him because he was strong and understanding. She made this very clear to herself, because she had a morbid fancy that Chris might be watching her. There were people who believed that sort of thing. To her excited fancy it seemed as though Chris's cynical smile might flash out from any dusky corner.

She knew she was not being quite rational. Which was strange, because she felt so strong, and because the voice with which she called Clayton's number was so steady. She knew, too, that she was no longer in love with Clay, because his steady voice over the telephone left her quite calm and unmoved.

"I want you to come up, Clay," she said. "If you can, easily."

"I can come at once. Is anything wrong?"

"Chris has been killed," she replied, and hung up the receiver. Then she sat down to wait, and to watch for Chris's cynical smile to flash in some dusky corner.

Clayton found her there, collapsed in her chair, a slim, gray-faced girl with the rouge giving a grotesque vitality to her bloodless cheeks. She got up very calmly and gave him the cablegram. Then she fainted in a crumpled heap at his feet.

Chapter XXVI

The new munition plant was nearing completion. Situated on the outskirts of the city, it spread over a vast area of what had once been waste land. Of the three long buildings, two were already in operation and the third was well under way.

To Clayton Spencer it was the realization of a dream. He never entered the great high-walled enclosure without a certain surprise at the ease with which it had all been accomplished, and a thrill of pride at the achievement. He found the work itself endlessly interesting. The casts, made of his own steel, lying in huge rusty heaps in the yard; the little cars which carried them into the plant; the various operations by which the great lathes turned them out, smooth and shining, only to lose their polish when, heated again, they were ready for the ponderous hammer to close their gaping jaws. The delicacy of the work appealed to him, the machining to a thousandth of an inch, the fastidious making of the fuses, tiny things almost microscopic, and requiring the delicate touch of girls, most of whom had been watchmakers and jewelry-workers.

And with each carload of the finished shells that left the plant he felt a fine glow of satisfaction. The output was creeping up. Soon they would be making ten thousand shells a day. And every shell was one more chance for victory against the Hun. It became an obsession with him to make more, ever more.

As the work advanced, he found an unexpected enthusiasm in Graham. Here was something to be done, a new thing. The steel mill had been long established. Its days went on monotonously. The boy found it noisy, dirty, without appeal to his imagination. But the shell plant was different. There were new problems to face, of labor, of supplies, of shipping and output.

He was, however, reluctantly coming to the conclusion that the break with Germany was the final step that the Government intended to take. That it would not declare war.

However, the break had done something. It had provided him with men from the local National Guard to police the plant, and he found the government taking a new interest, an official interest, in his safety. Agents from the Military Intelligence and the Department of Justice scanned his employment lists and sent agents into the plant. In the building where men and women were hired, each applicant passed a desk where they were quietly surveyed by two unobstrusive gentlemen in indifferent business suits who eyed them carefully. Around the fuse department, where all day girls and women handled guncotton and high-explosive powder, a special guard was posted, day and night.

Early in March Clayton put Graham in charge of the first of the long buildings to be running full, and was rewarded by a new look in the boy's face. He was almost startled at the way he took it.

"I'll do my very best, sir," he said, rather huskily. "If I can't fight, I can help put the swine out of business, anyhow."

He was by that time quite sure that Natalie had extracted a promise of some sort from the boy. On the rare occasions when Graham was at home he was quiet and suppressed.

He was almost always at Marion Hayden's in the evenings, and from things he let fall, Clayton gathered that the irresponsible group which centered about Marion was, in the boy's own vernacular, rather "shot to pieces." Tommy Hale had gone to England to join the Royal Flying Corps. One or two of them were in Canada, trying to enlist there, and one evening Graham brought home to dinner an inordinately tall and thin youngster in the kilts of a Scotch-Canadian regiment, with an astounding length of thin leg below his skirts, who had been one of Marion's most reckless satellites.

"Look like a fool, I know, sir," said the tall individual sheepishly. "Just had to get in it somehow. No camouflage about these skirts, is there?"

And Clayton had noticed, with a thrill of sympathy, how wistfully Graham eyed the debonnair young Scot by adoption, and how Buckham had hovered over him, filling his plate and his glass. Even Graham noticed Buckham.

"Old boy looks as though he'd like to kiss you, Sid," he said. "It's the petticoats. Probably thinks you're a woman."

"I look better with my legs under the table," said the tall boy, modestly.

Clayton was still determined that Graham should fight the thing out for himself. He wished, sometimes, that he knew Marion Hayden's attitude. Was she like Natalie? Would she, if the time came, use her undeniable influence for or against? And there again he resented the influence of women in the boy's life. Why couldn't he make his own decisions? Why couldn't they let him make his own decisions?

He remembered his father, and how his grandmother, in '61, had put a Bible into one pocket and a housewife into another, and had sent him off to war. Had the fiber of our women weakened since then? But he knew it had not. All day, in the new plant, women were working with high-explosives quite calmly. And there were Audrey and the Haverford women, strong enough, in all conscience.

Every mental path, those days, somehow led eventually to Audrey. She was the lighted window at the end of the long trail.

Graham was, as a matter of fact, trying to work out his own salvation. He blundered, as youth always blunders, and after a violent scene with Marion Hayden he made an attempt to break off his growing intimacy with Anna Klein-to find, as many a man had before him, that the sheer brutality of casting off a loving woman was beyond him.

The scene with Marion came one Sunday in the Spencer house, with Natalie asleep up-stairs after luncheon, and Clayton walking off a sense of irritation in the park. He did not like the Hayden girl. He could not fathom Natalie's change of front with regard to Graham and the girl. He had gone out, leaving them together, and Marion had launched her attack fiercely.

"Now!" she cried.

"I couldn't come last night. That's all, Marion."

"It is certainly not all. Why couldn't you come?"

"I worked late."

"Where?"

"At the plant."

"That's a lie, Graham. I called the plant. I'll tell you where you were. You were out with a girl. You were seen, if you want to know it."

"Oh, if you are going to believe everything you hear about me?"

"Don't act like a child. Who was the girl?"

"It isn't like you to be jealous, Marion. I let you run around all the time with other fellows, but the minute I take a girl out for a little spin, you're jealous."

"Jealous!" She laughed nastily. But she knew she was losing her temper; and brought herself up short. Let him think she was jealous. What really ailed her was deadly fear lest her careful plan go astray. She was terrified. That was all. And she meant to learn who the girl was.

"I know who it was," she hazarded.

"I think you are bluffing."

"It was Delight Haverford."

"Delight!"

She knew then that she was wrong, but it was her chance to assail Delight and she took it.

"That-child!" she continued contemptuously. "Don't you suppose I've seen how she looks at you? I'm not afraid of her. You are too much a man of the world to let her put anything over on you. At least, I thought you were. Of course, if you like milk and water?"

"It was not Delight," he said doggedly. "And I don't think we need to bring her into this at all. She's not in love with me. She wouldn't wipe her feet on me."

Which was unfortunate. Marion smiled slowly.

"Oh! But you are good enough for me to be engaged to! I wonder!"

He went to the window and stood for a moment looking out. Then he went slowly back to her.

"I'm not good enough for you to be engaged to, Marion," he said. "I —don't you want to call it a day?"

She was really terrified then. She went white and again, miserably, he mistook her agitation for something deeper.

"You want to break the engagement?"

"Not if you still want me. I only mean —I'm a pretty poor sort. You ought to have the best, and God help this country if I'm the best."

"Graham, you're in some sort of trouble?"

He drew himself up in boyish bravado. He could not tell her the truth. It opened up too hideous a vista. Even his consciousness of the fact that the affair with Anna was still innocent did not dull his full knowledge of whither it was trending. He was cold and wretched.

"It's nothing," he muttered.

"You can tell me. You can tell me anything. I know a lot, you see. I'm no silly kitten. If you're in a fix, I'll help you. I don't care what it is, I'll help you. I? I'm crazy about you, Graham."

Anna's words, too!

"Look here, Marion," he said, roughly, "you've got to do one of two things. Either marry me or let me go."

"Let you go! I like that. If that is how you feel?"

"Oh-don't." He threw up his arm. "I want you. You know that. Marry me-to-morrow."

"I will not. Do you think I'm going to come into this family and have you cut off? Don't you suppose I know that Clayton Spencer hates the very chair I sit on? He'll come and beg me to marry you, some day. Until then?"

"You won't do it?"

"To-morrow? Certainly not."

And again he felt desperately his powerlessness to loosen the coils that were closing round him, fetters forged of his own red blood, his own youth, the woman-urge.

She was watching him with her calculating glance.

"You must be in trouble," she said.

"If I am, it's you and mother who have driven me there."

He was alarmed then, and lapsed into dogged silence. His anxiety had forced into speech thoughts that had never before been articulate. He was astounded to hear himself uttering them, although with the very speaking he realized now that they were true.

"Sorry, Marion," he muttered. "I didn't mean all that. I'm excited. That's all."

When he sat down beside her again and tried to take her hand, she drew it away.

"You've been very cruel, Graham," she said. "I've been selfish. Every girl who is terribly in love is selfish. I am going to give you your ring, and leave you free to do whatever you want."

Her generosity overcame him. He was instantly ashamed, humbled.

"Don't!" he begged. "Don't let me go. I'll just go to the dogs. If you really care?"

"Care!" she said softly. And as he buried his head in her lap she stroked his hair softly. Her eyes, triumphant, surveyed the long room, with its satin-paneled walls, its French furniture, its long narrow gilt-framed mirrors softening the angles of the four corners.

Some day all this would be hers. For this she would exchange the untidy and imitation elegance of her present setting.

She stroked the boy's head absently.

Graham made an attempt to free himself the next day. He was about to move his office to the new plant, and he made a determination not to take Anna with him.

He broke it to her as gently as he could.

"Mr. Weaver is taking my place here," he said, avoiding her eyes.

"Yes, Graham."

"He'll-there ought to be some one here who knows the ropes."

"Do you mean me?"

"Well, you know them, don't you?" He had tried to smile at her.

"Do you mean that you are going to have another secretary at the plant?"

"Look here, Anna," he said impulsively. "You know things can't go on indefinitely, the way we are now. You know it, don't you."

She looked down and nodded.

"Well, don't you think I'd better leave you here?"

She fumbled nervously with her wrist-watch.

"I won't stay here if you go," she said finally. "I hate Mr. Weaver. I'm afraid of him. I —oh, don't leave me, Graham. Don't. I haven't anybody but you. I haven't any home-not a real home. You ought to see him these days." She always referred to her father as "him." "He's dreadful. I'm only happy when I'm here with you."

He was angry, out of sheer despair.

"I've told you," he said. "Things can't go on as they are. You know well enough what I mean. I'm older than you are, Anna. God knows I don't want any harm to come to you through me. But, if we continue to be together —"

"I'm not blaming you." She looked at him honestly. "I'd just rather have you care about me than marry anybody else."

He kissed her, with a curious mingling of exultation and despair. He left her there when he went away that afternoon, a rather downcast young figure, piling up records and card-indexes, and following him to the door with worshiping, anxious eyes. Later on in the afternoon Joey, wandering in from Clayton's office on one of his self-constituted observation tours, found her crying softly while she wiped her typewriter, preparatory to covering it for the night.

"Somebody been treatin' you rough?" he asked, more sympathetic than curious.

"What are you doing here, anyhow?" she demanded, angrily. "You're always hanging around, spying on me."

"Somebody's got to keep an eye on you."

"Well, you don't."

"Look here," he said, his young-old face twitching with anxiety. "You get out from under, kid. You take my advice, and get out from under. Something's going to fall."

"Just mind your own business, and stop worrying about me. That's all."

He turned and started out.

"Oh, very well," he said sharply. "But you might take a word of warning, anyhow. That cousin of yours has got an eye on you, all right. And we don't want any scandal about the place."

"We? Who are 'we'?"

"Me and Mr. Clayton Spencer," said Joey, smartly, and went out, banging the door cheerfully.

Anna climbed the hill that night wearily, but with a sense of relief that Rudolph had not been waiting for her at the yard gate. She was in no mood to thrust and parry with him. She wondered, rather dully, what mischief Rudolph was up to. He was gaining a tremendous ascendency over her father, she knew. Herman was spending more and more of his evenings away from home, creaking up the stairs late at night, shoes in hand, to undress in the cold darkness across the hall.

"Out?" she asked Katie, sitting by the fire with the evening paper. Conversation in the cottage was almost always laconic.

"Ate early," Katie returned. "Rudolph was here, too. I'm going to quit if I've got to cook for that sneak any longer. You'd think he had a meal ticket here. Your supper's on the stove."

"I'm not hungry." She ate her supper, however, and undressed by the fire. Then she went up-stairs and sat by her window in the gathering night. She was suffering acutely. Graham was tired of her. He wanted to get rid of her. Probably he had a girl somewhere else, a lady. Her idea of the life of such a girl had been gathered from novels.

"The sort that has her breakfast in bed," she muttered, "and has her clothes put on her by somebody. Her underclothes, too!"

The immodesty of the idea made her face burn with anger.

Late that night Herman came back.

Herman had been a difficult proposition for Rudolph to handle. His innate caution, his respect for law and, under his bullying exterior, a certain physical cowardice, made him slow to move in the direction Rudolph was urging. He was controversial. He liked to argue over the beer and schnitzel Rudolph bought. And Rudolph was growing impatient.

Rudolph himself was all eagerness and zeal. It was his very zeal that was his danger, although it brought him slavish followers. He was contemptuous, ill-tempered, and impatient, but, of limited intelligence himself, he understood for that very reason the mental processes of those he would lead. There was a certain simplicity even in his cunning. With Herman he was a ferret driving out of their hiding-places every evil instinct that lay dormant. Under his goading, Herman was becoming savage, sullen, and potentially violent.

He was confused, too. Rudolph's arguments always confused him.

He was confused that night, heavy with fatigue and with Rudolph's steady talk in his ear. He was tired of pondering great questions, tired of hearing about the Spencers and the money they were making.

Anna's clothing was scattered about the room, and he frowned at it. She spent too much money on her clothes. Always sewing at something —

He stooped down to gather up his shoes, and his ear thus brought close to the table was conscious in the silence of a faint rhythmical sound. He stood up and looked about. Then he moved the newspaper on the table. Underneath it, forgotten in her anxiety and trouble, lay the little gold watch.

He picked it up, still following his train of thought. It fitted into the evening's inflammable proceedings. So, with such trinkets as this, capital would silence the cry of labor for its just share in the products of its skill and strength! It would bribe, and cheaply. Ten dollars, perhaps, that ticking insult. For ten dollars —

He held it close to his spectacles. Ah, but it was not so cheap. It came from the best shop in the city. He weighed it carefully in his hand, and in so doing saw the monogram. A doubt crept into his mind, a cold and chilling fear. Since when had the Spencer plant taken to giving watches for Christmas? The hill girls who worked as stenographers in the plant; they came in often enough and he did not remember any watches, or any mention of watches. His mind, working slowly, recalled that never before had he seen the watch near at hand. And he went into a slow and painful calculation. Fifty dollars at least it had cost. A hundred stenographers-that would be five thousand dollars for watches.

Suddenly he knew that Anna had lied to him. One of two things, then: either she had spent money for it, unknown to him, or some one had given it to her. There was, in his mind, not much difference in degree between the two alternatives. Both were crimes of the first magnitude.

He picked the watch up between his broad thumb and forefinger, and then, his face a cold and dreadful mask, he mounted the stairs.

Chapter XXVII

Clayton Spencer was facing with characteristic honesty a situation that he felt was both hopeless and shameful.

He was hopelessly in love with Audrey. He knew now that he had known it for a long time. Here was no slender sentiment, no thin romance. With every fiber of him, heart and soul and body, he loved her and wanted her. There was no madness about it, save the fact itself, which was mad enough. It was not the single attraction of passion, although he recognized that element as fundamental in it. It was the craving of a strong man who had at last found his woman.

He knew that, as certainly as he knew anything. He did not even question that she cared for him. It was as though they both had passed through the doubting period without knowing it, and had arrived together at the same point, the crying need of each other.

He rather thought, looking back, that Audrey had known it sooner than he had. She had certainly known the night she learned of Chris's death. His terror when she fainted, the very way he had put her out of his arms when she opened her eyes-those had surely told her. Yet, had Chris's cynical spirit been watching, there had been nothing, even then.

There was, between them, nothing now. He had given way to the people who flocked to her with sympathy, had called her up now and then, had sent her a few books, some flowers. But the hopelessness of the situation held him away from her. Once or twice, at first, he had called her on the telephone and had waited, almost trembling, for her voice over the wire, only to ask her finally, in a voice chilled with repression, how she was feeling, or to offer a car for her to ride in the park. And her replies were equally perfunctory. She was well. She was still studying, but it was going badly. She was too stupid to learn all those pot-hooks.

Once she had said:

"Aren't you ever coming to see me, Clay?"

Her voice had been wistful, and it had been a moment before he had himself enough in hand to reply, formally:

"Thank you. I shall, very soon."

But he had not gone to the little flat again.

Through Natalie he heard of her now and then.

"I saw Audrey to-day," she said once. "She is not wearing mourning. It's bad taste, I should say. When one remembers that she really drove Chris to his death —"

He had interrupted her, angrily.

"That is a cruel misstatement, Natalie. She did nothing of the sort."

"You needn't bite me, you know. He went, and had about as much interest in this war as-as —"

"As you have," he finished. And had gone out, leaving Natalie staring after him.

He was more careful after that, but the situation galled him. He was no hypocrite, but there was no need of wounding Natalie unnecessarily. And that, after all, was the crux of the whole situation. Natalie. It was not Natalie's fault that he had found the woman of his heart too late. He had no thought of blame for her. In decency, there was only one thing to do. He could not play the lover to her, but then he had not done that for a very long time. He could see, however, that she was not hurt.

Perhaps, in all her futile life, Natalie had, for all her complaining, never been so content in her husband as in those early spring months when she had completely lost him. He made no demands whatever. In the small attentions, which he had never neglected, he was even more assiduous. He paid her ever-increasing bills without comment. He submitted, in those tense days when every day made the national situation more precarious, to hours of discussion as to the country house, to complaints as to his own lack of social instinct, and to that new phase of her attitude toward Marion Hayden that left him baffled and perplexed.

Then, on the Sunday when he left Graham and Marion together at the house, he met Audrey quite by accident in the park. He was almost incredulous at first. She came like the answer to prayer, a little tired around the eyes, showing the strain of the past weeks, but with that same easy walk and unconscious elegance that marked her, always.

She was not alone. There was a tall blonde girl beside her, hideously dressed, but with a pleasant, shallow face. Just before they met Audrey stopped and held out her hand.

"Then you'll let me know, Clare?"

"Thank you. I will, indeed, Mrs. Valentine."

With a curious glance at Clayton the girl went on. Audrey smiled at him.

"Please don't run!" she said. "There are people looking. It would be so conspicuous."

"Run!" he replied. He stood looking down at her, and at something in his eyes her smile died. "It's too wonderful, Clay."

For a moment he could not speak. After all those weeks of hunger for her there was no power in him to dissemble. He felt a mad, boyish impulse to hold out his arms to her, Malacca stick, gloves, and all!

"It's a bit of luck I hadn't expected, Audrey," he said, at last, unsteadily.

She turned about quite simply, and faced in the direction he was going.

"I shall walk with you," she said, with a flash of her old impertinence. "You have not asked me to, but I shall, anyhow. Only don't call this luck. It isn't at all. I walk here every Sunday, and every Sunday I say to myself-he will think he needs exercise. Then he will walk, and the likeliest place for him to go is the park. Good reasoning, isn't it?"

She glanced up at him, but his face was set and unsmiling. "Don't pay any attention to me, Clay. I'm a little mad, probably. You see" —she hesitated —"I need my friends just now. And when the very best of them all hides away from me?"

"Don't say that. I stayed away, because —" He hesitated.

"I'm almost through. Don't worry! But I was walking along before I met Clare —I'll tell you about her presently-and I was saying to myself that I thought God owed me something. I didn't know just what. Happiness, maybe. I've been careless and all that, but I've never been wicked. And yet I can look back, and count the really happy days of my life on five fingers."

She held out one hand.

"Five fingers!" she repeated, "and I am twenty-eight. The percentage is pretty low, you know."

"Perhaps you and I ask too much?"

He was conscious of her quick, searching glance.

"Oh! You feel that way, too? I mean-as I do, that it's all hardly worth while? But you seem to have everything, Clay."

"You have one thing I lack. Youth."

"Youth! At twenty-eight!"

"You can still mold your life, Audrey dear. You have had a bad time, but-with all reverence to Chris's memory-his going out of it, under the circumstances, is a grief. But it doesn't spell shipwreck."

"Do you mean that I will marry again?" she asked, in a low tone.

"Don't you think you will, some time? Some nice young chap who will worship you all the days of his life? That-well, that is what I expect for you. It's at least possible, you know."

"Is it what you want for me?"

"Good God!" he burst out, his restraint suddenly gone. "What do you want me to say? What can I say, except that I want you to be happy? Don't you think I've gone over it all, over and over again? I'd give my life for the right to tell you the things I think, but —I haven't that right. Even this little time together is wrong, the way things are. It is all wrong."

"I'm sorry, Clay. I know. I am just reckless to-day. You know I am reckless. It's my vice. But sometimes-we'd better talk about the mill."

But he could not talk about the mill just then. They walked along in silence, and after a little he felt her touch his arm.

"Wouldn't it be better just to have it out?" she asked, wistfully. "That wouldn't hurt anybody, would it?"

"I'm afraid, Audrey."

"I'm not," she said proudly. "I sometimes think-oh, I think such a lot these days-that if we talked these things over, I'd recover my-friend. I've lost him now, you see. And I'm so horribly lonely, Clay."

"Lost him!"

"Lost him," she repeated. "I've lost my friend, and I haven't gained anything. It didn't hurt anybody for us to meet now and then, Clay. You know that. I wish you would understand," she added impatiently. "I only want to go back to things as they were. I want you to come in now and then. We used to talk about all sorts of things, and I miss that. Plenty of people come, but that's different. It's only your occasional companionship I want. I don't want you to come and make love to me."

"You say you have missed the companionship," he said rather unsteadily. "I wonder if you think I haven't?"

"I know you have, my dear. And that is why I want you to come. To come without being afraid that I expect or want anything else. Surely we can manage that."

He smiled down at her, rather wryly, at her straight courageous figure, her brave eyes, meeting his so directly. How like her it all was, the straightforwardness of it, the absence of coquetry. And once again he knew, not only that he loved her with all the depths of him, of his strong body and his vigorous mind, but that she was his woman. The one woman in the world for him. It was as though all his life he had been searching for her, and he had found her, and it was too late. She knew it, too. It was in her very eyes.

"I have wanted to come, terribly," he said finally. And when she held out her hand to him, he bent down and kissed it.

"Then that's settled," she said, in a matter-of-fact tone. "And now I'll tell you about Clare. I'm rather proud of her."

"Clare?"

The tension had been so great that he had forgotten the blonde girl entirely.

"Do you remember the night I got a hundred dollars from you? And later on, that I asked you for work in your mill for the girl I got it for?"

"Do you mean?" He looked at her in surprise.

"That was the girl. You see, she rather holds onto me. It's awful in a way, too. It looks as though I am posing as magnanimous. I'm not, Clay. If I had cared awfully it would have been different. But then, if I had cared awfully, perhaps it would never have happened."

"You have nothing to blame yourself for, Audrey."

"Well, I do, rather. But that's not the point. Sometimes when I am alone I have wicked thoughts, you know, Clay. I'm reckless, and sometimes I think maybe there is only one life, and why not get happiness out of it. I realize that, but for some little kink in my brain, I might be in Clare's position. So I don't turn her out. She's a poor, cheap thing, but-well, she is fond of me. If I had children-it's funny, but I rather mother her! And she's straight now, straight as a string!"

She was sensitive to his every thought, and she knew by the very change in the angle of his head that he was thinking that over and not entirely approving. But he said finally:

"You're a big woman, Audrey."

"But you don't like it!"

"I don't like her troubling you."

"Troubling me! She doesn't borrow money, you know. Why, she makes more money from your plant than I have to live on! And she brings me presents of flowers and the most awful embroidery, that she does herself."

"You ought not to know that side of life."

She laughed a little bitterly.

"Not know it!" she said. "I've had to know it. I learned it pretty well, too. And don't make any mistake, Clay." She looked up at him with her clear, understanding gaze. "Being good, decent, with a lot of people is only the lack of temptation. Only, thank God, there are some who have the strength to withstand it when it comes."

And he read in her clear eyes her promise and her understanding; that they loved each other, that it was the one big thing in both their lives, but that between them there would be only the secret inner knowledge of that love. There would be no shipwreck. And for what she gave, she demanded his strength and his promise. It was to what he read in her face, not to her words, that he replied:

"I'll do my very best, Audrey dear."

He went back to her rooms with her, and she made him tea, while he built the fire in the open fireplace and nursed it tenderly to a healthy strength. Overnursed it, she insisted. They were rather gay, indeed, and the danger-point passed by safely. There was so much to discuss, she pretended. The President's unfortunate phrase of "peace without victory"; the deportation of the Belgians, the recent leak in Washington to certain stock-brokers, and more and more imminent, the possibility of a state of war being recognized by the government.

"If it comes," she said, gayly, "I shall go, of course. I shall go to France and sing them into battle. My shorthand looks like a music score, as it is. What will you do?"

"I can't let you outshine me," he said. "And I don't want to think of your going over there without me. My dear! My dear!"

She ignored that, and gave him his tea, gravely.

Chapter XXVIII

When Natalie roused from her nap that Sunday afternoon, it was to find Marion gone, and Graham waiting for her in her boudoir. Through the open door she could see him pacing back and forward and something in his face made her vaguely uneasy. She assumed the child-like smile which so often preserved her from the disagreeable.

"What a sleep I've had," she said, and yawned prettily. "I'll have one of your cigarets, darling, and then let's take a walk."

Graham knew Natalie's idea of a walk, which was three or four blocks along one of the fashionable avenues, with the car within hailing distance. At the end of the fourth block she always declared that her shoes pinched, and called the machine.

"You don't really want to walk, mother."

"Of course I do, with you. Ring for Madeleine, dear."

She was uncomfortable. Graham had been very queer lately. He would have long, quiet spells, and then break out in an uncontrollable irritation, generally at the servants. But Graham did not ring for Madeleine. He lighted a cigaret for Natalie, and standing off, surveyed her. She was very pretty. She was prettier than Toots. That pale blue wrapper, or whatever it was, made her rather exquisite. And Natalie, curled up on her pale rose chaise longue, set to work as deliberately to make a conquest of her son as she had ever done to conquer Rodney Page, or the long list of Rodney's predecessors.

"You're growing very handsome, you know, boy," she said. "Almost too handsome. A man doesn't need good looks. They're almost a handicap. Look at your father."

"They haven't hurt him any, I should say."

"I don't know." She reflected, eyeing her cigaret. "He presumes on them, rather. And a good many men never think a handsome man has any brains."

"Well, he fools them there, too."

She raised her eyebrows slightly.

"Tell me about the new plant, Graham."

"I don't know anything about it yet," he said bluntly. "And you wouldn't be really interested if I did."

"That's rather disagreeable of you."

"No; I'm just trying to talk straight, for once. We-you and I —we always talk around things. I don't know why."

"You look terribly like your father just now. You are quite savage."

"That's exactly what I mean, mother. You don't say father is savage. God knows he isn't that. You just say I act like father, and that I am savage."

Natalie blew a tiny cloud of cigaret smoke, and watched it for a moment.

"You sound fearfully involved. But never mind about that. I daresay I've done something; I don't know what, but of course I am guilty."

"Why did you bring Marion here to-day, mother?"

"Well, if you want to know exactly, I met her coming out of church, and it occurred to me that we were having rather a nice luncheon, and that it would be a pity not to ask some one to come in. It was a nice luncheon, wasn't it?"

"That's why you asked her? For food?"

"Brutally put, but correct."

"You have been asking her here a lot lately. And yet the last time we discussed her you said she was fast. That she wanted to marry me for my money. That people would laugh if I fell for it."

"I hardly used those words, did I?"

"For heaven's sake, mother," he cried, exasperated. "Don't quibble. Let's get down to facts. Does your bringing her here mean that you've changed your mind?"

Natalie considered. She was afraid of too quick a surrender lest he grow suspicious. She decided to temporize, with the affectation of frankness that had once deceived Clayton, and that still, she knew, affected Graham.

"I'll tell you exactly," she said, slowly. "At first I thought it was just an infatuation. And-you really are young, Graham, although you look and act like such a man. But I feel, now that time has gone on and you still care about her, that after all, your happiness is all that matters."

"Mother!"

But she held up her hand.

"Remember, I am only speaking for myself. My dearest wish is to make you happy. You are all I have. But I cannot help you very much. Your father looks at those things differently. He doesn't quite realize that you are grown up, and have a right to decide some things for yourself."

"He has moved me up, raised my salary."

"That's different. You're valuable to him, naturally. I don't mean he doesn't love you," she added hastily, as Graham wheeled and stared at her. "Of course he does, in his own way. It's not my way, but then —I'm only a woman and a mother."

"You think he'll object?"

"I think he must be handled. If you rush at him, and demand the right to live your own life —"

"It is my life."

"Precisely. Only he may not see it that way."

He took a step toward her.

"Mother, do you really want me to marry Marion?"

"I think you ought to be married."

"To Marion?"

"To some one you love."

"Circles again," he muttered. "You've changed your mind, for some reason. What is it, mother?"

He had an uneasy thought that she might have learned of Anna. There was that day, for instance, when his father had walked into the back room.

Natalie was following a train of thought suggested by her own anxiety.

"You might be married quietly," she suggested. "Once it was done, I am sure your father would come around. You are both of age, you know."

He eyed her then with open-eyed amazement.

"I'm darned if I understand you," he burst out. And then, in one of his quick remorses, "I'm sorry, mother. I'm just puzzled, that's all. But that plan's no good, anyhow. Marion won't do it. She will have to be welcome in the family, or she won't come."

"She ought to be glad to come any way she can," Natalie said sharply. And found Graham's eyes on her, studying her.

"You don't want her. That's plain. But you do want her. That's not so plain. What's the answer, mother?"

And Natalie, with an irritable feeing that she had bungled somehow, got up and flung away the cigaret.

"I am trying to give you what you want," she said pettishly. "That's clear enough, I should think."

"There's no other reason?"

"What other reason could there be?"

Dressing to dine at the Hayden's that night, Graham heard Clayton come in and go into his dressing-room. He had an impulse to go over, tie in hand as he was, and put the matter squarely before his father. The marriage-urge —surely a man would understand that. Even Anna, and his predicament there. Anything was better than this constant indirectness of gaining his father's views through his mother.

Had he done so, things would have been different later. But by continual suggestion a vision of his father as hard, detached, immovable, had been built up in his mind. He got as far as the door, hesitated, turned back.

It was Marion herself who solved the mystery of Natalie's changed attitude, when Graham told of it that night. She sat listening, her eyes slightly narrowed, restlessly turning her engagement ring.

"Well, at least that's something," she said, noncommittally. But in her heart she knew, as one designing woman may know another. She knew that Natalie had made Graham promise not to enlist at once, if war was declared, and now she knew that she was desperately preparing to carry her fear for Graham a step further, even at the cost of having her in the family.

She smiled wryly. But there was triumph in the smile, too. She had them now. The time would come when they would crawl to her to marry Graham, to keep him from going to war. Then she would make her own terms.

In the meantime the thing was to hold him by every art she knew.

There was another girl, somewhere. She had been more frightened about that than she cared to admit, even to herself. She must hold him close.

She used every art she knew. She deliberately inflamed him. And the vicious circle closed in about him, Natalie and Marion and Anna Klein. And to offset them, only Delight Haverford, at evening prayer in Saint Luke's, and voicing a tiny petition for him, that he might walk straight, that he might find peace, even if that peace should be war.

Chapter XXIX

Herman Klein, watch between forefinger and thumb, climbed heavily to Anna's room. She heard him pause outside the door, and her heart almost stopped beating. She had been asleep, and rousing at his step, she had felt under the pillow for her watch to see the time. It was not there.

She remembered then; she had left it below, on the table. And he was standing outside her door. She heard him scratching a match, striking it against the panel of her door. For so long as it would take the match to burn out, she heard him there, breathing heavily. Then the knob turned.

She leaped out of the bed in a panic of fear. The hall, like the room, was dark, and she felt his ponderous body in the doorway, rather than saw it.

"You will put on something and come down-stairs," he said harshly.

"I will not." She tried to keep her voice steady. "I've got to work, if you haven't. I've got to have my sleep." Her tone rose, hysterically. "If you think you can stay out half the night, and guzzle beer, and then come here to get me up, you can think again."

"You are already up," he said, in a voice slowed and thickened by rage. "You will come down-stairs."

He turned away and descended the creaking stairs again. She listened for the next move, but he made none. She knew then that he was waiting at the foot of the stairs.

She was half-maddened with terror by that time, and she ran to the window. But it was high. Even if she could have dropped out, and before she could put on enough clothing to escape in, he would be back again, his rage the greater for the delay. She slipped into a kimono, and her knees giving way under her she went down the stairs. Herman was waiting. He moved under the lamp, and she saw that he held the watch, dangling.

"Now!" he said. "Where you got this? Tell me."

"I've told you how I got it."

"That was a lie."

So-Rudolph had told him!

"I like that!" she blustered, trying to gain time. "I guess it's time they gave me something — I've worked hard enough. They gave them to all the girls."

"That is a lie also."

"I like that. Telling me I'm lying. You ask Mr. Graham Spencer. He'll tell you."

"If that is true, why do you shake so?"

"You scare me, father." She burst into frightened tears. "I don't know what's got into you. I do my best. I give you all I make. I've kept this house going, and" —she gained a little courage —"I've had darned little thanks for it."

"You think I believe the mill gave five thousand dollars in watches last Christmas? To-morrow I go, with this to Mr. Clayton Spencer, not to that degenerate son of his, and I ask him. Then I shall know."

He turned, as if about to leave her, but the alternative he offered her was too terrible.

"Father!" she said. "I'll tell you the truth. I bought it myself."

"With what money?"

"I had a raise. I didn't tell you. I had a raise of five dollars a week. I'm paying for it myself. Honest to heaven, that's right, father."

"So-you have had a raise, and you have not told me?"

"I give all the rest to you. What do I get out of all my hard work? Just a place to live. No clothes. No fun. No anything. All the other girls have a good time now and then, but I'm just like a prisoner. You take all I earn, and I get-the devil."

Her voice rose to a terrified squeal. Behind her she heard the slovenly servant creaking down the stairs. As Herman moved toward her she screamed.

"Katie!" she called. "Quick. Help!"

But Herman had caught her by the shoulder and was dragging her toward a corner, where there hung a leather strap.

Katie, peering round the door of the enclosed staircase, saw him raise the strap, and Anna's white face upraised piteously.

"For God's sake, father."

The strap descended. Even after Katie had rushed up the stairs and locked herself in the room, she could hear, above Anna's cries, the thud of the strap, relentless, terrible, lusty with cruelty.

Herman went to church the next morning. Lying in her bed, too sore and bruised to move, Anna heard him carefully polishing his boots on the side porch, heard him throw away the water after he had shaved, heard at last the slam of the gate as he started, upright in his Sunday clothes, for church.

Only when he had reached the end of the street, and Katie could see him picking his way down the blackened hill, did she venture up with a cup of coffee. Anna had to unlock her door to admit her, to remove a further barricade of chairs. When Katie saw her she almost dropped the cup.

"You poor little rat," she said compassionately. "Gee! He was crazy. I never saw such a face. Gee!"

Anna said nothing. She dropped on the side of the bed and took the coffee, drinking gingerly through a lip swollen and cut.

"I'm going to leave," Katie went on. "It'll be my time next. If he tries any tricks on me I'll have the law on him. He's a beast; that's what he is."

"Katie," Anna said, "if I leave can you get my clothes to me? I'll carry all I can."

"He'd take the strap to me."

"Well, if you're leaving anyhow, you can put some of my things in your trunk."

"Good and right you are to get out," Katie agreed. "Sure I'll do it. Where do you think you'll go?"

"I thought last night I'd jump in the river. I've changed my mind, though. I'll pay him back, and not the way he expects."

"Give it to him good," assented Katie. "I'd have liked to slip some of that Paris green of his in his coffee this morning. And now he's off for church, the old hypocrite!"

To Katie's curious inquiries as to the cause of the beating Anna was now too committal.

"I held out some money on him," was all she said.

Katie regarded her with a mixture of awe and admiration.

"You've got your nerve," she said. "I wonder he didn't kill you. What's yours is his and what's his is his own!"

But Anna could not leave that morning. She lay in her bed, cold compresses on her swollen face and shoulders, a bruised and broken thing, planning hideous reprisals. Herman made no inquiry for her. He went stolidly about the day's work, carried in firewood and coal from the shed, inspected the garden with a view to early planting, and ate hugely of the mid-day dinner.

In the afternoon Rudolph came.

"Where's Anna?" he asked briskly.

"She is in her room. She is not well."

If Rudolph suspected anything, it was only that Anna was sulking. But later on he had reason to believe that there trouble. Out of a clear sky Herman said:

"She has had a raise." Anna was "she" to him.

"Since when?" Rudolph asked with interest.

"I know nothing. She has not given it to me. She has been buying herself a watch."

"So!" Rudolph's tone was wary.

"She will buy herself no more watches," said Herman, with an air of finality.

Rudolph hesitated. The organization wanted Herman; he had had great influence with the millworkers. Through him many things would be possible. The Spencers trusted him, too. At any time Rudolph knew they would be glad to reinstate him, and once inside the plant, there was no limit to the mischief he could do. But Herman was too valuable to risk. Suppose he was told now about Graham Spencer and Anna, and beat the girl and was jailed for it? Besides, ugly as Rudolph's suspicions were, they were as yet only suspicions. He decided to wait until he could bring Herman proof of Graham Spencer's relations with Anna. When that time came he knew Herman. He would be clay for the potter. He, Rudolph, intended to be the potter.

Katie had an afternoon off that Sunday. When she came back that night, Herman, weary from the late hours of Saturday, was already snoring in his bed. Anna met Katie at her door and drew her in.

"I've found a nice room," Katie whispered. "Here's the address written down. The street cars go past it. Three dollars a week. Are you ready?"

Anna was ready, even to her hat. Over it she placed a dark veil, for she was badly disfigured. Then, with Katie crying quietly, she left the house. In the flare from the Spencer furnaces Katie watched until the girl reappeared on the twisting street below which still followed the old path-that path where Herman, years ago, had climbed through the first spring wild flowers to the cottage on the hill.

Graham was uncomfortable the next morning on his way to the mill. Anna's face had haunted him. But out of all his confusion one thing stood out with distinctness. If he was to be allowed to marry Marion, he must have no other entanglement. He would go to her clean and clear.

So he went to the office, armed toward Anna with a hardness he was far from feeling.

"Poor little kid!" he reflected on the way down. "Rotten luck, all round."

He did not for a moment believe that it would be a lasting grief. He knew that sort of girl, he reflected, out of his vast experience of twenty-two. They were sentimental, but they loved and forgot easily. He hoped she would forget him; but even with that, there was a vague resentment that she should do so.

"She'll marry some mill-hand," he reflected, "and wear a boudoir cap, and have a lot of children who need their noses wiped."

But he was uncomfortable.

Anna was not in her office. Her coat and hat were not there. He was surprised, somewhat relieved. It was out of his hands, then; she had gone somewhere else to work. Well, she was a good stenographer. Somebody was having a piece of luck.

Clayton, finding him short-handed, sent Joey over to help him pack up his office belongings, the fittings of his desk, his personal papers, the Japanese prints and rugs Natalie had sent after her single visit to the boy's new working quarters. And, when Graham came back from luncheon, Joey had a message for him.

"Telephone call for you, Mr. Spencer."

"What was it?"

"Lady called up, from a pay phone. She left her number and said she'd wait." Joey lowered his voice confidentially. "Sounded like Miss Klein," he volunteered.

He was extremely resentful when Graham sent him away on an errand. And Graham himself frowned as he called the number on the pad. It was like a girl, this breaking off clean and then telephoning, instead of letting the thing go, once and for all. But his face changed as he heard Anna's brief story over the wire.

"Of course I'll come," he said. "I'm pretty busy, but I can steal a half-hour. Don't you worry. We'll fix it up some way."

He was more concerned than deeply anxious when he rang off. It was unfortunate, that was all. And the father was a German swine, and ought to be beaten himself. To think that his Christmas gift had brought her to such a pass! A leather strap! God!

He was vaguely uneasy, however. He had a sense of a situation being forced on him. He knew, too, that Clayton was waiting for him at the new plant. But Anna's trouble, absurd as its cause seemed to him, was his responsibility.

It ceased to be absurd, however, when he saw her discolored features. It would be some time before she could even look for another situation. Her face was a swollen mask, and since such attraction as she had had for him had been due to a sort of evanescent prettiness of youth, he felt a repulsion that he tried his best to conceal.

"You poor little thing!" he said. "He's a brute. I'd like —" He clenched his fists. "Well, I got you into it. I'm certainly going to see you through."

She had lowered her veil quickly, and he felt easier. The telephone booth was in the corner of a quiet hotel, and they were alone. He patted her shoulder.

"I'll see you through," he repeated. "Don't you worry about anything. Just lie low."

"See me through? How?"

"I can give you money; that's the least I can do. Until you are able to work again." And as she drew away, "We'll call it a loan, if that makes you feel better. You haven't anything, have you?"

"He has everything I've earned.. I've never had a penny except carfare."

"Poor little girl!" he said again.

She was still weak, he saw, and he led her into the deserted cafe. He took a highball himself, not because he wanted it, but because she refused to drink, at first. He had never before had a drink in the morning, and he felt a warm and reckless glow to his very finger-tips. Bending toward her, while the waiter's back was turned, he kissed her marred and swollen cheek.

"To think I have brought you all this trouble!"

"You mustn't blame yourself."

"I do. But I'll make it up to you, Anna. You don't hate me for it, do you?"

"Hate you! You know better than that."

"I'll come round to take you out now and then, in the evenings. I don't want you to sit alone in that forsaken boarding-house and mope." He drew out a bill-fold, and extracted some notes. "Don't be silly," he protested, as she drew back. "It's the only way I can get back my self-respect. You owe it to me to let me do it."

She was not hard to persuade. Anything was better than going back to the cottage on the hill, and to that heavy brooding figure, and the strap on the wall. But the taking of the money marked a new epoch in the girl's infatuation. It bought her. She did not know it, nor did he. But hitherto she had been her own, earning her own livelihood. What she gave of love, of small caresses and intimacies, had been free gifts.

From that time she was his creature. In her creed, which was the creed of the girls on the hill, one did not receive without giving. She would pay him back, but all that she had to give was herself.

"You'll come to see me, too. Won't you?"

The tingling was very noticeable now. He felt warm, and young, and very, very strong.

"Of course I'll come to see you," he said, recklessly. "You take a little time off-you've worked hard-and we'll play round together."

She bent down, unexpectedly, and put her bruised cheek against his hand, as it lay on the table.

"I love you dreadfully," she whispered.

Chapter XXX

February and March were peaceful months, on the surface. Washington was taking stock quietly of national resources and watching for Germany's next move. The winter impasse in Europe gave way to the first fighting of spring, raids and sorties mostly, since the ground was still too heavy for the advancement of artillery. On the high seas the reign of terror was in full swing, and little tragic echoes of the world drama began again to come by cable across the Atlantic. Some of Graham's friends, like poor Chris, found the end of the path of glory. The tall young Canadian Highlander died before Peronne in March. Denis Nolan's nephew was killed in the Irish Fusileers.

One day Clayton came home to find a white-faced Buckham taking his overcoat in the hall, and to learn that he had lost a young brother.

Clayton was uncomfortable at dinner that night. He wondered what Buckham thought of them, sitting there around the opulent table, in that luxurious room. Did he resent it? After dinner he asked him if he cared to take a few days off, but the old butler shook his head.

"I'm glad to have my work to keep me busy, sir," he said. "And anyhow, in England, it's considered best to go on, quite as though nothing had happened. It's better for the troops, sir."

There was a new softness and tolerance in Clayton that early spring. He had mellowed, somehow, a mellowing that had nothing to do with his new prosperity. In past times he had wondered how he would stand financial success if it ever came. He had felt fairly sure he could stand the other thing. But success-Now he found that it only increased his sense of responsibility. He was, outside of the war situation, as nearly happy as he had been in years. Natalie's petulant moods, when they came, no longer annoyed him. He was supported, had he only known it, by the strong inner life he was living, a life that centered about his weekly meetings with Audrey.

Audrey gave him courage to go on. He left their comradely hours together better and stronger. All the week centered about that one hour, out of seven days, when he stood on her hearth-rug, or lay back in a deep chair, listening or talking-such talk as Natalie might have heard without resentment.

Some times he felt that that one hour was all he wanted; it carried so far, helped so greatly. He was so boyishly content in it. And then she would make a gesture, or there would be, for a second, a deeper note in her voice, and the mad instinct to catch her to him was almost overwhelming.

Some times he wondered if she were not very lonely, not knowing that she, too, lived for days on that one hour. She was not going out, because of Chris's death, and he knew there were long hours when she sat alone, struggling determinedly with the socks she was knitting.

Only once did they tread on dangerous ground, and that was on her birthday. He stopped in a jeweler's on his way up-town and brought her a black pearl on a thin almost invisible chain, only to have her refuse to take it.

"I can't Clay!"

"Why not?"

"It's too valuable. I can't take valuable presents from men."

"It's value hasn't anything to do with it."

"I'm not wearing jewelry, anyhow."

"Audrey," he said gravely, "it isn't the pearl. It isn't its value. That's absurd. Don't you understand that I would like to think that you have something I have given you?"

When she sat still, thinking over what he had said, he slipped the chain around her neck and clasped it. Then he stooped down, very gravely, and kissed her.

"For my silent partner!" he said.

In all those weeks, that was the only time he had kissed her. He knew quite well the edge of the gulf they stood on, and he was determined not to put the burden of denial on her. He felt a real contempt for men who left the strength of refusal to a woman, who pleaded, knowing that the woman's strength would save them from themselves, and that if she weakened, the responsibility was hers.

So he fed on the husks of love, and was, if not happy, happier.

Graham, too, was getting on better. For one thing, Anna Klein had been ill. She lay in her boarding-house, frightened at every step on the stairs, and slowly recovered from a low fever. Graham had not seen her, but he sent her money for a doctor, for medicines, for her room rent, enclosed in brief letters, purely friendly and interested. But she kept them under her pillow and devoured them with feverish eyes.

But something had gone out of life for Graham. Not Anna. Natalie, watching him closely, wondered what it was. He had been strange and distant with her ever since that tall boy in kilts had been there. He was studiously polite and attentive to her, rose when she entered a room and remained standing until she was seated, brought her the book she had forgotten, lighted her occasional cigaret, kissed her morning and evening. But he no longer came into her dressing-room for that hour before dinner when Natalie, in dressing-gown and slippers, had closed the door to Clayton's room and had kept him for herself.

She was jealous of Clayton those days. Some times she found the boy's eyes fixed on his father, with admiration and something more. She was jealous of the things they had in common, of the days at the mill, of the bits of discussion after dinner, when Clayton sat back with his cigar, and Graham voiced, as new discoveries, things about the work that Clayton had realized for years.

He always listened gravely, with no hint of patronage. But Natalie would break in now and then, impatient of a conversation that excluded her.

"Your father knows all these things, Graham," she said once. "You talk as though you'd just discovered the mill, like Columbus discovering America."

"Not at all," Clayton said, hastily. "He has a new viewpoint. I am greatly interested. Go on, Graham."

But the boy's enthusiasm had died. He grew self-conscious, apologetic. And Clayton felt a resentment that was close to despair.

The second of April fell on a Saturday. Congress, having ended the session the fourth of March, had been hastily reconvened, and on the evening of that day, Saturday, at half past eight, the President went before the two Houses in joint session.

Much to Clayton's disgust, he found on returning home that they were dining out.

"Only at the Mackenzies. It's not a party," Natalie said. As usual, she was before the dressing-table, and she spoke to his reflection in the mirror. "I should think you could do that, without looking like a thunder-cloud. Goodness knows we've been quiet enough this Lent."

"You know Congress has been re-convened?"

"I don't know why that should interfere."

"It's rather a serious time." He tried very hard to speak pleasantly. Her engrossment in her own reflection irritated him, so he did not look at her. "But of course I'll go."

"Every time is a serious time with you lately," she flung after him. Her tone was not disagreeable. She was merely restating an old grievance. A few moments later he heard her calling through the open door.

"I got some wonderful old rugs to-day, Clay."

"Yes?"

"You'll scream when you pay for them."

"I've lost my voice screaming, my dear."

"You'll love these. They have the softest colors, dead rose, and faded blue, and old copper tones."

"I'm very glad you're pleased."

She was in high good humor when they started. Clayton, trying to meet her conversational demands found himself wondering if the significance of what was to happen in Washington that night had struck home to her. If it had, and she could still be cheerful, then it was because she had forced a promise from Graham.

He made his decision then; to force her to release the boy from any promise; to allow him his own choice. But he felt with increasing anxiety that some of Natalie's weakness of character had descended to Graham, that in him, as in Natalie, perhaps obstinacy was what he hoped was strength. He wondered listening to her, what it would be to have beside him that night some strong and quiet woman, to whom he could carry his problems, his perplexities. Some one to sit, hand in his, and set him right as such a woman could, on many things.

And for a moment, he pictured Audrey. Audrey, his wife, driving with him in their car, to whatever the evening might hold. And after it was all over, going back with her, away from all the chatter that meant so little, to the home that shut them in together.

He was very gentle to Natalie that night.

Natalie had been right. It was a small and informal group, gathered together hastily to discuss the emergency; only Denis Nolan, the Mackenzies, Clayton and Natalie, and Audrey.

"We brought her out of her shell," said Terry, genially, "because the country is going to make history to-night. The sort of history Audrey has been shouting for for months."

The little party was very grave. Yet, of them all, only the Spencers would be directly affected. The Mackenzies had no children.

"Button, my secretary," Terry announced, "is in Washington. He is to call me here when the message is finished."

"Isn't it possible," said Natalie, recalling a headline from the evening paper, "that the House may cause an indefinite delay?"

And, as usual, Clayton wondered at the adroitness with which, in the talk that followed, she escaped detection.

They sat long at the table, rather as though they clung together. And Nolan insisted on figuring the cost of war in money.

"Queer thing," he said. "In ancient times the cost of war fell almost entirely on the poor. But it's the rich who will pay for this war. All taxation is directed primarily against the rich."

"The poor pay in blood," said Audrey, rather sharply. "They give their lives, and that is all they have."

"Rich and poor are going to do that, now," old Terry broke in. "Fight against it all you like, you members of the privileged class, the draft is coming. This is every man's war."

But Clayton Spencer was watching Natalie. She had paled and was fingering her liqueur-glass absently. Behind her lowered eyelids he surmised that again she was planning. But what? Then it came to him, like a flash. Old Terry had said the draft would exempt married men. She meant to marry Graham to a girl she detested, to save him from danger.

Through it all, however, and in spite of his anger and apprehension, he was sorry for her. Sorry for her craven spirit. Sorry even with an understanding that came from his own fears. Sorry for her, that she had remained an essential child in a time that would tax the utmost maturity. She was a child. Even her selfishness was the selfishness of a spoiled child. She craved things, and the spirit, the essence of life, escaped her.

And beside him was Audrey, valiant-eyed, courageous, honest. Natalie and Audrey! Some time during the evening his thoughts took this form: that there were two sorts of people in the world: those who seized their own happiness, at any cost; and those who saw the promised land from a far hill, and having seen it, turned back.

Chapter XXXI

Graham was waiting in Clayton's dressing-room when he went up-stairs. Through the closed door they could hear Natalie's sleepy and rather fretful orders to her maid. Graham rose when he entered, and threw away his cigaret.

"I guess it has come, father."

"It looks like it."

A great wave of tenderness for the boy flooded over him. That tall, straight body, cast in his own mold, but young, only ready to live, that was to be cast into the crucible of war, to come out-God alone knew how. And not his boy only, but millions of other boys. Yet-better to break the body than ruin the soul.

"How is mother taking it?"

Natalie's voice came through the door. She was insisting that the house be kept quiet the next morning. She wanted to sleep late. Clayton caught the boy's eyes on him, and a half smile on his face.

"Does she know?"

"Yes."

"She isn't taking it very hard, is she?" Then his voice changed. "I wish you'd talk to her, father. She's —well, she's got me! You see, I promised her not to go in without her consent."

"When did you do that?"

"The night we broke with Germany in February. I was a fool, but she was crying, and I didn't know what else to do. And" —there was a ring of desperation in his voice —"she's holding me to it. I've been to her over and over again."

"And you want to go?"

"Want to go! I've got to go."

He broke out then into a wild appeal. He wanted to get away. He was making a mess of all sorts of things. He wasn't any good. He would try to make good in the army. Maybe it was only the adventure he wanted-he didn't know. He hadn't gone into that. He hated the Germans. He wanted one chance at them, anyhow. They were beasts.

Clayton, listening, was amazed at the depth of feeling and anger in his voice.

"I'll talk to your mother," he agreed, when the boy's passion had spent itself. "I think she will release you." But he was less certain than he pretended to be. He remembered Natalie's drooping eyelids that night at dinner. She might absolve him from the promise, but there were other ways of holding him back than promises.

"Perhaps we would better go into the situation thoroughly," he suggested. "I have rather understood, lately, that you-what about Marion Hayden, Graham?"

"I'm engaged to her."

There was rather a long pause. Clayton's face was expressionless.

"Since when?"

"Last fall, sir."

"Does your mother know?"

"I told her, yes." He looked up quickly. "I didn't tell you. I knew you disliked her, and mother said?" He checked himself. "Marion wanted to wait. She wanted to be welcome when she came into the family."

"I don't so much dislike her as I —disapprove of her."

"That's rather worse, isn't it?"

Clayton was tired. His very spirit was tired. He sat down in his big chair by the fire.

"She is older than you are, you know."

"I don't see what that has to do with it, father."

In Clayton's defense was his own situation. He did not want the boy to repeat his mistakes, to marry the wrong woman, and then find, too late, the right one. During the impassioned appeal that followed he was doggedly determined to prevent that. Perhaps he lost the urgency in the boy's voice. Perhaps in his new conviction that the passions of the forties were the only real ones, he took too little count of the urge of youth.

He roused himself.

"You think you are really in love with her?"

"I want her. I know that."

"That's different. That's —you are too young to know what you want."

"I ought to be married. It would settle me. I'm sick of batting round."

"You want to marry before you enter the army?"

"Yes."

"Do you think for a moment that your wife will be willing to let you go?"

Graham straightened himself.

"She would have to let me go."

And in sheer despair, Clayton played his last card. Played it, and regretted it bitterly a moment later.

"We must get this straight, Graham. It's not a question of your entering the army or not doing it. It's a question of your happiness. Marriage is a matter of a life-time. It's got to be based on something more than —" he hesitated. "And your mother?"

"Please go on."

"You have just said that your mother does not want you to go into the army. Has it occurred to you she would even see you married to a girl she detests, to keep you at home?"

Graham's face hardened.

"So;" he said, heavily, "Marion wants me for the money she thinks I'm going to have, and mother wants me to marry to keep me safe! By God, it's a dirty world, isn't it?"

Suddenly he was gone, and Clayton, following uneasily to the doorway, heard a slam below. When, some hours later, Graham had not come back, he fell into the heavy sleep that follows anxiety and brings no rest. In the morning he found that Graham had gone back to the garage and taken his car, and that he had not returned.

Afterward Clayton was to look back and to remember with surprise how completely the war crisis had found him absorbed in his own small group. But perhaps in the back of every man's mind war was always, first of all, a thing of his own human contacts. It was only when those were cleared up that he saw the bigger problem. The smaller questions loomed so close as to obscure the larger vision.

He went out into the country the next day, a cold Sunday, going afoot, his head down against the wind, and walked for miles. He looked haggard and tired when he came back, but his quiet face held a new resolve. War had come at last. He would put behind him the selfish craving for happiness, forget himself. He would not make money out of the nation's necessity. He would put Audrey out of his mind, if not out of his heart. He would try to rebuild his house of life along new and better lines. Perhaps he could bring Natalie to see things as he saw them, as they were, not as she wanted them to be.

Some times it took great crises to bring out women. Child-bearing did it, often. Urgent need did it, too. But after all the real test was war. The big woman met it squarely, took her part of the burden; the small woman weakened, went down under it, found it a grievance rather than a grief.

He did not notice Graham's car when it passed him, outside the city limits, or see Anna Klein's startled eyes as it flashed by.

Graham did not come in until evening. At ten o'clock Clayton found the second man carrying up-stairs a tray containing whisky and soda, and before he slept he heard a tap at Graham's door across the hall, and surmised that he had rung for another. Later still he heard Natalie cross the hall, and rather loud and angry voices. He considered, ironically, that a day which had found a part of the nation on its knees found in his own house only dissension and bitterness.

In the morning, at the office, Joey announced a soldier to see him, and added, with his customary nonchalance:

"We'll be having a lot of them around now, I expect."

Clayton, glancing up from the visitor's slip in his hand, surprised something wistful in the boy's eyes.

"Want to go, do you?"

"Give my neck to go-sir." He always added the "sir," when he remembered it, with the air of throwing a sop to a convention he despised.

"You may yet, you know. This thing is going to last a while. Send him in, Joey."

He had grown attached to this lad of the streets. He found in his loyalty a thing he could not buy.

Jackson was his caller. Clayton, who had been rather more familiar with his back in its gray livery than with any other aspect of him, found him strange and impressive in khaki.

"I'm sorry I couldn't get here sooner, Mr. Spencer," he explained. "I've been down on the border. Yuma. I just got a short leave, and came back to see my family."

He stood very erect, a bronzed and military figure. Suddenly it seemed strange to Clayton Spencer that this man before him had only a few months before opened his automobile door for him, and stood waiting with a rug to spread over his knees. He got up and shook hands.

"You look like a different man, Jackson."

"Well, at least I feel like a man."

"Sit down," he said. And again it occurred to him that never before had he asked Jackson to sit down in his presence. It was wrong, somehow. The whole class system was absurd. Maybe war would change that, too. It was doing many queer things, already.

He had sent for Jackson, but he did not at once approach the reason. He sat back, while Jackson talked of the border and Joey slipped in and pretended to sharpen lead pencils.

Clayton's eyes wandered to the window. Outside in the yard were other men, now employees of his, who would soon be in khaki. Out of every group there in a short time some would be gone, and of those who would go a certain number would never come back. That was what war was; one day a group of men, laboring with their hands or their brains, that some little home might live; that they might go back at evening to that home, and there rest for the next day's toil. And the next, gone. Every man out there in the yard was loved by some one. To a certain number of them this day meant death, or wounding. It meant separation, and suffering, and struggle.

And all over the country there were such groups.

The roar of the plant came in through the open window. A freight car was being loaded with finished shells. As fast as it was filled, another car was shunted along the spur to take its place. Over in Germany, in hundreds of similar plants, similar shells were being hurried to the battle line, to be hurled against the new army that was soon to cross the seas.

All those men, and back of every man, a woman.

Jackson had stopped. Joey was regarding him with stealthy admiration, and holding his breast bone very high. Already in his mind Joey was a soldier.

"You did not say in your note why you wanted to see me, Mr. Spencer."

He roused himself with a visible effort.

"I sent for you, yes," he said. "I sent —I'll tell you why I sent for you, Jackson. I've been meaning to do it for several weeks. Now that this has come I'm more than glad I did so. You can't keep your family on what you are getting. That's certain."

"My wife is going to help me, sir. The boy will soon be weaned. Then she intends to get a position. She was a milliner when we were married."

"But-Great Scott! She ought not to leave a child as young as that."

Jackson smiled.

"She's going to fix that, all right. She wants to do it. And we're all right so far I had saved a little."

Then there were women like that! Women who would not only let their men go to war, but who would leave their homes and enter the struggle for bread, to help them do it.

"She says it's the right thing," volunteered Jackson, proudly. Women who felt that a man going into the service was a right thing. Women who saw war as a duty to be done, not a wild adventure for the adventurous.

"You ought to be very proud of her," he said slowly. "There are not many like that."

"Well," Jackson said, apologetically, "they'll come round, sir. Some of them kind of hate the idea, just at first. But I look to see a good many doing what my wife's doing."

Clayton wondered grimly what Jackson would think if he knew that at that moment he was passionately envious of him, of his uniform, of the youth that permitted him to wear that uniform, of his bronzed skin, of his wife, of his pride in that wife.

"You're a lucky chap, Jackson," he said. "I sent for you because I wanted to say that, as long as you are in the national service, I shall feel that you are on a vacation" —he smiled at the word —"on pay. Under those circumstances, I owe you quite a little money."

Jackson was too overwhelmed to reply at once.

"As a matter of fad," Clayton went on, "it's a national move, in a way. You don't owe any gratitude. We need our babies, you see. More than we do hats! If this war goes on, we shall need a good many boy babies."

And his own words suddenly crystallized the terror that was in him. It was the boys who would go; boys who whistled in the morning; boys who dreamed in the spring, long dreams of romance and of love.

Boys. Not men like himself, with their hopes and dreams behind them. Not men who had lived enough to know that only their early dreams were real. Not men, who, having lived, knew the vast disillusion of living and were ready to die.

It was only after Jackson had gone that he saw the fallacy of his own reasoning. If to live were disappointment, then to die, still dreaming the great dream, was not wholly evil. He found himself saying,

"To earn some honorable advancement for one's soul."

Deep down in him, overlaid with years of worldliness, there was a belief in a life after death. He looked out the window at the little, changing group. In each man out there there was something that would live on, after he had shed that sweating, often dirty, always weary, sometimes malformed shell that was the body. And then the thing that would count would be not how he had lived but what he had done.

This war was a big thing. It was the biggest thing in all the history of the world. There might be, perhaps, some special heaven for those who had given themselves to it, some particular honorable advancement for their souls. Already he saw Jackson as one apart, a man dedicated.

Then he knew that all his thinking was really centered about his boy. He wanted Graham to go. But in giving him he was giving him to the chance of death. Then he must hold to his belief in eternity. He must feel that, or the thing would be unbearable. For the first time in his life he gave conscious thought to Natalie's religious belief. She believed in those things. She must. She sat devoutly through the long service; she slipped, with a little rustle of soft silk, so easily to her knees. Perhaps, if he went to her with that?

Chapter XXXII

For a week after Anna's escape Herman Klein had sat alone and brooded. Entirely alone now, for following a stormy scene on his discovery of Anna's disappearance, Katie had gone too.

"I don't know where she is," she had said, angrily, "and if I did know I wouldn't tell you. If I was her I'd have the law on you. Don't you look at that strap. You lay a hand on me and I'll kill you. If you think I'm afraid of you, you can think again."

"She is my daughter, and not yet of age," Herman said heavily. "You tell her for me that she comes back, or I go and bring her."

"Yah!" Katie jeered. "You try it! She's got marks on her that'll jail you." And on his failure to reply her courage mounted. "This ain't Germany, you know. They know how to treat women over here. And you ask me" —her voice rose —"and I'll just say that there's queer comings and goings here with that Rudolph. I've heard him say some things that'll lock him up good and tight."

For all his rage, Teutonic caution warned him not to lay hands on the girl. But his anger against her almost strangled him. Indeed, when she came down stairs, dragging her heavy suitcase, he took a step or two toward her, with his fists clenched. She stopped, terrified.

"You old bully!" she said, between white lips. "You touch me, and I'll scream till I bring in every neighbor in the block. There's a good lamp-post outside that's just waiting for your sort of German."

He had refused to pay her for the last week, also. But that she knew well enough was because he was out of money. As fast as Anna's salary had come in, he had taken out of it the small allowance that was to cover the week's expenses, and had banked the remainder. But Anna had carried her last pay envelope away with her, and added to his anger at her going was his fear that he would have to draw on his savings.

With Katie gone, he set heavily about preparing his Sunday dinner. Long years of service done for him, however, had made him clumsy. He cooked a wretched meal, and then, leaving the dishes as they were, he sat by the fire and brooded. When Rudolph came in, later, he found him there, in his stocking-feet, a morose and untidy figure.

Rudolph's reception of the news roused him, however. He looked up, after the telling, to find the younger man standing over him and staring down at him with blood-shot eyes.

"You beat her!" he was saying. "What with?"

"What does that matter-She had bought herself a watch —"

"What did you beat her with?" Rudolph was licking his lips. Receiving no reply, he called "Katie!"

"Katie has gone."

"Maybe you beat her, too."

"She wasn't my daughter."

"No by God! You wouldn't dare to touch her. She didn't belong to you. You —"

"Get out," said Herman, somberly. He stood up menacingly. "You go, now."

Rudolph hesitated. Then he laughed.

"All right, old top," he said, in a conciliatory tone. "No offense meant. I lost my temper."

He picked up the empty coal-scuffle, and went out into the shed where the coal was kept. He needed a minute to think. Besides, he always brought in coal when he was there. In the shed, however, he put down the scuttle and stood still.

"The old devil!" he muttered.

But his rage for Anna was followed by rage against her. Where was she to-night? Did Graham Spencer know where she was? And if he did, what then? Were they at that moment somewhere together? Hidden away, the two of them? The conviction that they were together grew on him, and with it a frenzy that was almost madness. He left the coal scuttle in the shed, and went out into the air. For a half hour he stood there, looking down toward the Spencer furnace, sending up, now red, now violet bursts of flame.

He was angry enough, jealous enough. But he was quick, too, to see that that particular lump of potters' clay which was Herman Klein was ready for the wheel. Even while he was cursing the girl his cunning mind was already plotting, revenge for the Spencers, self-aggrandizement among his fellows for himself. His inordinate conceit, wounded by Anna's defection, found comfort in the early prospect of putting over a big thing. He carried the coal in, to find Herman gloomily clearing his untidy table. For a moment they worked in silence, Rudolph at the stove, Herman at the sink.

Then Rudolph washed his hands under the faucet and faced the older man. "How do you know she bought herself that watch," he demanded.

Herman eyed him.

"Perhaps you gave it to her!" Something like suspicion of Rudolph crept into his eyes.

"Me? A hundred-dollar watch!"

"How do you know it cost a hundred dollars?"

"I saw it. She tried that story on me, too. But I was too smart for her. I went to the store and asked. A hundred bucks!"

Herman's lips drew back over his teeth.

"You knew it, eh? And you did not tell me?"

"It wasn't my funeral," said Rudolph coolly. "If you wanted to believe she bought it herself?"

"If she bought it herself!" Rudolph's shoulder was caught in an iron grip. "You will tell me what you mean."

"Well, I ask you, do you think she'd spend that much on a watch? Anyhow, the installment story doesn't go. That place doesn't sell on installments."

"Who is there would buy her such a watch?" Herman's voice was thick.

"How about Graham Spencer? She's been pretty thick with him."

"How you mean-thick?"

Rudolph shrugged his shoulders.

"I don't mean anything. But he's taken her out in his car. And the Spencers think there's nothing can't be bought with money."

Herman put down the dish-cloth and commenced to draw down his shirt sleeves.

"Where you going?" Rudolph demanded uneasily.

"I go to the Spencers!"

"Listen!" Rudolph said, excitedly. "Don't you do it; not yet. You got to get him first. We don't know anything; we don't even know he gave her that watch. We've got to find her, don't you see? And then, we've got to learn if he's going there-wherever she is."

"I shall bring her back," Herman said, stubbornly. "I shall bring her back, and I shall kill her."

"And get strung up yourself! Now listen?" he argued. "You leave this to me. I'll find her. I've got a friend, a city detective, and he'll help me, see? We'll get her back, all right. Only you've got to keep your hands off her. It's the Spencers that have got to pay."

Herman went back to the sink, slowly.

"That is right. It is the Spencers," he muttered.

Rudolph went out. Late in the evening he came back, with the news that the search was on. And, knowing Herman's pride, he assured him that the hill need never learn of Anna's flight, and if any inquiries came he advised him to say the girl was sick.

In Rudolph's twisted mind it was not so much Anna's delinquency that enraged him. The hill had its own ideas of morality. But he was fiercely jealous, with that class-jealousy which was the fundamental actuating motive of his life. He never for a moment doubted that she had gone to Graham.

And, sitting by the fire in the little house, old Herman's untidy head shrunk on his shoulders, Rudolph almost forgot Anna in plotting to use this new pawn across the hearth from him in his game of destruction.

By the end of the week, however, there was no news of Anna. She had not returned to the mill. Rudolph's friend on the detective force had found no clew, and old Herman had advanced from brooding by the fire to long and furious wanderings about the city streets.

He felt no remorse, only a growing and alarming fury. He returned at night, to his cold and unkempt house, to cook himself a frugal and wretched meal. His money had run very low, and with true German stubbornness he refused to draw any from the savings bank.

Rudolph was very busy. There were meetings always, and to the little inner circle that met behind Gus's barroom one night later in March, he divulged the plan for the destruction of the new Spencer munition plant.

"But-will they take him back?" one of the men asked. He was of better class than the rest, with a military bearing and a heavy German accent, for all his careful English.

"Will a dog snatch at a bone?" countered Rudolph. "Take him back! They'll be crazy about it."

"He has been there a long time. He may, at the last, weaken."

But Rudolph only laughed, and drank more whisky of the German agent's providing.

"He won't weaken," he said. "Give me a few days more to find the girl, and all hell won't hold him."

On the Sunday morning after the President had been before Congress, he found Herman dressed for church, but sitting by the fire. All around him lay the Sunday paper, and he barely raised his head when Rudolph entered.

"Well, it's here!" said Rudolph.

"It has come. Yes."

"Wall Street will be opening champagne to-day."

Herman said nothing. But later on he opened up the fountain of rage in his heart. It was wrong, all wrong. We had no quarrel with Germany. It was the capitalists and politicians who had done it. And above all, England.

He went far. He blamed America and Americans for his loss of work, for Anna's disappearance. He searched his mind for grievances and found them in the ore dust on the hill, which killed his garden; in the inefficiency of the police, who could not find Anna; in the very attitude of Clayton Spencer toward his resignation.

And on this smoldering fire Rudolph piled fuel Not that he said a great deal. He worked around the cottage, washed dishes, threw pails of water on the dirty porches, swept the floor, carried in coal and wood. And gradually he began to play on the older man's vanity. He had had great influence with the millworkers. No one man had ever had so much.

Old Herman sat up, and listened sourly. But after a time he got up and pouring some water out of the kettle, proceeded to shave himself. And Rudolph talked on. If now he were to go back, and it were to the advantage of the Fatherland and of the workers of the world to hamper the industry, who so able to do it as Herman.

"Hamper? How?" Herman asked, suspiciously, holding his razor aloft. He had a great fear of the law.

Rudolph re-assured him, cunning eyes averted.

"Well, a strike," he suggested. "The men'll listen to you. God knows they've got a right to strike."

"I shall not go back," said Herman stolidly, and finished his shaving.

But Rudolph was satisfied. He left Herman sitting again by the fire, but his eyes were no longer brooding. He was thinking, watching the smoke curl up from the china-bowled German pipe which he had brought from the Fatherland, and which he used only on special occasions.

Chapter XXXIII

The declaration of war found Graham desperately unhappy. Natalie held him rigidly to his promise, but it is doubtful if Natalie alone could have kept, him out of the army. Marion was using her influence, too! She held him by alternating between almost agreeing to runaway marriage and threats of breaking the engagement if he went to war. She had tacitly agreed to play Natalie's game, and she was doing it.

Graham did not analyze his own misery. What he said to himself was that he was making a mess of things. Life, which had seemed to be a simple thing, compounded of work and play, had become involved, difficult and wretched.

Some times he watched Clayton almost with envy. He seemed so sure of himself; he was so poised, so calm, so strong. And he wondered if there had been a tumultuous youth behind the quiet of his maturity. He compared the even course of Clayton's days, his work, his club, the immaculate orderliness of his life, with his own disordered existence.

He was hedged about with women. Wherever he turned, they obtruded themselves. He made plans and women brushed them aside. He tried to live his life, and women stepped in and lived it for him. His mother, Marion, Anna Klein. Even Delight, with her friendship always overclouded with disapproval. Wherever he turned, a woman stood in the way. Yet he could not do without them. He needed them even while he resented them.

Then, gradually, into his self-engrossment there penetrated a conviction that all was not well between his father and his mother. He had always taken them for granted much as he did the house and the servants. In his brief vacations during his college days they had agreed or disagreed, amicably enough. He had considered, in those days, that life was a very simple thing. People married and lived together. Marriage, he considered, was rather the end of things.

But he was older now, and he knew that marriage was a beginning and not an end. It did not change people fundamentally. It only changed their habits.

His discovery that his father and mother differed about the war was the first of other discoveries; that they differed about him; that they differed about many matters; that, indeed, they had no common ground at all on which to meet; between them, although Graham did not put it that way, was a No-Man's Land strewn with dead happiness, lost desires, and the wreckage of years of dissension.

It was incredible to Graham that he should ever reach the forties, but he wondered some times if all of life was either looking forward or looking back. And it seemed to him rather tragic that for Clayton, who still looked like a boy, there should be nothing but his day at the mill, his silent evening at home, or some stodgy dinner-party where the women were all middle-aged, and the other men a trifle corpulent.

For the first time he was beginning to think of Clayton as a man, rather than a father.

Not that all of this was coherently thought out. It was a series of impressions, outgrowth of his own beginning development and of his own uneasiness.

He wondered, too, about Rodney Page. He seemed to be always around, underfoot, suave, fastidious, bowing Natalie out of the room and in again. He had deplored the war until he found his attitude unfashionable, and then he began, with great enthusiasm, to arrange pageants for Red Cross funds, and even to make little speeches, graceful and artificial, patterned on his best after-dinner manner.

Graham was certain that he supported his mother in trying to keep him at home, and he began to hate him with a healthy young hate. However, late in April, he posed in one of the pageants, rather ungraciously, in a khaki uniform. It was not until the last minute that he knew that Delight Haverford was to be the nurse bending over his prostrate figure. He turned rather savage.

"Rotten nonsense," he said to her, "when they stood waiting to be posed.

"Oh, I don't know. They're rather pretty."

"Pretty! Do you suppose I want it be pretty?"

"Well, I do," said Delight, calmly.

"It's fake. That's what I hate. If you were really a nurse, and was really in uniform —! But this parading in somebody else's clothes, or stuff hired for the occasion-it's sickening."

Delight regarded him with clear, appraising eyes.

"Why don't you get a uniform of your own, then?" she inquired. She smiled a little.

He never knew what the effort cost her. He was pale and angry, and his face in the tableau was so set that it brought a round of applause. With the ringing down of the curtain he confronted her, almost menacingly.

"What did you mean by that?" he demanded. "We've hardly got into this thing yet."

"We are in it, Graham."

"Just because I don't leap into the first recruiting office and beg them to take me-what right have you got to call me a slacker?"

"But I heard —"

"Go on!"

"It doesn't matter what I heard, if you are going."

"Of course I'm going," he said, truculently.

He meant it, too. He would get Anna settled somewhere-she had begun to mend-and then he would have it out with Marion and his mother. But there was no hurry. The war would last a long time. And so it was that Graham Spencer joined the long line of those others who had bought a piece of ground, or five yoke of oxen, or had married a wife.

It was the morning after the pageant that Clayton, going down-town with him in the car, voiced his expectation that the government would take over their foreign contracts, and his feeling that, in that case, it would be a mistake to profit by the nation's necessities.

"What do you mean, sir?"

"I mean we should take only a small profit. A banker's profit."

Graham had been fairly stunned, and had sat quiet while Clayton explained his attitude. There were times when big profits were allowable. There was always the risk to invested capital to consider. But he did not want to grow fat on the nation's misfortunes. Italy was one thing. This was different.

"But-we are just getting on our feet!"

"Think it over!" said Clayton. "This is going to be a long war, and an expensive one. We don't particularly want to profit by it, do we?"

Graham flushed. He felt rather small and cheap, but with that there was a growing admiration of his father. Suddenly he saw that this man beside him was a big man, one to be proud of. For already he knew the cost of the decision. He sat still, turning this new angle of war over in his mind.

"I'd like to see some of your directors when you put that up to them!"

Clayton nodded rather grimly. He did not anticipate a pleasant hour.

"How about mother?"

"I think we may take it for granted that she feels as we do."

Graham pondered that, too.

"What about the new place?"

"It's too soon to discuss that. We are obligated to do a certain amount. Of course it would be wise to cut where we can."

Graham smiled.

"She'll raise the deuce of a row," was his comment.

It had never occurred to him before to take sides between his father and his mother, but there was rising in him a new and ardent partisanship of his father, a feeling that they were, in a way, men together. He had, more than once, been tempted to go to him with the Anna Klein situation. He would have, probably, but a fellow felt an awful fool going to somebody and telling him that a girl was in love with him, and what the dickens was he to do about it?

He wondered, too, if anybody would believe that his relationship with Anna was straight, under the circumstances. For weeks now he had been sending her money, out of a sheer sense of responsibility for her beating and her illness. He took no credit for altruism. He knew quite well the possibilities of the situation. He made no promises to himself. But such attraction as Anna had had for him had been of her prettiness, and their propinquity. Again she was girl, and that was all. And the attraction was very faint now. He was only sorry for her.

When she could get about she took to calling him up daily from a drug-store at a near-by corner, and once he met her after dark and they walked a few blocks together. She was still weak, but she was spiritualized, too. He liked her a great deal that night.

"Do you know you've loaned me over a hundred dollars, Graham?" she asked.

"That's not a loan. I owed you that."

"I'll pay it back. I'm going to start to-morrow to look for work, and it won't cost me much to live."

"If you send it back, I'll buy you another watch!"

And, tragic as the subject was, they both laughed.

"I'd have died if I hadn't had you to think about when I was sick, Graham. I wanted to die-except for you."

He had kissed her then, rather because he knew she expected him to. When they got back to the house she said:

"You wouldn't care to come up?"

"I don't think I had better, Anna."

"The landlady doesn't object. There isn't any parlor. All the girls have their callers in their rooms."

"I have to go out to-night," he said evasively. "I'll come some other time."

As he started away he glanced back at her. She was standing in the doorway, eying him wistfully, a lonely and depressed little figure. He was tempted to throw discretion to the wind and go back. But he did not.

On the day when Clayton had broached the subject of offering their output to the government at only a banker's profit, Anna called him up at his new office in the munition plant.

He was rather annoyed. His new secretary was sitting across the desk, and it was difficult to make his responses noncommittal.

"Graham!"

"Yes."

"Is anybody there? Can you talk?"

"Not very well."

"Then listen; I'll talk. I want to see you."

"I'm busy all day. Sorry."

"Listen, Graham, I must see you. I've something to tell you."

"All right, go ahead."

"It's about Rudolph. I was out looking for a position yesterday and I met him."

"Yes?"

He looked up. Miss Peterson was absently scribbling on the cover of her book, and listening intently.

"He was terrible, Graham. He accused me of all sorts of things, about you."

He almost groaned aloud over the predicament he was in. It began to look serious.

"Suppose I pick you up and we have dinner somewhere?"

"At the same corner?"

"Yes."

He was very irritable all morning. He felt as though a net was closing in around him, and his actual innocence made him the more miserable. Miss Peterson found him very difficult that day, and shed tears in her little room before she went to lunch.

Anna herself was difficult that evening. Her landlady's son had given up a good job and enlisted. Everybody was going. She supposed Graham would go next, and she'd be left alone.

"I don't know. I'd like to."

"Oh, you'll go, all right. And you'll forget I ever existed." She made an effort. "You're right, of course. I'm only looking ahead. If anything happens to you, I'll kill myself."

The idea interested her. She began to dramatize herself, a forlorn figure, driven from home, and deserted by her lover. She saw herself lying in the cottage, stately and mysterious, while the hill girls went in and out, and whispered.

"I'll kill myself," she repeated.

"Nothing will happen to me, Anna, dear."

"I don't know why I care so. I'm nothing to you."

"That's not so."

"If you cared, you'd have come up the other night. You left me alone in that lonesome hole. It's hell, that place. All smells and whispering and dirt."

"Now listen to me, Anna. You're tired, or you wouldn't say that. You know I'm fond of you. But I've got you into trouble enough. I'm not-for God's sake don't tempt me, Anna."

She looked at him half scornfully.

"Tempt you!" Then she gave a little scream. Graham following her eyes looked through the window near them.

"Rudolph!" she whimpered. And began to weep out of pure terror.

But Graham saw nobody. To soothe her, however, he went outside and looked about. There were half a dozen cars, a group of chauffeurs, but no Rudolph. He went hack to her, to find her sitting, pale and tense, her hands clenched together.

"They'll pay you out some way," she said. "I know them. They'll never believe the truth. That was Rudolph, all right. He'll think we're living together. He'd never believe anything else."

"Do you think he followed you the other day?"

"I gave him the shake, in the crowd."

"Then I don't see why you're worrying. We're just where we were before, aren't we?"

"You don't know them. I do. They'll be up to something."

She was excited and anxious, and with the cocktail he ordered for her she grew reckless.

"I'm just hung around your neck like a stone," she lamented. "You don't care a rap for me; I know it. You're just sorry for me."

Her eyes filled again, and Graham rose, with an impatient movement.

"Let's get out of this," he said roughly. "The whole place is staring at you."

But on the road the fact that she had been weeping for him made him relent. He put an arm around her and drew her to him.

"Don't cry, honey," he said. "It makes me unhappy to see you miserable."

He kissed her. And they clung together, finding a little comfort in the contact of warm young bodies.

He went up to her room that night. He was more anxious as to Rudolph than he cared to admit, but he went up, treading softly on stairs that creaked with every step. He had no coherent thoughts. He wanted companionship rather than love. He was hungry for what she gave him, the touch of her hands about his neck, the sense of his manhood that shone from her faithful eyes, the admiration and unstinting love she offered him.

But alone in the little room he had a reaction, not the less keen because it was his fastidious rather than his moral sense that revolted. The room was untidy, close, sordid. Even Anna's youth did not redeem it. Again he had the sense, when he had closed the door, of being caught in a trap, and this time a dirty trap. When she had taken off her hat, and held up her face to be kissed, he knew he would not stay.

"It's awful, isn't it?" she asked, following his eyes.

"It doesn't look like you. That's sure."

"I hurried out. It's not so bad when it's tidy."

He threw up the window, and stood there a moment. The spring air was cool and clean, and there was a sound of tramping feet below. He looked down. The railway station was near-by, and marching toward it, with the long swing of regulars, a company of soldiers was moving rapidly. The night, the absence of drums or music, the businesslike rapidity of their progress, held him there, looking down. He turned around. Anna had slipped off her coat, and had opened the collar of her blouse. Her neck gleamed white and young. She smiled at him.

"I guess I'll be going," he stammered.

"Going!"

"I only wanted to see how you are fixed." His eyes evaded hers. "I'll see you again in a day or two. I —"

He could not tell her the thoughts that were surging in him. The country was at war. Those fellows below there were already in it, of it. And here in this sordid room, he had meant to take her, not because he loved her, but because she offered herself. It was cheap. It was terrible. It was-dirty.

"Good night," he said, and tried to kiss her. But she turned her face away. She stood listening to his steps on the stairs as he went down, steps that mingled and were lost in the steady tramp of the soldiers' feet in the street below.

Chapter XXXIV

With his many new problems following the declaration of war, Clayton Spencer found a certain peace. It was good to work hard. It was good to fill every working hour, and to drop into sleep at night too weary for consecutive thought.

Yet had he been frank with himself he would have acknowledged that Audrey was never really out of his mind. Back of his every decision lay his desire for her approval. He did not make them with her consciously in his mind, but he wanted her to know and understand, In his determination, for instance, to offer his shells to the government at a nominal profit, there was no desire to win her approbation.

It was rather that he felt her behind him in the decision. He shrank from telling Natalie. Indeed, until he had returned from Washington he did not broach the subject. And then he was tired and rather discouraged, and as a result almost brutally abrupt.

Coming on top of a hard fight with the new directorate, a fight which he had finally won, Washington was disheartening. Planning enormously for the future it seemed to have no vision for the things of the present. He was met vaguely, put off, questioned. He waited hours, as patiently as he could, to find that no man seemed to have power to act, or to know what powers he had.

He found something else, too —a suspicion of him, of his motives. Who offered something for nothing must be actuated by some deep and hidden motive. He found his plain proposition probed and searched for some ulterior purpose behind it.

"It's the old distrust, Mr. Spencer," said Hutchinson, who had gone with him to furnish figures and various data. "The Democrats are opposed to capital. They're afraid of it. And the army thinks all civilians are on the make-which is pretty nearly true."

He saw the Secretary of War, finally, and came away feeling better. He had found there an understanding that a man may-even should-make sacrifices for his country during war. But, although he carried away with him the conviction that his offer would ultimately be accepted, there was nothing actually accomplished. He sent Hutchinson back, and waited for a day or two, convinced that his very sincerity must bring a concrete result, and soon.

Then, lunching alone one day in the Shoreham, he saw Audrey Valentine at another table. He had not seen her for weeks, and he had an odd moment of breathlessness when his eyes fell on her. She was pale and thin, and her eyes looked very tired. His first impulse was to go to her. The second, on which he acted, was to watch her for a little, to fill his eyes for the long months of emptiness ahead.

She was with a man in uniform, a young man, gay and smiling. He was paying her evident court, in a debonair fashion, bending toward her across the table. Suddenly Clayton was jealous, fiercely jealous.

The jealousy of the young is sad enough, but it is an ephemeral thing. Life calls from many directions. There is always the future, and the things of the future. And behind it there is the buoyancy and easy forgetfulness of youth. But the jealousy of later years knows no such relief. It sees time flying and happiness evading it. It has not the easy self-confidence of the twenties. It has learned, too, that happiness is a rare elusive thing, to be held and nursed and clung to, and that even love must be won and held.

It has learned that love must be free, but its instinct is to hold it with chains.

He suffered acutely, and was ashamed of his suffering. After all, Audrey was still young. Life had not been kind to her, and she should be allowed to have such happiness as she could. He could offer her nothing.

He would give her up. He had already given her up. She knew it.

Then she saw him, and his determination died under the light that came in her eyes. Give her up! How could he give her up, when she was everything he had in the world? With a shock, he recognized in the thought Natalie's constant repetition as to Graham. So he had come to that!

He felt Audrey's eyes on him, but he did not go to her. He signed his check, and went out. He fully meant to go away without seeing her. But outside he hesitated. That would hurt her, and it was cowardly. When, a few moments later, she came out, followed by the officer, it was to find him there, obviously waiting.

"I wondered if you would dare to run away!" she said. "This is Captain Sloane, Clay, and he knows a lot about you."

Close inspection showed Sloane handsome, bronzed, and with a soft Southern voice, some-what like Audrey's. And it developed that he came from her home, and was on his way to one of the early camps. He obviously intended to hold on to Audrey, and Clayton left them there with the feeling that Audrey's eyes were following him, wistful and full of trouble. He had not even asked her where she was stopping.

He took a long walk that afternoon, and re-made his noon-hour resolution. He would keep away from her. It might hurt her at first, but she was young. She would forget. And he must not stand in her way. Having done which, he returned to the Shoreham and spent an hour in a telephone booth, calling hotels systematically and inquiring for her.

When he finally located her his voice over the wire startled her.

"Good heavens, Clay," she said. "Are you angry about anything?"

"Of course not. I just wanted to —I am leaving to-night and I'm saying good-by. That's all."

"Oh!" She waited.

"Have you had a pleasant afternoon?"

"Aren't you going to see me before you go?"

"I don't think so."

"Don't you want to know what I am doing in Washington?"

"That's fairly clear, isn't it?"

"You are being rather cruel, Clay."

He hesitated. He was amazed at his own attitude. Then, "Will you dine with me to-night?"

"I kept this evening for you."

But when he saw her, his sense of discomfort only increased. Their dining together was natural enough. It was not even faintly clandestine. But the new restraint he put on himself made him reserved and unhappy. He could not act a part. And after a time Audrey left off acting, too, and he found her watching him. On the surface he talked, but underneath it he saw her unhappiness, and her understanding of his.

"I'm going back, too," she said. "I came down to see what I can do, but there is nothing for the untrained woman. She's a cumberer of the earth. I'll go home and knit. I daresay I ought to be able to learn to do that well, anyhow."

"Have you forgiven me for this afternoon?"

"I wasn't angry. I understood."

That was it, in a nutshell. Audrey understood. She was that sort. She never held small resentments. He rather thought she never felt them.

"Don't talk about me," she said. "Tell me about you and why you are here. It's the war, of course."

So, rather reluctantly, he told her. He shrank from seeming to want her approval, but at the same time he wanted it. His faith in himself had been shaken. He needed it restored. And some of the exaltation which had led him to make his proffer to the government came back when he saw how she flushed over it.

"It's very big," she said, softly. "It's like you, Clay. And that's the best thing I can say. I am very proud of you."

"I would rather have you proud of me than anything in the world," he said, unsteadily.

They drifted, somehow, to talking of happiness. And always, carefully veiled, it was their own happiness they discussed.

"I don't think," she said, glancing away from him, "that one finds it by looking for it. That is selfish, and the selfish are never happy. It comes-oh, in queer ways. When you're trying to give it to somebody else, mostly."

"There is happiness, of a sort, in work."

Their eyes met. That was what they had to face, she dedicated to service, he to labor.

"It's never found by making other people unhappy, Clay."

"No. And yet, if the other people are already unhappy?"

"Never!" she said. And the answer was to the unspoken question in both their hearts.

It was not until they were in the taxicab that Clayton forced the personal note, and then it came as a cry, out of the very depths of him. She had slipped her hand into his, and the comfort of even that small touch broke down the barriers he had so carefully erected.

"I need you so!" he said. And he held her hand to his face. She made no movement to withdraw it.

"I need you, too," she replied. "I never get over needing you. But we are going to play the game, Clay. We may have our weak hours-and this is one of them-but always, please God, we'll play the game."

The curious humility he felt with her was in his voice.

"I'll need your help, even in that."

And that touch of boyishness almost broke down her reserve of strength. She wanted to draw his head down on her shoulder, and comfort him. She wanted to smooth back his heavy hair, and put her arms around him and hold him. There was a great tenderness in her for him. There were times when she would have given the world to have gone into his arms and let him hold her there, protected and shielded. But that night she was the stronger, and she knew it.

"I love you, Audrey. I love you terribly."

And that was the word for it. It was terrible. She knew it.

"To have gone through all the world," he said, brokenly, "and then to find the Woman, when it is too late. Forever too late." He turned toward her. "You know it, don't you? That you are my woman?"

"I know it," she answered, steadily. "But I know, too —"

"Let me say it just once. Then never again. I'll bury it, but you will know it is there. You are my woman. I would go through all of life alone to find you at the end. And if I could look forward, dear, to going through the rest of it with you beside me, so I could touch you, like this —"

"I know."

"If I could only protect you, and shield you-oh, how tenderly I could care for you, my dear, my dear!"

The strength passed to him, then. Audrey had a clear picture of what life with him might mean, of his protection, his tenderness. She had never known it. Suddenly every bit of her called out for his care, his quiet strength.

"Don't make me sorry for myself." There were tears in her eyes. "Will you kiss me, Clay? We might have that to remember."

But they were not to have even that, for the taxicab drew up before her hotel. It was one of the absurd anti-climaxes of life that they should part with a hand-clasp and her formal "Thank you for a lovely evening."

Audrey was the better actor of the two. She went in as casually as though she had not put the only happiness of her life away from her. But Clayton Spencer stood on the pavement, watching her in, and all the tragedy of the empty years ahead was in his eyes.

Chapter XXXV

Left alone in her untidy room after Graham's abrupt departure, Anna Klein was dazed. She stood where he left her, staring ahead. What had happened meant only one thing to her, that Graham no longer cared about her, and, if that was true, she did not care to live.

It never occurred to her that he had done rather a fine thing, or that he had protected her against herself. She felt no particular shame, save the shame of rejection. In her small world of the hill, if a man gave a girl valuable gifts or money there was generally a quid pro quo. If the girl was unwilling, she did not accept such gifts. If the man wanted nothing, he did not make them. And men who made love to girls either wanted to marry them or desired some other relationship with them.

She listened to his retreating footsteps, and then began, automatically to unbutton her thin white blouse. But with the sound of the engine of his car below she ran to the window. She leaned out, elbows on the sill, and watched him go, without a look up at her window.

So that was the end of that!

Then, all at once, she was fiercely angry. He had got her into this scrape, and now he had left her. He had pretended to love her, and all the time he had meant to do just this, to let her offer herself so he might reject her. He had been playing with her. She had lost her home because of him, had been beaten almost insensible, had been ill for weeks, and now he had driven away, without even looking back.

She jerked her blouse off, still standing by the window, and when the sleeve caught on her watch, she jerked that off, too. She stood for a moment with it in her hand, her face twisted with shame and anger. Then recklessly and furiously she flung it through the open window.

In the stillness of the street far below she heard it strike and rebound.

"That for him!" she muttered.

Almost immediately she wanted it again. He had given it to her. It was all she had left now, and in a curious way it had, through long wearing, come to mean Graham to her. She leaned out of the window. She thought she saw it gleaming in the gutter, and already, attracted by the crash, a man was crossing the street to where it lay.

"You let that alone," she called down desperately. The figure was already stooping over it. Entirely reckless now, she ran, bare-armed and bare-bosomed, down the stairs and out into the street. She had thought to see its finder escaping, but he was still standing where he had picked it up.

"It's mine," she began. "I dropped it out of the window. I —"

"You threw it out of the window. I saw you."

It was Rudolph.

"You —" He snarled, and stood with menacing eyes fixed on her bare neck.

"Rudolph!"

"Get into the house," he said roughly. "You're half-naked."

"Give me my watch."

"I'll give it to you, all right. What's left of it. When we get in."

He followed her into the hail, but when she turned there and held out her hand, he only snarled again.

"We'll talk up-stairs."

"I can't take you up. The landlady don't allow it."

"She don't, eh? You had that Spencer skunk up there."

His face frightened her, and she lied vehemently.

"That's not so, and you know it, Rudolph Klein. He came inside, just like this, and we stood and talked. Then he went away. He wasn't inside ten minutes." Her voice rose hysterically, but Rudolph caught her by the arm, and pushing her ahead of him, forced her up the stairs.

"We're going to have this out," he muttered, viciously.

Half way up she stopped.

"You're hurting my arm."

"You be glad I'm not breaking it for you."

He climbed in a mounting fury. He almost threw her into her room, and closing the door, he turned the key in it. His face reminded her of her father's the night he had beaten her, and her instinct of self-preservation made her put the little table between them.

"You lay a hand on me," she panted, "and I'll yell out the window. The police would be glad enough to have something on you, Rudolph Klein, and you know it."

"They arrest women like you, too."

"Don't you dare say that." And as he took a step or two toward her she retreated to the window. "You stay there, or I'll jump out of the window."

She looked desperate enough to do it, and Rudolph hesitated.

"He was up here. I saw him at the window. I've been trailing you all evening. Keep off that window-sill, you little fool! I'm not going to kill you. But I'm going to get him, all right, and don't you forget it."

His milder tone and the threat frightened her more than ever. He would get Graham; he was like that. Get him in some cruel, helpless way; that was the German blood in him. She began to play for time, with instinctive cunning.

"Listen, Rudolph," she said. "I'll tell you all about it. He did come up, but he left right away. We quarreled. He threw me over, Rudolph. That's what he did."

Her own words reminded her of her humiliation, and tears came into her eyes.

"He threw me over! Honest he did. That's why I threw his watch out of the window. That's straight, Rudolph. That's straight goods. I'm not lying now."

"God!" said Rudolph. "The dirty pup. Then-then you're through with him, eh?"

"I'm through, all right."

Her tone carried conviction. Rudolph's face relaxed, and seeing that, she remembered her half-dressed condition.

"Throw me that waist," she said.

"Come around and get it."

"Aw, Rudolph, throw it. Please!"

"Getting modest, all at once," he jeered. But he picked it up and advanced to the table with it. As she held out her hand for it he caught her and drew her forward toward him, across the table.

"You little devil!" he said, and kissed her.

She submitted, because she must, but she shivered. If she was to save Graham she must play the game. And so far she was winning. She was feminine enough to know that already the thing he thought she had done was to be forgiven her. More than that, she saw a half-reluctant admiration in Rudolph's eyes, as though she had gained value, if she had lost virtue, by the fact that young Spencer had fancied her. And Rudolph's morals were the morals of many of his kind. He admired chastity in a girl, but he did not expect it.

But she was watchful for the next move he might make. That it was not what she expected did not make it the less terrifying.

"You get your hat and coat on."

"I'll not do anything of the kind."

"D'you think I'm going to leave you here, where he can come back whenever he wants to? You think again!"

"Where are you going to take me?"

"I'm going to take you home."

When pleading made no impression on him, and when he refused to move without her, she threw her small wardrobe into the suitcase, and put her hat and coat on. She was past thinking, quite hopeless. She would go back, and her father would kill her, which would be the best thing anyhow; she didn't care to live.

Rudolph had relapsed into moody silence. Down the stairs, and on the street he preceded her, contemptuously letting her trail behind. He carried her suitcase, however, and once, being insecurely fastened, it opened and bits of untidy apparel littered the pavement. He dropped the suitcase and stood by while she filled it again. The softness of that moment, when, lured by her bare arms he had kissed her, was gone.

The night car jolted and swayed. After a time he dozed, and Anna, watching him, made an attempt at flight. He caught her on the rear platform, however, with a clutch that sickened her. The conductor eyed them with the scant curiosity of two o'clock in the morning, when all the waking world is awry.

At last they were climbing the hill to the cottage, while behind and below them the Spencer furnaces sent out their orange and violet flames, and the roar of the blast sounded like the coming of a mighty wind.

The cottage was dark. Rudolph put down the suitcase, and called Herman softly through his hands. Above they could hear him moving, and his angry voice came through the open window.

"What you want?"

"Come down. It's Rudolph."

But when he turned Anna was lying in a dead faint on the garden path, a crumpled little heap of blissful forgetfulness. When Herman came down, it was to find Rudolph standing over her, the suitcase still in his hand, and an ugly scowl on his face.

"Well, I got her," he said. "She's scared, that's all." He prodded her with his foot, but she did not move, and Herman bent down with his candle.

He straightened.

"Bring her in," he said, and led the way into the house. When Rudolph staggered in, with Anna in his arms, he found Herman waiting and fingering the leather strap.

Chapter XXXVI

Audrey had found something to do at last. It was Captain Sloane who had given her the idea.

"You would make a great hit, Audrey," he had said. "It's your voice, you know. There's something about it-well, you know the effect it always has on me. No? All right, I'll be good."

But she had carried the idea home with her, and had proceeded, with her customary decision, to act on it.

Then, one day in May, she was surprised by a visit from Delight Haverford. She had come home, tired and rather depressed, to find the Haverford car at the door, and Delight waiting for her in her sitting-room.

Audrey's acquaintance with Delight had been rather fragmentary, but it had covered a long stretch of time. So, if she was surprised, it was not greatly when Delight suddenly kissed her. She saw then that the girl had brought her some spring flowers, and the little tribute touched her.

"What a nice child you are!" she said, and standing before the mirror proceeded to take off her hat. Before her she could see the reflection of Delight's face, and her own tired, slightly haggard eyes.

"And how unutterably old you make me look!" she added, smiling.

"You are too lovely for words, Mrs. Valentine."

Audrey patted her hair into order, and continued her smiling inspection of the girl's face.

"And now we have exchanged compliments," she said, "we will have some tea, and then you shall tell me what you are so excited about."

"I am excited; I —"

"Let's have the tea first."

Audrey's housekeeping was still rather casual. Tidiness of Natalie's meticulous order would always be beyond her, but after certain frantic searches for what was needed, she made some delicious tea.

"Order was left out of me, somehow," she complained. "Or else things move about when I'm away. I'm sure it is that, because I certainly never put the sugar behind my best hat. Now—let's have it."

Delight was only playing with her tea. She flushed delicately, and put the cup down.

"I was in the crowd this morning," she said.

"In the crowd? Oh, my crowd!"

"Yes."

"I see," said Audrey, thoughtfully. "I make a dreadful speech, you know."

"I thought you were wonderful. And, when those men promised to enlist, I cried. I was horribly ashamed. But you were splendid."

"I wonder!" said Audrey, growing grave. Delight was astonished to see that there were tears in her eyes. "I do it because it is all I can do, and of course they must go. But some times at night—you see, my dear, some of them are going to be killed. I am urging them to go, but the better the day I have had, the less I sleep at night."

There was a little pause. Delight was thinking desperately of something to say.

"But you didn't come to talk about me, did you?"

"Partly. And partly about myself. I want to do something, Mrs. Valentine. I can drive a car, but not very well. I don't know a thing about the engine. And I can nurse a little. I like nursing."

Audrey studied her face. It seemed to her sad beyond words that this young girl, who should have had only happiness, was facing the horrors of what would probably be a long war. It was the young who paid the price of war, in death, in empty years. Already the careless gayety of their lives was gone. For the dream futures they had planned they had now to substitute long waiting; for happiness, service.

"The Red Cross is going to send canteen workers to France. You might do that."

"If I only could! But I can't leave mother. Not entirely. Father is going. He wants to go and fight, but I'm afraid they won't take him. He'll go as a chaplain, anyhow. But he's perfectly helpless, you know. Mother says she is going to tie his overshoes around his neck."

"I'll see if I can think of something for you, Delight. There's one thing in my mind. There are to be little houses built in all the new training-camps for officers, and they are to be managed by women. They are to serve food—sandwiches and coffee, I think. They may be even more pretentious. I don't know, but I'll find out."

"I'll do anything," said Delight, and got up. It was then that Audrey realized that there was something more to the visit than had appeared, for Delight, ready to go, hesitated.

"There is something else, Mrs. Valentine," she said, rather slowly. "What would you do if a young man wanted to go into the service, and somebody held him back?"

"His own people?"

"His mother. And —a girl."

"I would think the army is well off without him."

Delight flushed painfully.

"Perhaps," she admitted. "But is it right just to let it go at that? If you like people, it seems wrong just to stand by and let others ruin their lives for them."

"Only very weak men let women ruin their lives."

But already she began to understand the situation.

"There's a weakness that is only a sort of habit. It may come from not wanting to hurt somebody." Delight was pulling nervously at her gloves. "And there is this to be said, too. If there is what you call weakness, wouldn't the army be good for it? It makes men, some times, doesn't it?"

For a sickening moment, Audrey thought of Chris. War had made Chris, but it had killed him, too.

"Have you thought of one thing?" she asked. "That in trying to make this young man, whoever it is, he may be hurt, or even worse?"

"He would have to take his chance, like the rest."

She went a little pale, however. Audrey impulsively put an arm around her.

"And this-woman is the little long-legged girl who used to give signals to her father when the sermon was too long! Now-what can I do about this youth who can't make up his own mind?"

"You can talk to his mother."

"If I know his mother —? and I think I do-it won't do the slightest good."

"Then his father. You are great friends, aren't you?"

Even this indirect mention of Clayton made Audrey's hands tremble. She put them behind her.

"We are very good friends," she said. But Delight was too engrossed to notice the deeper note in her voice. "I'll see what I can do. But don't count on me too much. You spoke of a girl. I suppose I know who it is."

"Probably. It is Marion Hayden. He is engaged to her."

And again Audrey marveled at her poise, for Delight's little tragedy was clear by that time. Clear, and very sad.

"I can't imagine his really being in love with her."

"But he must be. They are engaged."

Audrey smiled at the simple philosophy of nineteen, smiled and was extremely touched. How brave the child was! Audrey's own courageous heart rather swelled in admiration.

But after Delight had gone, she felt depressed again, and very tired. How badly these things were handled! How strange it was that love so often brought suffering! Great loves were almost always great tragedies. Perhaps it was because love was never truly great until the element of sacrifice entered into it.

Her own high courage failed her somewhat. During these recent days when, struggling against very real stage fright, she made her husky, wholly earnest but rather nervous little appeals to the crowds before the enlisting stations, she got along bravely enough during the day. But the night found her sad, unutterably depressed.

At these times she was haunted by a fear that persisted against all her arguments. In Washington Clayton had not looked well. He had been very tired and white, and some of his natural buoyancy seemed to have deserted him. He needed caring for, she would reflect bitterly. There should be some one to look after him. He was tired and anxious, but it took the eyes of love to see it. Natalie would never notice, and would consider it a grievance if she did. The fiercely, maternal tenderness of the childless woman for the man she loves kept her awake at night staring into the darkness and visualizing terrible things. Clayton ill, and she unable to go to him. Ill, and wanting her, and unable to ask for her.

She was, she knew, not quite normal, but the fear gripped and held her. These big strong men, no one ever looked after them. They spent their lives caring for others, and were never cared for.

There were times when a sort of exaltation of sacrifice kept her head high, when the thing she was forced to give up seemed trifling compared with the men and boys who, some determinedly, some sheepishly, left the crowd around the borrowed car from which she spoke, and went into the recruiting station. There was sacrifice and sacrifice, and there was some comfort in the thought that both she and Clayton were putting the happiness of others above their own.

They had both, somehow, somewhere, missed the path. But they must never go back and try to find it.

Delight's visit left her thoughtful. There must be some way to save Graham. She wondered how much of Clayton's weariness was due to Graham. And she wondered, too, if he knew of the talk about Natalie and Rodney Page. There was a great deal of talk. Somehow such talk cheapened his sacrifice and hers.

Not that she believed it, or much of it. She knew how little such gossip actually meant. Practically every woman she knew, herself included, had at one time or another laid herself open to such invidious comment. They had all been idle, and they sought amusement in such spurious affairs as this, harmless in the main, but taking on the appearance of evil. That was part of the game, to appear worse than one really was. The older the woman, the more eager she was often in her clutch at the vanishing romance of youth.

Only-it was part of the game, too, to avoid scandal. A fierce pride for Clayton's name sent the color to her face.

On the evening after Delight's visit, she had promised to speak at a recruiting station far down-town in a crowded tenement district, and tired as she was, she took a bus and went down at seven o'clock. She was uneasy and nervous. She had not spoken in the evening before, and in all her sheltered life she had never seen the milling of a night crowd in a slum district.

There was a wagon drawn up at the curb, and an earnest-eyed young clergyman was speaking. The crowd was attentive, mildly curious. The clergyman was emphatic without being convincing. Audrey watched the faces about her, standing in the crowd herself, and a sense of the futility of it all gripped her. All these men, and only a feeble cheer as a boy still in his teens agreed to volunteer. All this effort for such scant result, and over on the other side such dire need! But one thing cheered her. Beside her, in the crowd, a portly elderly Jew was standing with his hat in his hand, and when a man near him made some jeering comment, the Jew brought his hand down on his shoulder.

"Be still and listen," he said. "Or else go away and allow others to listen. This is our country which calls."

"It's amusing, isn't it?" Audrey heard a woman's voice near her, carefully inflected, slightly affected.

"It's rather stunning, in a way. It's decorative; the white faces, and that chap in the wagon, and the gasoline torch."

"I'd enjoy it more if I'd had my dinner."

The man laughed.

"You are a most brazen combination of the mundane and the spiritual, Natalie. You are all soul-after you are fed. Come on. It's near here."

Audrey's hands were very cold. By the movement of the crowd behind her, she knew that Natalie and Rodney were making their escape, toward food and a quiet talk in some obscure restaurant in the neighborhood. Fierce anger shook her. For this she and Clayton were giving up the only hope they had of happiness-that Natalie might carry on a cheap and stealthy flirtation.

She made a magnificent appeal that night, and a very successful one. The lethargic crowd waked up and pressed forward. There were occasional cheers, and now and then the greater tribute of convinced silence. And on a box in the wagon the young clergyman eyed her almost wistfully. What a woman she was! With such a woman a man could live up to the best in him. Then he remembered his salary in a mission church of twelve hundred a year, and sighed.

He gained courage, later on, and asked Audrey if she would have some coffee with him, or something to eat. She looked tired.

"Tired!" said Audrey. "I am only tired these days when I am not working."

"You must not use yourself up. You are too valuable to the country."

She was very grateful. After all, what else really mattered? In a little glow she accepted his invitation.

"Only coffee," she said. "I have had dinner. Is there any place near?"

He piloted her through the crowd, now rapidly dispersing. Here and there some man, often in halting English, thanked her for what she had said. A woman, slightly the worse for drink, but with friendly, rather humorous eyes, put a hand on her arm.

"You're all right, m'dear," she said. "You're the stuff. Give it to them. I wish to God I could talk. I'd tell 'em something."

The clergyman drew her on hastily.

In a small Italian restaurant, almost deserted, they found a table, and the clergyman ordered eggs and coffee. He was a trifle uneasy. In the wagon Audrey's plain dark clothes had deceived him. But the single pearl on her finger was very valuable. He fell to apologizing for the place.

"I often come here," he explained. "The food is good, if you like Italian cooking. And it is near my work. I—"

But Audrey was not listening. At a corner, far back, Natalie and Rodney were sitting, engrossed in each other. Natalie's back was carefully turned to the room, but there was no mistaking her. Audrey wanted madly to get away, but the coffee had come and the young clergyman was talking gentle platitudes in a rather sweet but monotonous voice. Then Rodney saw her, and bowed.

Almost immediately afterward she heard the soft rustle that was Natalie, and found them both beside her.

"Can we run you up-town?" Natalie asked. "That is, unless—"

She glanced at the clergyman.

"Thank you, no, Natalie. I'm going to have some supper first."

Natalie was uneasy. Audrey made no move to present the clergyman, whose name she did not know. Rodney was looking slightly bored.

"Odd little place, isn't it?" Natalie offered after a second's silence.

"Rather quaint, I think."

Natalie made a desperate effort to smooth over an awkward situation. She turned to the clergyman.

"We heard you speaking. It was quite thrilling."

He smiled a little.

"Not so thrilling as this lady. She carried the crowd, absolutely."

Natalie turned and stared at Audrey, who was flushed with annoyance.

"You!" she said. "Do you mean to say you have been talking from that wagon?"

"I haven't said it. But I have."

"For heaven's sake!" Then she laughed and glanced at Rodney. "Well, if you won't tell on me, I'll not tell on you." And then seeing Audrey straighten, "I don't mean that, of course. Clay's at a meeting to-night, so I am having a holiday."

She moved on, always with the soft rustle, leaving behind her a delicate whiff of violets and a wide-eyed clergyman, who stared after her admiringly.

"What a beautiful woman!" he said. There was a faint regret in his voice that Audrey had not presented him, and he did not see that her coffee-cup trembled as she lifted it to her lips.

At ten o'clock the next morning Natalie called her on the 'phone. Natalie's morning voice was always languid, but there was a trace of pleading in it now.

"It's a lovely day," she said. "What are you doing?"

"I've been darning."

"You! Darning!"

"I rather like it."

"Heavens, how you've changed! I suppose you wouldn't do anything so frivolous as to go out with me to the new house."

Audrey hesitated. Evidently Natalie wanted to talk, to try to justify herself. But the feeling that she was the last woman in the world to be Natalie's father-confessor was strong in her. On the other hand, there was the question of Graham. On that, before long, she and Natalie would have, in one of her own occasional lapses into slang, to go to the mat.

"I'll come, of course, if that's an invitation."

"I'll be around in an hour, then."

Natalie was unusually prompt. She was nervous and excited, and was even more carefully dressed than usual. Over her dark blue velvet dress she wore a loose motor-coat, with a great chinchilla collar, but above it Audrey, who would have given a great deal to be able to hate her, found her rather pathetic, a little droop to her mouth, dark circles which no veil could hide under her eyes.

The car was in its customary resplendent condition. There were orchids in the flower-holder, and the footman, light rug over his arm, stood rigidly waiting at the door.

"What a tone you and your outfit do give my little street," Audrey said, as they started. "We have more milk-wagons than limousines, you know."

"I don't see how you can bear it."

Audrey smiled. "It's really rather nice," she said. "For one thing, I haven't any bills. I never lived on a cash basis before. It's a sort of emancipation."

"Oh, bills!" said Natalie, and waved her hands despairingly. "If you could see my desk! And the way I watch the mail so Clay won't see them first. They really ought to send bills in blank envelopes."

"But you have to give them to him eventually, don't you?"

"I can choose my moment. And it is never in the morning. He's rather awful in the morning."

"Awful?"

"Oh, not ugly. Just quiet. I hate a man who doesn't talk in the mornings. But then, for months, he hasn't really talked at all. That's why" —she was rather breathless —"that's why I went out with Rodney last night."

"I don't think Clayton would mind, if you told him first. It's your own affair, of course, but it doesn't seem quite fair to him."

"Oh, of course you'd side with him. Women always side with the husband."

"I don't 'side' with any one," Audrey protested. "But I am sure, if he realized that you are lonely —"

Suddenly she realized that Natalie was crying. Not much, but enough to force her, to dab her eyes carefully through her veil.

"I'm awfully unhappy, Audrey," she said. "Everything's wrong, and I don't know why. What have I done? I try and try and things just get worse."

Audrey was very uncomfortable. She had a guilty feeling that the whole situation, with Natalie pouring out her woes beside her, was indelicate, unbearable.

"But if Clay —" she began.

"Clay! He's absolutely ungrateful. He takes me for granted, and the house for granted. Everything. And if he knows I want a thing, he disapproves at once. I think sometimes he takes a vicious pleasure in thwarting me."

But as she did not go on, Audrey said nothing. Natalie had raised her veil, and from a gold vanity-case was repairing the damages around her eyes.

"Why don't you find something to do, something to interest you?" Audrey suggested finally.

But Natalie poured out a list of duties that lasted for the last three miles of the trip, ending with the new house.

"Even that has ceased to be a satisfaction," she finished. "Clayton wants to stop work on it, and cut down all the estimates. It's too awful. First he told me to get anything I liked, and now he says to cut down to nothing. I could just shriek about it."

"Perhaps that's because we are in the war, now."

"War or no war, we have to live, don't we? And he thinks I ought to do without the extra man for the car, and the second man in the house, and heaven alone knows what. I'm at the end of my patience."

Audrey made a resolution. After all, what mattered was that things should be more tolerable for Clayton. She turned to Natalie.

"Why don't you try to do what he wants, Natalie? He must have a reason for asking you. And it would please him a lot."

"If I start making concession, I can just keep it up. He's like that."

"He's so awfully fine, Natalie. He's —well, he's rather big. And sometimes I think, if you just tried, he wouldn't be so hard to please. He probably wants peace and happiness?"

"Happiness!" Natalie's voice was high. "That sounds like Clay. Happiness! Don't you suppose I want to be happy?"

"Not enough to work for it," said Audrey, evenly.

Natalie turned and stared at her.

"I believe you're half in love with Clay yourself!"

"Perhaps I am."

But she smiled frankly into Natalie's eyes.

"I know if I were married to him, I'd try to do what he wanted."

"You'd try it for a year. Then you'd give it up. It's one thing to admire a man. It's quite different being married to him, and having to put up with all sorts of things?"

Her voice trailed off before the dark vision of her domestic, unhappiness. And again, as with Graham and his father, it was what she did not say that counted. Audrey came close to hating her just then.

So far the conversation had not touched on Graham, and now they were turning in the new drive. Already the lawns Were showing green, and extensive plantings of shrubbery were putting out their pale new buds. Audrey, bending forward in the car, found it very lovely, and because it belonged to Clay, was to be his home, it thrilled her, just as the towering furnaces of his mill thrilled her, the lines of men leaving at nightfall. It was his, therefore it was significant.

The house amazed her. Even Natalie's enthusiasm had not promised anything so stately or so vast. Moving behind her through great empty rooms, to the sound of incessant hammering, over which Natalie's voice was raised shrilly, she was forced to confess that, between them, Natalie and Rodney had made a lovely thing. She felt no jealousy when she contrasted it with her own small apartment. She even felt that it was the sort of house Clayton should have.

For, although it had been designed as a setting for Natalie, although every color-scheme, almost every chair, had been bought with a view to forming a background for her, it was too big, too massive. It dwarfed her. Out-of-doors, Audrey lost that feeling. In the formal garden Natalie was charmingly framed. It was like her, beautifully exact, carefully planned, already with its spring borders faintly glowing.

Natalie cheered in her approval.

"You're so comforting," she said. "Clay thinks it isn't homelike. He says it's a show place-which it ought to be. It cost enough-and he hates show places. He really ought to have a cottage. Now let's see the swimming-pool."

But at the pool she lost her gayety. The cement basin, still empty, gleamed white in the sun, and Natalie, suddenly brooding, stood beside it staring absently into it.

"It was for Graham," she said at last. "We were going to have week-end parties, and all sorts of young people. But now!"

"What about now?"

Natalie raised tragic eyes to hers.

"He's probably going into the army. He'd have never thought of it, but Clayton shows in every possible way that he thinks he ought to go. What is the boy to do? His father driving him to what may be his death!"

"I don't think he'd do that, Natalie."

Natalie laughed, her little mirthless laugh.

"Much you know what his father would do! I'll tell you this, Audrey. If Graham goes, and anything-happens to him, I'll never forgive Clay. Never."

Audrey had not suspected such depths of feeling as Natalie's eyes showed under their penciled brows. They were desperate, vindictive eyes. Suddenly Natalie was pleading with her.

"You'll talk to Clay, won't you? He'll listen to you. He has a lot of respect for your opinion. I want you to go to him, Audrey. I brought you here to ask you. I'm almost out of my mind. Why do you suppose I play around with Rodney? I've got to forget, that's all. And I've tried everything I know, and failed. He'll go, and I'll lose him, and if I do it will kill me."

"It doesn't follow that because he goes he won't come back."

"He'll be in danger. I shall be worrying about him every moment." She threw out her hands in what was as unrestrained a gesture as she ever made. "Look at me!" she cried. "I'm getting old under it. I have lines about my eyes already. I hate to look at myself in the morning. And I'm not old. I ought to be at my best now."

Natalie's anxiety was for Graham, but her pity was for herself. Audrey's heart hardened.

"I'm sorry," she said. "I can't go to Clay. I feel as I think he does. If Graham wants to go, he should be free to do it. You're only hurting him, and your influence on him, by holding him back."

"You've never had a child."

"If I had, and he wanted to go, I should be terrified, but I should be proud."

"You and Clay! You even talk alike. It's all a pose, this exalted attitude. Even this war is a pose. It's a national attitude we've struck, a great nation going to rescue humanity, while the rest of the world looks on and applauds! It makes me ill."

She turned and went back to the house, leaving Audrey by the swimming-pool. She sat on the edge of one of the stone benches, feeling utterly dreary and sad. To make a sacrifice for a worthy object was one thing. To throw away a life's happiness for a spoiled, petulant woman was another. It was too high a price to pay. Mingled with her depression was pity for Clayton; for all the years that he had lived with this woman: and pride in him, that he had never betrayed his disillusion.

After a time she saw the car waiting, and she went slowly back to the house. Natalie was already inside, and she made no apologies whatever. The drive back was difficult. Natalie openly sulked, replied in monosyllables, made no effort herself until they were in the city again. Then she said, "I'm sorry I asked you to speak to Clay. Of course you needn't do it."

"Not if it is to do what you said. But I wish you wouldn't misunderstand me, Natalie. I'm awfully sorry. We just think differently."

"We certainly do," said Natalie briefly. And that was her good-by.

Chapter XXXVII

When Clayton had returned from Washington, one of the first problems put up to him had been Herman Klein's application to be taken on again. He found Hutchinson in favor of it.

"He doesn't say much," he said. "Never did. But I gather things are changed, now we are in the war ourselves."

"I suppose we need him."

"You bet we need him."

For the problem of skilled labor was already a grave one.

Clayton was doubtful. If he could have conferred with Dunbar he would have felt more comfortable, but Dunbar was away on some mysterious errand connected with the Military Intelligence Department. He sat considering, tapping on his desk with the handle of his pen. Of course things were different now. A good many Germans whose sympathies had, as between the Fatherland and the Allies, been with Germany, were now driven to a decision between the land they had left and the land they had adopted. And behind Herman there were thirty years of good record.

"Where is the daughter?"

"I don't know. She left some weeks ago. It's talk around the plant that he beat her up, and she got out. Those Germans don't know the first thing about how to treat women."

"Then she is not in Weaver's office?"

There was more talk in the offices than Hutchinson repeated. Graham's fondness for Anna, her slavish devotion to him, had been pretty well recognized. He wondered if Clayton knew anything about it, or the further gossip that Graham knew where Anna Klein had been hiding.

"What about Rudolph Klein? He was a nephew, wasn't he?"

"Fired," said Hutchinson laconically. "Got to spreading the brotherhood of the world idea—sweat brothers, he calls them. But he was mighty careful never to get in a perspiration himself."

"We might try Herman again. But I'd keep an eye on him."

So Herman was taken on at the new munition plant. He was a citizen, he owned property, he had a record of long service behind him. And, at first, he was minded to preserve that record intact. While he had by now added to his rage against the Fatherland's enemies a vast and sullen fury against invested capital, his German caution still remained.

He would sit through fiery denunciations of wealth, nodding his head slowly in agreement. He was perfectly aware that in Gus's little back room dark plots were hatched. Indeed, on a certain April night Rudolph had come up and called him onto the porch.

"In about fifteen minutes," he said, consulting his watch in the doorway, "I'm going to show you something pretty."

And in fifteen minutes to the dot the great railroad warehouses near the city wharf had burst into flames. Herman had watched without comment, while Rudolph talked incessantly, boasting of his share in the enterprise.

"About a million dollars' worth of fireworks there," he said, as the glare dyed their faces red. "All stuff for the Allies." And he boasted, "When the cat sits on the pickhandle, brass buttons must go."

By that time Herman knew that the "cat" meant sabotage. He had nodded slowly.

"But it is dangerous," was his later comment. "Sometimes they will learn, and then?"

His caution had exasperated Rudolph almost to frenzy. And as time went on, and one man after another of the organization was ferreted out at the new plant and dismissed, the sole remaining hope of the organization was Herman. With his reinstatement their hopes had risen again, but to every suggestion so far he had been deaf. He would listen approvingly, but at the end, when he found the talk veering his way, and a circle of intent faces watching him, he would say:

"It is too dangerous. And it is a young man's work. I am not young."

Then he would pay his score, but never by any chance Rudolph's or the others, and go home to his empty house. But recently the plant had gone on double turn, and Herman was soon to go on at night. Here was the gang's opportunity. Everything was ready but Herman himself. He continued interested, but impersonal. For the sake of the Fatherland he was willing to have the plant go, and to lose his work. He was not at all daunted by the thought of the deaths that would follow. That was war. Anything that killed and destroyed was fair in war. But he did not care to place himself in danger. Let those young hot-heads do the work.

Rudolph, watching him, bided his time. The ground was plowed and harrowed, ready for the seed, and Rudolph had only to find the seed.

The night he had carried Anna into the cottage on the hill, he had found it.

Herman had not beaten Anna. Rudolph had carried her up to her bed, and Herman, following slowly, strap in hand, had been confronted by the younger man in the doorway of the room where Anna lay, conscious but unmoving, on the bed.

"You can use that thing later," Rudolph said. "She's sick now. Better let her alone."

"I will teach her to run away," Herman muttered thickly. "She left me, her father, and threw away a good job —I —"

"You come down-stairs. I've something to say to you."

And, after a time, Herman had followed him down, but he still clung doggedly to the strap.

Rudolph led the way outside, and here in the darkness he told Anna's story, twisted and distorted through his own warped mind, but convincing and partially true. Herman's silence began to alarm him, however, and when at last he rose and made for the door, Rudolph was before him.

"What are you going to do?"

Herman said nothing, but he raised the strap and held it menacingly.

"Get out of my way."

"Don't be a fool," Rudolph entreated. "You can beat her to death, and what do you get out of it? She'll run away again if you touch her. Put that strap down. I'm not afraid of you."

Their voices, raised and angry, penetrated through Anna's haze of fright and faintness. She sat up in the bed, ready to spring to the window if she heard steps on the stairs. When none came, but the voices, lowered now, went on endlessly below, she slipped out of her bed and crept to the doorway.

Sounds traveled clearly up the narrow enclosed stairway. She stood there, swaying slightly, until at last her legs would no longer support her. She crouched on the floor, a hand clutching her throat, lest she scream. And listened.

She did not sleep at all. The night had been too full of horrors. And she was too ill to attempt a second flight. Besides, where could she go? Katie was not there. She could see her empty little room across, with its cot bed and tawdry dresser. Before, too, she had had Grahams protection to count on. Now she had nothing.

And the voices went on.

When she went back to bed it was almost dawn. She heard Herman come up, heard the heavy thump of his shoes on the floor, and the creak immediately following that showed he had lain down without undressing. By the absence of his resonant snoring she knew he was not sleeping, either. She pictured him lying there, his eyes on the door, in almost unwinking espionage.

At half past six she got up and went down-stairs. Almost immediately she heard his stockinged feet behind her. She turned and looked up at him.

"What are you going to do?"

"Going to make myself some coffee."

He came down, and sat down in the sitting-room. From where he sat he could survey the kitchen, and she knew his eyes were on her. His very quiet terrified her, but although the strap lay on the table he made no move toward it. She built a fire and put on the kettle, and after a time she brought him some coffee and some bread. He took it without a word. Sick as she was, she fell to cleaning up the dirty kitchen. She went outside for a pail, to find him behind her in the doorway. Then she knew what he intended to do. He was afraid, for some reason, to beat her again, but he was going to watch her lest again she make her escape. The silence, under his heavy gaze, was intolerable.

All day she worked, and only once did Herman lose sight of her. That was when he took a ladder, and outside the house nailed all the upper windows shut. He did it with German thoroughness, hammering deliberately, placing his nails carefully. After that he went to the corner grocery, but before he went he spoke the first words of the day.

"You will go to your room."

She went, and he locked her in. She knew then that she was a prisoner. When he was at the mill at night, while he slept during the day, she was to be locked up in her stuffy, airless room. When he was about she would do the housework, always under his silent, contemptuous gaze.

She made one appeal to him, and only one, and that was to his cupidity.

"I've been sick, but I'm able to work now, father."

He paid no attention to her.

"If you lock me up and don't let me work," she persisted, "you'll only be cutting off your nose to spite your face. I make good money, and you know it."

She thought he was going to speak then, but he did not. She put his food on the table and he ate gluttonously, as he always did. She did not sit down. She drank a little coffee, standing at the stove, and watched the back of his head with hate in her eyes. He could eat like that, when he stood committed to a terrible thing!

It was not until late in the day that it began to dawn on her how she was responsible. She was getting stronger then and more able to think. She followed as best she could the events of the last months, and she saw that, as surely as though a malevolent power had arranged it, the thing was the result of her infatuation for Graham.

She was in despair, and she began to plan how to get word to Graham of what was impending. She scrawled a note to Graham, telling him where she was and to try to get in touch with her somehow. If he would come around four o'clock Herman was generally up and off to the grocer's, or to Gus's saloon for his afternoon beer.

"I'll break a window and talk to you," she wrote. "I'm locked in when he's out. My window is on the north side. Don't lose any time. There's something terrible going to happen."

But several days went by and the postman did not appear. Herman had put a padlock on the outside of her bedroom door, and her hope of finding a second key to fit the door-lock died then.

It had become a silent, bitter contest between the two of them, with two advantages in favor of the girl. She was more intelligent than Herman, and she knew the thing he was planning to do. She made a careful survey of her room, and she saw that with a screw-driver she could unfasten the hinge of her bedroom door. Herman, however, always kept his tools locked up. She managed, apparently by accident, to break the point off a knife, and when she went up to her room one afternoon to be locked in while Herman went to Gus's saloon, she carried the knife in her stocking.

It was a sorry tool, however. Driven by her shaking hand, there was a time when she almost despaired. And time was flying. The postman, when he came, came at five, and she heard the kitchen clock strike five before the first screw fell out into her hand. She got them all out finally, and the door hung crazily, held only by the padlock. She ran to the window. The postman was coming along the street, and she hammered madly at the glass. When he saw her he turned in at the gate, and she got her letter and ran down the stairs.

She heard his step on the porch outside, and called to him.

"Is that you, Briggs?"

The postman was "Briggs" to the hill.

"Yes."

"If I slide a letter out under the door, will you take it to the post-office for me? It's important."

"All right. Slide."

She had put it partially under the door when a doubt crept into her mind. That was not Briggs's voice. She made a frantic effort to draw the letter back, but stronger fingers than hers had it beyond the door. She clutched, held tight. Then she heard a chuckle, and found herself with a corner of the envelope in her hand.

There were voices outside, Briggs's and Rudolph's.

"Guess that's for me."

"Like hell it is."

She ran madly up the stairs again, and tried with shaking fingers to screw the door-hinges into place again. She fully expected that they would kill her. She heard Briggs go out, and after a time she heard Rudolph trying to kick in the house door. Then, when the last screw was back in place, she heard Herman's heavy step outside, and Rudolph's voice, high, furious, and insistent.

Had Herman not been obsessed with the thing he was to do, he might have beaten her to death that night. But he did not. She remained in her room, without food or water. She had made up her mind to kill herself with the knife if they came up after her, but the only sounds she heard were of high voices, growing lower and more sinister.

After that, for days she was a prisoner. Herman moved his bed down-stairs and slept in the sitting-room, the five or six hours of day-light sleep which were all he required. And at night, while he was at the mill, Rudolph sat and dozed and kept watch below. Twice a day some meager provisions were left at the top of the stairs and her door was unlocked. She would creep out and get them, not because she was hungry, but because she meant to keep up her strength. Let their vigilance slip but once, and she meant to be ready.

She learned to interpret every sound below. There were times when the fumes from burning food came up the staircase and almost smothered her. And there were times, she fancied, when Herman weakened and Rudolph talked for hours, inciting and inflaming him again. She gathered, too, that Gus's place was under surveillance, and more than once in the middle of the night stealthy figures came in by the garden gate and conferred with Rudolph down-stairs. Then, one evening, in the dusk of the May twilight, she saw three of them come, one rather tall and military of figure, and one of them carried, very carefully, a cheap suitcase.

She knew what was in that suitcase.

Chapter XXXVIII

One morning, in his mail, Clayton Spencer received a clipping. It had been cut from a so-called society journal, and it was clamped to the prospectus of a firm of private detectives who gave information for divorce cases as their specialty.

First curiously, then with mounting anger, Clayton read that the wife of a prominent munition manufacturer was being seen constantly in out of the way places with the young architect who was building a palace for her out of the profiteer's new wealth. "It is quite probable," ended the notice, "that the episode will end in an explosion louder than the best shell the husband in the case ever turned out."

Clayton did not believe the thing for a moment. He was infuriated, but mostly with the journal, and with the insulting inference of the prospectus. He had a momentary clear vision, however, of Natalie, of her idle days, of perhaps a futile last clutch at youth. He had no more doubt of her essential integrity than of his own. But he had a very distinct feeling that she had exposed his name to cheap scandal, and that for nothing.

Had there been anything real behind it, he might have understood, in his new humility, in his new knowledge of impulses stronger than any restraints of society, he would quite certainly have made every allowance. But for a whim, an indulgence of her incorrigible vanity! To get along, to save Natalie herself, he was stifling the best that was in him, while Natalie —

That was one view of it. The other was that Natalie was as starved as he was. If he got nothing from her, he gave her nothing. How was he to blame her? She was straying along dangerous paths, but he himself had stood at the edge of the precipice, and looked down.

Suddenly it occurred to him that perhaps, for once, Natalie was in earnest. Perhaps Rodney was, too. Perhaps each of them had at last found something that loomed larger than themselves. In that case? But everything he knew of Natalie contradicted that. She was not a woman to count anything well lost for love. She was playing with his honor, with Rodney, with her own vanity.

Going up-town that night he pondered the question of how to take up the matter with her. It would be absurd, under the circumstances, to take any virtuous attitude. He was still undetermined when he reached the house.

He found Marion Hayden there for dinner, and Graham, and a spirited three-corner discussion going on which ceased when he stood in the doorway. Natalie looked irritated, Graham determined, and Marion was slightly insolent and unusually handsome.

"Hurry and change, Clay," Natalie said. "Dinner is waiting."

As he went away he had again the feeling of being shut out of something which concerned Graham.

Dinner was difficult. Natalie was obviously sulking, and Graham was rather taciturn. It was Marion who kept the conversation going, and he surmised in her a repressed excitement, a certain triumph.

At last Natalie roused herself. The meal was almost over, and the servants had withdrawn.

"I wish you would talk sense to Graham, Clay," she said, fretfully. "I think he has gone mad."

"I don't call it going mad to want to enlist, father."

"I do. With your father needing you, and with all the men there are who can go."

"I don't understand. If he wants to enter the army, that's up to him, isn't it?"

There was a brief silence. Clayton found Natalie's eyes on him, uneasy, resentful.

"That's just it. I've promised mother not to, unless she gives her consent. And she won't give it."

"I certainly will not."

Clayton saw her appealing glance at Marion, but that young lady was lighting a cigaret, her eyelids lowered. He felt as though he were watching a play, in which he was the audience.

"It's rather a family affair, isn't it?" he asked. "Suppose we wait until we are alone. After all, there is no hurry."

Marion looked at him, and he caught a resentment in her glance. The two glances struck fire.

"Say something, Marion," Natalie implored her.

"I don't think my opinion is of any particular importance. As Mr. Spencer says, it's really a family matter."

Her insolence was gone. Marion was easy. She knew Natalie's game; it was like her own. But this big square-jawed man at the head of the table frightened her. And he hated her. He hardly troubled to hide it, for all his civility. Even that civility was contemptuous.

In the drawing-room things were little better. Natalie had counted on Marion's cooperation, and she had failed her. She pleaded a headache and went up-stairs, leaving Clayton to play the host as best he could.

Marion wandered into the music-room, with its bare polished floor, its lovely painted piano, and played a little—gay, charming little things, clever and artful. Except when visitors came, the piano was never touched, but now and then Clayton had visualized Audrey there, singing in her husky sweet voice her little French songs.

Graham moved restlessly about the room, and Clayton felt that he had altered lately. He looked older, and not happy. He knew the boy wanted to talk about Natalie's opposition, but was hoping that he would broach the subject. And Clayton rather grimly refused to do it. Those next weeks would show how much of the man there was in Graham, but the struggle must be between his mother and himself.

He paused, finally.

Marion was singing.

> "Give me your love for a day;
> A night; an hour.
> If the wages of sin are Death
> I'm willing to pay."

She sang it in her clear passionless voice. Brave words, Clayton thought, but there were few who would pay such wages. This girl at the piano, what did she know of the thing she sang about? What did any of the young know?

They always construed love in terms of passion. But passion was ephemeral. Love lived on. Passion took, but love gave.

He roused himself.

"Have you told Marion about the new arrangement?"

"I didn't know whether you cared to have it told."

"Don't you think she ought to know? If she intends to enter the family, she has a right to know that she is not marrying into great wealth. I don't suggest," he added, as Graham colored hotly, "that it will make any difference. I merely feel she ought to know your circumstances."

He was called to the telephone, and when he came back he found them in earnest conversation. The girl turned toward him smiling.

"Graham has just told me. You are splendid, Mr. Spencer."

And afterward Clayton was forced to admit an element of sincerity in her voice. She had had a disappointment, but she was very game. Her admiration surprised him. He was nearer to liking her than he had ever been.

Even her succeeding words did not quite kill his admiration for her.

"And I have told Graham that he must not let you make all the sacrifices. Of course he is going to enlist."

She had turned her defeat into a triumph against Natalie. Clayton knew then that she would never marry Graham. As she went out he followed her with a faint smile of tribute.

The smile died as he turned to go up the stairs.

Natalie was in her dressing-room. She had not undressed, but was standing by a window. She made no sign that she heard him enter, and he hesitated. Why try to talk things out with her? Why hurt her? Why not let things drift along? There was no hope of bettering them. One of two things he must do, either tear open the situation between them, or ignore it.

"Can I get anything for your head, my dear?"

"I haven't any headache."

"Then I think I'll go to bed. I didn't sleep much last night."

He was going out when she spoke again.

"I came up-stairs because I saw how things were going."

"Do you really want to go into that, to-night?"

"Why not to-night? We'll have to go into it soon enough."

Yet when she turned to him he saw the real distress in her face, and his anger died.

"I didn't want to hurt you, Natalie. I honestly tried. But you know how I feel about that girl."

"Even the servants know it. It is quite evident."

"We parted quite amiably."

"I dare say! You were relieved that she was going. If you would only be ordinarily civil to her-oh, don't you see? She could keep Graham from going into this idiotic war. You can't. I can't. I've tried everything I know. And she knows she can. She's —hateful about it."

"And you would marry him to that sort of a girl?"

"I'd keep him from being blinded, or mutilated, or being killed."

"You can kill his soul."

"His soul!" She burst into hysterical laughter. "You to talk about souls! That's —that's funny."

"Natalie, dear." He was very grave, very gentle. "Has it occurred to you that we are hitting it off rather badly lately?"

She looked at him quickly.

"How? Because I don't think as you do? We got on well enough before this war came along."

"Do you think it is only that?"

"If it's the house, just remember you gave me carte blanche there."

He made a little gesture of despair.

"I just thought perhaps you are not as happy as you might be."

"Happiness again! Did you come up-stairs to-night, with this thing hanging over us, to talk about happiness? That's funny, too." But her eyes were suddenly suspicious. There was something strange in his voice.

"Let's forget that for a moment. Graham will make his own decision. But, before we leave that, let me tell you that I love him as much as you do. His going means exactly as much. It's only —"

"Another point we differ on," she finished for him. "Go on. You are suddenly concerned about my happiness. I'm touched, Clay. You have left me all winter to go out alone, or with anybody who might be sorry enough for me to pick me up, and now?" Suddenly her eyes sharpened, and she drew her breath quickly. "You've seen that scandalous thing in the paper!"

"It was sent to me."

"Who sent it?"

"A firm of private detectives."

She was frightened, and the terror in her face brought him to her quickly.

"Natalie! Don't look like that! I don't believe it, of course. It's stupid. I wasn't going to tell you. You don't think I believe it, do you?"

She let him put an arm around her and hold her, as he would a scared child. There was no love for her in it, but a great pity, and acute remorse that he could hold her so and care for her so little.

"Oh, Clay!" she gasped. "I've been perfectly sick about it!"

His conviction of his own failure to her made him very tender. He talked to her, as she stood with her face buried in the shoulder of his coat, of the absurdity of her fear, of his own understanding, and when she was calmer he made a futile effort to make his position clear.

"I am not angry," he said. "And I'm not fudging you in any way. But you know how things are between us. We have been drifting apart for rather a long time. It's not your fault. Perhaps it is mine. Probably it is. I know I don't make you happy. And sometimes I think things have either got to be better or worse."

"If I'm willing to go along as we are, I think you should be."

"Then let's try to get a little happiness out of it all, Natalie."

"Oh, happiness! You are always raving about happiness. There isn't any such thing."

"Peace, then. Let's have peace, Natalie."

She drew back, regarding him.

"What did you mean by things having to be better or worse?"

When he found no immediate answer, she was uneasy. The prospect of any change in their relationship frightened her. Like all weak women, she was afraid of change. Her life suited her. Even her misery she loved and fed on. She had pitied herself always. Not love, but fear of change, lay behind her shallow, anxious eyes. Yet he could not hurt her. She had been foolish, but she had not been wicked. In his new humility he found her infinitely better than himself.

"I spoke without thinking."

"Then it must have been in your mind. Let me see the clipping, Clay. I've tried to forget what it said."

She took it, still pinned to the prospectus, and bent over them both. When she had examined them, she continued to stand with lowered eyelids, turning and crumpling them. Then she looked up.

"So that is what you meant! It was a —well, a sort of a threat."

"I had no intention of threatening you, my dear. You ought to know me better. That clipping was sent me attached to the slip. The only reason I let you see it was because I think you ought to know how the most innocent things are misconstrued."

"You couldn't divorce me if you wanted to." Then her defiance faded in a weak terror. She began to cry, shameless frightened tears that rolled down her cheeks. She reminded him that she was the mother of his child, that she had sacrificed her life to both of them, and that now they would both leave her and turn her adrift. She had served her purpose, now let her go.

Utter hopelessness kept him dumb. He knew of old that she would cry until she was ready to stop, or until she had gained her point. And he knew, too, that she expected him to put his arms around her again, in token of his complete surrender. The very fact hardened him. He did not want to put his arms around her. He wanted, indeed, to get out into the open air and walk off his exasperation. The scent in the room stifled him.

When he made no move toward her she gradually stopped crying, and gave way to the rage that was often behind her tears.

"Just try to divorce me, and see!"

"Good God, I haven't even mentioned divorce. I only said we must try to get along better. To agree."

"Which means, I dare say, that I am to agree with you!" But she had one weapon still. Suddenly she smiled a little wistfully, and made the apparently complete surrender that always disarmed him.

"I'll be good from now on, Clay. I'll be very, very good. Only-don't be always criticizing me."

She held up her lips, and after a second's hesitation he kissed her. He knew he was precisely where he had been when he started, and he had a hopeless sense of the futility of the effort he had made. Natalie had got by with a bad half-hour, and would proceed to forget it as quickly as she always forgot anything disagreeable. Still, she was in a more receptive mood than usual, and he wondered if that would not be as good a time as any to speak about his new plan as to the mill. He took an uneasy turn or two about the room, feeling her eyes on him.

"There is something else, Natalie."

She had relaxed like a kitten in her big chair, and was lighting one of the small, gilt-tipped cigarets she affected.

"About Graham?"

"It affects Graham. It affects us all."

"Yes?"

He hesitated. To talk to Natalie about business meant reducing it to its most elemental form.

"Have you ever thought that this war of ours means more than merely raising armies?"

"I haven't thought about this war at all. It's too absurd. A lot of politicians?" She shrugged her shoulders.

"It means a great deal of money."

"Well, the country is rich, isn't it?"

"The country? That means the people."

"I knew we'd get to money sooner or later," she observed, resignedly. "All right. We'll be taxed, so we'll cut down on the country house-go on. I can say it before you do. But don't say we'll have to do without the greenhouses, because we can't."

"We may have to go without more than greenhouses."

His tone made her sit bolt upright. Then she laughed a little.

"Poor old Clay," she said, with the caressing tone she used when she meant to make no concession. "I do spend money, don't I? But I do make you comfortable, you know. And what is what I spend, compared with what you are making?"

"It's just that. I don't think I can consistently go on making a profit on this war, now that we are in it."

He explained then what he meant, and watched her face set into the hard lines he knew so well. But she listened to the end and when he had finished she said nothing.

"Well?" he said.

"I don't think you have the remotest idea of doing it. You like to play at the heroic. You can see yourself doing it, and every one pointing to you as the man who threw away a fortune. But you are humbugging yourself. You'll never do it. I give you credit for too much sense."

He went rather white. She knew the weakness in his armor, his hatred of anything theatrical, and with unfailing accuracy she always pierced it.

"Suppose I tell you I have already offered the plant to the government, at a nominal profit."

Suddenly she got up, and every vestige of softness was gone.

"I don't think you would be such a fool."

"I have done it."

"Then you are insane. There is no other possible explanation."

She passed him, moving swiftly, and went into her bedroom. He heard her lock the door behind her.

Chapter XXXIX

Audrey had made a resolution, and with characteristic energy had proceeded to carry it out. She was no longer needed at the recruiting stations. After a month's debate the conscription law was about to be passed, made certain by the frank statement of the British Commission under Balfour as to the urgency of the need of a vast new army in France.

For the first time the Allies laid their cards face up on the table, and America realized to what she was committed. Almost overnight a potential army of hundreds of thousands was changing to one of millions. The situation was desperate. Germany had more men than the Allies, and had vast eastern resources to draw on for still more. To the Allies only the untapped resources of America remained.

In private conference with the President Mr. Balfour had urged haste, and yet more haste.

Audrey, reading her newspapers faithfully, felt with her exaltation a little stirring of regret. Her occupation, such as it was, was gone. For the thin stream of men flowing toward the recruiting stations there was now to be a vast movement of the young manhood of the nation. And she could have no place in it.

Almost immediately she set to work to find herself a new place. At first there seemed to be none. She went to a hospital, and offered her strong body and her two willing hands for training.

"I could learn quickly," she pleaded, "and surely there will not be enough nurses for such an army as we are to have."

"Our regular course is three years."

"But a special course. Surely I may have that. There are so many things one won't need in France."

The head of the training school smiled rather wistfully. They came to her so often now, these intelligent, untrained women, all eagerness to help, to forget and unlive, if they could, their wasted lives.

"You want to go to France, of course?"

"If I can. My husband was killed over there."

But she did not intend to make capital of Chris's death. "Of course, that has nothing to do with my going. I simply want to work."

"It's hard work. Not romantic."

"I am not looking for romance."

In the end, however, she had to give it up. In some hospitals they were already training nurses helpers, but they were to relieve trained women for France. She went home to think it over. She had felt that by leaving the country she would solve Clayton's problem and her own. To stay on, seeing him now and then, was torture for them both.

But there was something else. She had begun, that afternoon, to doubt whether she was fitted for nursing after all. The quiet of the hospital, the all-pervading odor of drugs, the subdued voice and quiet eyes of the head of the training school, as of one who had looked on life and found it infinitely sad, depressed her. She had walked home, impatient with herself, disappointed in her own failure. She thought dismally:

"I am of no earthly use. I've played all my life, and now I'm paying for it. I ought to." And she ran over her pitiful accomplishments: "golf, bridge, ride, shoot, swim, sing (a little), dance, tennis, some French-what a sickening list!"

She was glad that day to find Clare Gould waiting for her. As usual, the girl had brought her tribute, this time some early strawberries. Audrey found her in the pantry arranging their leaves in a shallow dish.

"Clare!" she said. "Aren't you working?"

"I've gone on night-turn now."

The girl's admiration salved her wounded pride in herself. Then she saw, on a table, an envelope with her name on it. Clare's eyes followed hers.

"That's the rest of the money, Mrs. Valentine."

She colored, but Audrey only smiled at her.

"Fine!" she said. "Are you sure you can spare it?"

"I couldn't rest until it was all paid up. And I'm getting along fine. I make a lot, really."

"Tell me about the night work."

"We've gone on double turn. I rather like it at night. It's —well, it's like something on the stage. The sparks fly from the lathes, and they look like fireworks. And when they hammer on hot metal it's lovely."

She talked on, incoherent but glowing. She liked her big turret lathe. It gave her a sense of power. She liked to see the rough metal growing smooth and shining like silver under her hands. She was naively pleased that she was doing a man's work, and doing it well.

Audrey leaned back in her chair and listened. All this that Clare was talking about was Clayton's doing. He at least had dreamed true. He was doing a man's part, too, in the war. Even this girl, whose hand Natalie Spencer would not have touched, this girl was dreaming true.

Clare was still talking. The draft would be hard on the plant. They were short-handed now. There was talk of taking in more girls to replace the men who would be called.

"Do you think I could operate a lathe, Clare?"

"You! Why, Mrs. Valentine, it's not work for a lady! Look at my hands."

But Audrey made an impatient gesture.

"I don't care about my hands. The question is, could I do it? I don't seem able to do anything else."

"Why, yes." Clare was reluctant. "I can, and you're a lot cleverer than I am. But it's hard. It's rough, and some of the talk-oh, I hope you don't mean it, Mrs. Valentine."

Audrey, however, was meaning it. It seemed to her, all at once, the way out. Here was work, needed work. Work that she could do. For the first time in months she blessed the golf and riding that had kept her fit.

"Mr. Spencer is a friend of yours. He'll never let you do it."

"He is not to know, Clare," Audrey said briskly. "You are quite right. He would probably be very-mannish about it. So we won't tell him. And now, how shall I go about getting in? Will they teach me, or shall I have to lust learn? And whatever shall I wear?"

Clare explained while, for she was determined not to lose a minute, Audrey changed into her plainest clothes. They would be in time, if they hurried, before the employment department closed. There were women in charge there. They card-indexed you, and then you were investigated by the secret service and if you were all right, well, that was all.

"Mercy! It's enough," said Audrey, impatiently. "Do you mean to say they'll come here?"

She glanced around her rooms, littered with photographs of people well known to the public through the society journals, with its high bright silver vases, its odd gifts of porcelain, its grand piano taking up more than its share of room.

"If they come here," she deliberated, "they won't take me, Clare. They'll be thinking I'm living on German money!"

So, in the end, she did not go to the munition works. She went room-hunting instead, with Clare beside her, very uncomfortable on the street for fear Audrey would be compromised by walking with her. And at six o'clock that evening a young woman with a softly inflected voice and an air of almost humorous enjoyment of something the landlady failed to grasp, was the tenant, for one month's rent in advance, of a room on South Perry Street.

Clare was almost in tears.

"I can't bear to think of your sleeping in that bed, Mrs. Valentine," she protested. "It dips down so."

"I shan't have much time to sleep, anyhow. And when I do so I shall be so tired! —-What was the name I gave her, Clare?"

"Thompson. Mary Thompson."

"She surprised me, or I'd have thought of a prettier one." She was absurdly high-spirited, although the next day's ordeal rather worried her when she thought about it. She had, oddly enough, no trepidation about the work itself. It was passing the detectives in the employment department that worried her. As a matter of fact, however, there was no ordeal. Her card was carried to the desk in the corner, where the two men sat on whose decisions might so easily rest the safety of the entire plant, and they surveyed her carefully. Audrey looked ahead, and waited. They would come over and question her, and the whole fabric she had built would be destroyed. But nothing happened. She was told she would be notified in a day or two if she would be taken on, and with that she was forced to be content.

She had a bad moment, however, for Graham came through the office on his way out, and stopped for a moment directly in front of her. Her heart almost stopped beating, and she dropped her glove and stooped to pick it up. When she sat erect again he was moving on. But even her brief glance had showed her that the boy looked tired and depressed.

She went to her rented room at once, for she must be prepared for inquiries about her. During the interval she arranged for the closing of her apartment and the storing of her furniture. With their going would depart the last reminders of the old life, and she felt a curious sense of relief. They had little happiness to remind her of, and much suffering. The world had changed since she had gathered them together, and she had changed with it. She was older and sadder. But she would not have gone back. Not for anything would she have gone back.

She had one thing to do, however, before she disappeared. She had promised to try to find something for Delight, and she did it with her usual thoroughness and dispatch. She sent for her that last day in the apartment, when in the morning she had found at the Perry Street room a card telling her to report the following night. When Delight came in she found the little apartment rather bare and rather dreary, but Audrey was cheerful, almost gay.

"Going away for a little while," she explained. "I've stored a lot of stuff. And now, my dear, do you really want to work?"

"I just must do something."

"All right. That's settled. I've got the thing I spoke about, in one of the officers' training-camps. But remember, Delight, this is not going to be a romantic adventure. It's to be work."

"I don't want a romantic adventure, Mrs. Valentine."

"Poor little thing," Audrey reflected to herself. And aloud: "Good! Of course I know you're sincere about working. I—I understand, awfully well."

Delight was pleased, but Audrey saw that she was not happy. Even when the details had been arranged she still sat in her straight chair and made no move to go. And Audrey felt that the next move was up to her.

"What's the news about Graham Spencer?" she inquired. "He'll be drafted, I suppose."

"Not if they claim exemption. He's making shells, you know."

She lifted rather heavy eyes to Audrey's.

"His mother is trying that now," she said. "Ever since his engagement was broken?"

"Oh, it was broken, was it?"

"Yes. I don't know why. But it's off. Anyhow Mrs. Spencer is telling everybody he can't be spared."

"And his father?"

"I don't know. He doesn't talk about it, I think."

"Perhaps he wants him to make his own decision."

Delight rose and drew down her veil with hands that Audrey saw were trembling a little.

"How can he make his own decision?" she asked. "He may think it's his own, but it's hers, Mrs. Spencer's. She's always talking, always. And she's plausible. She can make him think black is white, if she wants to."

"Why don't you talk to him?"

"I? He'd think I'd lost my mind! Besides, that isn't it. If you-like a man, you want him to do the right thing because he wants to, not because a girl asks him to."

"I wonder," Audrey said, slowly, "if he's worth it, Delight?"

"Worth what?" She was startled.

"Worth your-worth our worrying about him."

But she did not need Delight's hasty and flushed championship of Graham to tell her what she already knew.

After she had gone, Audrey sat alone in her empty rooms and faced a great temptation. She was taking herself out of Clayton's life. She knew that she would be as lost to him among the thousands of workers in the munition plant as she would have been in Russia. According to Clare, he rarely went into the shops themselves, and never at night.

Of course "out of his life" was a phrase. They would meet again. But not now, not until they had had time to become resigned to what they had already accepted. The war would not last forever. And then she thought of their love, which had been born and had grown, always with war at its background. They had gone along well enough until this winter, and then everything had changed. Chris, Natalie, Clayton, herself-none of them were quite what they had been. Was that one of the gains of war, that sham fell away, and people revealed either the best or the worst in them?

War destroyed, but it also revealed.

The temptation was to hear Clayton's voice again. She went to the telephone, and stood with the instrument in her hands, thinking. Would it comfort him? Or would it only bring her close for a moment, to emphasize her coming silence?

She put it down, and turned away. When, some time later, the taxicab came to take her to Perry Street, she was lying on her bed in the dusk, face-down and arms outstretched, a lonely and pathetic figure, all her courage dead for the moment, dead but for the desire to hear Clayton's voice again before the silence closed down.

She got up and pinned on her hat for the last time, before the mirror of the little inlaid dressing-table. And she smiled rather forlornly at her reflection in the glass.

"Well, I've got the present, anyhow," she considered. "I'm not going either to wallow in the past or peer into the future. I'm going to work."

The prospect cheered her. After all, work was the great solution. It was the great healer, too. That was why men bore their griefs better than women. They could work.

She took a final glance around her stripped and cheerless rooms. How really little things mattered! All her life she had been burdened with things. Now at last she was free of them.

The shabby room on Perry Street called her. Work called, beckoned to her with calloused, useful hands. She closed and locked the door and went quietly down the stairs.

Chapter XL

One day late in May, Clayton, walking up-town in lieu of the golf he had been forced to abandon, met Doctor Haverford on the street, and found his way barred by that rather worried-looking gentleman.

"I was just going to see you, Clayton," he said. "About two things. I'll walk back a few blocks with you."

He was excited, rather exalted.

"I'm going in," he announced. "Regimental chaplain. I've got a year's leave of absence. I'm rather vague about what a chaplain does, but I rather fancy he can be useful."

"You'll get over, of course. You're lucky. And you'll find plenty to do."

"I've been rather anxious," Doctor Haverford confided. "I've been a clergyman so long that I don't know just how I'll measure up as a man. You know what I mean. I am making no reflection on the church. But I've been sheltered and-well, I've been looked after. I don't think I am physically brave. It would be a fine thing," he said wryly, "if the chaplain were to turn and run under fire!"

"I shouldn't worry about that."

"My salary is to go on. But I don't like that, either. If I hadn't a family I wouldn't accept it. Delight thinks I shouldn't, anyhow. As a matter of fact, there ought to be no half-way measures about our giving ourselves. If I had a son to give it would be different."

Clayton looked straight ahead. He knew that the rector had, for the moment, forgotten that he had a son to give and that he had not yet given.

"Why don't you accept a small allowance?" he inquired quietly. "Or, better still, why don't you let me know how much it will take and let me do it? I'd like to feel that I was represented in France-by you," he added.

And suddenly the rector remembered. He was most uncomfortable, and very flushed.

"Thanks. I can't let you do that, of course."

"Why not?"

"Because, hang it all, Clayton, I'm not a parasite. I took the car, because it enabled me to do my parish work better. But I'm not going to run off to war and let you keep my family."

Clayton glanced at him, at his fine erect old figure, his warmly flushed face. War did strange things. There was a new light in the rector's once worldly if kindly eyes. He had the strained look of a man who sees great things, as yet far away, and who would hasten toward them. Insensibly he quickened his pace.

"But I can't go myself, so why can't I send a proxy?"

Clayton asked, smiling. "I've an idea I'd be well represented."

"That's a fine way to look at it, but I can't do it. I've saved something, not much, but it will do for a year or two. I'm glad you made the offer, though. It was like you, and-it showed me the way. I can't let any man, or any group of men, finance my going."

And he stuck to it. Clayton, having in mind those careful canvasses of the congregation of Saint Luke's which had every few years resulted in raising the rector's salary, was surprised and touched. After all, war was like any other grief. It brought out the best or the worst in us. It roused or it crushed us.

The rector had been thinking.

"I'm a very fortunate man," he said, suddenly. "They're standing squarely behind me, at home. It's the women behind the army that will make it count, Clayton."

Clayton said nothing.

"Which reminds me," went on the rector, "that I find Mrs. Valentine has gone away. I called on her to-day, and she has given up her apartment. Do you happen to know where she is? She has left no address."

"Gone away?" Clayton repeated. "Why, no. I hadn't heard of it."

There in the busy street he felt a strange sense of loneliness. Always, although he did not see her, he felt her presence. She walked the same streets. For the calling, if his extremity became too great, he could hear her voice over the telephone. There was always the hope, too, of meeting her. Not by design. She had forbidden that. But some times perhaps God would be good to them both, if they earned it, and they could touch hands for a moment.

But-gone!

"You are certain she left no address?"

"Quite certain. She has stored her furniture, I believe."

There was a sense of hurt, then, too. She had made this decision without telling him. It seemed incredible. A dozen decisions a day he made, and when they were vital there was always in his mind the question as to whether she would approve or not. He could not go to her with them, but mentally he was always consulting with her, earning her approbation. And she had gone without a word.

"Do you think she has gone to France?" He knew his voice sounded stiff and constrained.

"I hope not. She was being so useful here. Of course, the draft law-amazing thing, the draft law! Never thought we'd come to it. But it threw her out, in a way, of course."

"What has the draft law to do with Mrs. Valentine?"

"Why, you know what she was doing, don't you?"

"I haven't seen her recently."

The rector half-stopped.

"Well!" he said. "Let me tell you, Clayton, that that girl has been recruiting men, night after night and day after day. She's done wonders. Standing in a wagon, mind you, in the slums, or anywhere; I heard her one night. By George, I went home and tore up a sermon I had been working on for days."

Why hadn't he known? Why hadn't he realized that that was exactly the sort of thing she would do? There was bitterness in his heart, too. He might easily have stood unseen in the crowd, and have watched and listened and been proud of her. Then, these last weeks, when he had been working, or dining out, or sitting dreary and bored in a theater, she had been out in the streets. Ah, she lived, did Audrey. Others worked and played, but she lived. Audrey! Audrey!

"—in the rain," the rector was saying. "But she didn't mind it. I remember her saying to the crowd, 'It's raining over here, and maybe it's raining on the fellows in the trenches. But I tell you, I'd rather be over there, up to my waist in mud and water, than scurrying for a doorway here.' They had started to run out of the shower, but at that they grinned and stopped. She was wonderful, Clayton."

In the rain! And after it was over she would go home, in some crowded bus or car, to her lonely rooms, while he rolled about the city in a limousine! It was cruel of her not to have told him, not to have allowed him at least to see that she was warm and dry.

"I've been very busy. I hadn't heard," he said, slowly. "Is it-was it generally known?"

Had Natalie known, and kept it from him?

"I think not. Delight saw her and spoke to her, I believe."

"And you have no idea where she is now."

"None whatever."

He learned that night that Natalie had known, and he surprised a little uneasiness in her face.

"I —heard about it," she said. "I can't imagine her making a speech. She's not a bit oratorical."

"We might have sent out one of the cars for her, if I'd known."

"Oh, she was looked after well enough."

"Looked after?"

Natalie had made an error, and knew it.

"I heard that a young clergyman was taking her round," she said, and changed the subject. But he knew that she was either lying or keeping something from him. In those days of tension he found her half-truths more irritating than her rather childish falsehoods. In spite of himself, however, the thought of the young clergyman rankled.

That night, stretched in the low chair in his dressing-room, under the reading light, he thought over things carefully. If he loved her as he thought he did, he ought to want her to be happy. Things between them were hopeless and wretched. If this clergyman, or Sloane, or any other man loved her, and he groaned as he thought how lovable she was, then why not want for her such happiness as she could find?

He slept badly that night, and for some reason Audrey wove herself into his dreams of the new plant. The roar of the machinery took on the soft huskiness of her voice, the deeper note he watched for and loved.

Chapter XLI

Anna Klein stood in her small room and covered her mouth with her hands, lest she shriek aloud. She knew quite well that the bomb in the suit-case would not suffice to blow up the whole great plant. But she knew what the result of its explosion would be.

The shells were not loaded at the Spencer plant. They were shipped away for that. But the fuses were loaded there, and in the small brick house at the end of the fuse building there were stored masses of explosive, enough to destroy a town. It was there, of course, that Herman was to place the bomb. She knew how he would do it, carefully, methodically, and with what a lumbering awkward gait he would make his escape.

Her whole mind was bent on giving the alarm. On escaping, first, and then on arousing the plant. But when the voices below continued, long after Herman had gone, she was entirely desperate. Herman had not carried out the suit-case. He had looked, indeed, much as usual as he walked out the garden path and closed the gate behind him. He had walked rather slowly, but then he always walked slowly. She seemed to see, however, a new caution in his gait, as of one who dreaded to stumble.

She dressed herself, with shaking fingers, and pinned on her hat. The voices still went on below, monotonous, endless; the rasping of Rudolph's throat, irritated by cheap cigarets, the sound of glasses on the table, once a laugh, guttural and mirthless. It was ten o'clock when she knew, by the pushing back of their chairs, that they were preparing to depart. Ten o'clock!

She was about to commence again the feverish unscrewing of the door hinges, when she heard Rudolph's step on the stairs. She had only time to get to the back of her room, beside the bed, when she heard him try the knob.

"Anna?"

She let him call her again.

"Anna!"

"What is it?"

"You in bed?"

"Yes. Go away and let me alone. I've got a right to sleep, anyhow."

"I'm going out, but I'll be back in ten minutes. You try any tricks and I'll get you. See?"

"You make me sick," she retorted.

She heard him turn and run lightly down the stairs. Only when she heard the click of the gate did she dare to begin again at the door. She got down-stairs easily, but she was still a prisoner. However, she found the high little window into the coal-shed open, and crawled through it, to stand listening. The street was quiet.

Once outside the yard she started to run. They would let her telephone from the drug-store, even without money. She had no money. But the drug-store was closed and dark, and the threat of Rudolph's return terrified her. She must get off the hill, somehow.

There were still paths down the steep hill-side, dangerous things that hugged the edge of small, rocky precipices, or sloped steeply to sudden turns. But she had played over the hill all her young life. She plunged down, slipping and falling a dozen times, and muttering, some times an oath, some times a prayer,

"Oh, God, let me be in time. Oh, God, hold him up a while until I —" then a slip. "If I fall now —"

Only when she was down in the mill district did she try to make any plan. It was almost eleven then, and her ears were tense with listening for the sound she dreaded. She faced her situation, then. She could not telephone from a private house, either to the mill or to the Spencer house, what she feared, and the pay-booths of the telephone company demanded cash in advance. She was incapable of clear thought, or she would have found some way out, un- doubtedly. What she did, in the end, was to board an up-town car and throw herself on the mercy of the conductor.

"I've got to get up-town," she panted. "I'll not go in. See? I'll stand here and you take me as far as you can. Look at me! I don't look as though I'm just bumming a ride, do I?"

The conductor hesitated. He had very little faith in human nature, but Anna's eyes were both truthful and desperate. He gave the signal to go on.

"What's up?" he said. "Police after you?"

"Yes," Anna replied briefly.

There is, in certain ranks, a tacit conspiracy against the police. The conductor hated them. They rode free on his car, and sometimes kept an eye on him in the rush hours. They had a way, too, of letting him settle his own disputes with inebriated gentlemen who refused to pay their fares.

"Looks as though they'd come pretty close to grabbing you," he opened, by way of conver- sation. "But ten of 'em aren't a match for one smart girl. They can't run. All got flat feet."

Anna nodded. She was faint and dizzy, and the car seemed to creep along. It was twenty minutes after eleven when she got out. The conductor leaned down after her, hanging to the handrail.

"Good luck to you!" he said. "And you'd better get a better face on you than that. It's enough to send you up, on suspicion!"

She hardly heard him. She began to run, and again she said over and over her little inarticulate prayer. She knew the Spencer house. More than once she had walked past it, on Sunday afternoons, for the sheer pleasure of seeing Graham's home. Well, all that was over now. Everything was over, unless —

The Spencer house was dark, save for a low light in the hall. A new terror seized her. Suppose Graham saw her. He might not believe her story. He might think it a ruse to see his father. But, as it happened, Clayton had sent the butler to bed, and himself answered the bell from the library.

He recognized her at once, and because he saw the distress on her face he brought her in at once. In the brief moment that it required to turn on the lights he had jumped to a sickening conviction that Graham was at the bottom of her visit, and her appearance in full light confirmed this.

"Come into the library," he said. "We can talk in there." He led the way and drew up a chair for her. But she did not sit down. She steadied herself by its back, instead.

"You think it's about Graham," she began. "It isn't, not directly, that is. And my coming is terrible, because it's my own father. They're going to blow up the munition plant, Mr. Spencer!"

"When?"

"To-night, I think. I came as fast as I could. I was locked in."

"Locked in?" He was studying her face.

"Yes. Don't bother about that now. I'm not crazy or hysterical. I tell you I heard them. I've been a prisoner or I'd have come sooner. To-day they brought something-dynamite or a bomb-in a suit-case —and it's gone to-night. He took it-my father."

He was already at the telephone as she spoke. He called the mill first, and got the night superintendent. Then he called a number Anna supposed was the police station, and at the same time he was ringing the garage-signal steadily for his car. By the time he had explained the situation to the police, his car was rolling under the porte-cochere beside the house. He was starting out, forgetful of the girl, when she caught him by the arm.

"You mustn't go!" she cried. "You'll be killed, too. It will all go, all of it. You can't be spared, Mr. Spencer. You can build another mill, but —"

He shook her off, gently.

"Of course I'm going," he said. "We'll get it in time. Don't you worry. You sit down here and rest, and when it's all straightened out I'll come back. I suppose you can't go home, after this?"

"No," she said, dully.

He ran out, hatless, and a moment later she heard the car rush out into the night.

Five minutes passed. Ten. Anna Klein stood, staring ahead of her. When nothing happened she moved around and sat down in the chair. She was frightfully tired. She leaned her head back and tried to think of something to calm her shaking nerves, —that this was Graham's home, that he sometimes sat in that very chair. But she found that Graham meant nothing to her. Nothing mattered, except that her warning had been in time.

So intent was she on the thing that she was listening for that smaller, near-by sounds escaped her. So she did not hear a door open up-stairs and the soft rustle of a woman's negligee as it swept from stair to stair. But as the foot-steps outside the door she stood up quickly and looked back over her shoulder.

Natalie stood framed in the doorway, staring at her.

"Well?" she said. And on receiving no answer from the frightened girl, "What are you doing here?"

The ugly suspicion in her voice left Anna speechless for a moment.

"Don't move, please," said Natalie's cold voice. "Stay just where you are." She reached behind the curtain at the doorway, and Anna heard the far-away ringing of a bell, insistent and prolonged. The girl roused herself with an effort.

"I came to see Mr. Spencer."

"That is a likely story! Who let you in?"

"Mr. Spencer."

"Mr. Spencer is not in."

"But he did. I'm telling you the truth. Indeed I am. I rang the bell, and he came to the door. I had something to tell him."

"What could you possibly have to tell my husband at this hour."

But Anna Klein did not answer. From far away there came a dull report followed almost immediately by a second one. The windows rattled, and the house seemed to rock rather gently on its foundation. Then silence.

Anna Klein picked up her empty pocket-book from the table and looked at it.

"I was too late," she said dully, and the next moment she was lying at Natalie's feet.

Chapter XLII

It was not until dawn that the full extent of the disaster was revealed. All night, by the flames from the sheds in the yard, which were of wood and still burning, rescue parties had worked frantically. Two of the long buildings, nearest to the fuse department, had collapsed entirely. Above the piles of fallen masonry might be seen, here and there, the black mass of some machine or lathe, and it was there the search parties were laboring. Luckily the fuse department had not gone double turn, and the night shift in the machine-shop was not a full one.

The fuse department was a roaring furnace, and repeated calls had brought in most of the fire companies of the city. Running back and forth in the light of the flames were the firemen and such volunteer rescuers as had been allowed through the police cordon. Outside that line of ropes and men were gathered a tragic crowd, begging, imploring to be allowed through to search for some beloved body. Now and then a fresh explosion made the mob recoil, only to press close again, importuning, tragic, hopeless.

The casualty list ran high. All night long ambulances stood in a row along the street, backed up to the curb and waiting, and ever so often a silent group, in broken step, carried out some quiet covered thing that would never move again.

With the dawn Graham found his father. He had thrown off his coat and in his shirt-sleeves was, with other rescuers, digging in the ruins. Graham himself had been working. He was nauseated, weary, and unutterably wretched, for he had seen the night superintendent and had heard of his father's message.

"Klein!" he said. "You don't mean Herman Klein?"

"That was what he said. I was to find him and hold him until he got here. But I couldn't find him. He may have got out. There's no way of telling now."

Waves of fresh nausea swept over Graham. He sat down on a pile of bricks and wiped his forehead, clammy with sweat.

"I hope to God he was burned alive," muttered the other man, surveying the scene. His eyes were reddened with smoke from the fire, his clothing torn.

"I was knocked down myself," he said. "I was out in the yard looking for Klein, and I guess I lay there quite a while. If I hadn't gone out?" He shrugged his shoulders.

"How many women were on the night shift?"

"Not a lot. Twenty, perhaps. If I had my way I'd take every German in the country and boil 'em in oil. I didn't want Klein back, but he was a good workman. Well, he's done a good job now."

It was after that that Graham saw his father, a strange, wild-eyed Clayton who drove his pick with a sort of mad strength, and at the same time gave orders in an unfamiliar voice. Graham, himself a disordered figure, watched him for a moment. He was divided between fear and resolution. Some place in that debacle there lay his own responsibility. He was still bewildered, but the fact that Anna's father had done the thing was ominous.

The urge to confession was stronger than his fears. Somehow, during the night, he had become a man. But now he only felt, that somehow, during the night, he had become a murderer.

Clayton looked up, and he moved toward him.

"Yes?"

"I've had some coffee made at a house down the street. Won't you come and have it?"

Clayton straightened. He was very tired, and the yard was full of volunteers now, each provided at the gate with a pick or shovel. A look at the boy's face decided him.

"I'll come," he said, and turned his pick over to a man beside him. He joined Graham, and for a moment he looked into the boy's eyes. Then he put a hand on his shoulder, and together they walked out, past the line of ambulances, into a street where the scattered houses showed not a single unshattered window, and the pavements were littered with glass.

His father's touch comforted the boy, but it made even harder the thing he had to do. For he could not go through life with this thing on his soul. There had been a moment, after he learned of Herman's implication, when he felt the best thing would be to kill himself, but he had put that aside. It was too easy. If Herman Klein had done this thing because of Anna and himself, then he was a murderer. If he had done it because he was a German, then he-Graham-had no right to die. He would live to make as many Germans as possible pay for this night's work.

"I've got something to tell you, father," he said, as they paused before the house where the coffee was ready. Clayton nodded, and together they went inside. Even this house was partially destroyed. A piece of masonry had gone through the kitchen, and standing on fallen bricks and plaster, a cheerful old woman was cooking over a stove which had somehow escaped destruction.

"It's bad," she said to Graham, as she poured the coffee into cups, "but it might have been worse, Mr. Spencer. We're all alive. And I guess I'll understand what my boy's writing home about now. They've sure brought the war here this night."

Graham carried the coffee into the little parlor, where Clayton sat dropped on a low chair, his hands between his knees. He was a strange, disheveled figure, gray of face and weary, and the hand he held out for the cup was blistered and blackened. Graham did not touch his coffee. He put it on the mantel, and stood waiting while Clayton finished his.

"Shall I tell you now, sir?"

Clayton drew a long breath.

"It was Herman Klein who did it?"

"Probably. I had a warning last night, but it was too late. I should have known, of course, but somehow I didn't. He'd been with us a long time. I'd have sworn he was loyal."

For the first time in his life Graham saw his father weaken, the pitiful, ashamed weakness of a strong man. His voice broke, his face twitched. The boy drew himself up; they couldn't both go to pieces. He could not know that Clayton had worked all that night in that hell with the conviction that in some way his own son was responsible; that he knew already what Graham was about to tell him.

"If Herman Klein did it, father, it was because he was the tool of a gang. And the reason he was a tool was because he thought I was-living with Anna. I wasn't. I don't know why I wasn't. There was every chance. I suppose I meant to some time. Anyhow, he thought I was."

If he had expected any outbreak from Clayton, he met none. Clayton sat looking ahead, and listening. Inside of the broken windows the curtains were stirring in the fresh breeze of early morning, and in the kitchen the old woman was piling the fallen bricks noisily.

"I had been flirting with her a little-it wasn't much more than that, and I gave her a watch at Christmas. He found it out, and he beat her. Awfully. She ran away and sent for me, and I met her. She had to hide for days. Her face was all bruised. Then she got sick from it. She was sick for weeks."

"Did he know where she was?"

"I think not, or he'd have gone to get her. But Rudolph Klein knew something. I took her out to dinner, to a roadhouse, a few days ago, and she said she saw him there. I didn't. All that time, weeks, I'd never —I'd never gone to her room. That night I did. I don't know why. I—"

"Go on."

"Well, I went, but I didn't stay. I couldn't. I guess she thought I was crazy. I went away, that's all. And the next day I felt that she might be feeling as though I'd turned her down or something. And I felt responsible. Maybe you won't understand. I don't quite myself. Anyhow, I went back, to let her know I wasn't quite a brute, even if—-But she was gone. I'm not trying to excuse myself. It's a rotten story, for I was engaged to Marion then."

Suddenly he sat down beside Clayton and buried his face in his hands. For some reason or other Clayton found himself back in the hospital, that night when Joey lay still and quiet, and Graham was sobbing like a child, prostrate on the white covering of the bed. With the incredible rapidity of thought in a mental crisis, he saw the last months, the boy's desire to go to France thwarted, his attempt to interest himself in the business, the tool Marion Hayden had made of him, Anna's doglike devotion, all leading inevitably to catastrophe. And through it all he saw Natalie, holding Graham back from war, providing him with extra money, excusing him, using his confidences for her own ends, insidiously sapping the boy's confidence in his father and himself.

"We'll have to stand up to this together, Graham."

The boy looked up.

"Then-you're not going to throw me over altogether —"

"No."

"But-all this —!"

"If Herman Klein had not done it, there were others who would, probably. It looks as though you had provided them with a tool, but I suppose we were vulnerable in a dozen ways."

He rose, and they stood, eyes level, father and son, in the early morning sunlight. And suddenly Graham's arms were around his shoulders, and something tight around Clayton's heart relaxed. Once again, and now for good, he had found his boy, the little boy who had not so long ago stood on a chair for this very embrace. Only now the boy was a man.

"I'm going to France, father," he said. "I'm going to pay them back for this. And out of every two shots I fire one will be for you."

Perhaps he had found his boy only to lose him, but that would have to be as God willed.

At ten o'clock he went up to the house, to change his wet and draggled clothing. The ruins were being guarded by soldiers, and the work of rescue was still going on, more slowly now, since there was little or no hope of finding any still living thing in that flame-swept wreckage. He found Natalie in bed, with Madeleine in attendance, and he learned that her physician had just gone.

He felt that he could not talk to her just then. She had a morbid interest in horrors, and with the sights of that night fresh in his mind he could not discuss them. He stopped, however, in her doorway.

"I'm glad you are resting," he said, "Better stay in bed to-day. It's been a shock."

"Resting! I've been frightfully ill."

"I'm sorry, my dear. I'll come in again on my way out."

"Clay!"

He turned in the doorway.

"Is it all gone? Everything?"

"Practically. Yes."

"But you were insured?"

"I'll tell you about that later. I haven't given it much thought yet. I don't know just how we stand."

"I shall never let Graham go back to it again. I warn you. I've been lying here for hours, thinking that it might have happened as easily as not while he was there."

He hardly listened. He had just remembered Anna.

"I left a girl here last night, Natalie," he said. "Do you happen to know what became of her?"

Natalie stirred on her pillows.

"I should think I do. She fainted, or pretended to faint. The servants looked after her."

"Has she gone?"

"I hope so. It is almost noon. Oh, by the way," she called, as he moved off, "there is a message for you. A woman named Gould, from the Central Hospital. She wants to see you at once. They have kept the telephone ringing all the morning."

Clare Gould! That was odd. He had seen her taken out, a bruised and moaning creature, her masses of fair hair over her shoulders, her eyes shut. The surgeons had said she was not badly hurt. She might be worse than they thought. The mention of her name brought Audrey before him. He hoped, wherever she was, she would know that he was all right.

As soon as he had changed he called the hospital. The message came back promptly and clearly.

"We have a woman named Gould here. She is not badly hurt, but she is hysterical. She wants to see you, but if you can't come at once I am to give you a message. Wait a moment. She has written it, but it's hardly legible."

Clayton waited.

"It's about somebody you know, who had gone on night turn recently at your plant. I can't read the name. It looks like Ballantine."

"It isn't Valentine, is it?"

"Perhaps it is. It's just a scrawl. But the first name is clear enough-Audrey."

Afterward he did not remember hanging up the receiver, or getting out of the house. He seemed to come to himself somewhat at the hospital, and at the door to Clare's ward his brain suddenly cleared. He did not need Clare's story. It seemed that he knew it all, had known it long ages before. Her very words sounded like infinite repetitions of something he had heard, over and over.

"She was right beside me, and I was showing her about the lathe. They'd told me I could teach her. She was picking it up fast, too. And she liked it. She liked it   "

The fact that Audrey had liked it broke down his scanty reserve of restraint. Clayton found himself looking down at her from a great distance. She was very remote. Clare pulled herself together.

"When the first explosion came it didn't touch us. But I guess she knew it meant more. She said something about the telephone and getting help and there'd be more, and she started to run. I just stood there, watching her run, and waiting. And then the second one came, and —"

Suddenly Clare seemed to disappear altogether. He felt something catch his arm, and the nurse's voice, very calm and quiet:

"Sit down. I'll get you something."

Then he was swallowing a fluid that burned his throat, and Clare was crying with the sheet drawn to her mouth, and somewhere Audrey —

He got up, and the nurse followed him out.

"You might look for the person here," she suggested. "We have had several brought in."

He was still dazed, but he followed her docilely. Audrey was not there. He seemed to have known that, too. That there would be a long search, and hours of agony, and at the end-the one thing he did not know was what was to be at the end.

All that afternoon he searched, going from hospital to hospital. And at each one, as he stopped, that curious feeling of inner knowledge told him she was not there. But the same instinct told him she was not dead. He would have known it if she was dead. There was no reasoning in it. He could not reason. But he knew, somehow.

Then, late in the afternoon, he found her. He knew that he had found her. It was as though, at the entrance of the hospital, some sixth sense had told him this was right at last. He was quite steady, all at once. She was here, waiting for him to come. And now he had come, and it would be all right.

Yet, for a time, it seemed all wrong. She was not conscious, had not roused since she was brought it. There were white screens around her bed, and behind them she lay alone. They had braided her hair in two long dark braids, and there was a bandage on one of her arms. She looked very young and very tired, but quite peaceful.

His arrival had caused a small stir of excitement, his own prominence, the disaster with which the country was ringing. But for a few minutes, before the doctors arrived, he was alone with her behind the screen. It was like being alone with his dead. Bent over her, his face pressed to one of her quiet hands, he whispered to her all the little tendernesses, the aching want of her, that so long he had buried in his heart. Things he could not have told her, waking, he told her then. It seemed, too, that she must rouse to them, that she must feel him there beside her, calling her back. But she did not move.

It was then, for the first time, that he wondered what he would do if she should die.

The doctors, coming behind the screen, found him sitting erect and still, staring ahead of him, with a strange expression on his face. He had just decided that he could not, under any circumstances, live if she died.

It was rather a good thing for Clayton's sanity that they gave him hope. He was completely unnerved, tired and desperate. Indeed, when they came in he had been picturing Audrey and himself, wandering hand in hand, very quietly and contentedly, in some strange world which was his rather hazy idea of the Beyond. It seemed to him quite sane and extraordinarily happy.

The effort of meeting the staff roused him, and, with hope came a return to normality. There was much to be done, special nurses, a private room, and-rather reluctantly —-friends and relatives to be notified. Only for a few minutes, out of all of life, had she been his. He must give her up now. Life had become one long renunciation.

He did not go home at all that night. He divided his time between the plant and the hospital, going back and forward. Each time he found the report good. She was still strong; no internal injuries had manifested themselves, and the concussion would probably wear off before long. He wanted to be there when she first opened her eyes. He was afraid she might be frightened, and there would be a bad minute when she remembered-if she did remember.

At midnight, going into the room, he found Mrs. Haverford beside Audrey's bed, knitting placidly. She seemed to accept his being there as perfectly natural, and she had no sick-room affectations. She did not whisper, for one thing.

"The nurse thinks she is coming round, Clayton," she said. "I waited, because I thought she ought to see a familiar face when she does."

Mrs. Haverford was eminently good for him. Her cheerful matter-of-factness her competent sanity, restored his belief in a world that had seemed only chaos and death. How much, he wondered later, had Mrs. Haverford suspected? He had not been in any condition to act a part. But whatever she suspected she knew was locked in her kindly breast.

Audrey moved slightly, and he went over to her. When he glanced up again Mrs. Haverford had gone out.

So it was that Audrey came back to him, and to him alone. She asked no questions. She only lay quite still on her white pillows, and looked at him. Even when he knelt beside her and drew her toward him, she said nothing, but she lifted her uninjured hand and softly caressed his bent head. Clayton never knew whether Mrs. Haverford had come back and seen that or not. He did not care, for that matter. It seemed to him just then that all the world must know what was so vitally important, so transcendently wonderful.

Not until Audrey's eyes closed again, and he saw that she was sleeping, did he loosen his arms from around her.

When at last he went out to the stiffly furnished hospital parlor, he found Mrs. Haverford sitting there alone, still knitting. But he rather thought she had been crying. There was an undeniably moist handkerchief on her knee.

"She roused a little while ago," he said, trying to speak quietly, and as though Audrey's rousing were not the wonder that it was. "She seemed very comfortable. And now she's sleeping."

"The dear child!" said Mrs. Haverford. "If she had died, after everything —" Her plump face quivered. "Things have never been very happy for her, Clayton."

"I'm afraid not." He went to a window and stood looking out. The city was not quiet, but its mighty roar of the day was lowered to a monotonous, drowsy humming. From the east, reflected against low-hanging clouds, was the dull red of his own steel mills, looking like the reflection of a vast conflagration.

"Not very happy," he repeated.

"Some times," Mrs. Haverford was saying, "I wonder about things. People go along missing the best things in life, and —I suppose there is a reason for it, but some times I wonder if He ever meant us to go on, crucifying our own souls."

So she did know!

"What would you have us do?"

"I don't know. I suppose there isn't any answer."

Afterward, Clayton found that that bit of conversation with Mrs. Haverford took on the unreality of the rest of that twenty-four hours. But one part of it stood out real and hopelessly true. There wasn't any answer!

Chapter XLIII

Anna Klein had gone home, at three o'clock that terrible morning, a trembling, white-faced girl. She had done her best, and she had failed. Unlike Graham, she had no feeling of personal responsibility, but she felt she could never again face her father, with the thing that she knew between them. There were other reasons, too. Herman would be arrested, and she would be called to testify. She had known. She had warned Mr. Spencer. The gang, Rudolph's gang, would get her for that.

She knew where they were now. They would be at Gus's, in the back room, drinking to the success of their scheme, and Gus, who was a German too, would be with them, offering a round of drinks on the house now and then as his share of the night's rejoicing. Gus, who was already arranging to help draft-dodgers by sending them over the Mexican border.

She would have to go back, to get in and out again if she could, before Herman came back. She had no clothes, except what she stood up in, and those in her haste that night were, only her print house-dress with a long coat. She would have to find a new position, and she would have to have her clothing to get about in. She dragged along, singularly unmolested. Once or twice a man eyed her, but her white face and vacant eyes were unattractive, almost sodden.

She was barely able to climb the hill, and as she neared the house her trepidation increased. What if Herman had come back? If he suspected her he would kill her. He must have been half mad to have done the thing, anyhow. He would surely be half mad now. And because she was young and strong, and life was still a mystery to be solved, she did not want to die. Strangely enough, face to face with danger there was still, in the back of her head, an exultant thrill in her very determination to live. She would start over again, and she would work hard and make good.

"You bet I'll make good," she resolved. "Just give me a chance and I'll work my fool head off."

Which was by way of being a prayer.

It was the darkest hour before the dawn when she reached the cottage. It was black and very still, and outside the gate she stooped and slipped off her shoes. The window into the shed by which she had escaped was still open, and she crouched outside, listening. When the stillness remained unbroken she climbed in, tense for a movement or a blow.

Once inside, however, she drew a long breath. The doors were still locked, and the keys gone. So Herman had not returned. But as she stood there, hurried stealthy footsteps came along the street and turned in at the gate. In a panic she flew up the stairs and into her room, where the door still hung crazily on its hinges. She stood there, listening, her heart pounding in her ears, and below she distinctly heard a key in the kitchen door. She did the only thing she could think of. She lifted the door into place, and stood against it, bracing it with her body.

Whoever it was was in the kitchen now, moving however more swiftly than Herman. She heard matches striking. Then:

"Hsst!"

She knew that it was Rudolph, and she braced herself mentally. Rudolph was keener than Herman. If he found her door in that condition, and she herself dressed! Working silently and still holding the door in place, she flung off her coat. She even unpinned her hair and unfastened her dress.

When his signal remained unanswered a second time he called her by name, and she heard him coming up.

"Anna!" he repeated.

"Yes?"

He was startled to hear her voice so close to the door. In the dark she heard him fumbling for the knob. He happened on the padlock instead, and he laughed a little. By that she knew that he was not quite sober.

"Locked you in, has he?"

"What do you want?"

"Has Herman come home yet?"

"He doesn't get home until seven."

"Hasn't he been back at all, to-night?"

She hesitated.

"How do I know? I've been asleep!"

"Some sleep!" he said, and suddenly lurched against the door. In spite of her it yielded, and although she braced herself with all her strength, his weight against it caused it to give way. It was a suspicious, crafty Rudolph who picked himself up and made a clutch at her in the dark.

"You little liar," he said thickly. And struck a match. She cowered away from him.

"I was going to run away, Rudolph," she cried. "He hasn't any business locking me in, I won't stand for it."

"You've been out."

"No!"

"Out—after him!"

"Honest to God, Rudolph, no. I hate him. I don't ever want to see him again."

He put a hand out into the darkness, and finding her, tried to draw her to him. She struggled, and he released her. All at once she knew that he was weak with fright. The bravado had died out of him. The face she had touched was covered with a clammy sweat.

"I wish to God Herman would come."

"What d' you want with him?"

"Have you got any whisky?"

"You've had enough of that stuff."

Some one was walking along the street outside. She felt that he was listening, crouched ready to run; but the steps went on.

"Look here, Anna," he said, when he had pulled himself together again. "I'm going to get out of this. I'm going away."

"All right. You can go for all of me."

"D'you mean to say you've been asleep all night? You didn't hear anything?"

"Hear what?"

He laughed.

"You'll know soon enough." Then he told her, hurriedly, that he was going away. He'd come back to get her to promise to follow him. He wasn't going to stay here and —

"And what?"

"And be drafted," he finished, rather lamely.

"Gus has a friend in a town on the Mexican border," he said. "He's got maps of the country to Mexico City, and the Germans there fix you up all right. I'll get rich down there and some day I'll send for you? What's that?"

He darted to the window, faintly outlined by a distant street-lamp. Three men were standing quietly outside the gate, and a fourth was already in the garden, silently moving toward the house. She felt Rudolph brush by her, and the trembling hand he laid on her arm.

"Now lie!" he whispered fiercely. "You haven't seen me. I haven't been here to-night."

Then he was gone. She ran to the window. The other three men were coming in, moving watchfully and slowly, and Rudolph was at Katie's window, cursing. If she was a prisoner, so was Rudolph. He realized that instantly, and she heard him breaking out the sash with a chair. At the sound the three figures broke into a run, and she heard the sash give way. Almost instantly there was firing. The first shot was close, and she knew it was Rudolph firing from the window. Some wild design of braining him from behind with a chair flashed into her desperate mind, but when she had felt her way into Katie's room he had gone. The garden below was quiet, but there was yelling and the crackling of underbrush from the hill-side. Then a scattering of shots again, and silence. The yard was empty.

The hill paid but moderate attention to shots. They were usually merely pyrotechnic, and indicated rejoicing rather than death. But here and there she heard a window raised, and then lowered again. The hill had gone back to bed. Anna went into her room and dressed. For the first time it had occurred to her that she might be held by the police, and the thought was unbearable. It was when she was making her escape that she found a prostrate figure in the yard, and knew that one of Rudolph's shots had gone home. She could not go away and leave that, not unless —A terrible hatred of Herman and Rudolph and all their kind suddenly swept over her. She would not run away. She would stay and tell all the terrible truth. It was her big moment, and she rose to it. She would see it through. What was her own safety to letting this band of murderers escape? And all that in the few seconds it took to reach the fallen figure. It was only when she was very close that she saw it was moving.

"Tell Dunbar he went to the left," a voice was saying. "The left! They'll lose him yet."

"Joey!"

"Hello," said Joey's voice. He considered that he was speaking very loud, but it was hardly more than a whisper. "That wasn't your father, was it? The old boy couldn't jump and run like that."

"Are you hurt?"

He coughed a little, a gurgling cough that rather startled himself. But he was determined to be a man.

"No. I just lay down here for a nap. Who was it that jumped?"

"My cousin Rudolph. Do you think I can help you into the house?"

"I'll walk there myself in a minute. Unless your cousin Rudolph —" His head dropped back on her arm. "I feel sort of all in." His voice trailed off.

"Joey!"

"Lemme alone," he muttered. "I'm the first casualty in the American army! I —" He made a desperate effort to speak in a man's voice, but the higher boyish notes of sixteen conquered. "They certainly gave us hell to-night. But we're going to build again; me and-Clayton Spen —"

All at once he was very still. Anna spoke to him and, that failing, gave him a frantic little shake. But Joey had gone to another partnership beyond the stars.

Chapter XLIV

The immediate outstanding result of the holocaust at the munitions works was the end of Natalie's dominion aver Graham. She never quite forgave him the violence with which he threw off her shackles.

"If I'd been half a man I'd have been over there long ago," he said, standing before her, tall and young and flushed. "I'd have learned my job by now, and I'd be worth something, now I'm needed."

"And broken my heart."

"Hearts don't break that way, mother."

"Well, you say you are going now. I should think you'd be satisfied. There's plenty of time for you to get the glory you want."

"Glory! I don't want any glory. And as for plenty of time-that's exactly what there isn't."

During the next few days she preserved an obstinate silence on the subject. She knew he had been admitted to one of the officers' training-camps, and that he was making rather helpless and puzzled purchases. Going into his room she would find a dressing-case of khaki leather, perhaps, or flannel shirts of the same indeterminate hue. She would shed futile tears over them, and order them put out of sight. But she never offered to assist him.

Graham was older, in many ways. He no longer ran up and down the stairs whistling, and he sought every opportunity to be with his father. They spent long hours together in the library, when, after a crowded day, filled with the thousand, problems of reconstructions, Clayton smoked a great deal, talked a little, rather shame-facedly after the manner of men, of personal responsibility in the war, and quietly watched the man who was Graham.

Out of those quiet hours, with Natalie at the theater or reading up-stairs in bed, Clayton got the greatest comfort of his life. He would neither look back nor peer anxiously ahead.

The past, with its tragedy, was gone. The future might hold even worse things. But just now he would live each day as it came, working to the utmost, and giving his evenings to his boy. The nights were the worst. He was not sleeping well, and in those long hours of quiet he tried to rebuild his life along stronger, sterner lines. Love could have no place in it, but there was work left. He was strong and he was still young. The country should have every ounce of energy in him. He would re-build the plant, on bigger lines than before, and when that was done, he would build again. The best he could do was not enough.

He scarcely noticed Natalie's withdrawal from Graham and himself. When she was around he was his old punctilious self, gravely kind, more than ever considerate. Beside his failure to her, her own failure to him faded into insignificance. She was as she was, and through no fault of hers. But he was what he had made himself.

Once or twice he had felt an overwhelming remorse toward her, and on one such occasion he had made a useless effort to break down the barrier of her long silence.

"Don't go up-stairs, Natalie," he had begged. "I am not very amusing, I know, but —I'll try my best. I'll promise not to touch on anything disagreeable." He had been standing in the hail, looking up at her on the stair-case, and he smiled. There was pleading behind the smile, an inarticulate feeling that between them there might at least be friendship.

"You are never disagreeable," she had said, looking down with hostile eyes. "You are quite perfect."

"Then won't you wait?"

"Perfection bores me to tears," she said, and went on up the stairs.

On the morning of Graham's departure, however, he found her prepared to go to the railway-station. She was red-eyed and pale, and he was very sorry for her.

"Do you think it is wise?" he asked.

"I shall see him off, of course. I may never see him again."

And his own tautened nerves almost gave way.

"Don't say that!" he cried. "Don't even think that. And for God's sake, Natalie, send him off with a smile. That's the least we can do."

"I can't take it as casually as you do."

He gave up then in despair. He saw that Graham watched her uneasily during the early breakfast, and he surmised that the boy's own grip on his self-control was weakened by the tears that dropped into her coffee-cup. He reflected bitterly that all over the country strong women, good women, were sending their boys away to war, giving them with prayer and exaltation. What was wrong with Natalie? What was wrong with his whole life?

When Graham was up-stairs, he turned to her.

"Why do you persist in going, Natalie?"

"I intend to go. That's enough."

"Don't you think you've made him unhappy enough?"

"He has made me unhappy enough."

"You. It is always yourself, Natalie. Why don't you ever think of him?" He went to the door. "Countermand the order for the limousine," he said to the butler, "and order the small car for Mr. Graham and myself."

"How dare you do that?"

"I am not going to let you ruin the biggest day in his life."

She saw that he meant it. She was incredulous, reckless, angry, and thwarted for the first time in her self-indulgent life.

"I hate you," she said slowly. "I hate you!"

She turned and went slowly up the stairs. Graham, knocking at her door a few minutes later, heard the sound of hysterical sobbing, within, but received no reply.

"Good-by, mother," he called. "Good-by. Don't worry. I'll be all right."

When he saw she did not mean to open the door or to reply, he went rather heavily down the stairs.

"I wish she wouldn't," he said. "It makes me darned unhappy."

But Clayton surmised a relief behind his regret, and in the train the boy's eyes were happier than they had been for months.

"I don't know how I'll come out, dad," he said. "But if I don't get through it won't be because I didn't try."

And he did try. The enormous interest of the thing gripped him from the start; There was romance in it, too. He wore his first uniform, too small for him as it was, with immense pride. He rolled out in the morning at reveille, with the feeling that he had just gone to bed, ate hugely at breakfast, learned to make his own cot-bed, and lined up on a vast dusty parade ground for endless evolutions in a boiling sun.

It was rather amusing to find himself being ordered about, in a stentorian voice, by Jackson. And when, in off moments, that capable ex-chauffeur condescended to a few moments of talk and relaxation, the boy was highly gratified.

"Do you think I've got anything in me?" he would inquire anxiously.

And Jackson always said heartily, "Sure you have."

There were times when Graham doubted himself, however. There was one dreadful hour when Graham, in the late afternoon, and under the eyes of his commanding officer and a group of ladies, conducting the highly formal and complicated ceremony of changing the guard, tied a lot of grinning men up in a knot which required the captain of the company and two sergeants to untangle.

"I'm no earthly good," he confided to Jackson that night, sitting on the steps of his barracks. "I know it like a-b-c, and then I get up and try it and all at once I'm just a plain damned fool."

"Don't give up like that, son," Jackson said. "I've seen 'em march a platoon right into the C.O.'s porch before now. And once I just saved a baby-buggy and a pair of twins."

Clayton wrote him daily, and now and then there came a letter from Natalie, cheerful on the surface, but its cheerfulness obviously forced. And once, to his great surprise, Marion Hayden wrote him.

"I just want you to know," she said, "that I am still interested in you, even if it isn't going to be anything else. And that I am ridiculously proud of you. Isn't it queer to look back on last Winter and think what a lot of careless idiots we were? I suppose war doesn't really change us, but it does make us wonder what we've got in us. I am surprised to find that I am a great deal better than I ever thought I was!"

There was comfort in the letter, but no thrill. He was far away from all that now, like one on the first stage of a long journey, with his eyes ahead.

Then one day he saw a familiar but yet strange figure striding along the country road. Graham was map-sketching that day, and the strange but familiar figure was almost on him when he looked up. It was extremely military, and looked like a general at least. Also it was very red in the face, and was clutching doggedly in its teeth an old briar pipe. But what had appeared from the front to be an ultra military figure on closer inspection turned out to be a procession. Pulling back hard on a rope behind was the company goat, Elinor.

The ultra-military figure paused by Graham's sketching-stool, and said, "Young man, do you know where this creature belongs? I found her trying to commit suicide on the rifle range-why, Graham!"

It was Doctor Haverford. He grew a trifle less military then, and borrowed some pipe tobacco. He looked oddly younger, Graham thought, and rather self-conscious of his uniform.

"Every inch a soldier, Graham," he chuckled. "Still have to use a hook and eye at the bottom of the coat-blouse," he corrected himself. "But I'm getting my waist-line again. How's the-whoa!" he called, as Elinor wrapped the rope around his carefully putted legs. "Infernal animal!" he grumbled. "I just paid a quarter to have these puttees shined. How's the family?"

"Mother has gone to Linndale. The house is finished. Have you been here long, sir?"

"Two weeks. Hang it all, Graham, I wish I'd let this creature commit suicide. She's —do you know Delight is here?"

"Here? Why, no."

"At the hostess house," said the chaplain, proudly. "Doing her bit, too. Mrs. Haverford wanted to come too, and sew buttons on, or something. But I told her two out of three was a fair percentage. I hear that Washington has sent for your father."

"I hadn't heard."

"He's a big man, Graham. We're going to hear from him. Only —I thought he looked tired when I saw him last. Somebody ought to look after him a bit." He was patiently untangling himself from Elinor's rope. "You know there are two kinds of people in the world: those who look after themselves and those who look after others. That's your father-the last."

Graham's face clouded. How true that was! He knew now, as he had not known before. He was thinking clearly those days. Hard work and nothing to drink had clarified his mind, and he saw things at home as they really were. Clayton's infinite patience, his strength and his gentleness. But he only said:

"He has had a hard year." He raised his eyes and looked at the chaplain. "I didn't help him any, you know, sir."

"Well, well, that's all over now. We've just one thing to think of, and that's to beat those German devils back to Berlin. And then burn Berlin," he added, militantly.

The last Graham saw of him, he was dragging Elinor down the road, and a faint throaty humming came back, which sounded suspiciously like "Where do we go from here, boys? Where do we go from here?"

Candidate Spencer took great pains with his toilet that afternoon. He polished his shoes, and shaved, and he spent a half hour on some ten sadly neglected finger-nails. At retreat he stood at attention in the long line, and watched the flag moving slowly and majestically to the stirring bugle notes. Something swelled almost to bursting in his throat. That was his flag.

He was going to fight for it. And after that was done he was going to find some girl, some nice girl-the sort, for instance, that would leave her home to work in a hostess house. And having found her, he would marry her, and love and cherish her all his life. Unless, of course, she wouldn't have him. He was inclined to think she wouldn't.

He ate very little supper that night, little being a comparative term, of course. And then he went to discover Delight. It appeared, however, that she had been already discovered. She was entirely surrounded by uniforms, and Graham furiously counted a colonel, two majors, and a captain.

"Pulling rank, of course!" he muttered, and retired to a corner, where he had at least the mild gratification of seeing that even the colonel could not keep Delight from her work.

"Silly asses!" said Graham, again, and then she saw him. There was no question about her being pleased. She was quite flushed with it, but a little uncomfortable, too, at Graham's attitude. He was oddly humble, and yet he had a look of determination that was almost grim. She filled in a rather disquieting silence by trying to let him know, without revealing that she had ever been anything else, how proud she was of him. Then she realized that he was not listening, and that he was looking at her with an almost painful intensity.

"When can you get away, Delight?" he asked abruptly.

"From here?" She cast an appraising glance over the room. "Right away, I think. Why?"

"Because I want to talk to you, and I can't talk to you here."

She brought a bright colored sweater and he helped her into it, still with his mouth set and his eyes a trifle sunken. All about there were laughing groups of men in uniform. Outside, the parade glowed faintly in the dusk, and from the low barrack windows there came the glow of lights, the movement of young figures, voices, the thin metallic notes of a mandolin.

"How strange it all is," Delight said. "Here we are, you and father and myself-and even Jackson. I saw him to-day. All here, living different lives, doing different things, even thinking different thoughts. It's as though we had all moved into a different world."

He walked on beside her, absorbed in his own thoughts, which were yet only of her.

"I didn't know you were here," he brought out finally.

"That's because you've been burying yourself. I knew you were here."

"Why didn't you send me some word?"

She stiffened somewhat in the darkness.

"I didn't think you would be greatly interested, Graham."

And again, struggling with his new humility, he was silent. It was not until they had crossed the parade ground and were beyond the noises of the barracks that he spoke again.

"Do you mind if I talk to you, Delight? I mean, about myself? I —since you're here, we're likely to see each other now and then, if you are willing. And I'd like to start straight."

"Do you really want to tell me?"

"No. But I've got to. That's all."

He told her. He made no case for himself. Indeed, some of it Delight understood far better than he did himself. He said nothing against Marion; on the contrary, he blamed himself rather severely. And behind his honest, halting sentences, Delight read his own lack of understanding. She felt infinitely older than this tall, honest-eyed boy in his stained uniform-older and more sophisticated. But if she had understood the Marion Hayden situation, she was totally at a loss as to Anna.

"But I don't understand!" she cried. "How could you make love to her if you didn't love her?"

"I don't know. Fellows do those things. It's just mischief-some sort of a devil in them, I suppose."

When he reached the beating and Anna's flight, however, she understood a little better.

"Of course you had to stand by her," she agreed.

"You haven't heard it all," he said quietly. "When I'm through, if you get up and leave me, I'll understand, Delight, and I won't blame you."

He told her the rest of the story in a voice strained with anxiety. It was as though he had come to a tribunal for judgment. He spared her nothing, the dinner at the road-house with Rudolph at the window, his visit to Anna's room, and her subsequent disappearance.

"She told the Department of Justice people that Rudolph found her that night, and, took her home. She was a prisoner then, poor little kid. But she overheard her father and Rudolph plotting to blow up the mill. That's where I came in, Delight. He was crazy at me. He was a German, of course, and he might have done it anyhow. But Rudolph told him a lot of lies about me, and-he did it. When I think about it all, and about Joey, I'm crazy."

She slipped her hand over his.

"Of course they would have done it anyhow," she said softly.

"You aren't going to get up and go away?"

"Why should I?" she asked. "I only feel-oh, Graham, how wretched you must have been."

Something in her voice made him sit up straighter. He knew now that it had always been Delight, always. Only she had been too good for him. She had set a standard he had not hoped to reach. But now things were different. He hadn't amounted to much in other things, but he was a soldier now. He meant to be a mighty good soldier. And when he got his commission —

"You won't mind, then, if I come in to see you now and then?"

"Mind? Why, Graham!"

"And you don't think I'm quite hopeless, do you?"

There were tears in her eyes, but she answered bravely:

"I believe in you every minute. But then I think I always have."

"Like fun you have!" But although he laughed, it was a shaky laugh. Suddenly he stood up and shook himself. He felt young and strong and extremely happy. There had been a bad time, but it was behind him now. Ahead there lay high adventure, and here, beside him in the dusk, was the girl of his heart. She believed in him. Work to do and a woman who believed in a fellow-that was life.

"Aren't you cold?" he asked, and drew the gaudy sweater tenderly around her shoulders.

Chapter XLV

The fact that Audrey Valentine, conspicuous member of a conspicuous social group that she was, had been working in the machine-shop of the Spencer munitions works at the time of the explosion was in itself sufficient to rouse the greatest interest. When a young reporter, gathering human-interest stories about the event from the pitiful wreckage in the hospitals, happened on Clare Gould, he got a feature-story for the Sunday edition that made Audrey's own world, reading it in bed or over its exquisite breakfast-tables, gasp with amazement.

For, following up Clare's story, he found that Audrey had done much more than run toward the telephone. She had reached it, had found the operator gone, and had succeeded, before the roof fell in on her, in calling the fire department and in sending in a general alarm to all the hospitals.

The reporter found the night operator who had received the message. He got a photograph of her, too, and, from the society file, an old one of Audrey, very delicate and audacious, and not greatly resembling the young woman who lay in her bed and read the article aloud, between dismay and laughter, to old Terry Mackenzie.

"Good heavens, Terry," she said. "Listen! I had heard the explosion, but did not of course know what it was. And then I got a signal, and it was the Spencer plant. A sweet Southern voice said, very calmly, 'Operator, this is important. Listen carefully. There has been an explosion at the Spencer plant and the ruins are on fire. There will probably be more explosions in a minute. Send in a general fire-alarm, and then get all the ambulances and doctors —' Then there was another explosion, and their lines went out of commission. I am glad she is not dead. She certainly had her nerve."

"Fame at last, Audrey!" said old Terry, very gently.

"It's shameless!" But she was a little pleased, nevertheless. Not at the publicity. That was familiar enough. But that, when her big moment came, she had met it squarely.

Terry was striding about the room. His visits were always rather cyclonic. He moved from chair to chair, leaving about each one an encircling ring of cigaret ashes, and carefully inspecting each new vase of flowers. He stopped in front of a basket of exquisite small orchids.

"Who sent this?" he demanded.

"Rodney Page. Doesn't it look like him?"

He turned and stared at her.

"What's come over Clayton Spencer? Is he blind?"

"Blind?"

"About Rodney. He's head over heels in love with Natalie Spencer, God alone knows why."

"I daresay it isn't serious. He is always in love with somebody."

"There's a good bit of talk. I don't give a hang for either of them, but I'm fond of Clayton. So are you. Natalie's out in the country now, and Rodney is there every week-end. It's a scandal, that's all. As for Natalie herself, she ought to be interned as a dangerous pacifist. She's a martyr, in her own eyes. Thank heaven there aren't many like her."

Audrey leaned back against her pillows.

"I wonder, Terry," she said, "if you haven't shown me what to do next. I might be able to reach some of the women like Natalie. There are some of them, and they've got to learn that if they don't stand behind the men, we're lost."

"Fine!" he agreed. "Get 'em to knit less and write more letters, cheerful letters. Tell 'em to remember that by the time their man gets the letter the baby's tooth will be through. There are a good many men in the army-camps to-day vicariously cutting teeth. Get after 'em, Audrey! A worried man is a poor soldier."

After he had gone, she had the nurse bring her paper and pencil, and she wrote, rather incoherently, it is true, her first appeal to the women of the country. It was effective, too. Audrey was an effective person. When Clayton came for his daily visit she had just finished it, and was reading it over with considerable complacency.

"I've become an author, Clay," she said, "I think myself I'm terribly good at it. May I read it to you?"

He listened gravely, but with a little flicker of amusement in his eyes. How like her it was, to refuse to allow herself even time to get entirely well! But when she finished he was thoughtful. She had called it "Slacker Women." That was what Natalie was; he had never put it into words before. Natalie was a slacker.

He had never discussed Natalie's attitude toward the war with Audrey. He rather thought she was entirely ignorant of it. But her little article, glowing with patriotism, frank, simple, and convincing, might have been written to Natalie herself.

"It is very fine," he said. "I rather think you have found yourself at last. There aren't a lot of such women and I daresay they will be fewer all the time. But they exist, of course."

She glowed under his approval.

There was, in all their meetings, a sub-current of sadness, that they must be so brief, that before long they must end altogether, that they could not put into words the things that were in their eyes and their hearts. After that first hour of her return to consciousness there had been no expressed tenderness between them. The nurse sat in the room, eternally knitting, and Clayton sat near Audrey, or read to her, or, like Terry, wandered about the room. But now and then Audrey, enthroned, like a princess on her pillows, would find his eyes on her, and such a hungry look in them that she would clench her hands. And after such times she always said: "Now, tell me about the mill." Or about Washington, where he was being summoned with increasing frequency. Or about Graham. Anything to take that look out of his eyes. He told her all his plans; he even brought the blue-prints of the new plant and spread them out on the bed. He was dreaming a great dream those days, and Audrey knew it. He was building again, this time not for himself, but for the nation.

After he had gone, looking boyish and reluctant, she would lie for a little while watching the door. Perhaps he had forgotten something, and would come back! One day he did, and was surprised to find her suddenly in tears.

"You came back!" she said half hysterically. "You came back."

That was the only time in all those weeks that he kissed her. The nurse had gone out, and suddenly he caught her in his arms and held her to him. He put her back very gently, and she saw that he was pale.

"I think I'd better go now, and not come back," he said.

And for two long and endless days he did not come. Then on the third he came, very stiff and formal, and with himself well in hand. Audrey, leaning back and watching him, felt what a boy he was after all, so determined to do the right thing, so obvious with his blue-prints, and so self-conscious.

In June she left the hospital and went to the country. She had already made a little market for her work, and she wanted to carry it on. By that time, too, she knew that the break must come between Clayton and herself if it came at all.

"No letters, no anything, Clay," she said, and he acquiesced quietly. But the night she left, the butler, coming downstairs to investigate a suspicious sound, found him restlessly pacing the library floor.

In August he went abroad, and some time about the middle of the month while he was in London, he received a cable from Graham. He had been commissioned a first lieutenant in the infantry. Clayton had been seeing war at first hand then, and for a few moments he was fairly terrified. On that first of August the Germans had used liquid fire for the first time, thus adding a new horror. Men in the trenches swept by it had been practically annihilated. Attacks against it were practically suicide. Already the year had seen the last of Kitchener's army practically destroyed, and the British combing the country for new divisions.

In the deadly give and take of that summer, where gains and losses were measured by yards, the advantage was steadily on the German side, and it would be a year before the small force of American regulars could be augmented to any degree by the great new army. It was the darkest hour.

Following on the heels of Graham's cable came a hysterical one from Natalie.

"Graham probably ordered abroad. Implore you use influence with Washington."

He resorted to his old remedy when he was in trouble. He walked the streets. He tried to allow for Natalie's lack of exaltation by the nature of her life. If she could have seen what he had seen, surely she would have felt, as he did, that no sacrifice could be too great to end this cancer of the world. But deep in his heart he knew that Natalie was-Natalie. Nothing would change her.

As it happened, he passed Graham on the Atlantic. There was a letter for him at the office, a boyish, exultant letter:

"Dad dear, I'm married!" it began. "Married and off for France. It is Delight, of course. It always was Delight, altho I know that sounds queer. And now I'm off to kill a Hun or two. More than that, I hope. I want two Germans for every poor devil they got at the works. That's the minimum. The maximum —!

"You'll look after Delight, I know. She has been perfectly bully, but it's hard on her. We were married two days ago, and already I feel as though I've always been married. She's going on with the canteen work, and I shall try not to be jealous. She's popular! And if you'd seen the General when we were married you'd have thought he was losing a daughter.

"I wired Mother, but she was too cut up about my leaving to come. I wish she had, for it was a strange sort of wedding. The division was about to move, and at the last minute five girls turned up to be married to fellows who were leaving. They came from all over, and believe me there was some excitement. All day the General and Chaplain Haverford were fussing about licenses, and those girls sat around and waited, and looked droopy but sort of happy-you know what I mean.

"It was nine o'clock in the evening before everything was ready. Delight had trimmed up the little church which is in the camp and had a flag over the altar. Then we had a multiple wedding. Honestly! The organ played a squeaky wedding march, and we went in, six couples. The church was full of soldiers, and —I don't mind saying I was ready to shed tears.

"We lined up, and Doctor Haverford married us. Delight says she is sure we are only one-sixth married. Quiet! You never heard such quiet-except for the General blowing his nose. I think myself he was weeping, and there was a rumor about the camp to that effect. You know-the flag over the altar, and all that. I tell you it made a fellow think.

"Well, I'm going over now. Quick work, isn't it? And to think that a few months ago I was hanging around the club and generally making a mess of life. That's all over now, thank God. I'm going to make good. Try to buck mother up. It's pretty hard for her. It's hard for all women, just waiting. And while I know I'm coming back, safe and sound, I'd like to feel that you are going to keep an eye on Delight. She's the most important thing in the world to me now."

Then scrawled in a corner he had added,

"You've been mighty fine with me always, dad. I was a good bit of a pup last winter. If I make anything of myself at all, it will be because I want to be like you."

Clayton sat for a long time with the letter in his hand. The happiness and hope that fairly radiated from it cheered and warmed him. He was nearly happy. And it came to him then that, while every man had the right to happiness, only those achieved it who craved it for others, and having craved it for them, at last saw the realization of their longing.

Chapter XLVI

Natalie had had a dull Spring. With Graham's departure for camp she moved to the country house, carrying with her vast amounts of luggage, the innumerable thing, large and small, which were necessary for her comfort. The installing of herself in her new and luxurious rooms gave her occupation for several days. She liked her new environment. She liked herself in it. The rose-colored taffetas of her bedroom brought out the delicacy of her skin. The hangings of her bed, small and draped, reflected a faint color into her face, and the morning inspection with a hand-mirror, which always followed her coffee, showed her at her best instead of her worst.

Of her dressing-room she was not so sure. It's ivory-paneled walls, behind whose sliding panels were hung her gowns, her silk and satin chiffon negligees, her wraps and summer furs-all the vast paraphernalia with which she armed herself, as a knight with armor-the walls seemed cold. She hated old-blue, but old-blue Rodney had insisted upon.

He had held a bit of the taffeta to her cheek.

"It is delicious, Natalie," he said. "It makes your eyes as blue as the sea."

"Always a decorator!" she had replied, smiling.

And, standing in her blue room, the first day of her arrival, and frowning at her reflection, she remembered his reply.

"Because I have no right, with you, to be anything else." He had stopped for a moment, and had absently folded and refolded the bit of blue silk. Suddenly he said, "What do you think I am going to do, now that our work together is done? Have you ever thought about that, Natalie?"

"You are coming often to enjoy your handiwork?"

He had made an impulsive gesture.

"I'm not coming. I've been seeing too much of you as it is. If you want the truth, I'm just wretchedly unhappy, Natalie. You know I'm in love with you, don't you?"

"I believe you think you are."

"Don't laugh." He almost snarled. "I may laugh at my idiocy, but you haven't any right to. I know I'm ridiculous. I've known it for months. But it's pretty serious for me."

He had meant it. There could be no doubt of that. It is the curious quality of very selfish women that they inspire a certain sort of love. They are likely to be loved often, even tho the devotion they inspire is neither deep nor lasting. Big and single-hearted women are loved by one man, and that forever.

Natalie had not laughed, but she had done what was almost as bad. She had patted him on the arm.

"Don't talk like that," she said, gently. "You are all I have now, Rodney, and I don't want to lose you. I'm suffering horribly these days. You're my greatest comfort."

"I've heard you say that of a chair."

"As for loving me, you must not talk like that. Under the circumstances, it's indelicate."

"Oh!" he had said, and looked at her quickly. "I can love you, but it's indelicate to tell you about it!"

"I am married, Rodney."

"Good God, do you think I ever forget it?"

There was a real change in their relationship, but neither of them understood it. The change was that Rodney was no longer playing. Little by little he had dropped his artistic posing for her benefit, his cynical cleverness, his adroit simulation of passion. He no longer dramatized himself, because rather often he forgot himself entirely. His passion had ceased to be spurious, and it was none the less real because he loved not a real woman, but one of his own artistic creation.

He saw in Natalie a misunderstood and suffering woman, bearing the burdens he knew of with dignity and a certain beauty. And behind her slightly theatrical silences he guessed at other griefs, nobly borne and only gently intimated. He developed, after a time, a certain suspicion of Clayton, not of his conduct but of his character. These big men were often hard. It was that quality which made them successful. They married tender, gentle girls, and then repressed and trampled on them.

Natalie became, in his mind, a crushed and broken thing, infinitely lonely and pathetic. And, without in the least understanding, Natalie instinctively knew it was when she was wistful and dependent that he found her most attractive, and became wistful and dependent to a point that imposed even on herself.

"I've been very selfish with you, Rodney, dear," she said, lifting sad eyes to his. "I am going to be better. You must come often this summer, and I'll have some nice girls for you to play with."

"Thank you," he said, stiffly.

"We'll have to be as gay as we can," she sighed. "I'm just a little dreary these days, you know."

It was rather absurd that they were in a shop, and that the clerk should return just then with curtain cords, and that the discussion of certain shades of yellow made an anti-climax to it all. But in the car, later, he turned to her, roughly.

"You needn't ask any girls for me," he said. "I only want one woman, and if I can't have her I don't want any one."

At first the very fact that he could not have her had been, unconsciously, the secret of her attraction. She was a perfect thing, and unattainable. He could sigh for her with longing and perfect safety. But as time went on, with that incapacity of any human emotion to stand still, but either to go on or to go back, his passion took on a more human and less poetic aspect. She satisfied him less, and he wanted more.

For one thing, he dreamed that strange dream of mankind, of making ice burn, of turning snow to fire. The old chimera of turning the cold woman to warmth through his own passion began to obsess him. Sometimes he watched Natalie, and had strange fancies. He saw her lit from within by a fire, which was not the reflection of his, but was recklessly her own. How wonderful she would be, he thought. And at those times he had wild visions of going away with her into some beautiful wilderness and there teaching her what she had missed in life.

But altho now he always wanted her, he was not always thinking of a wilderness. It was in his own world that he wanted her, to fit beautifully into his house, to move, exquisitely dressed, through ball-rooms beside him. He wanted her, at those times, as the most perfect of all his treasures. He was still a collector!

The summer only served to increase his passion. During the long hot days, when Clayton was abroad or in Washington, or working late at night, as he frequently did how, they were much together. Natalie's plans for gayety had failed dismally. The city and the country houses near were entirely lacking in men. She found it a real grievance.

"I don't know what we are coming to," she complained. "The country club is like a girl's boarding-school. I wish to heaven the war was over, and things were sensible again."

So, during his week-end visits, they spent most of the time together. There were always girls there, and now and then a few men, who always explained immediately that they had been turned down for the service, or were going in the fall.

"I'm sure somebody has to stay home and attend to things here," she said to him one August night. "But even when they are in America, they are rushing about, pretending to do things. One would think to see Clayton that he is the entire government. It's absurd."

"I wish I could go," he said unexpectedly.

"Don't be idiotic. You're much too old."

"Not as old as Clay."

"Oh, Clay! He's in a class by himself." She laughed lightly.

"Where is he now?"

"In France, I think. Probably telling them how to run the war."

"When is he coming back?"

"I don't know. What do you mean by wishing you could go?"

"Do you want me to tell you the truth?"

"Not if it's disagreeable."

"Well, I will, and it's not very agreeable. I can't keep this up, Natalie. I can't keep on coming here, being in Clayton's house, and eating his bread, while I'm in love with his wife. It isn't decent."

He flung away his cigaret, and bent forward.

"Don't you see that?" he asked gently. "Not while he is working for the country, and Graham is abroad."

"I don't see why war needs to deprive me of my friends. I've lost everything else."

His morals were matters of his private life, and they had been neither better nor worse than the average. But he had breeding and a sure sense of the fitness of things, and this present week-end visit, with the ostentatious care the younger crowd took to allow him time to see Natalie alone, was galling to him. It put him in a false position; what hurt more, perhaps, in an unfavorable light. The war had changed standards, too. Men were being measured, especially by women, and those who failed to measure up were being eliminated with cruel swiftness, especially the men who stayed at home.

With all this, too, there was a growing admiration for Clayton Spencer in their small circle. His name had been mentioned in connection with an important position in Washington. In the clubs there was considerable praise and some envy. And Rodney knew that his affair with Natalie was the subject of much invidious comment.

"Do you love him?" he asked, suddenly.

"I—why, of course I do."

"Do you mean that?"

"I don't see what that has to do with our friendship."

"Oh-friendship! You know how I feel, and yet you go on, bringing up that silly word. If you love him, you don't—love me, and yet you've let me hang around all these months, knowing I am mad about you. You don't play the game, Natalie."

"What do you want to say?"

"If you don't love Clayton, why don't you tell him so? He's honest enough. And I miss my guess if he wants a wife who-cares for somebody else."

She sat in the dusk, thinking, and he watched her. She looked very lovely in the setting which he himself had designed for her. She hated change; she loathed trouble, of any sort. And she was, those days, just a little afraid of that strange, quiet Clayton who seemed eternally engrossed in war and the things of war. She glanced about, at the white trellises that gleamed in the garden, at the silvery fleur de lis which was the fountain, at all the lovely things with which Clayton's wealth had allowed her to surround herself. And suddenly she knew she could not give them up.

"I don't see why you have to spoil everything," she said fretfully. "It had been so perfect. Of course I'm not going to say anything to Clay. He has enough to worry him now," she added, virtuously.

Suddenly Rodney stooped and kissed her, almost savagely.

"Then I'm going," he said. And to her great surprise he went.

Alone in his room up-stairs Rodney had, in his anger, a glimpse of insight. He saw her, her life filled with small emotions, lacking the courage for big ones. He saw her, like a child, clutching one piece of cake and holding out a hand for another. He saw her, taking always, giving never.

"She's not worth it," he muttered.

On the way to the station he reflected bitterly over the past year. He did not blame her so much as he blamed himself. He had been playing a game, an attractive game. During the first months of it his interest in Natalie had been subordinate to his interest in her house. He had been creating a beautiful thing, and he had had a very real joy in it. But lately he knew that his work on the house had been that he might build a background for Natalie. He had put into it the best of his ability, and she was not worth it.

For some days he neither wrote nor called her up. He was not happy, but he had a sense of relief. He held his head a trifle higher, was his own man again, and he began to make tentative inquiries as to whether he could be useful in the national emergency or not. He was half-hearted at first, but he found out something. The mere fact that he wanted to work in some capacity brought back some of his old friends. They had seemed to drop away, before, but they came back heartily and with hands out.

"Work?" said Terry Mackenzie, at the club one day, looking up from the billiard table, where he was knocking balls about, rather at haphazard. "Why, of course you can work. What about these new cantonments we're building all over the country? You ought to be useful there. They don't want 'em pretty, tho." And Terry had laughed. But he put down his cue and took Rodney by the arm.

"Let's ask Nolan about it," he said. "He's in the reading-room, tearing the British strategy to pieces. He knows everything these days, from the draft law to the month's shipping losses. Come along."

It was from Nolan, however, that Rodney first realized how seriously Clayton's friends were taking his affair with Natalie, and that not at first from anything he said. It was an indefinable aloofness of manner, a hostility of tone. Nolan never troubled himself to be agreeable unless it suited his inclination, and apparently Terry found nothing unusual in his attitude. But Rodney did.

"Something he could build?" said Nolan, repeating Terry's question. "How do I know? There's a lot of building going on, Page, but it's not exactly your sort." And there was a faint note of contempt in his voice.

"Who would be the man to see in Washington?" Rodney inquired.

"I'll look it up and let you know. You might call me up to-morrow."

Old Terry, having got them together, went back to his billiards and left them. Nolan sat down and picked up his paper, with an air of ending the interview. But he put it down again as Rodney turned to leave the room.

"Page!"

"Yes?"

"D'you mind having a few minutes talk?"

Rodney braced himself.

"Not at all."

But Nolan was slow to begin. He sat, newspaper on his knee, his deep-set eyes thoughtful. When he began it was slowly.

"I am one of Clay Spencer's oldest friends," he said. "He's a white man, the whitest man I know. Naturally, anything that touches him touches me, in a way."

"Well?"

"The name stands for a good bit, too. His father and his grandfather were the same sort. It's not often in this town that we have three generations without a breath of scandal against them."

Rodney flushed angrily.

"What has that got to do with me?" he demanded.

"I don't know. I don't want to know. I simply wanted to tell you that there are a good many of us who take a peculiar pride in Clayton Spencer, and who resent anything that reflects on a name we respect rather highly."

"That sounds like a threat."

"Not at all. I was merely calling your attention to something I thought perhaps you had forgotten." Then he got up' and his tone changed, became brisk, almost friendly. "Now, about this building thing. If you're in earnest I think it can be managed. You won't get any money to speak of, you know."

"I don't want any money," sullenly.

"Fine. You'll probably have to go west somewhere, and you'll be set down in the center of a hundred corn-fields and told to make them overnight into a temporary town. I suppose you've thought of all that?"

"I'll go wherever I'm sent."

"Come along to the telephone, then."

Rodney hesitated. He felt cheap and despicable, and his anger was still hot. They wanted to get him out of town. He saw that. They took little enough trouble to hide it. Well, he would go. He wanted to go anyhow, and he would show them something, too, if he got a chance. He would show them that he was as much a man as Clayton Spencer. He eyed Nolan's insolently slouching figure with furious eyes. But he followed him.

Had he secured an immediate appointment things might have been different for him. Like Chris Valentine, he had had one decent impulse, and like Chris too, there was a woman behind it. But Chris had been able to act on his impulse at once, and Rodney was compelled to wait while the mills of the government ground slowly.

Then, on the fourteenth of August, Natalie telegraphed him:

"Have had bad news about Graham. Can you come?"

He thought of Graham ill, possibly dead, and he took the next train, late in the evening. It was mid-week and Natalie was alone. He had thought of that possibility in the train and he was miserably uncomfortable, with all his joy at the prospect of seeing her again. He felt that the emergency must be his justification. Clayton was still abroad, and even his most captious critics would admit that Natalie should have a friend by if she were in trouble. Visions of Graham wounded filled his mind. He was anxious, restless and in a state of the highest nervous tension.

And there was no real emergency.

He found Natalie in the drawing-room, pacing the floor. She was still in her morning dress, and her eyes were red and swollen. She gave him both her hands, and he was surprised to find them cold as ice.

"I knew you would come," she said. "I am so alone, so terrified."

He could hardly articulate.

"What is it?"

"Graham has been ordered abroad."

He stood still, staring at her, and then he dropped her hands.

"Is that all?" he asked, dully.

"No."

"Good heavens, Natalie! Tell me. I've been frantic with anxiety about you."

"He was married to-night to Delight Haverford."

And still he stared at her.

"Then he's not hurt, or ill?"

"I didn't say he was. Good gracious, Rodney, isn't that bad enough?"

"But-what did you expect? He would have to go abroad some time. You knew that. I'm sorry, but-why in God's name didn't you say in your wire what the trouble was?"

"You sound exactly like Clay."

She was entirely incapable of understanding. She stood before him, straight and resentful, and yet strangely wistful and appealing.

"I send you word that my only son is going to France, that he has married without so much as consulting me, that he is going to war and may never come back. I needed you, and you said once that when I needed you, wherever you were, you would come. So I sent for you, and now you act like-like Clay."

"Have you any one here?"

"The servants. Good gracious, Rodney, are you worrying about that?"

"Only for you, Natalie."

"We resent anything that reflects on a name we respect rather highly." That was what Nolan had said.

"I'm sorry about Graham, dearest. I am sorry about any trouble that comes to you. You know that, Natalie. I'm only regretful that you have let me place you in an uncomfortable position. If my being here is known-Look here, Natalie, dear, I hate to bother you, but I'll have to take one of the cars and go back to the city to-night."

"Aren't you being rather absurd?"

He hesitated. He could not tell her of that awkward talk with Nolan. There were many things he would not tell her; his own desire to rehabilitate himself among the men he knew, his own new-born feeling that to take advantage of Clayton's absence on business connected with the war was peculiarly indefensible.

"I shall order the car at once," she said, and touched a bell. When she turned he was just behind her, but altho he held out his arms she evaded them, her eyes hard and angry.

"I wish you would try to understand," he said.

"I do, very thoroughly. Too thoroughly. You are afraid for yourself, not for me. I am in trouble, but that is a secondary consideration. Don't bother about me, Rodney. I have borne a great deal alone in my life, and I can bear this."

She turned, and went with considerable dignity out of the door.

"Natalie!" he called. But he heard her with a gentle rustle of silks going up the staircase. It did not add to his comfort that she had left him to order the car.

All through the night Rodney rode and thought. He was angry at Natalie, but he was angrier at himself. He felt that he had been brutal, unnecessarily callous. After all, her only son was on his way to war. It was on the cards that he might not come back. And he had let his uneasiness dominate his sympathy. He had lost her, but then he had never had her. He never could have her.

Half way to town, on a back road, the car broke down, and after vainly endeavoring to start it the chauffeur set off on foot to secure help. Rodney slept, uncomfortably, and wakened with the movement of the machine to find it broad day. That was awkward, for Natalie's car was conspicuous, marked too with her initials. He asked to be set down at a suburban railway station, and was dismayed to find it crowded with early commuters, who stared at the big car with interest. On the platform, eyeing him with unfriendly eyes, was Nolan. Rodney made a movement toward him. The situation was intolerable, absurd. But Nolan turned his back and proceeded to read his newspaper.

Perhaps not in years had Rodney Page faced the truth about himself so clearly as he did that morning, riding into the city on the train which carried, somewhere ahead, that quietly contemptuous figure that was Denis Nolan. Faced the truth, saw himself for what he was, and loathed the thing he saw. For a little time, too, it was given him to see Natalie for what she was, for what she would always be, her sole contribution to life the web of her selfishness, carefully woven, floating apparently aimlessly, and yet snaring and holding relentlessly whatever it touched. Killing freedom. He saw Clayton and Graham and himself, feeders for her monstrous complacency and vanity, and he made a definite determination to free himself.

"I'm through," he reflected savagely. "I'll show them something, too. I'll—"

He hesitated. How lovely she was! And she cared for him. She was small and selfish and unspeakably vain, but she cared for him.

The war had done something for Rodney Page. He no longer dreamed the old dream, of turning her ice to fire. But he dreamed, for a moment, something finer. He saw Natalie his, and growing big and fine through love. He saw himself and Natalie, like cards in the game of life, re-dealt. A new combination; a winning hand —

Chapter XLVII

Very quietly Audrey had taken herself out of Clayton's life. She sent him a little note of farewell:

"We have had ten very wonderful months, Clay," she wrote. "We ought to be very happy. So few have as much. And we both know that this can't go on. I am going abroad. I have an opportunity to go over and see what Englishwomen are doing in the way of standing behind their men at war. Then I am to tell our women at home. Not that they need it now, bless them!

"I believe you will be glad to know that I am to be on the same side of the ocean with Graham. I could get to him, I think, if anything should go wrong. Will you send him the enclosed address?

"But, my dear, the address is for him, not for you. You must not write to me. I have used up every particle of moral courage I possess, as it is. And I am holding this in my mind, as you must. Time is a great healer of all wounds. We could have been happy together; oh, my dear, so very happy together! Now that I am going, let me be frank for once. I have given you the finest thing I am capable of. I am better for caring for you as I have, as I do.

"But those days in the hospital told me we couldn't go on. Things like that don't stand still. Maybe-we are only human, Clay-maybe if the old days were still here we might have compromised with life. I don't know. But I do know that we never will, now.

"After all, we have had a great deal, and we still have. It is a wonderful thing to know that somewhere in the world is some one person who loves you. To waken up in the morning to it. To go to sleep remembering it. And to have kept that love fine and clean is a wonderful thing, too.

"I am not always on a pinnacle. There have been plenty of times when the mere human want of you has sent me to the dust. Is it wrong to tell you that? But of course not. You know it. But you and I know this; Clay, dear. Love that is hopeless, that can not end in marriage, does one of two things. Either it degrades or it exalts. It leaves its mark, always, but that mark does not need to be a stain."

Clayton lived, for a time after that, in a world very empty and very full. The new plant was well under way. Not only was he about to make shells for the government at a nominal profit, but Washington was asking him to assume new and wide responsibilities. He accepted. He wanted so to fill the hours that there would be no time to remember. But, more than that, he was actuated by a fine and glowing desire to serve. Perhaps, underlying it all was the determination to be, in every way, the man Audrey thought him to be. And there was, too, a square-jawed resolution to put behind Graham, and other boys like Graham, all the shells and ammunition they needed.

He worked hard; more than hard. Old Terry, meeting him one day in the winter that followed, was shocked at his haggard face.

"Better take a little time off, Clay," he suggested. "We're going to Miami next week. How about ten days or so? Fishing is good this year."

"Can't very well take a holiday just now. Too much to do, Terry."

Old Terry went home and told his wife.

"Looks like the devil," he said. "He'll go down sick one of these days. I suppose it's no use telling Natalie."

"None whatever," said Mrs. Terry. "And, anyhow, it's a thing I shouldn't care to tell Natalie."

"What do you mean, not care to tell Natalie?"

"Hard work doesn't make a man forget how to smile."

"Oh, come now. He's cheerful enough. If you mean because Graham's fighting?"

"That's only part of it," said Mrs. Terry, sagely, and relapsed into one of the poignant silences that drove old Terry to a perfect frenzy of curiosity.

Then, in January of 1918, a crisis came to Clayton and Natalie Spencer. Graham was wounded.

Clayton was at home when the news came. Natalie had been having one of her ill-assorted, meticulously elaborate dinner-parties, and when the guests had gone they were for a moment alone in the drawing-room of their town house. Clayton was fighting in himself the sense of irritation Natalie's dinners always left, especially the recent ones. She was serving, he knew, too much food. In the midst of the agitation on conservation, her dinners ran their customary seven courses. There was too much wine, too. But it occurred to him that only the wine had made the dinner endurable.

Then he tried to force himself into better humor. Natalie was as she was, and if, in an unhappy, struggling, dying world she found happiness in display, God knew there was little enough happiness. He was not at home very often. He could not spoil her almost childish content in the small things that made up her life.

"I think it was very successful," she said, surveying herself in one of the corner mirrors. "Do you like my gown, Clay?"

"It's very lovely."

"It's new. I've been getting some clothes, Clay. You'll probably shriek at the bills. But all this talk about not buying clothes is nonsense, you know. The girls who work in the shops have to live."

"Naturally. Of course there is other work open to them now."

"In munition plants, I daresay. To be blown up!"

He winced. The thought of that night the year before, when the plant went, still turned him sick.

"Don't buy too many things, my dear," he said, gently. "You know how things are."

"I know it's your fault that they are as they are," she persisted. "Oh, I know it was noble of you, and all that. The country's crazy about you. But still I think it was silly. Every one else is making money out of things, and you —a lot of thanks you'll get, when the war's over."

"I don't particularly want thanks."

Then the door-bell rang in the back of the house, and Buckham answered it. He was conscious at once that Natalie stiffened, and that she was watchful and a trifle pale. Buckham brought in a telegram on a tray.

"Give it to me, Buckham," Natalie said, in a strained voice. And held out her hand for it. When she saw it was for Clayton, however, she relaxed. As he tore it open, Clayton was thinking. Evidently Natalie had been afraid of his seeing some message for her. Was it possible that Natalie-He opened it. After what seemed a long time he looked up. Her eyes were on him.

"Don't be alarmed, my dear," he said. "It is not very bad. But Graham has been slightly wounded. Sit down," he said sharply, as he saw her sway.

"You are lying to me," she said in a dreadful voice. "He's dead!"

"He is not dead, Natalie." He tried to put her into a chair, but she resisted him fiercely.

"Let me alone. I want to see that telegram."

And, very reluctantly, at last he gave it to her. Graham was severely wounded. It was from a man in his own department at Washington who had just seen the official list. The nature of his wounding had not been stated.

Natalie looked up from the telegram with a face like a painted mask.

"This is your doing," she said. "You wanted him to go. You sent him into this. He will die, and you will have murdered him."

The thought came to him, in that hour of stress, that she was right. Pitifully, damnably right. He had not wanted Graham to go, but he had wanted him to want to go. A thousand thoughts flashed through his mind, of Delight, sleeping somewhere quietly after her day's work at the camp; of Graham himself, of that morning after the explosion, and his frank, pitiful confession. And again of Graham, suffering, perhaps dying, and with none of his own about him. And through it all was the feeling that he must try to bring Natalie to reason, that it was incredible that she should call him his own son's murderer.

"We must not think of his dying," he said. "We must only think that he is going to live, and to come back to us, Natalie dear."

She flung off the arm he put around her.

"And that," he went on, feeling for words out of the dreadful confusion in his mind, "if-the worst comes, that he has done a magnificent thing. There is no greater thing, Natalie."

"That won't bring him back to us," she said, still in that frozen voice. And suddenly she burst into hard, terrible crying.

All that night he sat outside her door, for she would not allow him to come in. He had had Washington on the telephone, but when at last he got the connection it was to learn that no further details were known. Toward dawn there came the official telegram from the War Department, but it told nothing more.

Natalie was hysterical. He had sent for a doctor, and with Madeleine in attendance the medical man had worked over her for hours. Going out, toward morning, he had found Clayton in the hall and had looked at him sharply.

"Better go to bed, Mr. Spencer," he advised. "It may not be as bad as you think. And they're doing fine surgery over there."

And, as Clayton shook his head:

"Mrs. Spencer will come round all right. She's hysterical, naturally. She'll be sending for you before long."

With the dawn, Clayton's thoughts cleared. If he and Natalie were ever to get together at all, it should be now, with this common grief between them. Perhaps, after all, it was not too late to re-build his house of life. He had failed. Perhaps they had both failed, but the real responsibility was his. Inside the room he could hear her moaning, a low, monotonous, heart-breaking moan. He was terribly sorry for her. She had no exaltation to help her, no strength of soul, no strength of any sort. And, as men will under stress, he tried to make a bargain with his God.

"Let him live," he prayed. "Bring him back to us, and I will try again. I'll do better. I've been a rotten failure, as far as she is concerned. But I'll try."

He felt somewhat better after that, altho he felt a certain ignominy, too, that always, until such a time, he had gone on his own, as it were, and that now, when he no longer sufficed for himself, he should beseech the Almighty.

Natalie had had a sleeping-powder, and at last he heard her moaning cease and the stealthy movements of her maid as she lowered the window shades. It was dawn.

During the next two days Clayton worked as he never had worked before, still perhaps with that unspoken pact in mind. Worked too, to forget. He had sent several cables, but no reply came until the third day. He did not sleep at night. He did not even go to bed. He sat in the low chair in his dressing-room, dozing occasionally, to waken with a start at some sound in the hall. Now and again, as the trained nurse who was watching Natalie at night moved about the hallways, he would sit up, expecting a summons that did not come.

She still refused to see him. It depressed and frightened him, for how could he fulfill his part of the compact when she so sullenly shut him out of her life?

He was singularly simple in his fundamental beliefs. There was a Great Power somewhere, call it what one might, and it dealt out justice or mercy as one deserved it. On that, of course, had been built an elaborate edifice of creed and dogma, but curiously enough it all fell away now. He was, in those night hours, again the boy who had prayed for fair weather for circus day and had promised in return to read his Bible through during the next year. And had done it.

In the daytime, however, he was a man, suffering terribly, and facing the complexities of his life alone. One thing he knew. This was decisive. Either, under the stress of a common trouble, he and Natalie would come together, to make the best they could of the years to come, or they would be hopelessly alienated.

But that was secondary to Graham. Everything was secondary to Graham, indeed. He had cabled Audrey, and he drew a long breath when, on the third day, a cable came from her. She had located Graham at last. He had been shot in the chest, and there were pneumonia symptoms.

"Shall stay with him,'" she ended, "and shall send daily reports."

Next to his God, he put his faith in Audrey. Almost he prayed to her.

Dunbar, now a captain in the Military Intelligence Bureau, visiting him in his office one day, found Clayton's face an interesting study. Old lines of repression, new ones of anxiety, marked him deeply.

"The boy, of course," he thought. And then reflected that it takes time to carve such lines as were written in the face of the man across the desk from him. Time and a woman, he considered shrewdly. His mind harked back to that dinner in the Spencer house when diplomatic relations had been broken off with. Germany, and war seemed imminent. It was the wife, probably. He remembered that she had been opposed to war, and to the boy's going. There were such women in the country. There were fewer of them all the time, but they existed, women who saw in war only sacrifice. Women who counted no cost too high for peace. If they only hurt themselves it did not matter, but they could and did do incredible damage.

Clayton was going through some papers he had brought, and Dunbar had time to consider what to him was an interesting problem. Mrs. Spencer had kept the boy from immediate enlistment. He had wanted to go; Dunbar knew that. If she had allowed him to go the affair with Anna Klein would have been ended. He knew all that story now. Then, if there had been no affair, Herman would not have blown up the munition works and a good many lives, valuable to themselves at least, might have been saved.

"Curious!" he reflected. "One woman! And she probably sleeps well at nights and goes to church on Sundays!"

Clayton passed back his papers, and ran a hand over his heavy hair.

"They seem to be all right," he said.

Dunbar rose.

"Hope the next news will be better, Mr. Spencer."

"I hope so."

"I haven't told you, I think, that we have traced Rudolph Klein."

Clayton's face set.

"He's got away, unfortunately. Over the border into Mexico. They have a regular system there, the Germans-an underground railway to Mexico City. They have a paymaster on our side of the line. They even bank in one of our banks! Oh, we'll get them yet, of course, but they're damnably clever."

"I suppose there is no hope of getting Rudolph Klein?"

"Not while the Germans are running Mexico," Captain Dunbar replied, dryly. "He's living in a Mexican town just over the border. We're watching him. If he puts a foot on this side we'll grab him."

Clayton sat back after he had gone. He was in his old office at the mill, where Joey had once formed his unofficial partnership with the firm. Outside in the mill yard there was greater activity than ever, but many of the faces were new. The engineer who had once run the yard engine was building bridges in France. Hutchinson had heard the call, and was learning to fly in Florida, The service flag over his office door showed hundreds of stars, and more were being added constantly. Joey dead. Graham wounded, his family life on the verge of disruption, and Audrey —

Then, out of the chaos there came an exaltation. He had given himself, his son, the wealth he had hoped to have, but, thank God, he had had something to give. There were men who could give nothing, like old Terry Mackenzie, knocking billiard-balls around at the club, and profanely wistful that he had had no son to go. His mind ranged over those pathetic, prosperous, sonless men who filed into the club late in the afternoons, and over the last editions and whisky-and-sodas fought their futile warfare, their battle-ground a newspaper map, their upraised voices their only weapons.

On parade days, when the long lines of boys in khaki went by, they were silent, heavy, inutile. They were too old to fight. The biggest thing in their lives was passing them by, as passed the lines of marching boys, and they had no part in it. They were feeding their hungry spirits on the dregs of war, on committee meetings and public gatherings, and they were being useful. But the great exaltation of offering their best was not for them.

He was living a tragedy, but a greater tragedy was that of the childless. And back of that again was the woman who had not wanted children. There were many men to-day who were feeling the selfishness of a woman at home, men who had lost, somehow, their pride, their feeling of being a part of great things. Men who went home at night to comfortable dwellings, with no vacant chair at the table, and dined in a peace they had not earned.

Natalie had at least given him a son.

He took that thought home with him in the evening. He stopped at a florist's and bought a great box of flowers for her, and sent them into her room with a little note,

"Won't you let me come in and try to comfort you?"

But Madeleine brought the box out again, and there was pity in her eyes.

"Mrs. Spencer can not have them in the room, sir. She says the odor of flowers makes her ill."

He knew Madeleine had invented the excuse, that Natalie had simply rejected his offering. He went down-stairs, and made a pretense of dining alone in the great room.

It was there that Audrey's daily cable found him. Buckham brought it in in shaking fingers, and stood by, white and still, while he opened it.

Clayton stood up. He was very white, but his voice was full and strong.

"He is better, Buckham! Better!"

Suddenly Buckham was crying. His austere face was distorted, his lean body trembling. Clayton put his arm around the bowed old shoulders.

And in that moment, as they stood there, master and man, Clayton Spencer had a flash of revelation. There was love and love. The love of a man for a woman, and of a woman for a man, of a mother for the child at her knee, of that child for its mother. But that the great actuating motive of a man's maturity, of the middle span, was vested along with his dreams, his pride and his love, in his son, his man-child.

Buckham, carrying his coffee into the library somewhat later, found him with his head down on his desk, and the cablegram clutched in his outstretched hands. He tip-toed out, very quietly.

Chapter XLVIII

Clayton's first impulse was to take the cable to Natalie, to brush aside the absurd defenses she had erected, and behind which she cowered, terrified but obstinate. To say to her,

"He is living. He is going to live. But this war is not over yet. If we want him to come through, we must stand together. We must deserve to have him come back to us."

But by the time he reached the top of the stairs he knew he could not do it. She would not understand. She would think he was using Graham to further a reconciliation; and, after her first joy was over, he knew that he would see again that cynical smile that always implied that he was dramatizing himself.

Nothing could dim his strong inner joy, but something of its outer glow faded. He would go to her, later. Not now. Nothing must spoil this great thankfulness of his.

He gave Madeleine the cable, and went down again to the library.

After a time he began to go over the events of the past eighteen months. His return from the continent, and that curious sense of unrest that had followed it, the opening of his eyes to the futility of his life. His failure to Natalie and her failure to him. Graham, made a man by war and by the love of a good woman. Chris, ending his sordid life in a blaze of glory, and forever forgiven his tawdry sins because of his one big hour.

War took, but it gave also. It had taken Joey, for instance, but Joey had had his great moment. It was better to have one great moment and die than to drag on through useless years. And it was the same way with a nation. A nation needed its hour. It was only in a crisis that it could know its own strength. How many of them, who had been at that dinner of Natalie's months before, had met their crisis bravely! Nolan was in France now. Doctor Haverford was at the front. Audrey was nursing Graham. Marion Hayden was in a hospital training-School. Rodney Page was still building wooden barracks in a cantonment in Indiana, and was making good. He himself—

They could never go back, none of them, to the old smug, complacent, luxurious days. They could no more go back than Joey could return to life again. War was the irrevocable step, as final as death itself. And he remembered something Nolan had said, just before he sailed.

"We have had one advantage, Clay. Or maybe it is not an advantage, after all. Do you realize that you and I have lived through the Golden Age? We have seen it come and seen it go. The greatest height of civilization, since the world began, the greatest achievements, the most opulent living. And we saw it all crash. It will be a thousand years before the world will be ready for another."

And later,

"I suppose every life has its Golden Age. Generally we think it is youth. I'm not so sure. Youth is looking ahead. It has its hopes and its disappointments. The Golden Age in a man's life ought to be the age of fulfillment. It's nearer the forties than the twenties."

"Have you reached it?"

"I'm going to, on the other side."

And Clayton had smiled.

"You are going to reach it," he said. "We are always going to find it, Nolan. It is always just ahead."

And Nolan had given him one of his quick understanding glances.

There could be no Golden Age for him. For the Golden Age for a man meant fulfillment. The time came to every man when he must sit at the west window of his house of life and look toward the sunset. If he faced that sunset alone —

He heard Madeleine carrying down Natalie's dinner-tray, and when she left the pantry she came to the door of the library.

"Mrs. Spencer would like to see you, sir."

"Thank you, Madeleine. I'll go up very soon."

Suddenly he knew that he did not want to go up to Natalie's scented room. She had shut him out when she was in trouble. She had not cared that he, too, was in distress. She had done her best to invalidate that compact he had made. She had always invalidated him.

To go back to the old way, to the tribute she enforced to feed her inordinate vanity, to the old hypocrisy of their relationship, to live again the old lie, was impossible.

He got up. He would not try to buy himself happiness at the cost of turning her adrift. But he must, some way, buy his self-respect.

He heard her then, on the staircase, that soft rustle which, it seemed to him, had rasped the silk of his nerves all their years together with its insistence on her dainty helplessness, her femininity, her right to protection. The tap of her high heels came closer. He drew a long breath and turned, determinedly smiling, to face the door.

Almost at once he saw that she was frightened. She had taken pains to look her best-but then she always did that. She was rouged to the eyes, and the floating white chiffon of her negligee gave to her slim body the illusion of youth, that last illusion to which she so desperately clung. But-she was frightened.

She stood in the doorway, one hand holding aside the heavy velvet curtain, and looked at him with wide, penciled eyes.

"Clay?"

"Yes. Come in. Shall I have Buckham light a fire?"

She came in, slowly.

"Do you suppose that cable is reliable?"

"I should think so."

"He may have a relapse."

"We mustn't worry about what may come. He is better now. The chances are that he'll stay better."

"Probably. I suppose, because I have been so ill —"

He felt the demand for sympathy, but he had none to give. And he felt something else. Natalie was floundering, an odd word for her, always so sure of herself. She was frightened, unsure of herself, and-floundering. Why?

"Are you going to be in to-night?"

"Yes."

She gave a curious little gesture. Then she evidently made up her mind and she faced him defiantly.

"Of course, if I had known he was going to be better, I'd —Clay, I wired yesterday for Rodney Page. He arrives to-night."

"Rodney?"

"Yes."

"I don't think I quite understand, Natalie. Why did you wire for him?"

"You wouldn't understand, of course. I was in trouble. He has been my best friend. I tried to bear it alone, but I couldn't. I —"

"Alone! You wouldn't see me."

"I couldn't, Clay."

"Why?"

"Because-if Graham had died —"

Her mouth trembled. She put her hand to her throat.

"You would have blamed me for his death?"

"Yes."

"Then, even now, if—"

"Yes."

The sheer cruelty of it sent him pale. Yet it was not so much deliberate as unconscious. She was forcing herself to an unwonted honesty. It was her honest conviction that he was responsible for Graham's wounding and danger.

"Let me get to the bottom of this," he said quietly. "You hold me responsible. Very well. How far does that take us? How far does that take you? To Rodney!"

"You needn't be brutal. Rodney understands me. He-he cares for me, Clay."

"I see. And, since you sent for him I take it you care for Rodney."

"I don't know. I—"

"Isn't it time you do know? For God's sake, Natalie, make up your mind to some course and stick to it."

But accustomed as he was to the curious turns of her mind, he was still astounded to have her turn on him and accuse him of trying to get rid of her. It was not until later that he realized in that attitude of hers her old instinct of shifting the responsibility from her own shoulders.

And then Rodney was announced.

The unreality of the situation persisted. Rodney's strained face and uneasy manner, his uniform, the blank pause when he had learned that Graham was better, and when the ordinary banalities of greeting were over. Beside Clayton he looked small, dapper, and wretchedly uncomfortable, and yet even Clayton had to acknowledge a sort of dignity in the man.

He felt sorry for him, for the disillusion that was to come. And at the same time he felt an angry contempt for him, that he should have forced so theatrical a situation. That the night which saw Graham's beginning recovery should be tarnished by the wild clutch after happiness of two people who had done so little to earn it.

He saw another, totally different scene, for a moment. He saw Graham in his narrow bed that night in some dimly-lighted hospital ward, and he saw Audrey beside him, watching and waiting and praying. A wild desire to be over there, one of that little group, almost overcame him. And instead—

"Natalie has not been well, Rodney," he said. "I rather think, if you have anything to say to me, we would better talk alone."

Natalie went out, her draperies trailing behind her. Clayton listened, as she moved slowly up the stairs. For the last time he heard that soft rustling which had been the accompaniment to so many of the most poignant hours of his life. He listened until it had died away.

Chapter XLIX

For months Rudolph Klein had been living in a little Mexican town on the border. There were really two towns, but they were built together with only a strip of a hundred feet between. Along this strip ran the border itself, with a tent pitched on the American side, and patrols of soldiers guarding it. The American side was bright and clean, orderly and self-respecting, but only a hundred feet away, unkempt, dusty, with adobe buildings and a notorious gambling-hell in plain view, was Mexico itself-leisurely, improvident, not overscrupulous Mexico.

At first Rudolph was fairly contented. It amused him. He liked the idleness of it. He liked kicking the innumerable Mexican dogs out of his way. He liked baiting the croupiers in the "Owl." He liked wandering into that notorious resort and shoving Hindus, Chinamen, and Mexicans out of the way, while he flung down a silver dollar and watched the dealers with cunning, avaricious eyes.

He liked his own situation, too. It amused him to think that here he was safe, while only a hundred feet away he was a criminal, fugitive from the law. He liked to go to the very border itself, and jeer at the men on guard there.

"If I was on that side," he would say, "you'd have me in one of those rotten uniforms, wouldn't you? Come on over, fellows. The liquor's fine."

Then, one day, a Chinaman he had insulted gave him an unexpected shove, and he had managed to save himself by a foot from the clutch of a quiet-faced man in plain clothes who spent a certain amount of time lounging on the other side of the border.

That had sobered him. He kept away from the border itself after that, although the temptation of it drew him. After a few weeks, when the novelty had worn off, he began to hunger for the clean little American town across the line. He wanted to talk to some one. He wanted to boast, to be candid. These Mexicans only laughed when he bragged to them. But he dared not cross.

There was a high-fenced enclosure behind the "Owl," the segregated district of the town. There, in tiny one-roomed houses built in rows like barracks were the girls and women who had drifted to this jumping-off place of the world. In the daytime they slept or sat on the narrow, ramshackle porches, untidy, noisy, unspeakably wretched. At night, however, they blossomed forth in tawdry finery, in the dancing-space behind the gambling-tables. Some of them were fixtures. They had drifted there from New Orleans, perhaps, or southern California, and they lacked the initiative or the money to get away. But most of them came in, stayed a month or two, found the place a nightmare, with its shootings and stabbings, and then disappeared.

At first Rudolph was popular in this hell of the underworld. He spent money easily, he danced well, he had audacity and a sort of sardonic humor. They asked no questions, those poor wretches who had themselves slid over the edge of life. They took what came, grateful for little pleasures, glad even to talk their own tongue.

And then, one broiling August day, late in the afternoon, when the compound was usually seething with the first fetid life of the day, Rudolph found it suddenly silent when he entered it, and hostile, contemptuous eyes on him.

A girl with Anna Klein's eyes, a girl he had begun to fancy, suddenly said,
"Draft-dodger!"

There was a ripple of laughter around the compound. They commenced to bait him, those women he would not have wiped his feet on at home. They literally laughed him out of the compound.

He went home to his stifling, windowless adobe room, with its sagging narrow bed, its candle, its broken crockery, and he stood in the center of the room and chewed his nails with fury. After a time he sat down and considered what to do next. He would have to move on some time. As well now as ever. He was sick of the place.

He began preparations to move on, gathering up the accumulation of months of careless living for destruction. He picked up some newspapers preparatory to throwing them away, and a name caught his attention. Standing there, inside his doorway in the Mexican dusk, he read of Graham's recent wounding, his mending, and the fact that he had won the Croix de Guerre. Supreme bitterness was Rudolph's then.

"Stage stuff!" he muttered. But in the depths of his warped soul there was bitter envy. He knew well with what frightened yet adoring eyes Anna Klein had devoured that news of Graham Spencer. While for him there was the girl in the compound back of the "Owl," with Anna Klein's eyes, filled when she looked at him with that bitterest scorn of all, the contempt of the wholly contemptible.

That night he went to the Owl. He had shaved and had his hair cut and he wore his only remaining decent suit of clothes. He passed through the swinging gate in the railing which separated the dancing-floor from the tables and went up to the line of girls, sitting in that saddest waiting of all the world, along the wall. There was an ominous silence at his approach. He planted himself in front of the girl with eyes like Anna Klein.

"Are you going to dance?"

"Not with you," she replied, evenly. And again the ripple of laughter spread.

"Why not?"

"Because you're a coward," she said. "I'd rather dance with a Chinaman."

"If you think I'm here because I'm afraid to fight you can think again. Not that I care what you think."

He had meant to boast a little, to intimate that he had pulled off a big thing, but he saw that he was ridiculous. The situation infuriated him. Suddenly he burst into foul-mouthed invective, until one of the girls said, wearily,

"Oh, cut that out, you slacker."

And he knew that no single word he had used against them, out of a vocabulary both extensive and horrible, was to them so degraded as that single one applied to him.

Late that night he received a tip from a dealer at one of vingt-et-un tables. There were inquiries being made for him across the border. That very evening he, the dealer, had gone across for a sack of flour, and he had heard about it.

"You'd better get out," said the dealer.

"I'm as safe here as I'd be in Mexico City."

"Don't be too sure, son. You're not any too popular here. There's such a thing as being held up and carried over the border. It's been done before now."

"I'm sick of this hole, anyhow," Rudolph muttered, and moved away in the crowd. The mechanical piano was banging in the dance-hall as he slipped out into the darkness, under the clear starlight of the Mexican night, and the gate of the compound stood open. He passed it with an oath.

Long before, he had provided for such a contingency. By the same agency which had got him to the border, he could now be sent further on. At something after midnight, clad in old clothes and carrying on his back a rough outfit of a blanket and his remaining wardrobe, he knocked at the door of a small adobe house on the border of the town. An elderly German with a candle admitted him.

"Well, I'm off," Rudolph said roughly.

"And time enough, too," said the German, gruffly.

Rudolph was sullenly silent. He was in this man's power, and he knew it. But the German was ready enough to do his part. For months he had been doing this very thing, starting through the desert toward the south slackers and fugitives of all descriptions. He gathered together the equipment, a map with water-holes marked, a canteen covered with a dirty plaid-cloth casing, a small supply of condensed foods, in tins mostly, and a letter to certain Germans in Mexico City who would receive hospitably any American fugitives and ask no questions.

"How about money?" Rudolph inquired.

The German shrugged his shoulders.

"You will not need money in the desert," he said. "And you haf spent much money here, on the women. You should have safed it."

"I was told you would give me money."

But the German shook his head.

"You viii find money in Mexico City, if you get there," he said, cryptically. And Rudolph found neither threats nor entreaties of any avail.

He started out of the town, turning toward the south and west. Before him there stretched days of lonely traveling through the sand and cactus of the desert, of blistering sun and cold nights, of anxious searches for water-holes. It was because of the water-holes that he headed southwest, for such as they were they lay in tiny hidden oases in the canyons. Almost as soon as he left the town he was in the desert; a detached ranch, a suggestion of a road, a fenced-in cotton-field or two, an irrigation ditch, and then—sand.

He was soft from months of inaction, from the cactus whisky of Mexico, too, that ate into a man like a corrosive acid. But he went on steadily, putting behind him as rapidly as possible the border, and the girls who had laughed at him. He traveled by a pointed mountain which cut off the stars at the horizon, and as the miles behind him increased, in spite of his growing fatigue his spirits rose. Before him lay the fulness of life again. Mexico City was a stake worth gambling for. He was gambling, he knew. He had put up his life, and his opponent was thirst. He knew that, well enough, too, and the figure rather amused him.

"Playing against that, all right," he muttered. He paused and turned around. The sun had lifted over the rim of the desert, a red disc which turned the gleaming white alkali patches to rose. "By God," he said, "that's the ante, is it —A red chip!"

A caravan of mules was coming up from the head of the Gulf of California. It moved in a cloud of alkali dust and sand, its ore-sacks coated white. The animals straggled along, wandering out of the line incessantly and thrust back into place by muleteers who cracked long whips and addressed them vilely.

At a place where a small rock placed on another marked a side trail to water, the caravan turned and moved toward the mountains. Close as they appeared, the outfit was three hours getting to the foot hills. There was a low meadow now, covered with pale green grass. Quail scurried away under the mesquite bushes, stealthily whistling, and here and there the two stones still marked the way.

With the instinct of desert creatures the mules hurried their pace. Pack-saddles creaked, spurs jingled. Life, insistent, thirsty life, quickened the dead plain.

A man rode ahead. He dug his spurs into his horse and cantered, elbows flapping, broad-brimmed hat drawn over his eyes. For hours he had been fighting the demon of thirst. His tongue was dry, his lips cracking. The trail continued to be marked with its double stones, but it did not enter the cool canyon ahead. It turned and skirted the base of the bare mountain slope. The man's eyes sharpened. He knew very definitely what he was looking for, and at last he saw it, a circle of flat stones, some twenty feet across, the desert sign for a buried spring.

But there was something inside the circle, something which lay still. The man put his horse to the gallop again. There was a canteen lying in the trail, a canteen covered with a dirty plaid casing. The horse's hoof struck it, and it gave out a dry, metallic sound.

"Poor devil!" muttered the rider.

He dismounted and turned the figure over.

"God!" he said. "And water under him all the time!"

Then he dragged the quiet figure outside the ring of stones, and getting a spade from his saddle, fell to digging in the center. A foot below the surface water began to appear, clear, cold water. He lay down, flat and drank out of the pool.

Clayton Spencer was alone in his house. In the months since Natalie had gone, he had not been there a great deal. He had been working very hard. He had not been able to shoulder arms, but he had, nevertheless, fought a good fight.

He was very tired. During the day, a sort of fierce energy upheld him. Because in certain things he had failed he was the more determined to succeed in others. Not for himself; ambition of that sort had died of the higher desire to serve his country. But because the sense of failure in his private life haunted him.

The house was very quiet. Buckham came in to mend the fire, issuing from the shadows like a lean old ghost and eyeing him with tender, faded old eyes.

"Is there anything else, sir?"

"Thanks, no. Buckham."

"Yes, Mr. Spencer."

"I have not spoken about it, but I think you have understood. Mrs. Spencer is-not coming back."

"Yes, Mr. Spencer."

"I had meant to close the house, but certain things-Captain Spencer's wife expects a child. I would rather like to have her come here, for the birth. After that, if the war is over, I shall turn the house over to them. You would stay on, I hope, Buckham."

"I'll stay, sir. I —" His face worked nervously. "I feel toward the Captain as I would to my own son, sir. I have already thought that perhaps-the old nursery has been cleaned and aired for weeks, Mr. Spencer."

Clayton felt a thrill of understanding for the old man through all the years he had watched and served them. He had reflected their joys and their sorrows. He had suffered the family destiny without having shaped it. He had lived, vicariously, their good hours and their bad. And now, in his old age, he was waiting again for the vicarious joy of Graham's child.

"But you'll not be leaving the house, sir?"

"I don't know. I shall keep my rooms. But I shall probably live at the club. The young people ought to be alone, for a while. There are readjustments-You never married, Buckham?"

"No, Mr. Spencer. I intended to, at one time. I came to this country to make a home, and as I was rather a long time about it, she married some one else."

Clayton caught the echo of an old pain in Buckham's repressed voice. Buckham, too! Was there in the life of every man some woman tragedy? Buckham, sitting alone in his west window and looking toward the sunset, Buckham had his memories.

"She lost her only son at Neuve Chapelle," Buckham was saying quietly. "In a way, it was as tho I had lost a boy. She never cared for the man she married. He was a fine boy, sir. I —you may remember the night I was taken ill in the pantry."

"Is her husband still living?"

"No, Mr. Spencer."

"Do you ever think of going back and finding her?"

"I have, sir. But I don't know. I like to remember her as she used to be. I have some beautiful memories. And I think sometimes it is better to live on memories. They are more real than-well, than reality, sir."

Long after Buckham had withdrawn, Clayton paced the floor of the library. Was Buckham right? Was the real life of a man his mental life? Was any love so great as a man's dream of love? Peace was on the way. Soon this nightmare of war would be over, and in the great awakening love would again take the place of hate. Love of man for man, of nation for nation. Peace and the things of peace. Time to live. Time to hope, with the death-cloud gone. Time to work and time to play. Time to love a woman and cherish her for the rest of life, if only —

His failure with Natalie had lost him something. She had cost him his belief in himself. Her last words had crystallized his own sense of failure.

"I admit all your good qualities, Clay. Heaven knows they are evident enough. But you are the sort people admire. They don't love you. They never will."

Yet that night he had had a curious sense that old Buckham loved him. Maybe he was the sort men loved and women admired.

He sat down and leaned back in his chair, watching the fire-logs. He felt very tired. What was that Buckham had said about memories? But Buckham was old. He was young, young and strong. There would be many years, and even his most poignant memories would grow dim.

Audrey! Audrey!

From the wall over the mantel Natalie's portrait still surveyed the room with its delicate complacence. He looked up at it. Yes, Natalie had been right, he was not the sort to make a woman happy. There were plenty of men, young men, men still plastic, men who had not known shipwreck, and some such man Audrey would marry. Perhaps already, in France —

He got up. His desk was covered with papers, neatly endorsed by his secretary. He turned out all the lights but his desk lamp. Natalie's gleaming flesh-tones died into the shadows, and he stood for a moment, looking up at it, a dead thing, remote, flat, without significance. Then he sat down at his desk and took up a bundle of government papers.

There was still work. Thank God for work.

Chapter L

Audrey was in Paris on the eleventh of November. Now and then she got back there, and reveled for a day or two in the mere joy of paved streets and great orderly buildings. She liked the streets and the crowds. She liked watching the American boys swaggering along, smoking innumerable cigarets and surveying the city with interested, patronizing eyes. And, always, walking briskly along the Rue Royale or the Avenue de l'Opera, or in the garden of the Tuileries where the school-boys played their odd French games, her eyes were searching the faces of the men she met.

Any tall man in civilian clothes set her heart beating faster. She was quite honest with herself; she knew that she was watching for Clay, and she had a magnificent shamelessness in her quest. And now at last The Daily Mail had announced his arrival in France, and at first every ring of her telephone had sent her to it, somewhat breathless but quite confident. He would, she considered, call up the Red Cross at the Hotel Regina, and they would, by her instructions, give her hotel.

Then, on that Monday morning, which was the eleventh, she realized that he would not call her up. She knew it suddenly and absolutely. She sat down, when the knowledge came to her, with a sickening feeling that if he did not come to her now he never would come. Yet even then she did not doubt that he cared. Cared as desperately as she did. The bond still held.

She tried very hard, sitting there by her wood fire in the orderly uniform which made her so quaintly young and boyish, to understand the twisted mental processes that kept him away from her, now that he was free. And, in the end, she came rather close to the truth: his sense of failure; his loss of confidence in himself where his love life was concerned; the strange twisting and warping that were Natalie's sole legacy from their years together.

For months she had been tending broken bodies and broken spirits. But the broken pride of a man was a strange and terrible thing.

She did not know where he was stopping, and in the congestion of the Paris hotels it would be practically impossible to trace him. And there, too, her own pride stepped in. He must come to her. He knew she cared. She had been honest with him always, with a sort of terrible honesty.

Surveying the past months she wondered, not for the first time, what had held them apart so long, against the urge that had become the strongest thing in life to them both. The strength in her had come from him. She knew that. But where had Clay got his strength? Men were not like that, often. Failing final happiness, they so often took what they could get. Like Chris.

Perhaps, for the first and last time, she saw Clayton Spencer that morning with her mind, as well as with her heart. She saw him big and generous and fine, but she saw him also not quite so big as his love, conventional, bound by tradition and early training, somewhat rigid, Calvinistic, and dominated still by a fierce sex pride.

At once the weaknesses of the middle span, and its safety. And, woman-fashion, she loved him for both his weakness and his strength. A bigger man might have taken her. A smaller man would have let her go. Clay was-just Clay; single-hearted, intelligent but not shrewd, blundering, honest Clay.

She was one great ache for the shelter of his arms.

She had a small sense of shame that, on that day of all others, she should be obsessed with her own affairs.

This was a great day. That morning, if all went well, the war was to cease. The curtain was to fall on the great melodrama, and those who had watched it and those who had played in it would with the drop of the curtain turn away from the illusion that is war, to the small and quiet things of home.

"Home!" she repeated. She had no home. But it was a great day, nevertheless. Only that morning the white-capped femme de chambre had said, with exaltation in her great eyes:

"So! It is finished, Madame, or soon it will be-in an hour or two."

"It will be finished, Suzanne."

"And Madame will go back to the life she lived before." Her eyes had turned to where, on the dressing-table, lay the gold fittings of Audrey's dressing-case. She visualized Audrey, back in rich, opulent America, surrounded by the luxury the gold trinkets would indicate.

"Madame must be lovely in the costume for a ball," she said, and sighed. For her, a farm in Brittany, the endless round of small duties; for the American —

Sitting there alone Audrey felt already the reactions of peace. The war had torn up such roots as had held her. She was terribly aware, too, that she had outgrown her old environment. The old days were gone. The old Audrey was gone; and in her place was a quiet woman, whose hands had known service and would never again be content to be idle. Yet she knew that, with the war, the world call would be gone. Not again, for her, detached, impersonal service. She was not of the great of the earth. What she wanted, quite simply, was the service of love. To have her own and to care for them. She hoped, very earnestly, that she would be able to look beyond her own four walls, to see distress and to help it, but she knew, as she knew herself, that the real call to her would always be love.

She felt a certain impatience at herself. This was to be the greatest day in the history of the world, and while all the earth waited for the signal guns, she waited for a man who had apparently determined not to take her back into his life.

She went out onto her small stone balcony, on the Rue Danou, and looked out to where, on the Rue de la Paix, the city traffic moved with a sort of sporadic expectancy. Men stopped and consulted their watches. A few stood along the curb, and talked in low voices. Groups of men in khaki walked by, or stopped to glance into the shop windows. They, too, were waiting. She could see, far below, her valet de chambre in his green felt apron, and the concierge in his blue frock coat and brass buttons, unbending in the new democracy of hope to talk to a cabman.

Suddenly Audrey felt the same exaltation that had been in Suzanne's eyes. Those boys below in uniform-they were not tragic now. They were the hope of the world, not its sacrifice. They were going to live. They were going to live.

She went into her bedroom and put on her service hat. And as she opened the door Suzanne was standing outside, one hand upraised. Into the quiet hallway there came the distant sound of the signal guns.

"C'est l'armistice!" cried Suzanne, and suddenly broke into wild hysterical sobbing.

All the way down-stairs Audrey was praying, not articulately, but in her heart, that this was indeed the end; that the grapes of wrath had all been trampled; that the nations of the world might again look forward instead of back. And-because she was not of the great of the earth, but only a loving woman-that somewhere Clay was hearing the guns, as she was, and would find hope in them, and a future.

When a great burden is lifted, the relief is not always felt at once. The galled places still ache. The sense of weight persists. And so with Paris. Not at once did the city rejoice openly. It prayed first, and then it counted the sore spots, and they were many. And it was dazed, too. There had been no time to discount peace in advance.

The streets filled at once, but at first it was with a chastened people. Audrey herself felt numb and unreal. She moved mechanically with the shifting crowd, looking overhead as a captured German plane flew by, trying to comprehend the incomprehensible. But by mid-day the sober note of the crowds had risen to a higher pitch. A file of American doughboys, led by a corporal with a tin trumpet and officered by a sergeant with an enormous American cigar, goose-stepped down the Avenue de l'Opera, gaining recruits at every step. It snake-danced madly through the crowd, singing that one lyric stand-by of Young America: "Hail! hail! the gang's all here!"

But the gang was not all there, and they knew it. Some of them lay in the Argonne, or at Chateau-Thierry, and for them peace had come too late. But the Americans, like the rest of the world, had put the past behind them. Here was the present, the glorious present, and Paris on a sunny Monday. And after that would be home.

> "Hail, hail, the gang's all here,
> What the hell do we care?
> What the hell do we care?
> Hail, hail, the gang's all here,
> What the hell do we care now?"

Gradually the noise became uproarious. There were no bands in Paris, and any school-boy with a tin horn or a toy drum could start a procession. Bearded little poilus, arm in arm from curb to curb, marched grinning down the center of the streets, capturing and kissing pretty midinettes, or surrounding officers and dancing madly; Audrey saw an Algerian, ragged and dirty from the battle-fields, kiss on both cheeks a portly British Admiral of the fleet, and was herself kissed by a French sailor, with extreme robustness and a slight tinge of vin ordinaire. She went on smiling.

If only Clay were seeing all this! He had worked so hard. He had a right to this wonderful hour, at least. If he had gone to the front, to see Graham-but then it must be rather wonderful at the front, too. She tried to visualize it; the guns quiet, and the strained look gone from the faces of the men, with the wonderful feeling that as there was to-day, now there would also be to-morrow.

She felt a curious shrinking from the people she knew. For this one day she wanted to be alone. This peace was a thing of the soul, and of the soul alone. She knew what it would be with the people she knew best in Paris, —hastily arranged riotous parties, a great deal of champagne and noise, and, overlying the real sentiment, much sentimentality. She realized, with a faint smile, that the old Audrey would have welcomed that very gayety. She was even rather resentful with herself for her own aloofness.

She quite forgot luncheon, and early afternoon found her on the balcony of the Crillon Hotel, overlooking the Place de la Concorde. Paris was truly awake by that time, and going mad. The long-quiet fountains were playing, Poilus and American soldiers had seized captured German cannon and were hauling them wildly about. If in the morning the crowd had been largely khaki, now the French blue predominated. Flags and confetti were everywhere, and every motor, as it, pushed slowly through the crowd, carried on roof and running board and engine hood crowds of self-invited passengers. A British band was playing near the fountain. A line of helmets above the mass and wild cheers revealed French cavalry riding through, and, heralded by jeers and much applause came a procession of the proletariat, of odds and ends, soldiers and shop-girls, mechanics and street-sweepers and cabmen and students, carrying an effigy of the Kaiser on a gibbet.

As the sun went down, the outlines of the rejoicing city took on the faint mist blue of a dream city. It softened the outlines of the Eiffel tower to strange and fairy-like beauty and gave to the trees in the Tuileries gardens the lack of definition of an old engraving. And as if to remind the rejoicing of the price of their happiness, there came limping through the crowd a procession of the mutilees. They stumped along on wooden legs or on crutches; they rode in wheeled chairs; they were led, who could not see. And they smiled and cheered. None of them was whole, but every one was a full man, for all that.

Audrey cried, shamelessly like Suzanne, but quietly. And, not for the first time that day, she thought of Chris. She had never loved him, but it was pitiful that he could not have lived. He had so loved life. He would have so relished all this, the pageantry of it, and the gayety, and the night's revelry that was to follow. Poor Chris! He had thrown everything away, even life. The world perhaps was better that these mutilees below had given what they had. But Chris had gone like a pebble thrown into a lake. He had made his tiny ripple and had vanished.

Then she remembered that she was not quite fair. Perhaps she had never been fair to Chris. He had given all he had. He had not lived well, but he had died well. And there was something to be said for death. For the first time in her healthy life she wondered about death, standing here on the Crillon balcony, with the city gone mad with life below her. Death was quiet. It might be rather wonderful. She thought, if Clay did not want her, that perhaps it would be very comforting just to die and forget about everything.

From beneath the balcony there came again, lustily the shouts of a dozen doughboys hauling a German gun:

"Hail! hail! the gang's all here!
What the hell do we care?
What the hell do we care?

Hail, hail, the gang's all here!
What the hell do we care now?"

Then, that night, Clay came. The roistering city outside had made of her little sitting-room a sort of sanctuary, into which came only faintly the blasts of horns, hoarse strains of the "Marseillaise" sung by an un-vocal people, the shuffling of myriad feet, the occasional semi-hysterical screams of women.

"Mr. Spencer is calling," said the concierge over the telephone, in his slow English. And suddenly a tight band snapped which had seemed to bind Audrey's head all day. She was calm. She was herself again. Life was very wonderful; peace was very wonderful. The dear old world. The good old world. The kind, loving, tender old world, which separated people that they might know the joy of coming together again. She wanted to sing, she wanted to hang over her balcony and teach the un-vocal French the "Marseillaise."

Yet, when she had opened the door, she could not even speak. And Clay, too, after one long look at her, only held out his arms. It was rather a long time, indeed, before they found any words at all. Audrey was the first, and what she said astounded her. For she said:

"What a dreadful noise outside."

And Clay responded, with equal gravity: "Yes, isn't it!"

Then he took off his overcoat and put it down, and placed his hat on the table, and said, very simply: "I couldn't stay away. I tried to."

"You hadn't a chance in the world, Clay, when I was willing you to come."

Then there was one of those silences which come when words have shown their absolute absurdity. It seemed a long time before he broke it.

"I'm not young, Audrey. And I have failed once."

"It takes two to make a failure," she said dauntlessly. "I—wouldn't let you fail again, Clay. Not if you love me."

"If I love you!" Then he was, somehow, in that grotesque position that is only absurd to the on-looker, on his knees beside her. His terrible self-consciousness was gone. He only knew that, somehow, some way, he must prove to her his humility, his love, his terrible fear of losing her again, his hope that together they might make up for the wasted years of their lives. "I worship you," he said.

The little room was a sanctuary. The war lay behind them. Wasted and troubled years lay behind them. Youth, first youth, was gone, with its illusions and its dreams. But before them lay the years of fulfilment, years of understanding. Youth demanded everything, and was discontented that it secured less than its demands. Now they asked but three things, work, and peace, and love. And the greatest of these was love.

Something like that he said to her, when the first inarticulateness had passed, and when, as is the way of a man with the woman who loves him, he tried to lay his soul as well as his heart at her feet. The knowledge that the years brought. That love in youth was a plant of easy growth, springing up in many soils. But that the love of the middle span of a man's life, whether that love be the early love purified by fire, or a new love, sowed in sacrifice and watered with tears, the love that was to carry a man and a woman through to the end, the last love, was God's infinitely precious gift. A gift to take the place of the things that had gone with youth, of high adventure and the lilt of the singing heart.

The last gift.